If I'm Ever Back This Way

Gavin Cologne-Brookes is Professor of American Literature at Bath Spa University, and lives in Wiltshire with his wife and daughters. His previous books are *The Novels of William Styron: From Harmony to History; Writing and America*, and *Dark Eyes on America: The Novels of Joyce Carol Oates*.

Acknowledgments and Permissions

Transcripts of interviews and some of the conversations with William Styron appear in *The Novels of William Styron: From Harmony to History* (Baton Rouge: Louisiana State University Press, 1995), and *The Mississippi Quarterly* (2008).

Transcripts of interviews and some of the conversations with Joyce Carol Oates appear in *Studies in the Novel* (2006).

Grateful acknowledgment is made to Rose Styron for permission to reproduce an adapted version of a letter from William Styron, dated 20 October 1987, and lines from her poem, "Censor" (*Thieves' Afternoon*, New York: Viking, 1973), 23-25; and to William Heyen for permission to reproduce "The Tooth" (*Crazy Horse in Stillness*, Brockport: BOA Editions, 1996), 24. Gratitude for specific help in bringing the book to fruition is also due to Mark Annand, Richard Francis, Tessa Hadley, Richard Kerridge, Matthew Martin, and Stuart Woodington.

If I'm Ever Back This Way is a fictionalized travel memoir. While based on the author's experiences, it is still first and foremost fiction, and should be read as such.

If I'm Ever Back This Way

Gavin Cologne-Brookes

X/A Books

© Gavin Cologne-Brookes 2008

All rights reserved; no part of this book may be reproduced in any manner without written permission from the publisher, except for brief quotations used in reviews, critical articles, or books.

First Edition

ISBN 978-0-9558211-0-3

Published by X/A Books
Glenverne
Folly Lane East
Lacock
Wiltshire SN15 2LL
England

Transferred to digital print on demand, 2008
Printed and bound by **CPI** Antony Rowe, Eastbourne, England

FOR NICKI, XENATASHA AND ANASTASIA

It's got to be the going not the getting there that's good.

—Harry Chapin, "Greyhound"

As for Greyhounds—I rode them for years and years. A strange, very American sort of romance to these lumbering buses, especially at night.

—Joyce Carol Oates, Correspondence

CONTENTS

Part One: Escape

1	The Kings and I	11
2	Back to the Future	19
3	Michigan Dream	31
4	Desmoinesia	44
5	The Soul-Saver of Omaha	52
6	Laundromance	62
7	Mitzvah	80
8	If I'm Ever Back This Way	94
9	Truckstop, Montana	100
10	Tampa to Tampa, A Whirlwind Tour	111
11	Born in the USA	149

Part Two: Return

12	The Real Enid Stevick	159
13	Lilacs and Magnolias	188
14	The House of Inexpressible Happiness	199
15	A Spell in Connecticut	214
16	Pistachios with Arthur Miller	232
17	Douglas and Donehogawa	249
18	Joyce Carol Ghost	262
19	Redshift	277
20	Star Spangled Man	293
21	In the Twinkling of an Eye	307
22	The Final Act	326

Part One

Escape

1

THE KINGS AND I

Eddie Cochran died on my birthday. The car he was in hit a lamppost outside our house on Rowden Hill, Chippenham, and sent my mother into labor. They delivered me by forceps, causing minor contusions to the head, sixteen hours later—at teatime as my parents used to say—Easter Sunday, April 17, 1960. Cochran died that same afternoon. It's a matter of record.

Two minutes to midnight: April 16, the pale Ford Consul with five occupants shoots for London from the Bristol Hippodrome, blurs past the hamlet of Pickwick, kills two miles in a hundred seconds, and flashes through a tunnel. One minute to midnight: my mother turns to my father in bed and says, "It's really kicking. Feel that!"

"Wow! That's something else."

"No," says my mother. "It's the baby."

"It's just an expression. You know: *She's somethin' else.*"

"Suppose she's a he?"

"Then he's Eddie. In fact, it's Eddie either way. Edward. Edwina. Eddie. Not that I care what it's called, so long as it's mine."

"Meaning?"

Midnight: "a screeching of brakes," a witness tells *The Wiltshire Times*, "a whistling noise," then *bang!*

The car rests half on the kerb, half in the road. "A remarkable feature of the accident" is that the rear of the car is "completely wrecked" but wheels apart there's "no damage to the front." Contrary to the entry in *The Encyclopaedia of Rock Stars*, Cochran hasn't been thrown head-first through the windshield but flung through an open rear door. He's lying near Gene Vincent on the grass verge. Further down the road, Pat Thompkins, his business manager, crawls toward Cochran's girlfriend, the writer of "Somethin' Else," Sharon Sheeley, who kneels among photos and sheet music. Cochran's trademark Gretch guitar lies like a flat-topped island in a stream of oil. People rush out with blankets and cushions. My father's about to join them.

"My waters," says my mother. "I think they've broken! Get me to hospital!"

"There's been a crash outside."

"My child is about to be born!"

He looks back at her from the window, blue and red lights pulsing his stubbly cheek. "*Our* child?"

But maybe there's no time to lose so out they go to drive the half-mile to Greenways Hospital up the road on the right. The scene of flashing lights resembles the end of *Rebel Without A Cause*.

"Eddie!" Sharon Sheeley cries as she's lifted into the ambulance. "Where's Eddie?"

My parents climb into their Bentley and follow the ambulance up to Greenways.

Easter Sunday morning the passengers are transferred to St. Martin's Hospital, Bath. Cochran, only twenty-one years old but already famous for songs like "Summertime Blues" and "Somethin' Else" dies of multiple head wounds and haemorrhages. Gene Vincent has broken a collarbone and ribs and further damaged a leg already crippled in a motorcycle smash. Sheeley has broken her back and pelvis. Thompkins and driver George Martin are unhurt. That same afternoon, even as the fifties are sealed into history, I am born: a matter of record.

"A curse," says my father, pacing past his new, jaundiced charge in the maternity ward. "All the kings die young. James Dean in 1955. Buddy Holly in 1959 in that plane crash with the Big Bopper and Ritchie Valens. And now Cochran, who sang about them!"

"We'll *have* to call him Eddie," says my mother. "It's a sign."

My father shakes his head. "Not Eddie, not Buddy, not Jimmy, not Bopper, none of them. Except maybe Elvis. He's *the* King of rock 'n' roll."

"No one in Chippenham is called Elvis," replies my mother. "How about John, as in that nice young Senator Kennedy? They say he might be President and there's no reason why *he* shouldn't live to be old."

"Don't bet on it."

Fearing they might end up calling me Cliff Richard, whose "Fall In Love With You" has hit UK Number 2 that weekend, I wail, so diverting their attention forever from the subject of naming me, or perhaps allowing my father to indulge his superstitions. Name it, you kill it, he used to say. A name is a coffin. So I grew up with only a series of nicknames. Each left me as I passed to another stage of life. My mother called me "Son" or "Child." My father referred to me by way of an ever-changing selection of acronyms the meaning of which I had to work out for myself. (GB was a favourite. I think it meant Got Born, as in When Eddie Died, though maybe it just meant Greyhound Bus.)

But name or no name, my life began even as the fifties became myth. In that era lay my parents' dream of a land they never visited. They considered emigrating but instead the culture came to us. They put me in a little baseball jacket, bought me those inch high Timpo Cowboys and Indians, sat me in front of *The Virginian* and *Casey Jones*, drip-fed me the music, and left me to grow up with the Ponitails asking, Why was I born too late? The last time I saw my mother, in August 1978, she was enraptured by the coincidence of Cochran's death and my birth and the fact that only that week she'd bought "Three Steps to Heaven." And throughout my childhood, my father quizzed me on *The Alamo*. Viewing the film as an accurate depiction of American history, he told me I should grow up to be like John Wayne as Davy Crockett or Richard Widmark as Jim Bowie.

"Richard Widmark!" my mother needled. "Now there's a man!"

But my parents' real love was Elvis. Like *The Alamo*, *Jailhouse Rock* hit cinemas in 1960. My father saw it five times. He saw all Elvis's movies, bought every record, and claimed he and my mother knew him in Germany between 1958 and September 1959, when they returned to England for their shotgun wedding.

"I'm not saying the King and I were buddies or anything," he'd say, "but, yeah, we hung out. He wasn't exactly your ordinary GI. He had a three-storied house in a cobbled town called Bad Neuheim, and a BMW sports car. The local papers called it *Der Elviswagon*.

We met at parties. Elvis was ever so friendly, especially to your mother." On August 17, 1977, the day we learned of that particular royal death, my father put a hand on my shoulder and showed me a ten cents military payment certificate inscribed with: "I knew your mother, brother. Elvis P." He took his hand off my shoulder to reclaim his perennial beer bottle and gestured with it at the certificate. "I said to Elvis, If I ever have a son, I'll want to prove to him that my wife and I knew you. No problem, Elvis replied, smiling strangely. What's his name gonna be? I said I wasn't sure so Elvis just signed it: 'I knew your mother, brother. Elvis P.' I said what about me. He said, 'Father don't rhyme with brother. Rhyme 'n' rhythm's where it's at, cat.' So you, see, son," said my father, "one day this certificate will be yours."

Years later, after my mother's death, my father gave it to me for good. It's on my study wall, behind a glass-framed collection of mementoes including such trivia as a stub for the Great Platte River Archway Monument (with a 10% discount to Wendy's in Grand Island, Hastings, Kearney, Lexington, North Platte and Ogallala); a complimentary ticket to the 1985 Bold City Classic between Florida A&M and Georgia Southern College at the Gator Bowl, Jacksonville; various boarding passes, including Seat 24C Continental Airlines to Houston and Seat 11F USAir from Rochester to New York/La Guardia; a receipt for purchases from City Lights Books, A Mars Pathfinder July 4, 1997 $3.00 stamp, and a Greyhound Lines Ameripass travel coupon from Chicago to Milwaukee.

The pale blue, Monopoly size certificate (Series

481, Number D10265391D) is top right and even more faded than when I first saw it. My father, too, is now gone and I've no idea if it's really Elvis's handwriting. But the point is that when I first flew to America, my parents' dreams weighed far more than my father's old canvas bag. Even as I escaped Britain, America seemed a way home. I wanted to discover the country whose images had helped shape my parents' lives. Like my father, I've always had trouble telling imagination from reality, but America merged them irrevocably. My journey was a kaleidoscope of images caused, like a hallucinogen, by that culture-drip I'd been on since childhood, and I became a gatherer of voices and visions.

So call me anything. Or nothing. I am nobody, or anyone. What matters are the mélange of personalities and lives set down here. If I have a voice it's that of the perpetual foreigner, drawn to America in a way that her voices and mine have become forever entangled. Unless I need to explain how or why I got to be somewhere or meet someone, I'll avoid further reference to my personal history. It's a kind of fiction, anyway.

Suffice to say that some years ago, with as little money as Melville's Ishmael, fewer prospects, and nothing remotely to interest me in my own country, I naively decided to see America in entirety. Since that proved impossible, I tried making a mental-map of its actual geography, culture and history. Failing again, I gave up serious seeking and just went. Like Studs Terkel, I listened, watched and recorded. To roam America became a way I had—as Ishmael describes oceanic travel—"of driving off the spleen and regulating the circulation." Whenever I grew "grim about the mouth" or felt "a damp, drizzly November" in my soul; or found myself contemplating the height of accessible buildings or the price of alcohol in ratio to strength, I decided it was time to renew the relationship. The United States was my shotgun substitute. I could lose myself there until I felt able to continue ordinary life. Where Cato fell on his sword and Ishmael set out to sea, I quietly took flight for the Promised Land, and for over a quarter of a century my ship was the Greyhound Bus. I developed a strange love for and dependence on (as it says under the name slot) the "safe, reliable, courteous" figure of the Driver. I almost never knew where I was going. He knew exactly. I could sleep. He (sometimes She) never slept and always showed. Stranded in Nowhereville, a gleaming red, white and blue Americruiser would always spirit me away.

They say you never forget your first time. Mine's more vivid to me than the here-and-now. I'm in Muskegon, Michigan, August 4, 1979, a dog day noon. I'm queasy from combining malt shakes with Egg McMuffins and because I'm about to embark on a journey with only the haziest sense of an end. I've no idea it will last so long. The depot's a hut with GREYHOUND in blue letters above the door and a Dog sign swinging in the wind. The ticket man's stamped my Ameripass and I'm waiting in the shadows on my father's canvas bag. A dust swirl skeems up against abandoned buildings across the street. Around the sunlit bend, the shining celebrity rumbles in to roll me forth. For now it's just a bus that can hold forty-seven passengers and a driver. Only years later will I understand what the Texan broadcaster Jim Lehrer means at the start of *A Bus of My Own*. "There stands an ordinary person with me on a street corner waiting for the light to change," he writes. "Along comes a bus, let's say a blue and white bus with a running dog and the word GREYHOUND on the side. The ordinary person either sees nothing or sees only a bus with a running dog and the word GREYHOUND on the side." But for Lehrer, whose parents owned a regional bus company, it means his family "freezing, laughing and crying in Kansas in 1947." It means "cap-badges, bus depot signs, cast-iron toy buses and ticket punches in leather holsters." It means "drivers in starched gray uniforms driving through snowstorms, ticket agents quoting from memory schedules and fares to cities and towns all over America." In time it will mean as much to me. Somehow it all connects with the family I've lost and looked for, and the family I now have—a wife and two daughters I'll barely mention in this narrative, but who are everything to me. As my trip unfolded, the country of my parents' imagination gradually became real to me. In turn that real country fed my imagination and made me whoever it is that I have turned out to be. For like America itself the Greyhound is really many rolled into one. The country has many voices: the dog has many tales.

2

BACK TO THE FUTURE

"America," says Brandon Dimmerstamm, Director of Camp Jakalak, "is an *idea*."

We've filed into the Council Circle, a sandy arena with seats rising around a crackling fire. Jowls aglow, this bullet-headed Georgian might as well be a Confederate General rousing his dazed and depleted band of officers for one last battle. They amount to forty-odd counselors and a dozen support workers: over fifty staff to look after, not two hundred campers, as the Camp Profile said, but the eighty-six who've actually enrolled.

"Have you got the spirit?" intones Dimmerstamm amid a horror show of shadows. He clears his throat. A black squirrel yackets in the treetops. "Have you got the *spirit?*" Yackety-yak goes the squirrel. "Nine score and twelve years ago, guys," continues Dimmerstamm in his sixty-a-day smoker's voice, "our fathers brought forth on this continent a new nation, conceived in liberty, and dedicated to the proposition that we're all kinda equal. We have come, this as every summer, to dedicate our time to the promotion of that ideal, that dream, and this camp. I don't kid myself the world's going to pay much attention to what I say here. But never forget, guys, you're descendants of that founding dream. Dedicate yourselves to the unfinished work of those whose spirits populate this camp and this country. Resolve that they did not live in vain; that this camp, under God, shall have this summer a rebirth, and that government of this camp by the counselors for the campers shall not perish from this Earth."

"All *right!*" someone shouts from the shadows.

"Hey guys," grumbles Dimmerstamm, as if he's just thought of it, "what say we sing them old Jakalak songs?"

That night, my first at the camp, I lie in Cabin C-9 of the Mohawk Unit, alone and afraid. Through the flaps, silhouettes of trees frame a faint gleam of moonlight on Lake Michigan. C-9, the last in a line of widely dispersed, semi-ruined cabins, is haunted by the ghost of Tom Paschenslaag, a camper who drowned in the lake seven summers ago, and so began Jakalak's loss of popularity and slow decline. Attempting to cross deep rapids, he became entangled below water. They took a fortnight to retrieve his body. Paschenslaag Memorial Chapel stands just off the narrow path that ends at my broken-hinged door. Spared the details of Paschenslaag's death, I might have slept. Instead, I sweat in my sleeping bag, unable to clear my head of a ditty sung me by faces lit from beneath by reddening embers. *Have you seen the ghost of Tom? / Long white bones and the skin all gone. / Po - o - o - o - or Tom, / Wouldn't it be chilly with no skin on!*

Past midnight, waiting for Paschenslaag to tap my shoulder, my mind races through these black Michigan woods, haunted not just by Paschenslaag's lonely ghost but by the Potawatomi, whose arrowheads Hemingway's father collected as a child, and who once sung around long vanished fireplaces in these same woods.

Only some way north of here the Ottowa and Chippewa or Ojibway roamed. Here, still, the Brimley Chippewa live on a reservation at Bay Mills near the Hiawatha Forest between Lakes Michigan, Superior and Huron. And I think maybe I, aged nineteen, am merely a ghost myself, doomed to chase my parents' dreams. *Oh God*, I'm thinking, *how did I get here?*

Imagine our world around thirty years ago, just before everything seemed to accelerate toward some point of impact: before e-mail and the Internet, before Microsoft and the mapping of Mars. Before Voyager II had shown us the gas giants up-close. Before Hubble had revealed star nurseries five thousand light years away in the Lagoon Nebula. Before we started cloning animals, or had to deal with AIDS or CJD or the post-antibiotic age. Before Nine Eleven and the War on Terror. When Rap still meant something teachers were allowed to do to your knuckles and Crack was just the sound it made. When iPods, Sat Nav and cell phones would have seemed miraculous and shuttles were local services and while there was already too much ozone in the streets there was still enough in the sky. When no one seriously expected the Midwest to burn up or sea levels to threaten cities. When Bill and Hillary Clinton were best known in Arkansas, and no one had ever had an arm transplant or embarked on the Human Genome Project. When George Bush Snr seemed a likely President but hardly the father of one. When getting back to a split second before the Big Bang and isolating quarks was science fiction, not scientific reality.

It's 1979. The Iranians are soon to depose the Shah and bring back Ayatollah Khomeini. John Wayne is dying of cancer and Jean Seberg will be found dead in Paris in September after years of hounding by the FBI. Margaret Thatcher comes to power in Britain, and Reagan will beat Carter in November. O. J. Simpson's retired fifteen years before most Europeans know who he is. Judy Garland's false eyelashes are sold for $125. Thirteen-year-old Mike Tyson, who like Brando in *On the Waterfront*, has been keeping racing pigeons, arrives at the Tryon School, a correction center in upstate New York, where former Golden Gloves champion Bobby Stewart introduces him to boxing. And where are you? Are you already middle-aged, or nowhere at all because you're not even born? Me, I was born yet unborn, just as now, on this page, I'm no age and any age, and can flick back and forth like I do with TV channels on my remote control. But if this is 1979 then I'm underground, an undeveloped bulb, unworldly as an Anchorite monk, unhappy as the face of Walter Matthau: choose your own metaphor, but use a lot of un-s. Unemployed, unqualified, and unable to prevent my mother's death or arrest my father's alcoholism.

America beckons. My dreams are adolescent in the extreme. I'll hang out in the parking lot of Arnold's with Ritchie, Ralph Malph and Fonzie, and wear a white T-shirt under a short-sleeved, checked shirt. I'll cruise for girls down the same roads as Paul LeMat and Harrison Ford in *American Graffiti*, and sit on a car with Richard Dreyfuss to watch a rerun of JFK's assassination. I'll give old Holden Caulfield a buzz and meet up in the goddam Wicker Bar of the Seton Hotel to shoot the shit about *The Great Gatsby*, for Chrissake. Then I'll light out for the Territories ahead of the rest.

My sense of American geography is no less naïve.

"Where will you go?" asks my father, holding the door open as I cross the threshold.

"Alaska," I reply, "then Hawaii."

So Alaska, the Last Wilderness, for its name if for nothing else, becomes my aim. I've seen a Patricia Moraz film, *Les Indiens Sont Encore Loin*—"The Indians Are Still Far Away." Isabelle Huppert plays a young girl searching for what Thomas Mann called "the unattainable place of inexpressible happiness." Obsessed with the lost lives of Native Americans, she's found dead in snowy woodland far from home. I understand the yearning for snowy woods but, for me, Alaska sounds like a world of symphonic promise where gargantuan grizzlies send hungry roars echoing down mountainsides to startle away Caribou padding through the tundra past rivers swollen with salmon. Alaska seems to hold all the mystery my young soul thinks it yearns for. Not that I'm too particular. If I find myself in Hawaii I'll be just as happy. I work two jobs, fifteen hours a day, skimping to save and planning my escape. I'm not *really* sweeping floors. The trade winds of my imagination have swept me nine thousand miles across the Atlantic, the American continent and the Pacific to technicolor islands concocted by James Michener and populated by the girls who surround Elvis in *Blue Hawaii*. I'm not *really* cleaning urinals. I'm flying into a Hawaiian sunset over the extinct volcano of Diamond Head ready to join the ghost of Jimi Hendrix for an impromptu jam session at the foot of Haleakala.

So when, one fine spring day, a letter arrives from Camp Jakalak granting my request for a summer job, I look up the camp's location to see how far it is from Alaska and Hawaii, intending to visit both. Headlines splash news about a radioactive leak at Three Mile Island. But nothing will deter me. I'm bound for the Promised Land in pursuit of happiness. By the time Margaret Thatcher is in 10 Downing Street, I have my visa and tickets. On Monday, June 11—the day of John Wayne's death, and coincidentally the fifty-fourth birthday of another of my father's heroes, novelist William Styron, and the publication day of *Sophie's Choice*— with rain clattering the portholes and sweeping in torrents across the runway, my Capitol Airways flight thunders skyward for America. I'm without identity or direction. I'm nobody, and I need to *become*.

"Go west, young man," says an elderly gentleman named Horace Greeley in the aisle seat when I tell him this is my first trip. "Go west and grow up with the country."

The plane rises, battered by rain clouds, and bursts through cumulous castles into a sun-filled sky. Soon we're drifting over an arctic dreamscape. Icebergs like cloud-boats litter a Prussian blue sea. Acres of dense pine forest spill across the landscape to the sandy lip of the New World. It's like being transported back to Nick Carraway's vision of the vanished trees that "once pandered in whispers to the last and greatest of all human dreams." I hold my breath, compelled into an aesthetic contemplation in witnessing "something commensurate," at last, to my "capacity for wonder": *The United States of America.*

Except that this turns out not to be not the United States at all, but Newfoundland. Pines give way to patches of grassland dotted with red or yellow two-seater planes. We drop below the tree line and refuel at Gander to fly south for New York and then chase the night to Chicago. 35,000 feet below, the lights of Philadelphia, city of the Declaration of Independence, throb in the night. There's no cloud over America. Lights speckle the continent from New York to the Midwest.

"Behold the gem-strung towns and cities of the good, green East, flung like star-dust through the field of night," says Thomas Wolfe, a giant of a man who got on in New York and is now in the window seat to my right. "Over there, look! Boston, tinged with the bracelet of its shining little towns! And there's the towering island of Manhattan surrounded thick as grain by the glitter of a hundred towns and cities!" He points out what he calls "the necklace of Long Island" and the "duller glare of Philadelphia." As we approach Chicago he calls it "a spreading constellation to the north" with Lake Michigan a "giant wink" blazing in the moonlight. I'm too shy to ask the man if he's descended from *the* Thomas Wolfe, but his sense of the promise of America captures precisely my own exhilaration as I look down across the country that night. "Go seeker, if you will, throughout the land," he urges into my adolescent ear, "and you will find us burning in the night. It's your oyster—yours to open if you will."

The next morning I wake at 5 a.m. in my room at the Chicago YMCA, my radio scraping out "Penny Lane." Chicago's smothered in gray mist. In the lobby an old black man asks for a cigarette. "Sheey-it," he says when I tell him I don't have any. *Wonderful*, I think. *This is America.* The Sears Tower looms in the distance beyond South Wabash Avenue. Black ladies, hats as bright as the two-seater planes in Newfoundland, step off a Union Baptist Church bus. I ask the driver, who looks like Chuck Berry, how to get to Chicago Midway Airport.

"I'll take you there myself," says Berry. "I've got no particular place to go."

He gets me there in time to fly Northwestern Airlines to Milwaukee and Muskegon. The pilot, Lee Marvin, swings me skyward—a lone passenger, aside from a flight attendant with Betty Davis eyes who serves me Seven-Up—flings me down on Milwaukee to pick up two more passengers, skims low enough to ripple the plane's shadow across Lake Michigan and drops us unceremoniously in Muskegon. Dimmerstamm, in a lime green Camp Jakalak jacket and baseball cap, saunters into the pine-panelled foyer.

"So," he says, handing me a Whatchamacallit, "how d'you like America?"

Camp Jakalak lies wedged between Star Lake and Lake Michigan. Dimmerstamm bumps his Cadillac round a sandy bend, past an isolated bar with an electronic Budweiser sign pulsing in the dark window, a small park with wooden picnic tables and a deserted softball diamond. We pass another shack, sagging on the road edge. "That's the supermarket," he says, "where you'll be buying all your sodas, submarine sandwiches and T-shirts."

"What kind of T-shirts do they have?"

"Two kinds," said Dimmerstamm. "Camp Jakalak ones which say Camp Jakalak and Star Lake ones which say, Where the hell is Star Lake?"

"So where *is* Star Lake?"

"Over there," says Dimmerstamm.

Once in camp I follow his directions along successive half-vanished woodland paths to my far-flung cabin, waving away green caterpillars that hang on threads from the trees. Every fifty yards or so I pass a derelict cabin. C-9 is in the deepest backwoods where the caterpillars hang thickest and the poison ivy spreads darkest. Dust specks dance among the few sunbeams that break the woodland gloom. Like Robinson Crusoe, I lie back and dream a survival inventory. *Firstly, health and fresh water. Secondly, shelter from the heat of the sun. Thirdly, security from ravenous creatures, whether men or beasts. Fourthly, a view to the sea, that if God send any ship in sight. . . .* And start awake to someone shouting, "Fuckin' *worms!*"

A lanky figure is waving tanned arms through the trees. "Damned dogfuckin' *worms!* They tangle in your hair and fall on your face. Sonofabitch-shittin' *worms!*" Soon this crazed figure looms in the doorway, "So hey, bud, why Michigan?"

"In search," I say primly, "of the unattainable place of inexpressible happiness."

He scratches his belly beneath his maroon and yellow SEMINOLES half-shirt. "Come to visit the Amedicans, have you?" he mimics. "How jolly." He puts out a brown hand. "Darius Desoutter of Jacksonville, Flawda. But you can call me 'Redeye.' Let's go eat."

We join Dimmerstamm and the other counselors for yams, grits, and cold pork thrown at us by Texan Ted, a bad-tempered cook who looks, I'm shocked to discover when I see the film the following year, like

Jack Nicholson in *The Shining*. Then we troop off to the Council Circle for Dimmerstamm's pep-talk, them old camp songs, helpful reminiscences about Tom Paschenslaag, and information on the arriving campers, freckled, baseball bat-toting Alfred E. Neumans with astronaut haircuts one and all. For five weeks I spend daytimes teaching tennis with a counselor named Randy O'Pant, whose jacket sports nine Jakalak medals for the nine years he's been returning (one side Jesus, the other the camp motto, "My own self at my very best all the time"). Afternoons I teach soccer, burdened by the help of a Canadian linebacker named Melvin Weilschnecker, who is terrific at sprinting but has muscles so hardened that he can't turn corners. We devise a system whereby I run up and down one side, and Weilschnecker the other. But the campers drift to other sports until soccer is canceled. I take on tennis full-time, and Weilschnecker is put in charge of long-distance canoeing.

Time passes smooth as the waters of Star Lake until suddenly, three weeks before camp ends, a squall of Summer Love blows in from Nebraska in the shape of a seventeen-year-old, Polish-Italian Catholic girl named Carlotta Domarski. She looks at me across Star View, the log cabin where we eat, with big brown eyes that stop my heart, and a voice from the rafters says: *This is she.* The rest of the world goes on stand-by. Like brainwashed *Star Trek* extras, Carlotta and I float out onto the porch overlooking the lake, down over a fence and deep into the woods. Through the cold night we lie in the dirt gazing up through a single gap in the black foliage at the constellations. The moon, near fullness, slides into the gap. Since I've taken to imitating James Dean, I'm wearing only a white T-shirt and thin red jacket. I'm freezing. Carlotta puts a hand on my stomach. Neither of us speaks but my teeth are chattering worse than Leonardo DiCaprio's at the end of *Titanic*.

"You're shivering," she whispers, pulling me toward her. "I bet," she purrs, "you've never kissed an American girl." In truth, I've never kissed anyone much. I'm unsure if I should close my mouth and open my eyes, or open my eyes and close my mouth. I open my mouth a little, close my eyes, and wait. Nothing happens. "You're not asleep, are you?" she says.

I open an eye. "No," I explain. "I was waiting."

"Aha," she murmurs, Her teeth shine in the dark. "I bet you've had little experience of American girls, let alone *Catholic* ones. Not *Polish-Italian* Catholic ones."

So we keep warm in the freezing Michigan woods, working on our night moves, until suddenly the trees turn gray. The same the next night, and the next. This, I think, is my youth finally *happening*. All that matters about daytime is that it brings on the night. All that matters about the night is that I spend it with Carlotta. Some nights we find a crater of sand in a clearing or a forgotten path in the abandoned Pioneer Unit. The ghost of Paschenslaag drifts off in disgust. Other nights we stumble hand in hand up a giant sand dune called Shifting Mountain, down through Shifting Mountain Draw the half-mile to the dunes overlooking Lake Michigan. The orange moon rises to a hard bright disc doubled in the lake, and completes a circle with its watery reflection, fading and enlarging as it sinks into itself. The Aurora Borealis drifts in vertical lines like a vast radiator across the sky. But every night merges all too soon with dawn until daylight startles us awake and, bemused by the concertina time of love, we slip back to camp, footsteps quiet as snakes in sand. And just as the nights pass so too do our final weeks at Camp Jakalak. Soon, our only job left is to pack. The present, so delicious, so visceral, is about to become memory.

Carlotta stands before me, voice half-drowned by the rumble of the bus. "We're like painted spheres in the Universe," she says. "We bump for a millisecond, and bounce off toward distant constellations, but we leave a little paint mark on each other. Will you visit Omaha?"

The last bus gone, Jakalak is ready to return to its ghosts. Darius "Redeye" Desoutter flies to Jacksonville. Weilschnecker takes the straight road to Windsor, Ontario. Only Dimmerstamm, Texan Ted and I remain, standing beneath the Jakalak sign amid the footprints of a summer. Jack Nicholson lookalike that he is, Ted's been rumored all season to resemble a fifties cook who died tasting a broth concocted for a camp out. Now he finally turns with a strange expression, says, "So long, boys. Remember me," and saunters off into the forest, fading before our eyes. In our last look around Star View, Dimmerstamm and I spot him, not a day younger, in one of the group photos from the fifties that line the walls. Spooked by the whispering trees, I help Dimmerstamm lock up and he drives me to Muskegon before heading home to Georgia. So it is that I take my seat on my first Americruiser. I feel as if I'm plunging off the edge of the world. The bulky driver eases into his seat. The door hisses shut. "Let us advance," he says over the intercom, "upon the Chaos and the Dark."

3

MICHIGAN DREAM

So much for bold words: no sooner has my first Greyhound raced off, with me sitting forward in my seat, eager, apprehensive yet expecting to roll a thousand miles, than it grunts to a halt in Grand Rapids for a lunchtime rest-stop. Grand Rapids is not much of a place to rest or even stop. The town of spectacular vistas set on a white river promised by its name is just a conglomeration of red-painted buildings and dusty streets. I'd have got out of there as soon as possible if I hadn't unexpectedly met Marilyn Monroe.

Of course, she doesn't look like the Marilyn Monroe everybody thinks they know. She's in disguise as the proprietor of a run-down coffee shop and has gone back to her Norma Jean-look, with freckles and darker, graying hair. She's in her early fifties, but I know it's her as soon as I hear those wispy tones. I'm moping over my Jakalak farewells when she breathes in my ear, "Young man, why do you seem so sad? What are looking for?" Her dark turquoise eyes are hollowed out the way beautiful women's eyes sink beneath their brows and accentuate when they get older, but they're large and kind. "Here," she says. "I brought you over some complimentary gum." It's Wrigley's Big Red, the color of the lipstick she used to wear.

My heart thuds. "I—I can't believe it."

"It's only gum. It doesn't cost much anyway."
"No, I can't believe it's you."
"What do you mean, honey?"

In the dust-spotted sunlight, her face resembles the furrows of the Grand Canyon, but the bone structure is as firm as ever. To see her in a deserted coffee shop in Michigan tugs my heart.

"I mean—I'll pay for it. I'll pay for the gum."
"You won't," she breathes in that same soft voice she has in *Some Like It Hot*. "I own the place. Besides, you look like Walt."
"Walt?"
"My husband."

Miller and DiMaggio, yes, but Walt? "Don't tell me: Walt Disney."

"Don't mock me," she murmurs. "Walt Whitman."

I squint toward the sun-hazy door. Either she's mad or I am, but I've nothing to lose so play the game and ask the obvious question, "What are you doing running a coffee shop in Michigan?" I'm tempted to add that she's supposed to be seventeen years dead and buried in Westwood, Los Angeles, but it seems rude.

"Walt and I have run this shop since August 4, 1962," she replies. "This is our anniversary. Except he's no longer here."

"I'm sorry."

"That's okay. It's nice to have someone come in. It's been so quiet for so many years."

"Why stay?" I ask as naturally as possible.

"It was Walt's dream. He worked thirty years in the mines in southern Illinois, and all he ever wanted from life, after our daughter died, was to own a coffee shop in Grand Rapids."

"Why here?"

"It sounded nice. He was kind of shocked when we got here, but he'd had the dream so long. You know how it is when you fix on an image of something? Maybe you don't. You're so young." Her head shakes gently, more as if she has Parkinson's than as a sign of regret. She gazes through back-to-front letters on the window. I want to ask about her daughter, but that may tip her over the edge. I know she *can't* be Marilyn Monroe, but she's identical, right down to that fine, downy hair on her cheeks. Later I'll examine Marilyn's teeth in photos and see no obvious differences. And she's wearing Chanel No. 5.

She seems to have drifted into reminiscence, but then smiles directly at me. "Still! You do look like my Walt. Ever see *Carousel*? Guy returns from Heaven. His poor wife can't see him, but he leaves her a little star. He has a daughter too, but my girl's in Heaven with her daddy. He was a poet, you know."

"I guessed."

"Not for money. But he wrote them for me. *I bequeath myself to the dirt to grow from the grass I love,* he wrote. *If you want me again look for me under your boot-soles. / You will hardly know who I am or what I mean, / But I shall be good health to you nevertheless, / And filter and fibre your blood. / Failing to fetch me at first keep encouraged, / Missing me one place search another, / I stop somewhere waiting for you.* Isn't that pretty?"

"Is it original?"

She holds my gaze. "I've memorized huge chunks

of what he wrote me, all handwritten in little homemade booklets. He called them *Sheaves of Corn*. Walt was the sweetest man, and you *so* resemble him." Her eyes are the only wet things on this dry afternoon. I thank her for the gum. "Where are you headed next, honey?"

"Alaska."

"Ah, yes," she says. "The Last Wilderness. I hope you find what you seek or make yourself into whatever you want to become. You've a long journey ahead and one day you'll tell about it, and when you do, remember to mention me."

"I'll do that, Marilyn."

Her eyes widen. "Mrs Whitman," she breathes in a sing-song, girlish voice. "And if you ever call by Grand Rapids again, bring me a *star*."

I head for the door but turn back. She's become so pale and forlorn since her screen days. I want to make her happy. If she is Marilyn Monroe, I want her to see I know without embarrassing her, and if she isn't I want Mrs Whitman to feel good about the way she looks.

"You know something?" I unwrap a stick of gum. "I may resemble your Walt, but *you* look like Marilyn Monroe. That's why I said it. You even sound like her."

"Oh, why keep up the pretence?" she breathes. "How did you guess?"

"Doesn't everyone?"

"People see what they're looking for."

The door swings shut. I've forgotten the time. The bus has left. The desk clerk reassures me that my canvas bag will be in Lost Property in Omaha, but there's only one bus a day.

"You missed a bus, son?" says a middle-aged, bespectacled man with the triangle of an ironed handkerchief in the top pocket of his suit. "I'm going Detroitways."

"He's heading west, Mr Loman," says the ticket clerk.

"I've got twenty-four hours to wait," I shrug. "I may as well go east."

"I just dropped my son, Biff," smiles Mr Loman. "He's at college upstate and we meet in Grand Rapids. You'll be okay with me."

The ticket clerk nods. "Mr Loman knows Michigan like the back of his hand."

I glance at the back of Mr Loman's hairless, sun-blotched hand and suppose it's the hand of a man you can trust, so off we drive toward the cacophonic metropolis of Detroit. I know it's too far to go at present, but decide to take what comes until the bus back in Grand Rapids tomorrow. Only as he turns the ignition do I note his distinct resemblance to Henry Fonda in *On Golden Pond*, spectacles glinting as he peers through the windshield, hands tight on the wheel. But I dismiss it. Two incognito movie stars in one day is stretching it, especially in Michigan. He drives me as far as the state capital, Lansing. Some way along Highway 96, a little shaky, he pulls out a wad of papers wedged above the sunshade.

"Drawings," he says. "By Biff. He's been dead ten years."

My heart sinks. He drops the papers on my lap. They're crude pencil sketches on brittle, yellowed paper. Human figures in line-drawn landscapes.

"They're very good."

"You think so?" Mr Loman gives a wry smile. "I think they're crap. I'm glad he's gone. Incidentally, don't you know hitchhiking is illegal in Michigan?"

We speed past flat farmland. Hunched forward, he grips the wheel with both hands, as if it's pulling us along the road. He's begun to sweat. A drop rides down his temple like ice on a stove. He mops his brow and pushes his ironed handkerchief back in his top pocket, checking in the mirror to be sure it's neat. He seems like the kind of man who always went on driving vacations with his wife until one day he got tired of her, opened the passenger door, and pushed her out. Here I am in her seat, and probably the dead son's age.

"How old was Biff?"

"He's thirty-four."

"He's alive, then?"

"The dead are always alive," says Mr Loman. "He died aged nineteen, hitchhiking."

My mind works overtime. For all I know, he and the ticket clerk are in cahoots, and I'm just another illegal hitchhiker, and Mr Loman is a crank, or a crazed, bereaved father, or not a father at all. It occurs to me that his name's not even Mr Loman, and that "Biff" never existed. "Is your wife alive?"

"Oh, sure!"

"Where is she?"

"In the back seat."

"There's no one in the back seat."

Mr Loman, definitely looking like Henry Fonda now, smiles and says, "There's no one *on* the back seat. Say, did you know Michigan has the longest coastline of any state?"

"If you're not meeting Biff," I ask with some trepidation, "where are you going?"

"I've got just the book for you," he says. "Open the glove box." I open the glove box. "Go on," he says, "take out what you find in there. It's yours." I pull out a book called *If You Don't Know Where You're Going, You'll Probably End Up Somewhere Else* by David Campbell, and flick through it as we pass a red barn with a two-tiered, Dutch-style roof. Telegraph poles line the road like crosses down the Appian Way.

Mid-afternoon Mr Loman drops me on an empty Lansing street beside a barber's pole striped red, white and blue. A nearby hydrant's shadow is a black nudge against sharp sunlight. Above the green shop fronts the two storied building stretches red beneath a cloudless sky. Three consecutive upper windows have half-drawn yellow blinds as if drowsing into a siesta.

Mr Loman reaches that hairless hand through the window. I offer the book. He winks. "I said it's yours. I'm *already* somewhere else."

In a downtown parking lot a youth in a Silver Bullet Band T-shirt is climbing in through the window of a battered Pontiac plastered with Michigan State stickers. He's only going as far as "Moo U" in East Lansing but is happy to take me if I can climb through the window. He looks (and I've come to expect this by now) like Jeff Bridges in *The Last Picture Show*.

"Moo U?"

"Yeah, don't call it that," says Jeff. "I'm from Ohio, but my dad got transferred here. Cow College was the only place I could get in. But, hey, don't mind me. I'm just bitching. I flunked a math exam."

"Why don't the doors open?" I'm breathless from clambering in.

"I've soldered them shut."

He gives me the kind of hair-raising ride out to Michigan State you might expect from a student who has just failed an exam. Glad to get out, I hang around campus the rest of the day, spend the night beneath a bush, wake at dawn and hitch a ride from a carpenter doing some work at the music school at Interlochen. He has to fetch supplies from Traverse City so drops me there. White sail boats drift around Traverse Bay. I take snaps of a water tower with a spherical bulge on top that dominates the townscape, get carded in Antlers Liquor Bar, and finally hitch a ride in Charlie Michilimackinac's pick-up. He pronounces it "Michilimack-i-*naw*" and says it's Ojibway for Mackinac. He's a stocky man of about thirty on his way home to Mount Pleasant for the first time in a decade. He left to get an education at a community college in Kalamazoo and then at Wayne State in Detroit. He's coming back to teach "Integrity Studies" because not enough people in Michigan have integrity.

"Gerald Ford lost his when he left Grand Rapids and retired to California," he says. "Me, I'm heading north after a year or two. I'm gonna cross the Mackinac Bridge to the Upper Peninsular where wildlife outnumber people, and not one of them bears, raccoons, elks, chipmunks and such is without integrity."

We lapse into silence while I think of something to say. In the end I ask, "What do you think of General Custer?"

"One of the great villains of American history," he

replies, "a glory-seeker, the embodiment of evil, and a misguided fool. The Lakotas were defending their homeland in the Valley of the Greasy Grass, fighting yards from their village when they killed him."

That wasn't quite how my father's 1950 *Buffalo Bill Wild West Annual* portrayed it. "But the Little Big Horn was a great victory for the Indians."

"Not in the long run."

Charlie drops me at the fork for Big Rapids on Route 131. I trudge south along a snaking road between miles of green crops, its yellow line fuzzing into a heat haze. Eventually an old bus like the one that passes Cary Grant in *North by Northwest* spumes to a dusty halt. Through the driver's window a gaunt double of Uncle Sam, complete with Stars and Stripes top hat, beckons me aboard. The bus is empty except for a slopping fish tank, several transparent bags of white plastic crosses and, laid out along a double seat, a comatose woman.

"I," says the Uncle Sam figure, rising to greet me, "am Reverend Fish Flesch. And over there," he points to the woman, "is Reverend Fina Flesch, my co-habitual partner, and this," he pulls at the trout-like skin of his tattooed forearm, "is the flesh. *I* am the flesh. And you," he thrusts his hooked nose an inch from my face, spewing tuna breath, "are an Angel." Then he plunges back down into the driver's seat, peers at me in his rear mirror, bundles the bus into gear and splutters us off into the Twilight Zone. "Wasn't that you I saw prayin' by the road side?"

The shadows lengthen. Reverend Flesch's pustulous face fills the rear-view mirror. Beneath psoriatic lids his pupils flit around his convex eyes like panicking fish. Outside the light fades across the flat grassland, the sun perilously poised in the salmon pink sky. "Yea," he chants as we bump down the road. "None of us is of this world in spirit, but merely in flesh. Given the glorious chance, we'd any of us give up our filthy forsaken bodies. I mean who wants to *live?* Ain't I right? I'm from Missouri"—he pronounces it "Missoura"—"but I'm Reverend of the World. And these," he hands me some calling cards, "are letters from Jesus."

I WILL MAKE YOU *FISHERS OF MEN*
WHAT DO YOU SEE?

J E S U S

FISH & FINA FLESCH VICTORINE LINEBARGER

"And those," he points over at the sacks of plastic crosses, "are "Guilts'." I decide the next crossroads is my stop. "You intend to get off without buying some Guilts?" he says. "And at a *crossroads?*"

"I'm doing a study of signposts."

"At night?"

"To see how well they show up."

"Without a car?"

"To pedestrians."

"If you ask me," he says, picking at his psoriatic eyelids, "you're a little insane. But I'll show you my Guilts anyway." He stops the bus and flings me a cross the size of his bony hand. "They relieve you of any amount of sin, depending on their size. For real big sins—say, murder, or being a member of the Ku Klux Klan like Fina's Pappy was—I can carve a cross of

If I'm Ever Back This Way

blood into your forehead with this here Bowie knife. But the white crosses are best. That's an eight-inch Guilt you got, at ten dollar a piece. That's a mighty pile of guilt to sell off. Jes' see the *craft*. Last a young'un like you six month and more." He rumples in his bag. "Or these here three-inch Guilts cost you fifty cents a piece, or five for three dollar. Angel discount."

"I have a lot of signposts to check before dawn."

"You don't want to chew Peyote? My magic Mescaline may make you a little sick. Ask Fina." He prods his comatose wife. "But the *visions!* I'm offerin' you the way to truth. Beware *crossroads!*"

In the middle of this latest speech, I grab my bag, kick open the door and run. When I glance back, the dilapidated bus has swung off into the night. I'm at the loneliest crossroads in Michigan and don't get a ride into Grand Rapids until dawn. I head for Mrs Whitman's coffee shop, but it's shut and there's no sign of Mrs Whitman, or anyone, let alone Marilyn Monroe. "William Gates's Fu---ture Warehouse," says a notice, with the "rni" scrubbed out. "Relocation here September 1." I slump on the doorstep. Someone's already replaced the glass or scrubbed out COFFEE SHOP from Marilyn's windows. Either side of her doorway, they shine dark as the eyes of a seal pup. Clumps of grass grow on the sidewalk where yesterday it was clean and brushed. I wander down to a diner for breakfast. *Do you know where you're going to?* asks Diana Ross from inside the jukebox. Two teenagers canoodle in a corner booth. A sorrowful-eyed waitress clips over.

"That building down the road was a coffee shop yesterday!" I muse.

"Is that right?" she says. "Everything around here changes so fast you'll be in the future before you know it. Or maybe you was in some kind of timewarp."

On comes a succession of Bob Seger songs, including "Mainstreet" and "Fire Lake." I picture Traverse City in midday sun, and lonely people in shaded windows like the paintings of Edward Hopper: *Sunlight in a Cafeteria, Office in a Small City, New York Office.* I know *I'll* never end up boxed in some office in a small city. And if we all end up in a box sooner or later, I'm sure it will be later. I have a whole life ahead of me. I finish my scrambled eggs to the ecstatic whine of a lead guitar.

Back at the depot, I board the bus to resume my journey. Someone turns on a radio to a song called "Let Time Go Lightly." "Turn that off, would you?" calls the driver. Next to me a raven-haired girl is reading Emily Dickinson. "*Because I could not stop for Death—*" I read over her shoulder, "*He kindly stopped for me— / The Carriage held but just Ourselves / And Immortality.*" I watch the passing farms and assume I won't return to Michigan. If I close my eyes all that has passed still seems present. I can see Carlotta and me on the sand dunes in the moonlight, Reverend Flesch, Mr Loman, Marilyn Monroe-Whitman, Charlie Michilimackinac, Traverse City. You don't pass through Michigan. You need a reason to go there. In fact I will come back but not for many years. As I sit on the bus this first time the dilapidated towns seem to echo not only to the ghosts of that first American summer but to the summers of Hemingway's youth. ("Nick felt quite sure that *he* would never die.") To the Potawatomi; the ancient Indian Copper Culture; French *voyageurs*; the *coureurs de bois.* In that blithe way of youth, I never imagine I'll need to return. I think I'm heading onward, ever outward as the Greyhound rolls down toward Indiana and I start reading *If You Don't Know Where You're Going, You'll Probably End Up Somewhere Else.*

"Pass me a cigarette," says someone behind me. "I think there's one in my raincoat."

"We smoked the last one an hour ago," comes the reply.

Michigan, I decide, has to be a beginning rather than an ending. From here I'll see the rest of America, the *whole* of America. I'll find happiness or pursue it forever. I take out my journal. "This is not the end," I scrawl to the motion of the bus, "nor is it the beginning. But I think perhaps it is the end of the beginning." The bus crosses into Indiana and turns west toward Gary and Chicago.

4

DESMOINESIA

Deep in the night in the deep Midwest the bus jolts me half awake in a place called DESMOINESIA. I close my eyes, at last drifting through some strange land beyond the rainbow. *Desmoinesia!* Amnesia. How much better to forget the past, never to search but to ride in and out of lives like Alan Ladd in *Shane*. Everything in Michigan happened, but even now I'm inventing and realigning, and will weave this summer's tapestry for years to come. *Desmoinesia!* There's nothing easier. I choose to make it mean Remembering to Forget. But just as I'm folding myself back into sleep, an ancient, large-limbed man in a black suit worn to a shine asks if the aisle seat's free.

"Sure," I yawn. "Did you get on at Desmoinesia?"

"Des Moines. You're in Iowa, boy."

Desmoinesia collapses like a shack of dream dust and blows away across the prairies. Instead, I get Roosevelt Franklin's own private Iowa. It's well past midnight, but this old-timer's wide-awake, haggard but patrician-featured, identical to the picture of his Presidential almost-namesake sinking deathward in that chair between Stalin and Churchill at Yalta. I shift to the window and put my red jacket over the air-conditioning. He eases down, leaning heavily on hands the size of ploughshares. He's got a voice like Louis Armstrong.

"Last time I took one of these son-of-a-gun buses," he rasps, "a twister whizzed us Ozways." Through the tinted window a green moon tracks us over ripened corn. Roosevelt coughs, a guttural throat-scraper followed by a little swallow that jumps his decrepit Adam's apple like the last throb of a dying heart. "I retired five years ago, after forty years in insurance in Des Moines." He touches my arm and I look into his rheumy, insomniac's eyes. "Now I'm heading for Nebraska to sort out some bastards."

Through the night I get edited highlights of his life story. Born in Omaha, he moved to Des Moines after combat as a submarine navigator in the Pacific. "All Iowa's fertile whereas you can only grow stuff in Nebraska along the valley of the Platte River. Western Nebraska's just prairie." As he talks my souvenir Greyhound pillow deflates. I put my arm under my head, ready for sleep. "Now *Iowa's* just one state, mind, but we've got the best topsoil in the US," he's saying as I look at my watch just before 1.00 a.m. "Robert Frost said it looked like you could eat it without vegetables." He wipes an eye with a hand that could till and furrow five counties in an afternoon. "We command the Corn Belt! Son, you're watching the world's breadbasket fly by in the moonlight. *Russia's* a big importer. Them Ruskies love Iowa. Old Nikita Khruschev, he came to Iowa back in the fifties to see how farmers like my father did it."

"Your father was a farmer?"

"Until they stopped him! I'm bussing to Omaha because a typhoon's developing against corporate farming. Turns out he lost his farm not because of soil erosion but because some damned insurance company bought up ranches around us and irrigated all the water out of our land. We're up in arms to get the law down on the bastards. We've got the National Farmers' Union onto it and just about everyone else." He runs his tongue along his crusty lower lip, and taps the backers off on his huge fingers. "Hell, we've even got the Catholic Church behind us."

The night rolls on and I think of this giant bus rumbling through the American heartland, and how you wouldn't even see the road let alone the bus from space. Roosevelt Franklin's voice wanders in and out of my dreams. ("South of here, see, is Red Cloud and Willa Cather country.") His father came from Liverpool in 1920 and made it through snowstorm, drought and deluge without quitting.

"My father was a boomer," he says with a nudge, "a *boomer*, you know what a boomer is? My father planted acres of hope. But you've got to cope if any of it withers. You've got to have acres of hope, just don't expect it all to ripen, is all. When he found out his life wasn't going to happen he became *angry*. Angry at exploitation by all them out-of-state banks and corporations. But he never quit. He intended to succeed or die."

"What happened?"

"He died. But he never quit."

"Was he happy at all?"

"No. And yes. But life is always no and yes."

"It is?"

"Yes and no. Some hope ripens, other hope withers. That's why there are so many paths to bitterness. My elder brother worked the farm, and I went job hunt-

If I'm Ever Back This Way

ing. Before I knew it, the corporation that employed me stood on my own family. Remember." He touches my arm and whistles out his musty, plaque-coated breath. "There are *many paths to bitterness*."

He falls silent only as dawn cracks on the horizon. I sleep and dream of being chased across a muddy field by an oafish woman named Desdemona who is hitting me on the head with a skillet. I escape onto a bus. Buddy Holly and the Crickets are at the back playing "That'll Be the Day." I'm sick of the damned bus, Holly says to his guitarist, Tommy Allsup, after the final chord. Eight breakdowns, can you believe it? The Big Bopper's in a sleeping bag on the seat in front. You want another number, Bopper? says Holly. The Big Bopper grunts, How about "The Purple People Eater Meets the Witch Doctor?" Holly says he doesn't know that one but could do a version of "Chantilly Lace." You *knows* what I like! growls the Big Bopper, some goddam sleep! Then Ritchie Valens yawns, Why don't we catch a plane? Dwyer's Flying Service'll get us to Green Bay on one of their Beechcraft Bonanzas. In *this* weather? says Holly's bassist, Waylon Jennings. Hey, Bopper, give me your sleeping bag for my seat on the plane. Holly laughs: You piece of yellow shit, Waylon. What's gonna happen? Frightened you'll lose your bass in the snow? Waylon blushes: Lose my *ass* is what I'm worried about. I've got a whole career ahead of me and I don't need to come down at 172 miles an hour in some goddam snowstorm in a cornfield just outside Mason City and lie there unrecovered for ten days. Come now, says Holly, don't you want to be a legend? That's no kind of life, says Waylon, just being a groove on a record with a one-off appearance in some teenager's dream on a bus through Iowa twenty years after we're dead. Suddenly, they all stare at me and I look out of the window and see we're not on a bus at all, but a Beechcraft Bonanza light plane and it's plunging earthward. *"This'll be the day—"*

When I awake my skull's rattling on the metal sill. Green rolling hills have replaced the crops. Drizzle zips the window like Sioux arrows. Omaha looms ahead, gray against the sullen sky.

"Nebraskans," Roosevelt Franklin's saying, "don't waste time sleeping. We're set firm as rock: middle of America, middle of the road. Cornhuskers are strong, proud sustainers who aim to see what needs doing's done right. Rest of the country makes fun of us, but the Midwest makes me proud. Who do you suppose is the largest hog producing state in the country?"

"Nebraska?" I look at my watch. It's just before seven.

"Iowa. You know the second largest cattle state?"

"Iowa?"

"Nebraska. Iowa is third, Texas first. You know where Shaeffer pens are made? Fort Madison, Iowa. You know who started out in Iowa, doing commercials for H. R. Gross on Des Moines radio WHO? Ronald Reagan. Iowa's always been important for politics. It holds the first Presidential caucus in January. You know who was born in Omaha? Gerald Ford."

"I thought he was from Michigan."

"Ach," winces Roosevelt Franklin. "He moved there. But Nebraska has enough big names. Take William Jennings Bryan with his 'Cross of Gold' speech."

"I've heard of him. Wasn't he the man who said

everything bad in America came from people teaching evolution, and that we'd be better of burning every book except Genesis?"

"He should have been President. You want more big names? Take Fred Astaire, Willa Cather, Marlon Brando, Montgomery Clift, Johnny Carson, Ted Hustead. Nebraska breeds the best."

"Ted who?"

"Founder of the Wall Drugstore, South Dakota."

"What about Jean Seberg?"

"She's a Communist."

"I don't think so."

"She supports the Black Panthers. She's a Pinko. Anyways, she's no patriot. She moved to France."

"Didn't they *all* move away?"

"Only boomers stick it. Men like me, and billionaires like Warren Buffett."

"Couldn't Brando have been a contender?"

"Not in Omaha."

"You seem to have everything but a seaside. Is there enough water around?"

"You kidding? How would all them cattle munch across all them hundred-thousand acre ranches without water? Bring it to the surface, you'd drown the state to the height of five tall men standing feet on shoulders! I know this land edge to edge. I used to cycle, but my hips have disintegrated." He makes peddling motions with his ploughshare hands. "I did the RAGBRAI for twenty years—the *Des Moines Register*'s annual bike ride M'ouri to M'ippi. No hills in the Cornbelt? Try fives hundred miles on a cycle saddle! How old are you, son?"

"Nineteen."

"I'm sixty-nine. It irritates the hell out of me. But *you!* All that lovely time ahead!"

"I don't know what to do with it," I tell him. "I don't know where I'm going."

"What are you looking for?"

"Happiness. I thought I might try Alaska."

He laughs, teeth bright as corn at sunrise. "Just enjoy *youth*. See me? You'll be here *tomorrow*."

The bus pulls into Omaha in pelting rain. Roosevelt Franklin encircles my hand in his and says he's real glad I've found Omaha, and not just gone to New York or San Francisco. I thank him for his crop information.

"Where did you say you were going next?" he calls as I push through the glass doors.

"Maybe Alaska. But it's got to be the going not the getting there."

"That's the spirit," he winks. "We'll make you an American yet. Don't forget, plant acres of hope while remembering that there are many paths to bitterness. But you'll be okay if you keep singing in your sleep."

I want to call out that I'll put him in a book one day, and I imagine him waving a ploughshare hand and saying, "Aw, go ahead. I'll have taken my last bus west anyways! Write about old Roosevelt Franklin from—where was it?—*Desmoinesia*." But he's already gone and I'm through the doors into the spacious terminal with its open plan Burger King. In the rain Omaha looks like Guildford, Surrey, except the sloping road outside the depot is wider than the street of any English city. Empty of people, it stretches downhill toward skyscrapers misty through the rain. Another Hopper city. Another waystop on the road to somewhere. *There are many paths to bitterness*, is the phrase I'll most remember. But I'm sure there are paths out of bitterness too. As Roosevelt Franklin says, whatever else, I'll be old tomorrow, but I'm young today.

5

THE SOUL-SAVER OF OMAHA

Dottie West, the country singer, grew up in a tiny farming community near McMinnville, Tennessee, and had her first big break in 1963 when Jim Reeves recorded her song, "Is This Me?" When she sings for Carlotta and me that last summer of the seventies, I've heard of Dolly Parton and Tammy Wynette and Patsy Cline, but I've never heard of Dottie West. I've no idea how successful she's been or about her descent into alcohol-fuelled, divorce-littered near-ruin, or that a few years later, in the midst of a comeback, she'll die in a car crash on her way to the Grand Ole Opry.

After I say goodbye to Roosevelt Franklin I eat breakfast in the depot Burger King watching the warm summer rain and thinking maybe I'll stay in Omaha or else travel forever. I finish my meal, open my father's canvas bag, and pull out old T-shirts and a grubby pair of jeans and bin them. I'm a caterpillar shedding skins across the country. All that's bad has passed. All that's good lies ahead. I can disappear, change my name, steal into town, ride the bus forever around the continent, team up with some other lowdown loser as Bus Cassidy and the Greyhound Kid, or phone Carlotta. I phone Carlotta.

An hour later she walks into the depot. The rain's stopped and the sun gleams on the downtown office

If I'm Ever Back This Way

blocks. Omaha's a Cubist cityscape of light and dark angles, deserted as San Francisco in *Vertigo*. Cars are fleeting shadows. The sun catches Carlotta's solid brown calf muscles and the redness in her auburn hair, brushed to a shine. She's chewing Hubba Bubba.

"I've got to work all day until eight," she says opening the car door. "You think you can handle my parents?"

She drops me at their suburban home on South 131 Avenue. Two-storied from the front, a deck stretches out from the living room, with a garden below, looked out over by the basement windows. A blue mail tin is nailed to a stick on the front lawn. Charlie Brown and Lucy wander past as we pull into the driveway.

"This," Carlotta introduces her mother, "is Mrs Domarski to you, Mom to me. Irma to everyone else." Mrs Domarski, eyes narrowing needle-thin, pinches my hand like a scorpion. "And this," Carlotta turns to her father, a short, cleft-chinned man with limp gray hair and weary eyes, "is Mr Domarski, or Pa, or Sherwin." Then she disappears, explaining she has to change for work, and I feel like Gulliver with a couple of Lilliputians looking up at me. Neither of them reach my elbows. Mrs Domarski bustles off to the kitchen and Mr Domarski looks up at me, yawning.

"So," he says, "you rode the Dog. You shoulda gone Big Red."

"Big Red?" I'm thinking of the gum Marilyn Monroe or Mrs Whitman gave me.

"Sherwin's a Trailways driver," explains Mrs Domarski bringing in a tray with three glasses of iced tea. "He works the nightshift then sleeps all day while I work downtown at J.C. Penney. You like driving, don't you, Sherwin, but you sure get tired."

Mr Domarski yawns again. "It ain't what you'd call a vocation."

"Catch ya later!" calls Carlotta, squeezing through the front door in an alligator outfit.

"She still at the Jungle Café?"

"It's well paid, honey." Mrs Domarski has the hint of a Polish accent to match those Slavic eyes. "Are you cool enough?"

"He's hot," says Mr Domarski. "He don't want no coffee. You want iced tea, fella? Do we have iced tea, lady?"

"I *gotten* us iced tea."

We sit in the shade on the deck. The thermometer in the sun reads 105 degrees.

"Omaha's not what it used to be," Mrs Domarski sighs.

"It is too," says Mr Domarski.

"It is *not*." Her jaw sets firm. "Asians are buying here. The new people aren't even Christian, let alone Catholic."

An instant, silent comradeship grows up between Mr Domarski and me. We look at the sun on the trees outside, watch the thermometer rise. "But, lady," he says, "our parents were immigrants. My mother was Italian, my father Polish. Your mother was Polish, your father Hungarian. They were *immigrants*, no difference."

"Maybe so," says Mrs Domarski. "But *we* weren't. Anyway, where's their *religion?*"

"They've got religion."

"They don't."

"They do. They've got Islam or Buddhism or Hinduism."

"They don't got Catholicism."

"Irma," says Mr Domarski patiently, "The Moorish-American Science Temple was founded in 1913. This was the foundation of black Muslims in America. Your parents didn't arrive until the 1920s."

Mrs Domarski deigns not to respond.

Carlotta's home around sunset. It's been a long, long day, too hot to take a walk. I've drunk gallons of iced tea and Mrs Domarski's fed us spinach, egg and bacon sandwiches, and apple pie. That night and the next, Mr Domarski's out driving for Trailways. Carlotta and I sit up and watch TV with Mrs Domarski. Her needle-thin eyes pierce me as if she's shunned the use of a voodoo doll and gone for me direct. On the first night, she escorts us to our separate rooms. On the second night, Carlotta turns off the TV but gestures for me to stay put. The three of us sit for hours listening to June bugs batter the screen door.

"Carlotta," Mrs Domarski says after the first hour. "It's my job to save souls."

"Mine, too, Mom."

"I'm worried about your father's."

"Me too, Mom."

"And I'm worried about yours."

"My soul's intact, Mom."

"Is it?" She turns to me and jabs her needle eyes through my cornea. "Where do you go to church?"

'Here and there, ma'am." I've picked up "ma'am" from Darius. "Ma'am" and "sir." People seem to like it.

"Two places?"

"The Church of the Eclectic, ma'am. If I walk past a place of worship I just go in."

"Don't you attend your parents' church?"

"They're in Heaven."

"Oh that's too bad," says Mrs Domarski, which strikes me as an odd thing for a Catholic to say. "You poor soul," she says about ten minutes later. But she doesn't look eager to adopt me. The June bugs batter the screen like little devils. Eventually she pushes herself up from her easy chair and says, "Your soul needs its sleep, Carlotta."

"It'll be right up, mom."

For another half-hour Mrs Domarski's shadow lingers at the top of the stairs. "Carl-*otta?*" she calls down at intervals, "you coming to bed now?"

"Coming, mom!" Carlotta nods for me to go outside the French doors and wait.

Twenty minutes later we're on the grass beneath the decking. Carlotta's taken off her jeans and put on running shorts. The garden is like a flea circus putting on a fireworks show: crickets clickety-clacking, lightning bugs dotting the bushes like fallen stars.

After a while, she sits up, says, "Hey, look what I got," and pulls out a pack of Hubba Bubba. We chew and blow philosophically, listening to the crickets and watching the stars above the silhouettes of trees. Carlotta can blow bubbles the size of her face.

"Last year I came damned close to losing my soul again." She pauses to blow a bubble. It bursts on her nose.

"Again?"

If I'm Ever Back This Way

"Yeah. God made the phone ring."

"Good of him."

"He's as bad as Mom. Dad's okay, though. He says that if I'm good in my heart my soul's sound. If I have a soul, that is. He doesn't believe in them."

"Unlike your mother."

"Right. She's the Soul-Saver of Omaha."

"Tomorrow's our last night."

"I know," says Carlotta. "Want to go to a fair?"

So the evening before I leave we drive to Douglas County for the Waterloo Fair.

"You must be looking forward to home," says Carlotta. "Everyone does."

"Not me."

"But your parents, your friends? I'm a real homebod. This little acorn will never fall far. Why did you tell my parents you're an orphan?"

"Because I am," I tell her, "nearly." I start reading the leaflet. Billed in the *Omaha World-Herald* as Douglas County's entertainment package bargain of the year, the Waterloo Fair includes livestock judging, but there's also Championship Slo-pitch Softball, The Nebraska Bantam Show, a Hog Carcass Contest, a Tractor Operator Contest, and Furniture Interview Judging. "You think this involves interviewing furniture, or sitting on furniture to judge interviews?"

"You're avoiding the subject."

I read on. The advertised acts are Gene Watson from Palestine, Texas; Dave and Sugar, "country singer and movie screen star" Jerry Reed, famed for "When You're Hot, You're Hot" and "Guitar Man," and Dottie West, whose first single, recorded with Jim Reeves,

"Love is No Excuse," was Number One in *Billboard* magazine when Reeves died in a plane crash.

"I gotta see Dottie," says Carlotta.

It's dusk when we arrive. The fair resembles a stage set for *Oklahoma!* The streaky sunset soon loses out to the lights of the stalls. Cow dung mingles with whiffs of electricity and sugar cane. A couple of cowboys bang shut a long white hut full of livestock and stroll over the cable-strewn grass to watch Jerry Reed twang "Tupelo Mississippi Fish." Further on Reed bows out to a tape of "Lola" itself drowned by screams from the Ferris wheel.

"Way up high," sings Carlotta, "is where you lost me / On the Ferris wheel. Oh, my God!" She points at a pretty, middle-aged woman wearing a Stetson and spangled shirt, "Look! That's Dottie West! Dottie! Dottie!" She runs up to her. "This guy's never heard of you."

"That's okay," says Dottie West with a sweet smile. "I've never heard of him."

"Would you sing one for us?"

"Sure," says Dottie. She turns to me. "You live here, darlin'?" I tell her I'm leaving tomorrow. "You're leaving this here gal?" she says. "You're a fool, boy. Listen in a half hour."

We gorge on hot dogs, ice cream, cola, cotton candy, caramel apples, throw darts for pink rabbits, shoot at a string of ducks, ride the blue and red bird cage from hell, walk around, eat some more, then wash everything down with Mountain Dew and Mello Yello.

"Come on," says Carlotta, "another ride!" The metal bar clangs shut and the machine jerks forward, circling, spinning, sliding round. "Faster, faster!" cries

Carlotta. "Make it turn, make it role, make it jump!" The lights blur. The ride ends and we totter across the damp grass. It's later than we thought. The coconut shy's deserted. The boards have gone up on the target shooting. Autumn slips into my mind like a creepy evening shadow. Carlotta's watching me with her Slavic eyes. "You're always deep in your own thoughts," she says, "like you go to another world."

"I'm thinking I'm right where I want to be for the rest of my life."

"Me, too," she says. "Right here with you. You'll come back, won't you?"

"Of course."

"Or at least remember me?"

"I'll be back."

"People never come back. I'll get crowded out."

"It'll be the same for you," I say. "You'll marry a farm boy or grain importer and forget all about me."

I don't know that. We don't know anything. We only guess. When you're a teenager you think you'll never change. But Carlotta and I are flies in amber, drunk on those scenes and smells, inhaling the remnants of an evening almost gone. Dottie West's on stage, singing "Country Sunshine" to a thinning crowd.

"And this," she says, "is a song for two lovebirds who neglected to tell me their names. The guy's going off and leaving one of our young country girls, and you ask me he's a damned fool." There's a desultory cheer. "It's called, 'If You Go Away.'"

There's a slightly bigger cheer and I try to put an arm round Carlotta, but she runs off calling, "Come on! One more ride!"

I'm a step behind. "You don't want to hear the song?"

"The evening's folding up. We haven't time."

She makes it sound like a board game, a book. But maybe it is. Maybe when I leave everything packs up, and I'll go somewhere else and the same group of actors will unpack new stuff and entertain me. Maybe in future years, I'll get this evening out of some dark cupboard and take a look. Dottie's voice fades behind us as if we're deserting her. But we're rushing to live. Carlotta finds the last ride open, a giant black spider. We squeeze into a small cup on the end of a leg and lurch to a string of Eagles hits. First "Hotel California," then "New Kid in Town," then "The Last Resort." The cups rise and fall like boats leaving harbor. The panorama of the closing fair bobs like lights from shore. We rise and fall to the beat, our stomachs a second behind, squeezed into our tiny cup as if nothing can separate us. Then, in mid-ride, Carlotta's dark eyes widen so much they catch the fairground lights. Her cheeks blow out, her mouth opens, and she vomits into my lap.

Five full minutes the ride lurches on. Carlotta and I sit in sticky silence and try not to breathe. There's no escape. The ride will last and last. Time, which seemed so fleeting, now seems eternal. The operator has probably seen us up there in the darkness and recalled his own youth. Carlotta sobs gently, face buried in my chest while I sit stoically upright and wipe her cheek with my sleeve. When, finally, the ride creaks to a halt and the music fades, she runs to hide behind the closed shooting gallery. I buy cokes and find her kneeling, head down, murmuring, "Forgive me, forgive me." Together, we scrub grass on the stain on my shirt and jeans.

I hand her a coke. "Forgive what?"

"You're so sweet," she sobs.

"Sweet and sour."

"You're a real nice guy—a *gentleman*."

"Tell Mom." I scrape dried puke from her chin.

"The sad thing is that I'll be the girl who blew chunks all over you at the fair."

"You'll be the girl Dottie dedicated a song to."

"Promise?"

The next morning, Mrs Domarski's eyes sparkle with joy at the news that I'm leaving.

Mr Domarski winks and yawns. "Take Big Red next time, you hear?"

Carlotta drives me downtown and waves me off as I board the Greyhound south for Jacksonville to visit Darius Desoutter before looping back up to New York and the flight home. Much of the way to Florida I sleep and dream, or daydream, or read *If You Don't Know Where You're Going, You'll Probably End Up Somewhere Else*. But the rest of the time I watch America pass by. At least I'm going somewhere, I reflect, even if for now it feels like backward. Northbound I hum Eagles tunes and picture myself as a white maggot winding its way toward the core of the Big Apple. For the Eagles, to name a place 'Paradise' is to lose it. For me, in the melancholy splendor of adolescence, to suspect a place is Paradise means it's time to leave.

6

LAUNDROMANCE

But even when we know that we can't repeat the past we can still be foolish enough to try. If we lose someone we look for them in others. New friends attract us because they remind us of old ones. Even in ongoing relationships we repeat certain rituals to remind ourselves of what that person means. So I became one of F. Scott Fitzgerald's "boats against the current, borne back ceaselessly" to America. One pull forward, two strokes back. It's the way of the world. Or so I think when, one June morning nine months after the Waterloo Fair, I fly to New York, catch the Greyhound to Stroudsburg, Pennsylvania, and take a job at Camp Pocono. Twenty years old, my sole purpose in returning to America is to rediscover Summer Love. I've crammed my father's old canvas bag with affection and I intend to empty it out wherever it's wanted. A freckled Arrivals official whose little dog sniffs my suitcase for either fruit or drugs, but evidently not Love, is my first potential client.

"Go for it, Skip girl!" she says in a twee twangy voice, dancing around on the end of the terrier's lead. But Skip scampers away to another bag. I turn my attention to a Chinese-American policewoman who discourages me with a single adjustment of her large black holster. I'm not disheartened. Darius is meeting me off the Greyhound. He's fixed us both up with a Pocono job.

During the winter we each received a letter from Dimmerstamm announcing that Camp Jakalak had "closed forever" due to "growing deficits and diminishing uptake." The ride to camp, and Darius's promises of the girls he's already lined up for me, inflate my hopes further. He meets me in the camp truck. In the cab with him is a dark-skinned, hazel-eyed girl named Daniella Paella. As we weave our way through the Pocono Mountains, all kinds of auguries spring out at us. *You are entering the Land of Love,* reads a heart-shaped wooden sign splintered at the edges.

"Y'all catch that?" drawls Darius.

"I'm ready."

"*Are* you?" says Daniella, giving me a long, ambiguous look.

"What about Carlotta?" says Darius.

"If Carlotta were *here*."

"One thing I forgot to say. Pocono is a Jewish camp. Watch out for the JAPS, Jewish American Princesses, dangerous women."

I can hear air hissing out of my heart. Since last summer I've read *Sophie's Choice* and *Portnoy's Complaint.*

"*I'm* a JAP," says Daniella, "and there's nothing dangerous about *me*. Right, Redeye?"

"Daniella has an Amish mother and a Jewish-Catholic father, would you believe?"

Daniella gives me that look again. "My mother was brought up in an Old Order Amish community in Lancaster County. Even today her family drive horse-drawn carriages and the men dress in wide-brimmed hats and broadfall pants held up by suspenders. The women twist their hair in a bun beneath bonnets or prayer veils. My father's a Bethlehem steelworker. My parents had to elope."

"Bethlehem?"

"Bethlehem, Pennsylvania," Daniella explains. "She never went back to Lancaster. I suppose she was shunned or excommunicated. *His* parents were indifferent. His father was a Catholic Spaniard, his mother a Portuguese Jew brought up in a rural part of the San Joquin Valley. Grandpa was born on the boat in New York Harbor just in from Spain. He went out to California in the twenties, became a bootlegger, bought a dairy farm and married my grandmother. Daddy came east and met my mother. My grandparents could hardly complain."

"So what are you?"

"A Spanish-Portuguese Jewish-Catholic German Pietist. And you?"

"A foreigner." A foreigner, I don't add, entirely smitten by Daniella's large hazel eyes and glamorous origins. I sit back and watch the low hills sail by and wish *my* kin had included a Spanish-Portuguese bootlegger born in New York Harbor, and I'd not simply been born to a couple from Chippenham. "Is Pennsylvania known for anything else?"

"William Penn, Eddie Fisher, Chubby Checker, the Appalachians, the Allegheny National Forest," says Daniella. "Oh, and the Pennsylvania Turnpike."

"Ha!" says Darius.

I, on the other hand, am impressed. Especially when Daniella tells me the turnpike was completed in 1940 as America's first all-weather, limited access superhighway. But Pennsylvania's main attraction for me remains romance. Everywhere signs announce the Poconos as the eastern seaboard's favored honeymoon spot. Motels advertise heart-shaped bathtubs, gigantic circular beds, seven-foot high, transparent jacuzzis shaped like champagne glasses. The first few days of camp I spend the kosher lunches scanning for another Carlotta. A lot of the girl counselors seem much older than I am; some even teeter on twenty-two. But "with the sunshine and the great bursts of leaves" I once again have Fitzgerald's "familiar conviction that life is starting over again with summer." I'm happy with the sense of new experiences ahead and my mood is jolly and energetic, spurred by the anticipation of emotional satisfaction. I brush off some early disappointments like cobwebs from the cabin rafters. I'm assigned to repair flaps with the nicely named Carly Treal. She turns out to be large-boned and gat-toothed: the Wife of Bath in shorts and T-shirt. Daniella Paella is prettier, but Darius moves in before I can recover from jetlag. Soon I'm shifting furniture with a black-haired, black-eyed girl who looks like Cher. The foul dust of past summers mingles with her flowery perfume. The scent of pollen wafts in through the open windows from a yellow carpet of dandelions and buttercups spreading over the green fields toward a horizon of pine trees and puffy clouds. Naturally, Cher too has a boyfriend, Matt Zabel, a potbellied, psychopathic park ranger who teaches target-shooting.

 I cool my unfocused ardor by plunging into Crystal Lake, a muddy pond in the center of camp, then bake beneath the sultry sun on a floating dock. Periodically either Cher or Carly Treal swims out to lie with me, as does Daniella Paella once, long enough to mention that I resemble Clint Eastwood before Darius launches out to whisk her away. The heat keeps up for days and the green Poconos lie hazy and shadow-strewn beneath towering cumulous. Oh youth, oh bliss, what a summer this is to be! Far from idling through these afternoons, I'm bronzing my puny, winter-white body for the Land of Love.

Finally, the day before the campers arrive, while Darius and the other counselors play softball on the forest-cleared field, I meet a seventeen-year-old camp waitress. She wears a strange kind of smock and smokes a briar pipe but has a soft face, shiny, part-braided brown hair, and gray-blue eyes. Her name is Pickawillany Dinwiddie.

"Are you into Wowism?" she says when we first meet. "You know, like everything's either Wow or Mom? *I* am. Uncle Russell's into Momism. But that's because he's *old*."

"What's old?"

"This." She pulls forward a tall, sinister figure with heavy lids and a perm—basically Donald Sutherland as the teacher who seduces the Karen Allen character in *Animal House*.

"But I'm not old," says Uncle Russell in a gravel-strewn voice. "I'm thirty-three!"

"He's old," giggles Pickawillany Dinwiddie.

Beneath a tree by the lake I dream away the warm evenings smoking ten-cent sugar-coated cigars from the Seven-Eleven, certain that Pickawillany Dinwiddie will be my Summer Love. The only problem is to convince her. When the days begin to pass without her showing much interest I hear my heart hissing again and yearn to jump on the bus and find Carlotta. Camp has hardly begun but already it seems a mistake to try to repeat. This time around I see more clearly the rules and regulations that bind me. The two line leaders Amos Clark and his deputy Zachariah Dayan exacerbate my restlessness. The shaven Amos, from the well-healed Riverside area of the Bronx, resembles a donut in spectacles. The dark, unshaven Zach has dropped from a passing UFO. His petite body is visibly riddled with tiny tunnels drilled with pencil lead and wallpapered with rules. The Abbot and Costello of apparatchiks, these two busy beings compel campers and counselors alike into obedience all summer.

Still, ever the optimist and determined to honor my pledge to myself, I track Pickawillany as doggedly as the scout tracks Paul Newman and Robert Redford in *Butch Cassidy and the Sundance Kid*. Daily I watch for signs of her preoccupations and dispositions. Each mealtime she sits at our table and squeezes my knee. On Duty Nights in the lakeside pagoda in front of the cabins I squint over my sweet dime cigars hoping she might pass by in the moonlight and notice my resemblance to Clint Eastwood. Shadowy couples snigger past in mocking procession. Of Pickawillany, however, I see no sign until one dusk, wearied by my stint in the pagoda and the whine of mosquitoes, I stroll toward the dark woods. There, silhouetted like Scarlett O'Hara against the red evening sky, Pickawillany hangs cradled in the arms of a tall, thin man who looks nothing like Clark Gable but a lot like Donald Sutherland. Savagely miserable, I trail cigar smoke through the inky woods, doomed, I feel sure, to find friendship only among dead authors, love only in the pages of novels or the impersonal flicker of the cinema screen. When, long after midnight, I slink back into camp, Amos lurks in the shadows like a last donut in a closing shop.

"Where have you *been?*" he bubbles with deep-fried fury. "Next time, you say exactly where you're going, and for exactly how long."

"Were life so simple!"

"Cut the schmutz, putz. Who were you with?"

"With?" I sigh. "No one, Amos."

I cross the dark grass, leaving him to make notes on his Leadership pad. Other counselors are hanging out in the dining hall over Sprite and Pepsi. Only Carly Treal sits alone, reading Chaucer.

"I saw Pickawillany Dinwiddie with Uncle Russell," I mumble sadly.

"They're an item," she whistles through her gat-teeth. "Didn't you know?"

Reckless and desperate, I smile at her. "Like to take a walk?"

"I am not," she whistles, "that sort of girl!"

Later she passes me with a bespectacled, balding fellow who looks a bit like Woody Allen. He gives me a cheesy grin. Her eyes are granite. I shrink into the darkness, only to bump into John Cork and Derek Fly, bobbing out of a laurel bush. John Cork and Derek Fly are Australian computer analysts on a year's sabbatical to travel the world. America, or at least Pennsylvania, fails to impress them. They're roaming camp in green and yellow, knee-length shorts, and decide to confide in me as a fellow foreigner.

"Keep it under your corks, mate," says John, "but Australian skies are bluer."

"That's right," says Derek, "bluer. They're kind of anemic here. Not that you poms would notice, seeing as Blighty's got a concrete sky. But in the long run, when the climate turns nasty, you Brits will be better off."

"You know the future?"

"Sure," says John. "Here's something to keep under your corks, mate: The future belongs to computer analysts."

"That's right," says Derek. "The richest man in the world come the New Millennium will be whoever finds a way to mass market interactive personal computers."

"Computers talking to each other?"

"Sure," says John, "In a few years time practically the whole world will be computer-linked and we'll correspond instantly by electronic messages. Then we'll link up the solar system so astronauts can crapshoot from Saturn. As for life on Earth: ever heard of a portable cellular telephone?"

"No."

"An Information Pod?" says Derek.

"Should I have?"

"All in good time," they say together.

Of course, I assume they're barmy, not least because they also believe that America will be attacked by a fleet of hijacked commercial airliners and that a "demonic control center" will rule the world without anyone knowing. In the autumn they intend to head for Idaho to join the militia. "Safest place in the world," says Derek. "No earthquakes, floods, nuclear missiles, or drought."

That night, with the campers asleep and an immense downpour drumming on the cabin roof, I think about my father. *You'll end up in a factory*, comes his voice. *Your sort always does. You'll never complete anything.* I can't imagine a future for *myself*, let alone the world. I expect to dry like driftwood on life's beach, blanched as bone before twenty-one. Nobody will love me. I'll never find direction. I'll die on the road and be buried in a ditch, beneath a makeshift cross, scrawled UNKNOWN TRAVELER. I don't know where I'm going, and probably won't even end up somewhere else. *What you must do*, pelts my father into my rain-soaked delirium, *is complete something*. I toss and turn amid the thunder and lightning. To try to quell the voice in my head, the *Where go? What do?* of early manhood, I fumble in the dark and stuff a tape in my recorder. *How can you sleep at night?* mocks John Lennon. "For God's sake!" I tell him, "I *can't!*"

The next morning I resolve to shed my self-pity and look outward. It's a beautiful summer morning. A bluebird rises from the mud-green lake. I pick myself up, dust myself down, and stride out ahead of my line of campers, past the puddles from the night's rain. Eleven-year-olds love heroes and I intend to be a hero for a change. I'll help them find what they want even if I can't find it myself. With Pickawillany in the clutches of Donald Sutherland, I resolve to turn my attention to other things. Once I do so, the summer drifts by pleasantly enough. Every afternoon the campers and counselors plunge into the cold, muddy waters of Crystal Lake in the lap of the Poconos. Whenever I feel low I seek solace in reading, and these summer scenes, when I think back on them now, are double-exposed with images from *Moby-Dick*.

"Having little or no money in my purse, and nothing particular to interest me on land," Ishmael tells me, "I thought I would sail about a little and see the watery part of the world. Why don't you do the same?"

"I'm not much of a sailor."

"Ah," says Ishmael, "but your sea is America and your boat is the bus."

"I never thought of it that way."

"I know."

So on Ishmael's advice I plan another bus trip. My sea will be the prairies and deserts. I've read Whitman since childhood, but now, as well as Melville, I contemplate Dickinson, Thoreau, Hawthorne and, at a flag-raising one morning, Robert Frost. Amoz and Zachariah are predictably aggressive at this little American ceremony, demanding everyone be on time, so one day we're amazed to see Amos arrive at the gathering *late*, and on a day he's due to read.

"Two paths diverged in a wood, and I—," he wheezes, sweat setting like glaze, "I took the one less traveled by, and that has made all the difference." At this point a pretty counselor, brace flashing in the sun, asks if that's why he's late. "No, no, no, Mary-Ann," splutters Amos through misting spectacles. He goes on with the poem, but I've stopped listening. I'm thinking how witty this girl is and which path *I'll* take and what difference it will make; whether I'll find one of life's clearings or tread deeper into the dark woods, and whether this Mary-Ann could accompany me. For a few nights I sit outside the bunks on duty with my ten-cent cigars for company, and wonder if *Mary-Ann* will think I look like Clint Eastwood. Meanwhile, I plunge on with *Moby-Dick*.

"Methinks," says Ishmael beside me, staring out over muddy little Crystal Lake as if it were the Atlantic Ocean at New Bedford and the rare old Pequod were about to dock and take us aboard, "we have hugely mistaken this matter of Life and Death. Methinks," he says, in his quaint way, tapping ash from a cheroot and spewing smoke as he talks, "that what they call my shadow here on Earth is my true substance. Methinks that in looking at things spiritual, we are too much like oysters observing the sun through water, and thinking that thick water is the thinnest of air."

"You make me pensive," I tell him.

"Life is a pensive matter."

"I can't stop thinking of Mary-Ann."

"There are plenty of fish in the ocean."

"I don't want *any* fish."

"Or oyster."

"Right. Or whale. I want a soulmate."

"Ah!"

"I feel like nothing's changing outside, but inside I'm evolving. Does that make sense?"

"You are like a wilful traveler in Lapland refusing to wear colored or coloring glasses, so you gaze yourself blind upon the white shroud that wraps all the prospect around you. Your ghost-girl is a symbol. Dear boy, you are engaged on the fiery hunt!"

He talks in such an opaque and antiquated way that half the time I don't know what he's on about. But that's part of his charm. His melancholy somehow leaves me feeling better. Moreover the sunnier I grow inside, the stormier the weather becomes, confining us to indoor activities, and providing me with more chances of seeing Mary-Ann. Then, one rainy day, we have indoor roller-skating. We move round in two circles, one inside the other, stopping when the music stops and introducing ourselves to whoever's opposite, and saying whatever enters our head. This is how I first speak to Mary-Ann.

"Mary-Ann Steiner," she says. "*Gather ye rosebuds while ye may, / Old time is still a-flying: And this same flower that blooms today, / Tomorrow will be dying.*"

Lightning flashes at the windows. My heart kicks my concave chest into convexity.

'Where's that from?'

"Some school book."

The world takes on an instant, purple hue. Such learning! Wit *and* learning.

"Where are you from?"

"Harrisburg. My father's a doctor."

"What will you do?"

"Med School. And you?"

"Alaska." I palpitate. This further hint of her brilliance is one more aphrodisiac. And she's talking to *me!* If I can communicate with pre-Meds, perhaps I'm not stupid after all. Maybe I can bask in the reflected glory of a high-achiever. Later I quiz Darius. "Is Mary-Ann Steiner a JAP?"

"Mary-Ann Steiner!" drawls Darius. "Her teeth are held in by her wealth. But she's okay otherwise. A word of warning, though: she belonged to Barry Buck."

Barry Buck's an ex-counselor, a college footballer caught with another girl in his cabin and dropped at dawn at the Stroudsburg Seven-Eleven to find his way home. This is a common event, the camp equivalent of a firing squad. The Seven-Elevening of Barry Buck is the fifth of the season. The most colorful example was a huge counselor named Tiny Petrovitch who came back to camp drunk one night and urinated on the sleeping Zachariah. Drinking is strictly prohibited. Urinating on the assistant line leader's bed carries no extra penalty, so Tiny was simply Seven-Elevened and Zachariah presumably took a shower. As for Barry Buck, I reason callously, his hard luck is my chance of a little romance before the summer's done. So the broken-hearted Mary-Ann Steiner becomes my mission. I'll make her happy. I'll invite her to a movie. And I do.

"I've got to do laundry," is her overwhelmingly grateful response, "but sure, why not?"

So we catch the bus into town to do laundry and see *Caddy Shack*. Mary-Ann has green eyes, blonde hair, and behind that gleaming, multi-layered brace, green teeth. Green teeth are a bit repellent, I reason, but better than no teeth, and if Love's blind I'm short sighted at the best of times. This, added to the fact that my react-to-light spectacles, bought in a Stroudsburg mall, are proving better at darkening than getting lighter, enables me to fall irrevocably in love before the end of the movie. Mary-Ann takes longer, but I detect a new light in her eye on the way to the Laundromat, and become convinced of it during the washing cycle, with drying time still to come.

"Mary-Ann," I say above the whirr of the machines, "let's go outside."

"Okay," she says without a hint of enthusiasm.

My stomach's rumbling. I've managed to keep Mary-Ann awake through the movie with the promise of an anchovy pizza after we've done our laundry. But she's almost sleep-walking now. Outside the Laundromat, I murmur lines I've rehearsed in the cinema.

"This night will soon be twenty or thirty years ago. Seize the moment, Mary-Ann."

She begins to talk about her disgraced boyfriend.

"Do you love him?"

"Oh, yes," she says. "He's my world."

"But he's gone."

"I guess."

I've nothing to lose and no more room for delay. She starts back talking about Barry Buck but I'm thinking this is it, *gather ye rosebuds while ye may*. The Laundromat's a microcosm, a testing ground for my ability to make the right moves when it really counts. Either you go for it, or become a coward soul who quits. As she drones on, her lips move across her shadowed teeth in the chiaroscuro of the Laundromat doorway. Life, I'm thinking, sweat prickling my back, is a football game, and Barry's been sin-binned. Suddenly it's Superbowl XIII in the Orange Bowl, Miami. I'm running. I've found a gap. I'm twisting to see the flight of the seventy-five yard pass. "Barry, yes," she's saying, "he's got bunions but he's also got biceps. He's *so* sweet, *so* gorgeous. I'd forgive him anything. He only ends up with other girls because they throw themselves at him." But Barry is history. Barry's been Seven-Elevened. *Gather ye rosebuds while ye may*. The ball spins down through the air. I reach for it as I cross the line. Beneath the light of a giant yellow M, I lung at her rotted teeth like my grandfather parachuting into Arnhem in 1944. I swoop, dip and speed into the shadow beneath her nose as if it's the ground accelerating toward me, and attach my lips to hers.

Touchdown.

Our mouths undulate together, mine in the spasms of simulated passion, Mary-Ann's in the dual role of chewing and talking. She starts, accidentally I think, sharing her gum with me. I seem to be kissing her teeth. I start imagining a garden fence, then dried wood, then George Washington's sheep bone dentures, which I've seen the previous summer in the Smithsonian. I pull away.

"So, you see," she's saying, "that's why I'll love him forever." She tries to spit out her gum but it's tangled in the brace. She has to draw it out in long pink strands. "Look what you've done, you jerk, you've got my gum all wound up in my wires. What were you *doing?*"

"I was just trying to gather my rosebuds while I could."

"*That's* what you think I am?" She screws up her nose and pulls another sliver of gum from her green teeth. "A goddam *rosebud?*"

If the kiss means nothing to her, for me it's a moment of summer romance to savor. At least I tried. And maybe we can be company for each other in the final weeks. Proud of my bold plunge, I search for mental affinity to bolster the newly acquired physical bond.

"You and I," I whisper into the warm darkness,

If I'm Ever Back This Way

"are too much like—like *oysters*."

"Oysters?"

"Oysters, yes. Observing the sun through water, thinking thick water the thinnest air."

"First I'm a rosebud, now I'm a goddam *oyster*. You'd best go see if you've any detergent in your laundry."

Despite this setback, I leave the evening in buoyant mood, so I'm distressed when she sends Darius as an emissary of woe to explain that, unlike Daniella Paella, she doesn't need love right now (and doesn't much like being wooed as a flower or shellfish). She's too cut up about Barry Buck, who has written from Nantucket, where he's taken a gardening job at a harborside inn. The summer's purple sheen evaporates and I plunge into a mid-Atlantic size depression. I feel low and aimless, bereft of hope, as if the golden palace I've clambered so eagerly toward is a tin hut after all. The gaudy dream is mine alone and nothing of it now is any use. Congratulations, you asshole, I mock my reflection in the cabin mirror, eyes bleary from secret nips of Jack Daniel's: Romeo to Malvolio in a blink.

But all romantics must learn to re-inflate their hearts. What the hell, I decide when I eventually do so. Life is fleeting, ephemeral. I've been haunted all summer by the realization that whatever happens will soon be decades gone, so I can hardly think such dalliance *matters*. Recognition of the Absurd dared me kiss a green-toothed, brace-bedecked broad outside a Laundromat in the first place, and perhaps some same sense of the Absurd led her to let me. It's just that she ought really to take whatever romance she can before those teeth crumble altogether.

Admonishing myself for such bitterness, I rise from my bunk, hollow with love-belly sickness, quietly moaning *que sera sera*, strap on my watch, don my (now permanently dark) react-to-light spectacles, and open the cabin door to a new day. It's August. Camp's almost over, and my old fears that life's draining away with nothing accomplished taunt me from the bushes. All that time wasted on *love!* Amid the mayhem of cars and buses, there stands Mary-Ann, still looking—with her mouth shut anyhow—beautiful in the sunshine.

"Aren't you saying goodbye to anyone?"

"Only," I tell her, "to a certain kind of me."

She looks puzzled. "It's just that I wanted to say, you know, I did enjoy the movie, the pizza. I mean I do *care* for you. It's just not been a good time for me."

"That's okay. If you hadn't made that joke about Amos at Flag-raising, I'd not have looked twice at you."

"What joke?" says Mary-Ann.

"About Amos taking the path less traveled by, and being late."

"Huh? So *that's* what you thought I was, a goddam joker?"

As for Pickawillany, like me she has one night left at camp. I sit out on the steps of my empty cabin, smoking dreamily, and she comes, at last, to sit beside me.

"Why are you so often alone?"

"I don't know," I reply. "Maybe I don't want to subject people to my cigars."

'It means I can smoke my pipe." She gets her briar pipe from her smock and lights it.

'Where's Uncle Russell?"

"Am I my lover's keeper? I think he left this morning. He said something about giving Mary-Ann a ride."

So we sit and smoke a while. "Smoking and dreaming go together," I suggest.

"Plus it discourages mosquitoes," says Pickawillany. "Mosquitoes are strictly Mom. You've got to have something to disperse them."

"Smoking'll do it."

"Really. Discourage mosquitoes, attract dreams. Some invention."

We lapse into silence again and I think about how Mary-Ann would have taken this conversation literally, and how maybe all along Pickawillany has been my potential soulmate. It's just that she chose gnarled old Uncle Russell. In any case, I've never quite told her how much I like her, and maybe she's never quite told me the same. It's nice to think that, anyway, and I don't want to shatter my delusions by asking. By the time she ups and leaves it's after midnight. I agree to look her up in Chicago if I go that way, but Darius is staying with Daniella Paella in Bethlehem and they've invited me along, so Pickawillany's path and mine have probably diverged forever. Off in the distance, someone's playing Gershwin on a saxophone. I don't know if it's "Our Love Is Here To Stay" or "Let's Call The Whole Thing Off." I like the sound and light another cigar.

7

MITZVAH

There's another version of this Pocono summer. Once Pickawillany's safely in Uncle Russell's arms and Mary-Ann's told me she's not a goddam oyster, I look for spiritual solace to escape the humdrum veniality of life in the flesh. I find it from two people: the camp rabbi, Bruce (known as "Springstein") and the Hollywood screenwriter, Ben Hecht.

Hecht I meet when, wandering through the dusty rooms of high summer, I come across the all-but-abandoned Camp Library. There are signs of carnal activity on the unswept floor, but it looks like years since anyone's gone there to read. On a warped, dust-caked shelf lie some abandoned books. These scattered remnants from summers past consist of *Let Us Now Praise Famous Men*, *The Little House on the Prairie*, several copies of *Walden* and *The Scarlet Letter*, Dos Passos's *USA,* and Hecht's autobiography, *A Child of the Century* splayed open with its spine half-severed. I pull it from the shelf and collapse in a dust-flecked sunbeam. The semi-transparent pages come free as I turn them, some dissolving like the wings of a dead moth. The book is a palimpsest of its readers' minds. Whoever had it before focused not on wisdom but vocabulary. Inside both covers they've listed words for no reason I can fathom. They start with *paramour, prefatory* and *orifice*, and run through *bigoted, demented, genocide, bilious eye* and (twice) *eviscerate*. I don't know if they're all words from the book or just some rainy-day word game. The only chapter I read in detail—"Who Am I?"—has underlining in three faded colors. There are two kinds of people, Hecht tells me: the alive and the half-alive. One kind are those he trailed, as a journalist, from trains to hotels and back because "they were the people who ran the world." "Armed with certitudes and as alike as the teeth of a comb," they are "the mindless, moodless hunters of success."

"I couldn't understand," he explains, "how men and women who differed in no way from the dullest of failures I knew in my daily life could be such thumping successes. Later I understood. They were successful for the same reason that their kind were usually failures. Their success was founded on the fact that they were not themselves. They had borrowed identity from the world and not out of their own souls. This feat produced equally the leader and the led. I've found most 'greatness' in people to be of this quality. Lacking individuality, they can only become big with the world. They feel their importance as their only identity. Of true greatness there is a fine definition in the Old Testament. It is told in Exodus that Moses spent forty days with God and that when he returned to the common ways of man his face was radiant—but he did not know it. To such radiance I've always bowed."

"So fame's not the answer?"

"Certainly not."

I continue to flick through the pages. "What about growing up in general? What defines 'adulthood'?"

"Youth is our brief sanity. It's our fleeting performance as individuals."

"Why shouldn't adults remain individuals?"

"The young eventually realize the being they were born is too odd for them to use."

"So what do we do?"

"We throw away who we are and become everybody else."

Ah, everybody else! "What about love? What's love got to do with anything?"

"*Amour!* Of all the worlds in which a man lives the most difficult for him to understand—and remember—is the world of love." The afternoon wears on. The shaft of sunlight fingers the pine panels. I begin to fancy that Hecht's there with me in the room. I can hear his rough, peevish voice. "If you ask a man how many times he's loved—unless there's love in his heart at the moment—he is likely to answer, 'Never.'"

"Once," I blurt out, thinking of Pickawillany, but then of Mary-Ann, and then Carlotta.

Now Hecht, like Bogie in Woody Allen's *Play It Again, Sam*, steps out himself from the shadows. I recognize him from the book's photographs. My heart kicks, just as with Mary-Ann at the Laundromat. The sun catches the rim of his fedora. A Gable moustache gives his mouth a jaunty look, but his eyes are in shadow, as if he's become the abyss.

"He will say," whispers Hecht, "if his heart is loveless, that often he thought he loved, but that, victim or hero of love, he was mistaken. For only love can believe in love—or even remember it."

"Oh *I* remember it, Mr Hecht."

He motions me silent. "Such a man, forced to recall himself as a lover, will admit to folly or youthful oddity outgrown. Ah, he will say, there was little sense in it!"

"True," I agree. "I was deluded. Mary-Ann loves Barry Buck and has wired-up green teeth."

"Little sense, indeed!" thunders Hecht. "Your soul was in it, your sanity and mania wrestled over it."

"Steady on."

"The successes and failures of your life will be moulded by it."

Unnerved, I try to close the book but Hecht points to another translucent paragraph and steamrollers me in that way of the elderly and slightly deaf.

"All that was sweet in living lay in its warm hours. In those hours you bloomed like a field of poppies, your heart opened to rain, wind and light. You looked out of yourself with new eyes. You visited humanity, and beheld the nearness of God."

"I beheld no deity in the Laundromat." I'm not just annoyed at his quasi-poetic didacticism, but deep down angry that my anticipated Summer Love has come to nothing.

He shakes his head. "Remember amour and you see death, not love. Your heart kneels at many graves. Where you loved most wildly the silence is deepest."

"I've never loved wildly, Mr Hecht, not with reciprocation. If I love, they don't, and if they do, I don't. Besides, a snatched kiss outside a Pennsylvania Laundromat with a girl with barricaded gnashers is hardly a love affair."

"A love affair may be small, but the love that

launches it never is. Whether it ends quickly or lasts forever, this love comes out of the same deeps of one's being. One brings a full self to all beginnings." I consider asking him how to become a screenwriter, but he's already shrinking back into the shadows and I can hear voices outside. "A man's desire to hear the intimate cry of another's heart never lessens," are his final words. I see his eyes at last and they're full of tears. He smiles his Gable smile and is gone. What sad words for an old man to say, I muse. But what will *I* have to say to youth if I get old? Will I find wisdom? Will anyone ever open a book of *mine?* I close *A Child of the Century* with a puff of dust, and this time there's no ghostly hand to open it, so I return to the living sunshine of another day in the Poconos and decide to talk with Rabbi Bruce.

Rabbi Bruce is a slight, bespectacled figure, much respected around camp. He holds services at an outdoor synagogue of wooden seats sloping down through dappled sunlight to the lake. He delivers his sermons in a passionate, squeaky voice that calls to mind an orange squeezer. I find him slamming a softball into a mitt.

"Have you got time to tell me about Judaism, Springstein," I ask him. "Do you mind me calling you 'Springstein'?"

"Not at all. I'm rather proud of the nickname. I'm from New Jersey myself. But Springsteen's of Catholic stock, I believe, not Jewish. If it matters."

"I'm part-Jewish myself," I tell him, "from a long way back."

"Naturally," he says, "though some would say being 'part-Jewish' is like being 'part-Christian' or 'part-elephant.' It doesn't work like that."

"How does it work?"

We set off around the lake, circling it before Rabbi Bruce has finished. The whole way he carries his mitt and ball. There's a game coming up but he doesn't rush his explanations.

"You've got your three basic types," he says. "Orthodox, Conservative, and the nearest you'll get to acceptance: Reform. Try New York's Temple Emanu-El synagogue."

"So can I be a Jew for the summer? Can I learn from you about how to live?"

He smiles. "We won't throw you out. Do you have a sense of direction?"

"I'm looking."

"Good. Judaism's not so much about belief as about a way of being and seeing. It has to do with history and tradition."

"So you're not like a vicar?"

"A Rabbi is a teacher. I guide people toward being better human beings. You cannot be a good Jew and ignorant or uninterested in wider issues. If you don't seek to learn you have no hope of understanding God's will."

"So I need to study?"

"Study is always important."

"More than completion?"

Rabbi Bruce smiles. "Life is a constant search."

"It's about going not getting there? How about *American* Jews?" We're entering a darker part between the cabins and the lake. "Are they Jewish-American, or American-Jewish?"

"Many American Jews see themselves as mainly American. But America has something like forty percent of all ethnic Jews. That brings its own dilemmas: do we take on American identities wholesale, or do we seek to preserve our ethnic identity? Europe, frankly, didn't want us, although maybe things have changed since my parents and grandparents time. But here a lot of us assimilate. A big percentage of Jews marry Christians."

"That's good, isn't it?"

"Not everyone thinks so. Some would rather bring the European Shtetl to America." We reach the end of the line and head back round the lake. A hundred yards away, counselors have begun the softball. "But most of the parents who send kids to Camp Pocono just want them to have a sense of their backgrounds. Reform Judaism has no problem with Americanization. We *are* Americans. But we want to preserve ancient customs, kosher food and so on."

"Do you still see yourselves as chosen people."

"Sure: chosen to help the world. If you don't feel chosen how can you help bring about justice?" He touches my shoulder. "Perhaps your arrival at camp is part of that process." And off he wanders to his softball game.

Not long afterwards, Rabbi Bruce has a Judeo-American peace service. Weak sunlight spatters the bright shirts and caps through the gloom. Against the pea green backdrop of Crystal Lake, he intones Yiddish utterances an octave above even the youngest campers.

"*Shalom aleichem malachai hashareit malachei elyon,*" he sings, "*mimelech malechei hamelachim hakadosh baruch Hu. Boachem leshalom—*" Then he reads in English from the service booklet. "Life is short. Time is counted. Peace is something we haven't achieved."

"War is wasteful," we chant. "Men are killed but hatred and violence remain."

"It is just like some people to be selfish," reads Rabbi Bruce. "They're doing okay. They live in an eighty thousand dollar house and have two cars, so what do they care whether there's peace elsewhere in the world?"

"I prefer this in Hebrew!" whispers Pickawillany.

"Every now and then," reads Rabbi Bruce, "I stop and think about how absurd war is. Soldiers, people alive trained to kill, to die. I don't understand."

"Iran is what it's all about," murmurs a camper named Spillberg.

"Really," mutters one called Goldsmith. "War sucks."

"Pirates suck!"

"Orioles is like a pile of shit, diaper-face!"

"The Bible states that nation shall not lift up sword against nation. With the hope that this can happen let us join together and sing about a time without war. *Lo Yis a Goy el Goy Cherev, lo Yilmadu od Michamah.*"

"Peace is good," we chant. "It is a time when men stop fighting and the people are saved. Flowers live, trees live, plants live, people live; gee, why doesn't everyone like peace as much as we do? We have a dream that someday the slums will be pretty countryside and that pollution will turn into nice blue sky. Let us hope that someday our dreams will come true."

Darius snorts. "That's what it was like when America began." But he's overtaken by a startling launch into song. *To dream the impossible dream....*

I turn to Darius. "Haven't I heard this before?"

"It's from *The Man from La Mancha*, a musical about Don Quixote."

"Ouch!" exclaims Goldsmith. "You schmuck."

Soon it's intonation time again. *Hineh mahtovu manayim shevet achim gam yachad.* "It will be nice when children can play in fields without bombs flying overhead," reads Rabbi Bruce. "We join together in a song which expresses the hope that our brothers and sisters in Israel shall be able to live in peace in the years to come." I drift in and out of concentration. Pickawillany has to take a camper to the restroom. When she returns she stops to talk with Uncle Russell high in the bleachers. Mary-Ann's down below me. Fuck love and peace, I think bitterly. The sunlight shifts until it catches Rabbi Bruce's glasses like two coins and beams straight at me. *Oseh Shalom Bimromav,* we stumble on with the Hebrew script, *hu yaaseh shalom alenuh V'Al Kol Yisrael v'imru amen. Yaaseh Shalom, shalom alenuh V'Al Kol Yisrael.*

Rabbi Bruce is in no mood to shorten the service. "There are times, God, when everything seems to be going the wrong way," he reads. "I wake up in the morning and the first thing I hear is that the Phillies lost."

"Or would have done if the strike was off!" says Spillberg.

The singing restarts: *How many roads . . . ?*

"Springsteen wrote this," I hear Mary-Ann tell her campers. "Not the Rabbi, the singer. It's awesome!"

—*the answer is blowing in the wind.*

"Dear God," we end. "I guess we are saying help us to give peace a chance, starting right here at Camp Pocono." *Shabbat Shalom. Shalom Chaverim, l'hitraot, l'hitraot, shalom.*

"Phillies suck," says Spillberg.

On the final day, I catch up with Rabbi Bruce once more. "Tell me," I ask him, "do I need to become a Jew to find the place of inexpressible happiness?"

"Heaven, you mean? Judaism is not primarily about immortality. Hell is inconsistent with reason. We trust in God for final judgment. Notions of an afterlife comfort those of us who lost so many relatives in the Holocaust, but we should think only in terms of a *mitzvah*, a good deed. An evil act begets its own punishment. Good deeds beget rewards in themselves. Don't link hopes of immortality with moral action."

"So I did a *mitzvah?*" I venture, "working here and finding out about Judaism?"

"Not really," smiles Rabbi Bruce, "but you will."

Chuffed, I resolve to *mitzvah* my way around the States. Maybe it'll pay my way. For the rest of the summer I'll be an American Jew. I'll forget love and myself, and help others. Something like that, anyway.

"Incidentally," I ask him as he climbs into his mud-colored jalopy. "Do you know much about joining the Amish?"

Ahead of me in line at the glass doors of the Indianapolis terminal one hot afternoon a week after camp a woman in a tank top and leather skirt holds her little boy's hand. A rose and dagger tattoo peeps through the dirty blonde hair that falls between her shoulder blades. She could be anything from eighteen to thirty-five. I glance behind me at a man who has just belched. He's wearing a yellow baseball cap and denim jacket. The

If I'm Ever Back This Way

cap shades his face except for the tip of his nose, his sallow cheeks and furrowed chin. He's leaning on a walking stick with a steel tip.

The woman says to the boy, "Soon be home, Carter."

The man taps my shoulder. "Where go, friend?"

"South."

"Ma'am?"

"The hell out of Hoosierland."

"Tch." He rubs his furrowed chin. We move forward. He pushes his bag with his stick. "Where's home, Ma'am?"

"Chattanooga."

The driver opens the glass door out to the bays.

"I'm Duane Allman."

"You're not Duane Allman."

"I'm not *the* Duane Allman, who died on his motorcycle in 1970. Greatest guitarist ever. But I'm still Duane Allman, and I *nearly* died in a motorcycle crash, and I *used* to play guitar. Need a family?"

"I got family."

"Two's no family."

"We don't need nothing, mister."

"Don't nobody need nothing."

I follow the woman and Carter onto the bus and sit across from them. Duane drops down next to me. We roll out of downtown with the sun in thin cloud. The windows catch rain spots south through Kentucky, over the banks of the Ohio and into Louisville. The woman sings softly to Carter about being born the daughter of a coalminer in Butcher Holler.

"That's pretty," says Duane. "I bet you *are* Loretta

Lynn."

"She's Mommy," says Carter.

"Tch." The sky has darkened. Raindrops distort the rust-colored clouds. Duane flicks on his overhead light, casting an even deeper shadow beneath his yellow cap. In Louisville, he leans across the aisle to her and says, "I could make you rich."

It's when he prods her knee to get her attention that I finally dredge up a line from a thousand westerns and tell him to leave her alone.

Duane turns slowly until beneath the shadow of his cap an eye seems to glitter. "Gonna make me?"

"You heard me." My heart slams like a drum.

He pushes his cap up. His left eye is bloodshot. In place of his right eye festers a purple crater the size of a pool ball. He stabs his stick at my chest.

"I could hook and hang a pig with this."

"Put it away, honey," pipes up a big black lady in the seat ahead.

Duane waves his stick at her. "Could stick a pig with this, lady."

"You gonna hurt yo'self."

"Tch." He leans toward me, points the stick at my cheek. "If you survive this journey," he hisses beerily, "consider yourself a lucky boy. Last person to mess with me was a penitentiary stress-advice counselor. I crushed his cranium with an adjustable spanner."

In Chattanooga Carter and his mother are up the aisle and gone. As she edges between the knees of sleeping passengers her shoulder blades come together like clipped wings and eclipse the rose and dagger tattoo. Mercifully for me, if not them, Duane leaves, too. I have survived my attempt at a *mitzvah*. During the driver change I grab a sandwich and call the Desoutter home on Mayapple Road, Jacksonville. There's no reply.

Further south, bursts of rain blast the window like waves against a ship. I shut my eyes and when I open them the driver's flicking the main light on and announcing Lookout Mountain. The lashing rain sparkles on the windows.

"If it weren't raining," says the new driver over the intercom, "and if it weren't dark, you'd see Lookout Mountain." Someone laughs. Several overhead lights are on and people are chatting. Ahead of me the black lady is telling a thin white girl in the window seat that her son, Irwin, is studying dentistry at Meharry Medical School. Maybe it's the rain, or the fact we're well south, or because the new driver thinks he's a tour guide, but the atmosphere in the bus has changed. "Lookout Mountain," he announces, "was the scene of the Battle Above the Clouds, a key moment in the Civil War. Not many folks know this but Abraham Lincoln and Jefferson Davis were both born in Kentucky."

Soon enough we cross the state line, enter what W.E.B. Du Bois called "the hot red soil of Georgia" and head for "the breathless city of a hundred hills." At the Atlanta depot yellowish lights slash the wet streets. It's rained the whole way through Kentucky, Tennessee and into Georgia. Naturally the song on my mind is "Rainy Night in Georgia."

"Welcome to Atlanta," says the driver, "birthplace of Coca-Cola, May 8, 1886, when a guy named John Stith Pemberton mixed water, sugar, kola nut fluid and a bunch of other unknown herbs into a big pot in the hope of curing hangovers. Atlanta is also the one-time home and full-time resting place of Margaret Mitchell, known as Peggy, buried thirty years ago this August on Peachtree Avenue just down that way, and of Martin Luther King Jr, buried on Auburn. Welcome to the President's State, and thank you for traveling Greyhound."

"Free at last," says the black lady, squeezing herself up from her seat. "Thank God Almighty, free at last!"

We reach Jacksonville well after midnight. I still get no answer from the Desoutter number, so sit in one of those black plastic TV chairs and check my map thinking where else to go. On my walkman, Arlo Guthrie sings "Highway in the Wind."

The departures board indicates a four a.m. Miami bus. Or I could wait until dawn and get a local to the address on Mayapple Road. Or I could go to Charleston at five. The desk clerk's dozing. It's one a.m. and there's no one home on Mayapple Road. I could go north through Charleston to Washington, or maybe South. I trace a finger to Miami and along to Key West. The desk clerk harrumphs, opens his eyes, shakes his head and closes them again. I, too, close my eyes. A *mitzvah* is a *mitzvah*, like Rabbi Bruce said. Don't expect a reward. There seems nothing out there for me except darkness and rain.

8

IF I'M EVER BACK THIS WAY

Flying from Seattle to Vancouver early on a sunny evening the following year, the plane hugs the Pacific coastline and dotted islands up to English Bay, the city of Victoria on Vancouver Island (birthplace of folk legend Ian Tyson, author of "Four Strong Winds") and the panoramic beauty of Vancouver itself. I've secured a job at Duthie's bookstore on the corner of Robson and Hornby, near Robson Square. It's there, in my first week, that I meet Lena Skinelly.

Wearing the determined expression that will become familiar to me, she marches across the street to the bookshop. I've never seen anyone walk so fast and in such a direct line toward whatever it is they want. The glass door opens as she reaches it and she strides in without pause, comes straight up to the desk and says, "I'm looking for a book about Lilooet myths." By the time we find what she wants, she's told me she's a twenty-five-year-old Lilooet widow. Her husband, Cultus, died the previous year in a skiing accident on Grouse Mountain. She rents an apartment on English Bay and works three nights a week at the Astrodome to help pay her studies at Simon Fraser.

"Is that enough?"

"That plus money from the land my people sold for development."

Three days later, she's back to tell me she's going to take me to Stanley Park. She walks out and I follow. I can hardly keep up. This becomes the pattern of the summer. She leads, I follow, until eventually I turn to go the other way and she catches up, overtakes me, gives me a long hard look then lets me be. Lena Skinelly is inescapable unless she decides to release you. Most late afternoons through the summer we take the same walk. On her free nights we generally end up at the Rose and Crown, an English-style pub with floral-patterned cottage sofas. She says she takes me there to make me "feel at home." Aside from the fan on the ceiling and the waitress service, we might be in England. Lena and I drink beer after beer and talk into the night.

"You must be devastated by your husband's death," I suggest when we're drunk.

"Not really," she says. "Shocked maybe, but Cultus was a womanizer. 'Cultus' was his nickname. It's Lilooet for 'bad.' He got it as a teenager and he never improved. Are you a good or a bad man?"

I slug my Labatts' Blue. "Middling."

"Come home to my place and sleep on the couch."

"Why would I do that?"

"Women shouldn't have to go home alone."

We take a bus down Robson and walk to her apartment. Her cousin, Jania, curls in a sky blue dress on the couch watching TV. She's half-Lilooet and has lighter skin.

"I've brought this English guy home to sleep on the couch," Lena tells her.

"Get out of here," says Jania. "I'm watching TV."

So Lena and I go into Lena's bedroom. She shows

me her photo album. The previous summer she's been in England visiting an English boyfriend. "We write each other long letters," she says. Around the walls are photographs of the Reservation where her grandmother lives. Her parents have a log cabin on the outskirts of Vancouver. "They're alcoholics," she says offhandedly.

When I awake the morning sun catches her dark profile. Gulls are screaming on the driftwood-spattered beach. Cargo ships lie moored in the shallow waters of the bay.

"I've got to go."

She opens her eyes. "It's Saturday. Let's spend the day at the beach."

At the beach, a short, wiry, balding New Zealander named Barnaby Munderton tells us he's traveling the world looking for his wife. I ask where he lost her.

"I've never met her," replies Barnaby, "but I know she's out there."

"What kind of wife do you want?" asks Lena.

"The good kind."

That night the three of us drink at the Rose and Crown. Around midnight, I put on my jacket to go.

"A girl can't walk home alone," says Lena.

"I've heard that line before."

"True lines are often repeated."

"Be a gentleman," says Barnaby.

I take Lena home and Jania's still watching TV on the sofa so we go into Lena's room. And the next morning I awake to the sun on her dark profile and gulls screaming above the drift-wood littered bay.

"I'd better be off."

"Where to on Sunday?" she says. "Stumped you!"

"You know a cricketing term?"

"From last summer."

She shows me her boyfriend's letters. They're brief, mostly responding to questions.

"I'd better go."

"My parents are expecting us for a barbecue. Surely you want to see how a Lilooet household lives?"

We reach the dark cabin around midday. Out back there's a junk-strewn yard and a bottle-opener on the wall of the deck that leads out of the tatty kitchen. No one's home. We sit on the deck and drink Molson Canadian until dusk. I light the barbecue. While we're cooking steak, she says, "So what'll you do with your life?" but just then the phone rings. Lena answers it and comes back. "It's my parents," she says. "They've been found drunk by the roadside."

"Are they coming to the barbecue?"

"They're spending the night in jail. I have to go fetch them in the morning."

"What'll *you* do?"

"What I usually do," says Lena. "Go fetch them."

"I mean with your life?"

"I'm at college," she says. "That's good enough for now."

"What are you studying?"

"Tourism. I want to get back to England."

The weeks pass and the same events seem to recur every weekend and most week nights until, back at work one Monday, I realize I need to reboard the bus. Lena keeps hinting for us to go out again that night.

"Let's keep the weekend going," she says.

I really don't want to but I go all the same. Barnaby's waiting in the Rose and Crown. While we drink together I hatch my plan. Near the end of the evening, when Barnaby's gone to the bathroom, Lena puts her hand on mine.

"Walk me home, please," she says. "A girl can't go home alone."

I know it's time to leave Vancouver. "I'm not coming home with you," I tell her. "I leave tomorrow."

She gives me a long look. "Will you come back?"

"Not soon."

"Vancouver will have changed."

"And so will we."

"Still," she says. "Did you have a good summer?"

"Yes."

"And will you write?"

"Of course. I'll look for you if I'm ever back this way."

Barnaby comes out of the bathroom pulling up his zipper.

"One more beer?" he says.

"No, thanks," I say.

"You two off then?"

"He won't walk me home," says Lena.

"Be a gentleman, mate," says Barnaby.

I shake my head. "Would you walk her home for me?"

Barnaby and Lena glance at each other.

Lena and I write back and forth for a few months, but after a while there doesn't seem much to say and one or other of us writes the last letter without either knowing it *is* the last, and we never see or hear from each other again.

If I'm Ever Back This Way

I climb back on the Greyhound, with its large red maple leaf on the door, and put on my walkman. Neil Young sings his version of "Four Strong Winds" as if in my head while the sun glints orange on the Astrodome and the waters of English Bay. *I'll look for you if I'm ever back this way.* But by the time I return to Vancouver I'm a different person, and Vancouver's a different city, with a whole new section of skyscrapers. Granville Island's been developed and there's an influx of money from the Far East and especially Hong Kong. I never find out what happens to Lena, or her parents, or her pale, skinny cousin, Jania. Perhaps Lena comes to England, but more likely she's somewhere in Canada and happily married. Either that or, I like to think, in New Zealand, regretting nothing.

9

TRUCKSTOP, MONTANA

"In America," says a large woman with cropped, graying hair, sitting next to me as we pull into a truckstop somewhere between Butte and Billings, "there's more space where nobody is than where anybody is. How do you do, I'm Gertrude Stein."

"Your observation about America," I tell her, "sadly holds true for the human heart."

"In that case, young man," she replies, "take more chances."

The driver turns off the engine. You can hear the rain on the roof. Flashing puddles cover the gravel in unruly patterns. A Budweiser sign pulses in the dark window of the lone hut below a battered café sign. On the door a handwritten placard reads, "No dogs *'ALLOW'* and no BEAR FEET." I've been on the bus two days and lost track of time. I feel unknown, utterly alone, going nowhere, yet happy. A weary blonde waitress scribbles my order of steak and eggs. Her lipstick accentuates her thin mouth beneath eyes the color of an ocean she's maybe never seen. Ginsberg's *Howl and Other Poems*, the Pocket Poets Series edition published by City Lights bookstore on Columbus Avenue in San Francisco, peeks out of my jacket pocket. I bought it in a second hand bookstore in Spokane a few hours ago. I've tried imagining myself as that "Adonis of Denver," Neil

If I'm Ever Back This Way

Cassidy. ("Joy to the memory of . . . gaunt waitresses" etc.) But I'm no Beat womaniser just a twenty-two-year-old romantic, getting a kick from solitude.

"How do you want your steak?" sighs the waitress.

"Do you have a name?"

"Ántonia." She pronounces it "Anton-ee-ah" like the Cather novel. "How do you want the steak?"

"Rare." I'm suffering from bus-madness and look at her with eyes that say, *I love you.*

"Eggs?"

"Overeasy." *I love you. I really do.* She fills my coffee without even looking at the cup. I try to catch her eye but she swishes away.

Waiting for my steak and eggs, I write of how I left Vancouver the night before with the sun orange on the glassy waters of English Bay and dipped down into America and the night to sweep east from Seattle listening to Neil Young and then Harry Chapin. I feel like I'm in utter wilderness. My head's still full of Chapin's song about a waitress and a nightwatchman in Watertown, New York. "I spent a year there one afternoon," he introduces the song. It's another one about loneliness, isolation, the spaces between people. But nowhere in the east can compete with the lonely feeling Montana gives you. Half of me loves loneliness and wants to stay here forever with Ántonia, settle down on some homestead like the parents of the boy in *Shane*. The other half wants to be Shane himself, moving through, moving in, moving on. Maybe if I live in Montana I can have both: love a person so far from the life I've left yet stay in one place, because to travel seems to mean an inexorable return to my old world. Full of vague yearnings, struck with Greyhound cabin-fever, I decide to propose marriage and take it from there.

She comes back with the eggs and says, "Enjoy your meal" another shop-worn phrase from her purely functional repertoire. I thank her and smile.

"Uhuh." She doesn't even look at me.

I glance at a newspaper and realize it's August 16, the third anniversary of my mother's death. It's also the fourth anniversary of Elvis Presley's death, and a month since a tractor-trailer ran into the back of Harry Chapin's car on the Long Island Expressway. There's an article about the Harry Chapin Memorial Fund and a benefit concert to be held this time next year at the Nassau Veterans' Memorial Coliseum in Uniondale, New York. It says Chapin raised over five million dollars for good causes in his lifetime. *There's* a life, I think, and glance up just as his ghost ambles past. He looks right at me and says, "I've got it all figured out."

"What's the deal?"

"Everybody's lonely."

"Well, maybe I can do something about one person's loneliness."

"Two," he says, and passes not only through the door but right through a big-bellied trucker on his way in. The trucker looks round but nothing's there.

Face it, I tell myself, this waitress, Ántonia, doesn't give a damn about you and never will. This is busmadness, where you've been alone so long you're not only seeing ghosts but thinking the slightest interaction augurs a lifetime's companionship. Every word is an effort and you feel like Willie Nelson's "Red-Headed Stranger," who comes into Montana and shoots a woman for touching his horse. Or the slow-motion dreamers of "My Heroes Have Always Been Cowboys," depressed from being so long alone.

"Uhuh," she's said, not even looking at me, let alone smiling, so I continue to write about what happened earlier, thinking crazily to myself that I'll play hard to get. I write about how I woke this morning with the usual crick-neck to watch the sun rising over flat ground somewhere in Washington. The bus was unexpectedly crowded. I prefer those journeys with two or three passengers, so you feel it's the edge of the abyss and the driver will be some ghost or the devil taking you to another world or your own past. But instead I got a crying child and a chicken-necked woman in a purple kimono and ankle socks.

"I've come a long way, long long way," she kept saying. "It's about killed me dead."

I'd left Spokane with a double seat but we picked up a young couple on the outskirts. He looked Mexican and carried a pair of bright red boxing gloves; His blonde girlfriend sat on his lap and they necked so vigorously I got elbowed into the air-conditioning. They jumped off at Coeur d'Alene to be replaced from Idaho to Missoula by a brawny Montana damsel with corn-fed teeth, hair like wheat, and a nose that glistened like Coeur d'Alene Lake. Her real name was Jannine Taylor but she called herself Andromeda and intended to become a vet.

In Missoula we were deep in tree clad mountains. The town seemed to be sinking between the hills. Rain battered the porches of the shacks. Pabst signs flashed red, white and blue in the dark windows of the bars. I thought of a Bob Seger song where he stops for a beer, meets a girl, tells her his plans, and off they go. I had no girl right now but I was certainly happy, if not inexpressibly. I hurried across the puddled gravel into a saloon where a line of cowboys turned to look at me, eyes gleaming between hat rims and hunched shoulders. I sat at the bar and ordered a Schlitz and sour cream and onion potato chips. They were exchanging jokes about people from Wyoming.

"What's a Wyoming virgin?" said one named Slim Chisom. "A girl who can outrun her brothers." They all laughed uproariously. Slim was on a roll. "Don't marry a virgin, says the Wyoming father to his son," he said. "Because if she ain't good enough for her own folks, she ain't good enough for our'n."

"I'll tell ya, Slim Chisom," said an older man, "ain't no joke y'ever tell I ain't heard fifty times."

Slim Chisom reached for his holster, then put his hand in his pocket, as if realizing, suddenly, that the nineteenth century is history and these jokes are probably pretty old, even in Montana.

Settling back into the bus, warm out of the rain, I ate soggy tomato and salmon sandwiches, listened to a Doors tape and watched the puddles and the arrows of rain hitting the green windows all the way to Butte and beyond.

My waitress, Ántonia, nudges me. I look up from my pad. Perhaps she's got the hint, has packed her bags and is joining me. But then I remember I've yet to ask.

"More coffee?"

She's looking at me now, so I blurt it out. "Will

If I'm Ever Back This Way

you marry me?"

If she says yes I'll suggest we find a church right away. Then we'll either stay in this truckstop forever and I'll wash the dishes, or I'll bring her home to England, my wife from between Butte and Billings, from Truckstop, Montana.

"What?" she says.

"Marry me," I say—the imperative now. "I'll whisk you away from all this. Take a chance. Marry me. Let's see what happens."

The strange thing is that she doesn't laugh and doesn't smack me (of course, she depends on tips, that's the system), but she doesn't act as if I'm a weirdo either or get wary of me, or call the management, or any of the other things she might have done. In fact she doesn't answer at all, just smiles for the first time. It's a sad smile, but it's like the first hint of sun near the end of a rainy day. Not only that, she keeps holding that coffee jug in one hand and just stands there.

"Hey, gal," calls the big-bellied trucker who didn't see Chapin's ghost walk right through him. "Coffee!"

"Jes' hold ya horses," Ántonia says. Then turns back to me. "What if I said yes?"

"Try me."

"Where do you live?"

"England."

"England? You expect me to drop everything and come to *England?*"

My God, I think, *she's taking me seriously.* "You needn't drop anything, Ántonia." I look at the coffee pot. "You could just put it down. And we needn't go to England. We could marry here."

"Then what?"

The trucker is calling for coffee again.

"Excuse me," she says and whirls away.

She doesn't come back. It's time for the bus to leave and I haven't had my answer yet. When I go to the cash desk she just slaps the check down on the table, eyes on the till, but surely she's not forgotten. I'm walking out. The wispy white streaks race beneath the bruise-colored clouds. I swivel round, push back through the door, go up behind her while she refills the coffee pot.

"Well?"

She turns to me with those ocean-colored eyes. *I really am I in love,* I think, *I'll never forget you.* "I've thought about it," she says. "In fact, I've not stopped thinking since you said it."

"And?"

"Maybe," she says.

"Really?"

"Why don't you write me a letter?"

"Okay," I grin idiotically.

She gives me a café card. "It'll reach me here."

The driver's hooting. Ántonia and I smile at each other. I feel terribly sad. We might have known each other. We might have liked each other. It's possible I'd hate her parents, or get bored, or we'd fall out or have nothing in common, but I don't know that. Maybe this, I think now, as the bus hoots one more time, is a crossroads in my life I'm not going to take. I *could* take it. I don't have to get on that bus, and even if I don't I could take one tomorrow or next week. But of course I will take it. Sooner or later I always get back on the bus. I chastise myself over this, but I know it's true and that in the end this is just a story.

So I grab the card, and do one of the few things about the whole incident I don't regret—by which I mean I do regret not staying, perhaps, though of course I'd act the same again. I don't regret asking her to marry me because surely she'll remember it always—but what I do next is kiss her forehead, and tell her I love her.

She smiles the saddest smile I've ever seen, and says, "No you don't, but thanks." The bus is pulling out and I belong on it. Unlike the old advertisement for Wrigley's Gum, when the dust settles, I'm not standing there, bag in hand. She gets on with her life at the truckstop between Butte and Billings, and I get on my way.

Desolate, I'll reach Billings soon after midnight. I'll walk into a café across the road from the depot and sit at a counter to eat a plate of waffles and maple syrup. Another waitress will serve me. I'll imagine she's Ántonia as she'll look in twenty years' time. The roads will be slick with rain but the skies will have cleared and the night will be warm, so I'll sit out and watch the reflections of passers-by jagged in the shiny sidewalk. From Billings eastward into the night we'll hit small dust towns which look like the US might have looked in the thirties—very *Grapes of Wrath* even if we'll be a long way from Steinbeck country. But parts of Montana will be breathtaking. One section will look like a moonscape of broken rock, as if Moses has smashed giant tablets and left them strewn across the world, reminding me of a joke Rabbi Bruce told me: the good news is there are only ten of them. The bad news is what they include. Through the night I'll listen to a beautiful dark girl telling someone about her life in Hawaii. She'll talk in the seats behind me all night about some fiancé named Jim—her *third* fiancé—who doesn't smother her, like Brett in Ohio did. Brett used to call Hawaii, like *every day* to talk to her from Cleveland, and send like "fourteen letters a *day*, for Chrissake!" I'll listen and dream and watch the darkness, and contemplate asking her to marry me, and feel certain that I too will go to Hawaii one day, maybe when I'm old.

Meanwhile, Interstate 94 will take us through Dickinson and Bismark and all the way through North Dakota to Fargo. Then we'll head southeast to Minneapolis and St. Paul, childhood home of F. Scott Fitzgerald, and he'll lean over and nudge me.

"That's my Middle West," he'll say, "not the wheat or the prairies or the lost Swede towns, but the thrilling returning trains of my youth, and the street lamps and sleigh bells in the frosty dark and the shadows of holly wreaths thrown by lighted windows on the snow. I am part of that."

And I too will feel as if I'm coming home somehow and should spend the rest of my days in Minnesota—birth-state, incidentally, of Eddie Cochran, though his family moved to Los Angeles when he was twelve—where life will seem, that night, so broad and easy an expanse. But all too soon I'll be off again, maybe thinking of some other girl I'll meet on the bus that night, and will be just getting to know when she abandons me in Milwaukee yet somehow remains with me, like Ántonia, to this day.

We are like painted spheres in the universe, I remember Carlotta saying, and now and then we hit another and the collision rebounds us off further than ever into deepest space, bent on a new trajectory and spinning endlessly until our next random collision. But every collision leaves you with the paintwork of another's being scratched on your surface, yours on theirs.

Leaving Minneapolis I'll catch sight of a Twins' baseball game floodlit against a rumbling sky and will half-want to go back and watch it except the bus will be so far out of the city already and I'll have told Pickawillany when I'll be arriving. Besides, to stay would be to embark on another of the lives I might have led, but you can't, alas, lead more than one. So there I'll be, suddenly, in Chicago. I'll spend five days with Pickawillany, but time will have passed, and I'll feel wistful as I leave. It will have been a sad stopping, rainy and lonely days that the past can keep for itself. But I'll have other places to go, and a lot of sitting around in bars or truckstops watching waitresses and trying to imagine their lives.

Will you marry me?

How much of our lives are spent in our imagination! Did she forget me asking? Did she know I didn't mean it, or was she smarter about me than I was about myself, realizing the sadness behind the question, and so doing me the respect of taking it seriously? What shocked me was that she should have listened at all, turning an absurdity into a possibility. Maybe this is how the world works. Maybe, too, I set off something in her she has never forgotten, or maybe men asked her that question every other day. Anyway, *I* asked her, and I'm glad I did and that our story never had an ending.

Ántonia, my waitress from Truckstop, Montana, a mother now, perhaps. I never sent you that letter I promised. Perhaps you never expected one. Why do we take some opportunities and discard others? Can it be any other way? Have you ever stood on a porch somewhere wondering what *my* name was? Or was I just another customer you forgot as soon as I left?

I never asked your last name, or where you lived, or who with, if anyone, or what your parents did, or whether you were happy. Only, *Will you marry me?* And you said, *Maybe.*

10

TAMPA TO TAMPA, A WHIRLWIND TOUR

I return to England and two years pass. I've fled Chippenham for university, but it's not going well. I've made unwise promises to a girl named Tina and argued with my father. I want to say that like Huck Finn's Pap he's been handy with the stick, but it's not the full truth. I've crashed a car and have a cut on my chin that will later scar, causing more than one person to mention my resemblance to Harrison Ford. Back home my father tries to force me to go to hospital. *You're going to the hospital*, he's shouting. *I'm not going to the hospital. My mother died in that hospital*, I shout, and then, absurdly, *Eddie Cochran died in that hospital*. My father shouts back, *You're not Eddie Cochran* and I shout, *Then who am I? And who's my real father?*

The fight starts around then. He threatens me but he's still grieving five years after my mother's death. Somehow he manages to leave me with a cut across my right cornea, permanently blurring my vision in that eye. For my part I break a rib high in the middle of his chest, about where Minnesota is. The last time I see him, the bony lump sticks out like an accusing finger. We don't mention it.

Tina and I have met while working in The Pheasant, a pub on that same Bath Road that Cochran traveled to his death. The night before I fly I'm in there with her, trying to explain why I have to leave.

"There's no cure," I tell her, "for the summertime blues."

"How about winter?"

"I've got to go." I look out at the orange-lit street with its grubby bus stops and rows of houses. "There's too many places to see. If I stay here, things will change anyway."

"I feel sorry for you," she says. "You'll never be free."

"I'm free as a bird."

She grips my arm. "What about university?"

"I learn more from music."

"How long are you going for?"

"Two weeks, maybe three." *Forever.*

"What do you want?"

"I don't want to be trapped, and tomorrow discover it's too late."

"Someday," she says, "your childish dreams must end." Evidently, song clichés are contagious. "You're running against the wind. You hide behind music and books."

"John Lennon said only rock 'n' roll was real to him. Now he's dead."

"You and I are real. I'll come with you."

"No." I clip like Steve McQueen in *Bullitt*. "Some journeys you take alone."

"Like dying," says Tina. People are watching us. Cameras are rolling. "You once told me you loved me."

My hand's on the latch. "I said I'd never been in love."

"You told me security was important."

"I was so much older then," I mutter. "It's time to be young again."

I walk down the rainy street, beneath the train tunnel up Rowden Hill past the lamppost that killed Cochran, and into my childhood home for the last time. The next morning, after my father's left for work, I pack his old canvas bag, put on a blue rollneck like McQueen's, grab a copy of *Don Quixote*, close my bank account, pocket the remaining money left me in my mother's will, and find a travel agent.

"Where can I fly today?"

"Luxembourg?" suggests the desk girl. "You could practically pick your seat."

"In the States."

"Tampa. But it leaves in four hours. There's a two-hour check-in time."

The last passenger to board, I slink into my seat between an old lady from Nashville and a Swiss-Italian oceanographer, open *Don Quixote* as we taxi and begin with Quixote's Background and First Sally as we rise. *In a village of La Mancha the name of which I have no desire to recall, there lived not so long ago one of those gentleman who always have a lance in the rack, an ancient buckler, a skinny nag, and a greyhound for the chase....* Only as we cross what in those days were the frozen wastes of Greenland, just after Quixote has tilted at windmills, do I consider my aim. Someone is sure to be around somewhere on the continent. But I'll take things as they come, go where I'm led, read whatever falls into my lap. The old lady from Nashville, who's been talking past me to the Swiss-Italian oceanographer about her dead husband, falls asleep over her bourbon, and the oceanographer introduces himself as Marco de Voto from Tour-de-Peilz. He's studying at Gainesville.

"It's hard being an oceanographer in Switzerland," he says. "And you?"

"Studying happiness."

"In Tampa?"

Marco's hiring a car so I accept a ride to Gainesville. He drops me around six p.m. in the fly-ridden depot. Rain falls in globular spats on the dusty road and soon it's a river. A dark girl sits in the passenger seat of a pink Cadillac. Opposite me in the depot a Hispanic woman joggles a boy on her knee.

It's a bad time to visit Darius. He's living with his eldest brother, Dirk, a hippie veteran of the Miami riots. They're dustbowl poor because they've quit their part-time jobs to concentrate on exams.

"So this is your British sponger," says Dirk, shaking my hand. Like Darius he's wild-eyed. Indeed, amid the generally fiery Desoutters, he stands out as venomously bad-tempered and sharp-tongued. Despite his passion for The Grateful Dead, Frank Zappa and Jimmy Buffett, he's the least laid-back ex-hippy imaginable.

"Hello, Dirk. I seem to remember Darius telling me you're a teacher in Delaware."

"*Was*. It interfered with my 'tin cup chalice' lahfstyle. Too much crap so I'm back studying in Tallahassee. Like Jimmy says: 'changes in latitudes, changes in attitudes,' dig?"

But studying isn't conducive to his "lahfstyle" either. He grows more aggressive and angrier as the exams approach. Their rented house, overshadowed by a Live Oak covered in cobweb-like Spanish moss, is a wreck. They argue about it constantly. Most exchanges are of the "Git that fucking chair fixed, Redeye!" "Then gimme some fucking *rent* money, asshole!" variety. The sun-bleached roof sags while the warped deck rises to meet it. The broken screen has been turned into a hammock and doubles as my bed. A basketball hoop juts netless from the trunk of the oak above a rusted refrigerator wedged like an iceberg amid the weeds.

"Damn it," Darius says, turning to me. "Welcome to White Trash Central!"

While Darius and Dirk study, I read *Don Quixote* at the beach. Darius joins me one afternoon.

"Why *Don Quixote*?"

"He's on a quest."

"Chasing happiness?" He looks at me as if I'm crazy, but with envy too. Maybe I'll find it. "I gotta study another hour," he says. "There's a Willy Nelson album in the living room. Play yourself two songs, 'On the Road Again' and 'Blue Eyes Cryin' in the Rain.' They'll help your quest."

Both songs bother me. I realize I don't ever want to see Tina again. So I sit out in the yard by the refrigerator and write a truly horrible letter.

Dear Tina,

As you know I've flown to America for a little Time-Out. The fact is—and there's no other way I can think of putting this—I never want to see you again. You will get over it. Bon voyage.

Yours etc.

Then I cross out *Yours* because I'm not hers, and put *Goodbye* but that's too abrupt. So I bin it, and go out with Darius and Dirk to the bars.

"Y'all ought to visit our middle brother, Drummond," says Darius over a pitcher of Busch. "Head for the mountains. Drum's in Oregon, visiting friends for a wedding. You got any balls you'll go out there."

"Go for it," says Dirk. "Y'all 'sail on sailor' or remain forever a cowardly limey bastard."

Darius drops me at the depot in the pink dawn and I have my ticket stamped for Chicago and points west. It's time to grow up with the country. As I climb aboard the bus, he admits he envies me "hitting the road again."

"Will you go north to see Daniella?"

"We've lost touch. You'll see Pickawillany?"

"If she's there."

With an angular wave, he slopes away in his cut-off jeans. I'm in the front of the cool, stationary bus, waiting for it to roll me toward first Chicago and Pickawillany, who's written saying she hopes I'll drop by, then Portland, Oregon, in pursuit of the unattainable place of inexpressible happiness. The sun rises red over Tallahassee. Through the open door I watch a black Greyhound employee sway on a stepladder, shins against the final step. He's trying to knock a dead bird from the rafters. It swings between sun and shadow.

He grins down at me. "Seems this bird don't *wanna* be free!"

I sleep until late afternoon in Alabama. Birmingham is sticky as flypaper. Ninety-five degrees flashes a downtown sign. Outside my window, three young black girls say goodbye to a fourth. One hugs her and won't let go. When they disentangle they smile and wipe the tears from each other's eyes. The red soil and clap board houses of the Deep South slide by. Across the aisle two girls giggle. One's a brunette with brown-eyes and a maroon dress. The other's a blonde with blue eyes and a cobalt blue dress. I could fall for either. I've taken to jotting poems as a form of journal. I decide to write one especially for them. It takes a while and I get absorbed in my task, but when I look up to give it to the girls they've gone. I write Tina another letter.

Dear Tina,
As you know, I'm travelling in a far distant land where no one knows me. This is the way I intend to live. We all have to find our own best kind of life. I hope you find yours. Salud
Very best wishes etc.

I bin the letter in Huntsville. Back on the bus, a fierce-eyed black guy in a shimmering orange Hawaiian shirt occupies my seat. I challenge him—bravely given that, except during his periodic fits of giggling, he resembles Mohammed Ali in his prime.

"This seat," he jabs a finger, "belongs to Greyhound Inc. of Phoenix, Arizona."

"Yes, but that's my bag in the rack above, and you're sitting on my jacket."

"No, Captain," he giggles. "I *ate* your jacket." He shifts to the window. I sit down. It's the James Dean jacket I froze in through my Michigan nights with Carlotta. "You mind if Jeremiah takes off his shirt?" The bus rolls back from its moorings and forward through the fiery skies of downtown Huntsville. "You think *they* mind? Jeremiah don't want more trouble. Jeremiah's sick of trouble. But if Jeremiah *cain't* take his shirt off, he's gonna get *hot*, means *mad*, means *crazy!*"

"Go ahead," I tell him. "Take your shirt off."

"Long as Jeremiah gulps his medicine, he's silent as a *lamb*. But they didn't want him out. Here, pull this sleeve, Captain." I help Jeremiah take off his Hawaiian shirt. "Say, Captain, you know what makes Jeremiah *real* mad?" He motions me out of the way so he can stand up. "He cain't never git enough to *eat*." He's off down the aisle, shirtless, to harangue the driver about how hot it is. I look everywhere for my jacket, but he's soon back again. "Jeremiah needs a drink," he frowns. "Drink and food. That driver, he's crazy. You's the only one aside from Jeremiah ain't crazy." He points to a scar on his arm. "The doctor jabbed Ole Jeremiah. They say *he's* crazy? Shi-it! They don't know nothing, Captain. Whole *world* crazy except Jeremiah—and *you*. Where you heading?"

"Chicago."

"There's a stinking carnival in Milwaukee. You like music? Big Band? Benny Goodman playin' Carnegie Hall? You like jazz? I has everythin': Coleman Hawkins, Sonny Rollins, Miles Davis, Louis Armstrong dueting with Ella Fitzgerald, Charlie Mingus. I has the Duke Ellington band at Newport in 'fifty-six doin' that crazy quarter-hour Diminuendo in Blue and Crescent in Blue! Hey, you like blues? Robert Johnson?"

"He's playing in Milwaukee?"

"Are you kiddin' me? A cuckold killed him with poisoned whisky in thirty-eight! But he was the father of rock. 'Hellhound on my Trail'? 'Crossroads Blues'? Check it out, Captain," he laughs uproariously, teeth like elephant tusks. Suddenly I see he's pulled a penknife from his jeans pocket. "S'okay," he frowns. "Jeremiah's hongry, so he's gonna eat his shirt." He stretches his shimmering shirt taut. "Here, hold this." I hold one end of the shirt. He rips through it, puts the knife back in his pocket, rolls the orange cotton to the size of a kumquat, and slips it into his mouth.

"You can't do that. It won't digest."

He motions with his head, swallows, and says. "So where's your *jacket*, wise guy?" By the outskirts of Chattanooga he's eaten all but the sleeves and buttons, which rattle in an orange pile on the chrome sill. "Land ho, Captain! Jeremiah needs a drink." He jumps up as the bus grinds to a halt at a hut on a scabby lot with BUS in the dusty window and a Dog sign lit from inside. When the bus pulls out he's cross-legged and shirtless in the dust in front of the drinks dispenser, chugging a Dr Pepper. His orange sleeves lie beside me. I tell the driver.

"He didn't want to come," the driver says over his shoulder. "I didn't insist."

"He ate my jacket!"

The driver shrugs. "You want to follow him until it's out of his system?"

I sleep through Indianapolis and wake as the bus winds through the Chicago streets at dawn. We plunge through a maze of tunnels into the Arrival bays. I take the escalator up to the polished floors of the main terminal and wander the streets until it's a reasonable hour to call Pickawillany. Lake Michigan glitters. The wet parts of the concrete beach reflect the sky like a mirror. I sit on a bench and write:

Listen Tina,
I've thought long and hard about our relationship and have concluded that it must come to a swift

end. I've neither the time nor the inclination for so serious a matter and apologize for not informing you sooner. Please do not call me at all. Maybe some day I'll see you and we'll talk. Until then, Good Luck. Shalom.

I screw it up and toss it away. If I'd known how hard it is to write a letter finishing a relationship I'd never have let it begin.

Pickawillany's bobbed her hair and dyed it mauve. Her pupils are large as a cat's in dim light but stay that way even in sunshine. Most of the time she wears a T-shirt and army surplus trousers. She's in her "urban guerrilla phase," she says, out to bug her square parents and her "yuppie" sister, Chrissie, who's doing all the right things and has a job downtown.

The Dinwiddie house is in the affluent suburb of Glen Ellyn. Mr Dinwiddie is a half-Cherokee salesman who travels in toothpaste. He's always wanted to live in San Francisco but the job sends him to places like Cincinnati. Mrs Dinwiddie is a chunky social worker with Pickawillany's gray-blue eyes. After a summer job at JC Penny's, Pickawillany is starting at the Kansas City Art Institute and has become a post-punk as a first step toward being an artist. She wants a ring through her nose but her parents say that if she has one she'll be paying her own way through college.

"Mom said I could have a magnet stud," she tells me, "until I told her about a friend who'd done that but wore wire spectacles. The magnet shot up inside her nostril and lodged near her sinuses. To get it out they practically took her face off."

"Whatever happened to Uncle Russell?"

"I blew him away. He must be crowding forty. Practically a corpse."

We spend a couple of days on the Lakeside beach, taking the double-decker train between Glen Ellyn and Union Train Station on 210 South Canal Street, peering at the Chicago skyline through the tiny greenish, submarine windows. I don't know how Uncle Russell felt, but I'm three years older than Pickawillany and in her home environment feel like an old man tagging along with her and her friends. I buy them beer. We take it to a wooded hillside near her old high school and sit on a path deep in the bushes to drink. Pickawillany shows me a series of tunnels around the neighborhood. They use them to escape the police. The friends leave and the two of us finish the beer beneath a tree in a Glen Ellyn park until she knows her parents are out. Back in the garden, she hooks up a hammock. At twenty-three, I feel like the oldest man in the world.

The next morning Pickawillany drives me downtown and the bus rolls me away. She's given me a poem, carefully folded, and told me not to read it until I'm out of Chicago. I read it over coffee in Iowa City. *You're leaving when the dusk is forming / Leaving for a year or two./ Write a picture, paint a letter, / always say goodbye to you./ Always leaving, like a shadow, / at least I know you never lie. / I always know you won't be staying, / but I'll see you in the years gone by.* I have a mind to catch the next bus back to Chicago and stay in Glen Ellyn with Pickawillany forever. I can't understand why I always choose to leave, or even if I have a choice. But I tell myself the best thing in life is the first day or two you visit anyone, and the only way to keep happy is to keep moving. "Comes a time," says Neil Young from the next seat, "when you travel. Comes a time when you—"

"I know," I sigh. "But I don't think I'll ever settle anywhere long."

Willie Nelson, I suddenly realize, is in the seat across the aisle, and he and Young are advising me.

"Aged twenty-two," says Young, "who does know what to do?"

"My sentiments entirely," I tell him, "give or take a year."

"Don't grow up to be a cowboy," says Nelson, his beard and pigtails catching light from behind. "You'll roam alone for Eternity."

"I'll tell you something," says Young. "One thing you always carry inside is your home life, your childhood, the child within you."

Young and Nelson fade in the darkness. It's a clear night and the sun hits the crescent moon in a bright curve. The moon seems to pulse but it's my own heartbeat. What I see in the eyes of others is my own heartbeat too. I'm so impressed with this sad insight that it makes me happy.

Later, a meaty Argentine wrestler, nose studded with blackheads, sees I'm reading *Don Quixote*. "Ah, yes," he says, leaning across the aisle. "You have read Jorge Luis Borges? In *Labyrinths* Borges has a character who writes the whole of *Don Quixote*, word for word, without seeing the original."

"Why would he do that?"

"Aha," says the wrestler. "It is a labyrinth, is it not? He has a story called 'Paradiso, XXXI, 108.' *Who of us has never felt, while walking through the twilight or writing a date from the past, that something infinite has been lost?* You see, he is talking about the face of Christ, lost forever in the mists of history, and how the ticket clerk could have that face, or a fellow passenger. *Who knows whether tonight we shall not see it in the labyrinths of our dreams and not even know it tomorrow?"*

Just then a smartly-dressed woman with gray hair and horn-rimmed spectacles leans over and says, "Did you say the face of Christ?"

"I did, ma'am," says the Argentine wrestler.

"Well," says the woman, "the book Elvis Presley took to the bathroom with him the last time he was seen alive was called *The Scientific Search For the Face of Jesus.*"

"No kidding," says the Argentine wrestler. But the woman has leaned back into the shadows. "Do you ever think about faces?" he says to me, "how many faces you see in a lifetime? The only face I want to see is not that of a deity, but of my fiancée."

"The face I see," I tell him, "is the face of my soulmate. I might find her and I might not, or I might find and lose her."

"You don't have a soulmate?"

"No, but I have a friend interested in souls."

I phone Carlotta from Des Moines. She says it's inconvenient for a day or two, so I change buses and loop down to Kansas City via St. Louis, out through the plains of Kansas, then to the foot of the Rockies where Denver rises in the mist. The night bus back to Lincoln leaves me early the next morning sitting on a baggage trolley outside the depot. Carlotta finds me a place to stay at the university and I spend a day or two meeting her sorority friends. Her soul remains intact. She tells me she got "seriously burned" by a long-term boyfriend the past year. She's had more assurances from God that she is spiritually pure, including another of those phone calls just as the windows were steaming up. I suspect it was from her mother. She doesn't appreciate this suggestion and I realize it's time to move on.

"Where are you going?" she asks.

"Oregon."

"Why Oregon?"

"Why not?" We say goodbye and I catch a bus back along Route 80 to Cheyenne, which I reach on Frontier Day. My chisel-jawed seat companion resembles Trampus from *The Virginian*.

"Hell's Bells," he says. "It's Wild West Week."

"I've seen all this before," says some fantasist in the seat behind who calls himself Jack Kerouac. "Big crowds of businessmen in boots and ten gallon hats, with hefty wives in cowgirl attire, bustle and whoopee on the wooden sidewalks of old Cheyenne, with the long stringy boulevard lights of new downtown Cheyenne off in the distance. Blank guns go off. The saloons are filled to the sidewalk."

Trampus, Jack and I hit the bars then sleep it off at the depot. I curl up with my father's canvas bag until eight in the morning among the dreary murmurs and noises. At dawn, Trampus is nowhere to be seen, Kerouac goes his way to Denver, and I mine to Boise, Idaho and then Portland by way of Utah to see Salt Lake City in its sandy shell. The rest of the way to Portland I read

Don Quixote. I'm beginning to see myself as the Don, though I'm currently escaping my Dulcinea rather than trying to win her.

"That is the way with women," Don Quixote tells Sancho Panza as we cross into Washington. "They spurn those that care for them, and love those that hate them."

"Aren't men the same?"

"But assuming that two individuals are equally beautiful," he goes on, wincing from the lack of leg room, "it does not mean that their desires are the same; for not all beauty inspires love, but may sometimes merely delight the eye and leave the will intact. If it were otherwise, all would wander vaguely and aimlessly with nothing upon which to settle their affections."

"Ah," I respond, "so we all seek the particular."

"Sometimes you look for one thing," says Quixote, "and you find another."

Reflected in the Willamette River, Portland changes hue beneath a cloud-strewn sky. We pass the Portland Oregon Temple and a sign for John's Landing, and cross the river, the city to the left now, spread out amid the widening water and a mass of bridges. I'm four thousand miles from Florida, six thousand miles from England. *So many miles. How many miles will be enough?* Over the Columbia, there's a green bridge ribbed and criss-crossed like the Queensboro Bridge. Sometimes I feel I can hold all America in my mind at once in some strangely catalogued way, and that one day I'll resurrect everything and everyone I've seen and heard, and so become part of it myself.

"Well, y'all *did* have the balls to come to Oregon!" says Drum at the depot.

I recognize him instantly. Black hair, dark skin, hooked nose, he's a fairground mirror version of Dirk and Darius. Where they are lithe and taut, Drum is large and soft-bellied. He's Darius and Dirk without the edge. If anything, he looks Native American. He has a massive wood-carved face that in repose is like the photograph of the Cheyenne Chief, Dull Knife, in Dee Brown's *Bury My Heart at Wounded Knee*. Drum is home from home in Oregon. He went to college at his father's *alma mater*, some private place he doesn't name. Along with his black labrador, Mr Dog, he's mainly up in Oregon for the wedding of two friends, former classmate, Dr Calvin Krycjak, and the love of Drum's life, Marlene.

"I'm here to see a friend marry my woman," he explains on the way up to West Hills.

"*Your* woman?"

He nods. "Once upon a time." Drum occasionally talks about Marlene on our travels, and seems churned up inside. She speckles his conversation like ash from Mount St Helens. "I've traveled 5000 miles to see two friends marry," he says, gunning his metallic blue Chevrolet pick-up out of the city. "Y'ever hear of such devotion? Their vows will riddle my chest."

Krycjak lives with Marlene in a West Hills apartment overlooking the city. Willowy, with curly, light brown hair and a droopy moustache, every aspect of Krycjak seems to sag. He slouches. His eyes fall away toward low-slung ears. It's as if his whole body is so self-satisfied it no longer bothers to keep up appearances. Certainly he seems to have it made. He has a banjo, a waterbed, and Marlene. A dark-skinned nurse with lustrous hip-length hair, Marlene makes me wish I too were a doctor living in West Hills with a fiancée, a waterbed, and a banjo. At least I'm not in Drum's position. Once, in college, she told Drum she'd gladly marry him. But at the time Drum himself was engaged. I'll finish with her! he said. No, she said. I wouldn't let you fuck up your life for me. Later he found out she'd said much the same thing to several of them, but always had her eye on Krycjak because he was pre-Med.

"What happened to your fiancée?"

"Ex-fiancée," says Drum. "But we're still close. You'll meet her."

We stay with Krycjak and Marlene for the two days before their wedding, drinking beer and listening, at Drum's morose insistence, to Patsy Cline. He plays "Three Cigarettes in an Ashtray" over and over until Krycjak tries to liven it up with his banjo.

"One more twang," says Drum, "and I'll defenestrate you."

"Come on, guys," says Marlene, "we're here for our *wedding*."

On the horizon, the diminished Mount St Helens looks defeated while the pinnacled Mount Hood looks distinctly smug. Krycjak hands me a bottle of Blitz Weinhard as we sit on the deck. I ask him if he likes living in Oregon.

"Oh, sure." He oozes self-satisfaction like the foam from his Blitz. "Who wouldn't? There's always the danger of Californification, of course. We don't want anyone fucking up Oregon that way."

"Cali-fornication," says Gilmer Zeach, another ex-college buddy who's just arrived. Gilmer's a painter with a long face and shaved head. He's hitch-hiked up from Los Angeles with his parrot, Emerson. Gilmer lives with his blind mother and the home help has refused to look after Emerson while he's gone.

Krycjak is still on about Oregon. "People remember the 1968 Democratic Primary when Robert Kennedy lost to McCarthy. One minute he's here in Oregon, safe and carefree, the next he's shot dead in Hollywood. There's Oregon, and there's the rest of America, and not much to connect us."

"And where are *you* from, Krycjak?" says Drum, winking at me.

"Normal, Illinois."

All the next day it rains. A ring of mist severs the horizon from the volcanic peaks of the Cascades, crowned by the snow-clad Mount Hood. I'm down to my last hundred dollars plus three hundred for the flight. The night before the wedding, Krycjak, Drum, Gilmer, myself, Emerson the parrot and Mr Dog pool our resources for a room at a Holiday Inn while Marlene stays with girlfriends in the house. From midday onward I enter a haze of Daiquiris and Tequila Sunrises in a Mexican restaurant. By evening I'm jitterbugging in some hotel on a miniscule dance floor with a giant named Nadia Freneau. When Nadia Freneau thunders off, I'm pulled back to a table where Drum, Gilmer and assorted shadows have lined me up tequilas. I down them all and stumble to reception to ask the way to our Holiday Inn. I don't realize I'm already in it, so have no chance of finding it again. I wander across what seems to be a parking lot to a secluded grove, find a bush and lie down to look at the stars and work out the meaning of it all, but immediately pass out. At least I assume I pass out because what happens next can only be a vivid, surreal dream. Bobby Kennedy comes and sits next to me under the bush.

"So this is where to get away from it all," he says with his nasal, Boston twang.

"Well, the beach is better," I advise.

"Nah," he replies. "The place is swarming with photographers."

"Where do you go next?"

"Los Angeles."

"Don't do it," I tell him. "Stay in Oregon, or go back to Washington DC, or anywhere. Just don't go to LA. They'll kill you."

"It's got to happen somewhere," he says. "By the way, have you met Jack?"

And there, in the bush's blue shadows, silhouetted against the stars, squats JFK.

"Oh wow," I stutter. "I've always wanted to meet you, or would have. But you were dead before my fourth birthday."

"What do you mean?" He gives me an amused smile-frown.

"You don't know about Dallas?"

"Dallas?"

"The open-topped limousine, and Jackie in that pink dress with the black lapels, and the motorcade down Dealey Plaza?"

Bobby puts a hand on my arm. "It's okay," he nods. "Jack's in denial."

"He doesn't know he's dead?"

"He thinks he's still President. It's awful sad."

Of course, this is all rather strange, the Kennedys

and I sitting beneath a bush in Oregon. But like so much that summer, I just go with the flow. It turns out Bobby's in denial himself, evidently roaming Oregon, thinking he never did actually go down to Los Angeles. JFK thinks he's lived through a two-term Presidency, and is up here campaigning for Bobby to succeed him. I don't like to put them right, but I don't have to because I wake to a whooshing sound. When I burst my head through the gorse bush and blink at another tequila sunrise, I find I've passed out on the central reservation of a six-lane highway.

Back at the Holiday Inn, I curse the fact I've forgotten to ask the Kennedys about Marilyn Monroe, and whether they might possibly have paid her off and exiled her to run a Grand Rapids coffee shop. I find the room and recover with a Bloody Mary. Drunk again by midday, I reel to the wedding ceremony, held outdoors in burning heat. There's nothing to do but dip a glass beneath the flow of pink champagne cascading from a silver fountain at the back of the make-shift aisle. Krycjek and Marlene take their vows in front of a rose-covered archway. From beneath a nearby tree, a beautiful girl serenades them off-key with songs like "Kum-ba-yah" and "If I Had a Hammer" while her younger brother strums Heavy Metal.

Also beneath the tree is a blonde woman in a wheelchair.

"My old fiancée," gestures Drum. "Christine Svenson."

I follow him over. Christine is very pretty with green eyes. She's a paraplegic. It happened after she and Drum split. She dove off a cliff into a river. No one said it had to do with Drum, but no one said it hadn't. She doesn't mind talking about the accident.

"I hit my neck or head, but I was able to get out of the water," she tells me. "Then once I sat on the grass my body seized up and that was it."

She has to sit in the shade because she has problems with her sweat glands. This is the only tree available and we can hardly hear ourselves talk. Her smile grows sour as the lemons around the smoked salmon and thin as the low clouds that gather before the setting sun. The day after the wedding Drum and I visit her at home with her widowed father. He has all the money imaginable. Their vast house overlooks a lake and has a pool and almost anything else she might want. Drum and I help her into the pool. Clinging to the side, the ends of her blonde hair soaked dark-reddish, you wouldn't know she's a paraplegic. I fantasize about staying on as her helper and falling in love. It's not going to happen, of course, and Drum's not staying with her either.

"We've got to hit the road, Christine," he says late in the afternoon. "I've got school in a few days. And my friend has to get back to his life in England."

She holds my gaze. "What do you do in England?"

"I'm between things."

She smiles. I can't think what to say. I smile back, but slowly her smile fades and I look down. Her hands are curled up. She only has partial use of them. She's thin but with a little pot belly from being so often in a sitting position. I glance into her eyes again. She's been watching me look at her. Together, the three of us observe the slowing ripples of the pool. Early the next morning Drum and I drive in near silence to Lakeview.

"What y'all need, what *I* need," he says eventually, "is good, clean mountain air. You ready to hike? We'll go get supplies in Lakeview, then head for Mount Jefferson, and *no beer*."

"Or tequila."

"Just the Great Outdoors."

So we hike three days on Mount Jefferson then five in the Warner Wilderness of Northern California. We see no one, just porcupine, antelope, humming birds, deer, beaver, golden eagles and stunning scenery—mountains, lakes, wild flowers, valleys—the plains of Heaven painted by John Martin. At the end of each day's hike, I read *Don Quixote*. I feel heartsick about Christine. I can't imagine what her future holds. The moment has passed and I hate myself for not saying something to brighten her life, though even now I can't think what I could have said. *Don Quixote* is an escape, even though I'm the Don still, with his ever-changing vision of Dulcinea, who's certainly not an ugly peasant, but Pickawillany and Carlotta and Christine all mixed together. *My God*, I think. *Why can't I marry them all and live in a big house surrounded by women and father numerous children in a rambling Montana ranch like some Old Testament patriarch and make them all happy?* I don't bother compiling answers to this but lie on the grass between rocks and wild flowers and read.

"I was born a free being," Dulcinea is telling Quixote. "To live freely I chose the solitude of the fields; these mountain trees are my company, the clear-running waters in these brooks are my mirror, and to the trees and waters I communicate my thoughts and lend of them my beauty."

Between hikes we rest up near Lakeview with Ma McShudder. Ma lives on a smallholding up a dust track in the dry grass off Route 2. She's the aging mother of another of Drum's ex-college buddies, Shoulders McShudder. Shoulders couldn't be at the wedding because he makes good money every summer working on the Alaska pipeline to supplement his Lakeview income as a winter farmhand. Alone all summer, Ma's only too pleased to have us stay. It's exactly what I pictured as a child and I see myself as a farm boy with a dog and stick. Across the cornfields, purple hills range against the thunderheads. It's basically where Ricky and Uncle Sandy lived in *Champion, The Wonder Horse*, except it's in color, though even then the weather before rain turns the landscape sepia.

An alcoholic and late-onset diabetic, Ma stays up all night drinking Blitz and watching her fuzzy TV. She can watch two programs at once, she says. However much Drum tells her this is because of interference from the hills and she needs a proper aerial, she blames Shoulders' father, Thunder McShudder, who died of a heart attack on the floor in the space between Ma and the TV ten years before.

"It ain't never been the same since," she sighs.

"You must miss him."

"*Miss* him! He's still here, messing up my *TV!*"

Nights Drum and I go into town to a bar with a juke box and get drunk and dance with the local talent: an elderly lady in bellbottoms.

She crinkles a smile. "You want to come home for a good ole time?"

"Not really," I reply, though I'm poorer than ever

and the possibility of being a gigolo crosses my mind. But I'm happy to drink and dance with her into the early hours to endless repetitions of "Tulsa Time."

Meanwhile back at the ranch, Ma's breakfasts are drawn-out events. Egg and bacon, followed by more egg and bacon, then endless waffles and maple syrup, followed by popcorn.

"That sonofabitch, Thunder, he loved my waffles."

"Waffled his way to a coronary," whispers Drum.

Waking in the morning to the smell of bacon after the third day my heart, once so buoyant, sinks at the thought of another of Ma's breakfasts. But through the window the cornfields stretch to those dark hills and I feel like Ricky. Plus I've nothing to do all day or night but drink beer and read and go out for groceries. That, and get the letter to Tina right, which I finally do.

Dear Tina,

I'm in prison in Oregon on manslaughter charges. The trial will be long, and there's the probability of a hefty sentence if found guilty. I'm under an assumed-name, so they don't know who I am. I have one day of bail left, which is how I've managed to send this letter. Pray for me but don't expect ever to see me again.

Yours in deepest gloom etc.

I write this sitting in the backyard by a small pond and an artesian well, my face itching from the beard I'm trying to grow. I skim the last hundred or so pages of *Don Quixote* as my good intentions finally wilt. That opening sentence, about a gentleman with "a greyhound for the chase" seemed so appropriate for bus travel, but it's a long book and I feel I read that line in another lifetime, just as England now seems so small and far away. By August I'm totally out of money but luckily Drum's driving the pick-up to Florida. It's blindingly hot, and Gilmer, who's joined us from Portland with Emerson and happens to live in Orange County, Los Angeles, suggests we'd be better off driving down the coast and along Interstate 10 from LA.

"Why the fuck," says Drum, "would I drive to LA when I'm heading for Florida?"

"It's cooler down the coast," says Gilmer.

"And New Mexico? And *Texas?*"

"There's a meteor shower forecast. You'll catch it best from the desert."

Drum's a pushover. We bid farewell to Ma McShudder, and head south into California and diagonally across to Redding on 299 and over to the coast above Eureka and down.

"What the hell," he says to Gilmer. "Down the coast we'll go, you, me, Mr Dog, Emerson the Parrot, and an Englishman, in that order."

Fed up with the jibes and with jostling between a wagging tail and fluttering green feathers, I opt for the open back of the pick-up and lie watching the sky while we speed down 101 toward San Francisco. Much of the coastline is rugged and lonely, a land of rolling fog, waves tearing at the high cliffs, deep green forests stretching inland. We hit redwoods occasionally, winding through them like an ant on a forest floor. The sequoias loom above us, white by our headlamps. It grows cold and I tap on the window for Drum to let me in.

"Check out these fuckers," says Gilmer, craning to look at the trees. "It's a temple older than America itself.

But so much of it's gone. Once there were millions of acres of redwoods up this coast. But we've chopped most of them down."

We speed across the Golden Gate Bridge in the moonlight and into the lights of the city, bouncing down all those hills, windows open to the freezing coastal air. Emerson has crapped all over the cabin.

"Damn," says Drum, "why give a thousand mile ride to a *parrot?* Still, Dirk would appreciate it, being a Parrothead."

"Parrothead?"

"Jimmy Buffett fans are known as Parrotheads," says Gilmer. "But Emerson is not a Buffett fan, Drum."

"And I," says Drum, "am not a parrot fan."

We stop for gas and I set foot in what Thomas Wolfe called "the fabled town."

"San Francisco!" yells Drum. "Y'ever been to 'Frisco before?"

"No, but I've seen *Vertigo*, and I know a Carlotta."

"I love Hitchcock," says Gilmer. "Remember where Kim Novak falls in the water beneath the Golden Gate? That's Old Fort Point. Remember the art gallery where he sees her gazing at the portrait of Carlotta? That's the Palace of the Legion of Honor. What a movie! Mind you, there's nothing to touch Roy Rogers in *Springtime in the Sierras*."

San Francisco is soon far behind and I've barely seen it. But I know it exists now, like a myth becoming fact. Years later I'll read Steinbeck's *Travels with Charley* and how San Francisco "put on a show" for him. "The afternoon sun painted her white and gold—rising on her hills like a noble city in a happy dream." But such a view—not to mention Haight-Ashbury, Golden Gate Park, Human Be-Ins and so on—will all have to wait. Drum and Gilmer have no time to stop. We drive on through San José, Santa Cruz, past Steinbeck's hometown of Monterey. Somewhere near Salinas Drum and Gilmer start singing "Me and Bobby McGee." Santa Cruz spreads in a dawn mist and Drum guns the pick-up right on by. By mid-morning the sun's beating relentlessly on the windshield. Everything we drink is warm and sticky in seconds. Emerson wilts. When the first feathers fall out Gilmer looks worried.

"He's molting maybe," I suggest.

"He's revolting," says Drum. "Why take a goddam parrot to a wedding?"

"Hush," hisses Gilmer. "You'll hurt his feelings."

When he's not worrying about Emerson, Gilmer keeps up a monologue about California as relentless as the heat. "A tenth of the nation live here—yet you've seen yourselves how empty the Warner Wilderness is. We're so vast we *are* a nation—all but."

"So why not become one?" says Drum.

"Central Valley could swallow Florida whole. We've got every kind of fruit from apricots to zucchini, every kind of plant from alfalfa to wheat, and every kind of nut from almonds to—"

"Gilmer Zeach," laughs Drum.

Gilmer mutters "Walnuts, actually," but Drum has offended him and we drive on in silence, except for Emerson cackling *Blitz Weinhard,* and Mr Dog growling in response. South of Monterey we hit the wild coastline of Big Sur and ninety miles of spectacular coastal views, then join 101 at San Luis Obispo through Santa Maria into Santa Barbara County. The road's long and sun-parched, with white instead of yellow central lines. We pass a sign for Buellton with a black on yellow EXIT 30 mph sign, and Shell and Exxon signs off the side road. Up ahead the hills in the hazy sunshine are blue with foliage and patchy with sandy earth. 101 takes us all through Santa Barbara, set in its crescent-shaped valley between the honey-colored Santa Ynez Mountains and the Pacific and along the coast by Montecito Carpinteria and Ventura, turning inward from the Pacific across the top of Malibu Creek State Park into Los Angeles County. In the suburb of Encino I take over the driving and negotiate the Ventura Freeway. Emerson adopts my shoulder, with Gilmer asleep the other side and Drum and Mr Dog in the back. Suddenly I'm on the San Diego Freeway.

"Emerson, we're *here!*" shouts Gilmer.

But there are no landmarks, only the endless sprawl of a highway winding between distant rows of compact dwellings on green and yellow hills. Californians in shiny cars fall into line around our battered pick-up as if accompanying a decaying deity toward the smog-bound sun.

"Check out the slurbs, man," says Quincy. But he's mostly distracted by the deterioration in Emerson's health from hours in a sun-washed cabin. "Stay on the Freeway," he says, "and you can't go wrong."

Hands locked white and rigid against the wheel, I take us over the Santa Monica Mountains, past Beverly Hills to the left, over Santa Monica Boulevard and the Santa Monica Freeway, past signs for Culver City and Los Angeles International Airport, through Hawthorne and Torrence and Carson, over the Los Angeles River, until finally Gilmer says, "Next left," and I pull into a gas station so he can drive us to his home in Long Beach.

"Where are the pedestrians?"

"There are no pedestrians in Southern California," says Gilmer. "In Beverly Hills they don't even have sidewalks. Everybody drives."

"Where's the center?"

"There isn't one. The city is five hundred square miles of sprawl."

Gilmer lives in a small house near the ocean with a garden full of orange, lemon and lime trees. He mushes cheese, tabasco and avocado on toast for us. Orange County, Gilmer tells me, was the birthplace of Richard Nixon, who lived at San Clemente as his western White House. I hardly see LA at all. I just sleep. For Jean Baudrillard, LA is the future. "In years to come," he says, "cities will stretch out horizontally and will be non-urban (Los Angeles). After that, they will bury themselves in the ground and will no longer even have names. Everything will become infrastructure bathed in artificial light and energy. The brilliant superstructure, the crazy verticality will have disappeared. New York is the final fling in this baroque verticality."

When I eventually read Baudrillard's *America*, I see how easily we impose our own visions on a country and landscape. "On the aromatic hillsides of Santa Barbara," he writes, "the villas are all like funeral homes. Between the gardenias and the eucalyptus trees, among the profusion of plant genuses and the monotony of the human species, lies the tragedy of a utopian dream made reality." So here I am in paradise itself, which maybe isn't a fairground ride in Omaha, but California, just as the Eagles said. "Santa Barbara is a paradise," writes Baudrillard. "Disneyland is a paradise; the US is a paradise. Paradise is just paradise. Mournful, monotonous, and superficial though it may be, it is paradise." Yet only because it isn't mine and I don't have to pay taxes here. Besides, the charm of paradise is not just to do with the beauty that is not mine, but the ugliness that I have no stake in either. The beauty of being foreign is never permanent. So I prepare myself, mentally, for the inevitable return journey, which will begin as soon as we head east. Our only delay is a stop in Santa Monica.

Baudrillard is at my elbow. "One of the finest things there is, at dawn: the Santa Monica pier," he says, "with the white waves rolling in, the sky gray over Venice, the pale green or turquoise hotel overlooking the sands, and the endless line of run-down motels with their grimy little lamps, their graffiti-covered walls. The first waves, already frequented by a few insomniac surfers, the oh-so-melancholy palm trees with their Roaring Twenties grace, and the merry-go-round." He sighs, eyes misty behind those Gallic spectacles. "Here at dawn, it is one of the most insignificant shorelines in the world, just a place to go fishing. The Western World ends on a shore devoid of all signification, like a journey that loses all meaning when it reaches its end."

Time indeed to leave. I've reached the furthest point of my journey and every wheel-turn will now bring me nearer my point of departure.

"No time to lose," agrees Drum. "I got school soon. Reality beckons."

We leave Gilmer's house just as a pet ambulance is taking Emerson away on a little stretcher and attached to a drip. He looks awfully green. Gilmer is bawling. The housekeeper comes to sit with Gilmer's blind mother. Gilmer climbs into the pet ambulance with Emerson and they're gone. Drum, Mr Dog and I clamber back into Drum's battered pick-up and begin our long dusty haul along Interstate 10 the three thousand miles to Florida. "You know," says Drum as we rumble east. "I'd have liked to have seen San Diego. I've got a cousin there, an oceanographer like that Italian guy you mentioned, works at the Scripps Institute at La Jolla."

"There's always somewhere else."

"Sure is," says Drum, and guns the pick-up toward Arizona and the promised shower of shooting stars. The heat feels drier as we speed inland through San Bernadino to Phoenix to Tuscon, cutting through Las Cruces and the bottom end of New Mexico to El Paso where we veer into Mexico and spin down a dirt road through scrubland, stopping at a tin cabin where a one-legged man is selling T-shirts and Mountain Dew. Back in Texas, Emmy Lou Harris comes on the radio singing "Riding on the Wheels of Love." The music echoes across the barren earth. One hand on the wheel, Drum spews tobacco into a coffee flask. I chew gum, but it dries my mouth out like the landscape. "We haven't even reached Texas!" snorts Drum, spitting into his flask, "and Country already rules the waves."

Through Arizona and New Mexico we give rides to Boxcar Willie, Hank Williams, Chet Atkins, George Hamilton IV, Waylon Jennings, Skeeter Davis, Dolly Parton, Johnny Cash and a host of singers neither of us have heard of. Then in jumps Marty Robbins singing "By the Time I Get to Phoenix," and we shout the song out at the desert, Drum spitting into his flask, me sipping warm Coors. Next in is Bobby Goldsboro singing "Honey," that sentimental song about a man whose wife plants a tree and promptly dies of an unspecified illness.

"All country songs seem to be about loss."

"*Life* is loss," says Drum. "Haven't you noticed?"

We hit Texas. Somewhere between El Paso and San Antonio, Dottie West sings, "If You Go Away."

"I once met Dottie West."

"Sure you did."

Between San Antonio and Houston, Cochran sings "Three Steps to Heaven."

"You're not going to believe this either," I say, "but Eddie Cochran died as the result of a car crash in my street in England. As a matter of fact—"

"Eddie who?" says Drum.

I start reading a book Gilmer's given me: *Silent Spring* by Rachel Carson. I'm reading it as part of my summer policy of going with the flow. I'm playing the picaresque hero borne by fate and others' goodwill around the country. I read what I'm given. On the back cover it says Carson, a genetic biologist, died in 1964—three years after the book's publication—the same year as Ben Hecht. Like Hecht, she belonged to a world that existed before I was born. But it's my world yet.

"This is the story of the use of toxic chemicals in the countryside and the widespread destruction of wildlife in America," Carson tells me. "What has already silenced the voices of spring in countless towns in America?" She's writing at the start of an era that will bring the ecocrisis to the fore as humankind's greatest problem. Aged twenty-three, I listen attentively. "This pollution is for the most part irrecoverable," she says. "The chain of evil it initiates not only in the world that must support life but in living tissues is for the most part irreversible."

"You mean we're in a mess," I respond bleakly.

"And then there's the intensification of agriculture. Nature works in terms of variety," she explains. "Man has displayed a passion for simplifying it. Disease swept through the elms carried by a beetle that would only have a limited chance to build up large populations and to spread from tree to tree if the elms were only occasional trees in a richly diversified planting."

I drop the book to my lap. "Have you read this?"

"*Don Quixote*?"

"No, it's about the environment. *Silent Spring*."

"I heard somewhere the world's gonna get hotter. I can hardly bear it as it is!"

Something clicks in my brain. I must not only travel but also read. I must find something worthwhile to do with my life. Or else why live? All this traveling has to have a point. There's nothing for it, I decide. I'm going to have to save the world.

That afternoon we stop for ice cream and Mr Dog's tail swooshes my Pistachio and Chocolate out of its cornet, so he's banished to the back of the truck. In mid-Texas, a thunderstorm forces us off the road. Mr Dog clambers in from the driving rain and shakes himself. All the dust turns to mud to go with the melted ice cream. When we start again Mr Dog's so happy his tail whips it into a smoothie. Texas seems interminable, as if renewing itself like an immortal rattlesnake.

"Join up all the Texan roads you'd reach beyond the Moon," says Drum. "And that's a fact."

Only the promised meteorite storm breaks the monotony. Halfway through Texas our watches—maybe due to some kind of magnetism from the storm—get onto a weird kind of Texas time. Hundreds of hours pass between dawn and nightfall. Drum begins to worry he'll be late for school. The truck seems unable to go above forty. Even our voices slow to a Texan drawl.

"Someone has slowed everything down."

"Or speeded it up," says Drum. "Check out the rearview mirror. You look middle-aged." He swivels the mirror. I recoil in horror. Kenny Rogers stares back.

"Maybe Texas is circular, guys," suggests Kenny. "Like the Universe."

"Kenny Rogers is in the mirror," I tell Drum.

"You've been in Texas too long."

Kenny leans toward me. Mr Dog growls. "Don't take that dog to town," says Kenny.

Texas Time passes as slowly as if I were sitting with Carlotta waiting for her mother to go to bed. We pass the miles by rewriting Gene Pitney's "Twenty-Four Hours from Tulsa" as "Ninety-Six Hours in Texas." There's no need even to read a map. Interstate 10 takes us across the country.

"I have a dream," I confide in Drum as I take over the wheel, "that one day, whatever I'm doing in life, I'm going to hire a car and start in New York and drive the whole way around America."

"Ain't no dream." He spits in his flask. "Next?"

"Something'll come along. Alaska maybe."

"And if it don't?"

"Start round again."

"And that girl you told me about?" He spews a long stream of brown like diarrhoea. "You are one common as shit piece of manhood."

Texas continues to unroll like an unending beige carpet. At one point I fall asleep at the wheel but we just rumble through the cacti until I jolt awake fifty yards into the wilderness. Drum takes back the wheel and I resume reading Carson.

"Drum, a twenty-five percent solution of DDT spilt on skin kills in an hour."

"Say, look!"

Like a soaring, skimming kite, an eagle weaves toward us. The speck turns to a line, the line to wings, a head, and two sparkling eyes, and *clunk!* It crashes against the windscreen. We screech to a halt and turn in our seats as it thumps down onto the shimmering road.

"It had the whole sky to fly in."

"Either it intended to eat us," says Drum, "or it was just plain bored."

Houston's shady parks and gleaming buildings seem more like civilization again. Soon a radio station's playing Springsteen, and at normal speed. We're coming out of Texas Time while Springsteen tells us two lanes can take us anywhere.

"Then let's hope they take us home," says Drum. Sure enough, we're soon wading through the steamy heat of Louisiana. "From near Salinas," he says, "we're now, as Kristofferson says, busted flat in Baton Rouge."

We detour to New Orleans for a Dixie in the French Quarter as a steamer paddles by in the delta mist, then head northeast through Mobile, which I know from Dylan's "Stuck Inside of Mobile with the Memphis Blues Again." It was playing in The Pheasant the night I decided to leave England forever.

"What kept you?" says Darius in Tallahassee.

"Texas," say Drum and I together.

Darius slings a bag in the back and we drive the final three hours to Jacksonville. Except for flight money, I'm skint. Dirk, Drum and Darius pay my fare to Tampa. The Florida greenery whizzes by the bus window. I finish *Silent Spring* at the airport. It's a long way from *Don Quixote*, but maybe there's some connection.

"This is an era of specialists," says Carson, "each of whom sees his own problem and is unaware or intolerant of the larger frame."

The trick seems to be to get a broad vision, something encompassing, organic: to be a traveler, not an expert, or an expert in the art of the picaresque. Diversification, I decide, is the key to health. Thoreau was wrong to say "simplify, simplify, simplify!" Or is specialism the answer? It turns out that the man next to me on the plane home is a bow-tied biologist who calls himself Professor Thomas but resembles Hoagy Carmichael. He's a specialist in eye pigments.

"And what do *you* do?" he asks.

"Mostly," I tell him sheepishly, "I sit on buses. But I've spent part of the summer in a pick-up. You think it's okay to diversify?"

"Sure," he says. "But don't forget the bus. That's your specialism. Get in close enough to your available window, it reveals the world."

"So the bus window's a way to view everything?

Thanks for the tip."

"Don't thank me, thank Schopenhauer. We gain true wisdom not by measuring the boundless world—nor, incidentally, by traveling personally through endless space—but by trying to know and understand one individual phenomenon."

As the plane roars skyward, I think perhaps I'm learning something after all. My window is the bus. It's all about connections, whether you specialize or panoramarize. What connects *Don Quixote* and *Silent Spring?* I know I can't be Don Quixote all my life, confusing my dream—or my parents' dream—of America, with the place itself, and with living a real life. Some day I have to get off the bus and off the road.

"The transformation of matter into energy in the cell is an ever-flowing process," says Carson, "like a wheel endlessly turning. Grain by grain, molecule by molecule, carbohydrate fuel in the form of glucose is fed into this wheel; in its cyclic passage the fuel molecule undergoes fragmentation and a series of minute chemical changes. When the turning wheel comes full circle the fuel molecule has been stripped down to a form in which it is ready to combine with a new molecule coming in and to start the cycle anew."

As with Hecht the year before, I feel I've been given another vital message by someone now long gone. I reach England exhilarated that maybe I really have been on some grand journey of discovery. But one step forward, as they say, two steps back. I get home to find my father three weeks dead—cremated by his brother, since I was nowhere to be found. There's also a letter from Tina breaking off our relationship, and another from the university. I've been given another chance to take my exams. The great business of living, of connected living, is about to begin. Even as I enter the world of guilt and responsibility, some kind of truth by which to live seems within my grasp.

11

BORN IN THE USA

"America's future rests on a thousand dreams inside our hearts," says Ronald Reagan on his re-election campaign trail in Hammonton, New Jersey, in September, 1984. "It rests in the message of hope so many young people admire: New Jersey's own Bruce Springsteen. And helping you make those dreams come true is what this job of mine is all about."

"I don't know whether to be embarrassed for me or for the President," replies Springsteen.

But Reagan himself is not remotely embarrassed. I see him a few weeks later when he comes to Rochester, New York. Really, I want to meet Springsteen. Once, at Wembley Arena, he spoke to me. He was doing all the songs from *The River* but I came to hear earlier ones and asked for "Backstreets." I was in the third row. He knelt down, looked me in the eye, and said, "We'll get that one for you later." I'll see Springsteen play again when he visits upstate New York in January 1985, a few weeks after Reagan, but by then he's a megastar playing in the huge Carrier Dome in Syracuse. Still, Reagan's press office has announced that the President of the United States listens to Springsteen's records all the time. So, if I'm not destined to discuss life with the Boss himself, it seems wise to seize the chance to meet the president of his fan club.

This is one of my new aims. I've decided to *meet* some of the celebrities and heroes of my dreams. I've also decided to complete whatever I start. Up to now I haven't known where I'm going, so I've ended up all over the place. *What you must do*, I remember my father telling me during one of his diatribes, *is complete something*. He never saw me complete anything. He didn't believe I could. *Your sort never completes*, he said. Well, I have. I've completed my degree and won a scholarship to SUNY Brockport. I just wish my parents knew. And now I'm here to talk with a President.

It's Thursday, November 1, a bitter, overcast autumn day. A large crowd flows through the city to the venue. Mounted police line the route as the motorcade sweeps in, the shining black limousines, the Presidential crest, a shadowy face and waving arm.

"Here comes the bastard," says an aging, sundried hippy with binoculars. He says his name is Zonk. "I revile his politics, man," says Zonk. "Most right-wing governor California ever had. Git back west, asshole."

"He's the President of your country!" says a man who looks like Clark Kent. "Your country, right or wrong." His wife, who reaches his midriff and has dark staring eyes like a chinchilla, nods in agreement.

"I got no country and I got no flag," says Zonk.

"So why are you here?" I ask him.

"Compiling evidence against the Potus," says Zonk. "If Mussolini or Hitler came to talk, wouldn't you want to see what they were like?"

The mounted police funnel us inside like cowboys corralling cattle. At the door, I hand an FBI agent (or at least some extra in suit and shades) a list of questions. I tell him I'm from the London *Times* and could the President please answer some of them in his address. The FBI agent says the President's address is planned in advance. There's no room for dialogue.

"Oh, go on," I urge him, "*please!*"

The agent/extra sighs, but seems happy to have lines to speak. "I'll get it to him," he says with an air of importance. Maybe he thinks this is his big break.

I catch up with Zonk. Inside, the stadium is full around the sides, but empty in the middle because in front of Reagan there's a media stand. Someone's orchestrating practice chants of "four more years" for the small crowd of high school kids who've been allowed on the main floor. The rest of us are a hundred yards back. Through Zonk's binoculars I can see an army of gray-suited extras the size of my Timpo cowboys. They're milling around the podium with its Presidential crest, and arranging a bunch of stiff, plastic-looking local dignitaries, all to the animated movements of a high school band no one this far back can hear. On either side of this assembly hang two giant American flags, the stripes vertical, and above Reagan a tarpaulin like a vast black cloud, ready to rain down a host of balloons. A placard behind the grouping reads:

REAGAN — ROCHESTER
a Picture of the Future

The cameras start to roll. Stirring songs of the blessed country crackle from speakers—"The Star-Spangled Banner," "America the Beautiful." The man we're about to see is not a politician hoping for your vote, but the

President, at once America's figurehead, and the most powerful man in the world: former B-movie actor, union leader and Governor of California, and now halfway through his career as an eight-year king. Five Rumanian refugees are brought on stage to wave Stars and Stripes and symbolize gained freedom in the Land of the Free.

Then comes Reagan himself, later than scheduled, like a rock star entering only once the crowd are restless. He says nothing about Springsteen this time, but he does talk about America. If he's been given my questions, his answers are pretty cryptic.

"Where is America going?" is my first.

"America," Reagan replies, "is going for gold."

"America went for gold in the 1840s," I point out in my second question, having already anticipated his first answer, "which is why there was all that trouble with the Hunkpapa and Minneconjou Sioux in the Powder River Country, isn't it? What are you offering the American people, Mr President?"

Reagan's evasive. He talks about Walter Mondale and Geraldine Ferraro threatening America with "Mondale Mortgages." It's my fault for asking a question that gets him onto domestic issues, and he's answered my question on international affairs—at least with reference to the Los Angeles Olympics—with his "going for gold" statement. This is the Cold War era, and Reagan and the Iron Lady are promenading the Western battlements arm in clanking arm—or "shoulder to shoulder" as Yo' Blair will say of Britain's stance after Nine Eleven. The Russians have not long before shot down a Korean airliner in Soviet airspace. In October there have been massive anti-nuclear protests in several of the world's capitals. So it's important, I feel, to find out as much as possible from the man in charge.

"We're in a dangerous situation, aren't we?"

Reagan hums and ha-s. "I, too, have had an attempt on my life," he says, "as has Mrs Thatcher. It's a brutal world and the Russians are up to no good."

"Hinckley wasn't Russian, and nor are the IRA."

He sighs and mumbles something about state-sponsored terrorism.

"And America hasn't been involved in that? What about Nicaragua?"

Anticipating his weariness with such questions, I chance a personal one. "Tell me about your father."

The crowd goes deathly quiet. Reagan blinks in the harsh light, searches around as if the right words are on an autocue somewhere. But such subject matter is beyond the remit of his speechmakers. His bodyguards seem to be scrutinizing the crowd behind their shades, looking for the culprit. I'm glad *they* don't have binoculars. The President's going to have to find his own words. Jack Reagan was an alcoholic. I wish I hadn't asked, and that Oprah Winfrey would come on and put an arm around the Presidential shoulders.

"I remember bending over him," Jack's son begins, stuttering a little, "smelling the sharp odor of whiskey from the speakeasy. I got a fistful of his overcoat. Opening the door, I managed to drag him inside and get him to bed. In a few days, he was the bluff, hearty man I knew and loved and will always remember."

"But come on," I prod. "Your father was an alcoholic. You're avoiding the issue."

"Jack was a handsome man—tall, swarthy, filled

with contradictions."

"What effect did it have on you?"

"He died when I was nineteen."

"You must have been devastated."

"He was a sentimental Democrat."

"So you've shaped your career away from him. You must be aware of him all the time."

But Reagan's had enough. "America," he repeats in that patient, soft voice, "is going for gold." People start to clap. Reagan claps the crowd. The crowd claps him louder. He waves up at different angles into the dark arena. "America," he repeats a third time, "is going for gold." He talks of the terrible price of electing the Democrats; of "our children's fate," the country's past, a possible freeze in weapons; the banishment one day of nuclear weapons through unclear means. Then, as the band starts up, someone cuts the tarpaulin and thousands of red, white and blue balloons weave downward onto the school kids like a mushroom cloud in reverse.

REAGAN — ROCHESTER
a Picture of the Future

is obscured by the balloons. Even Zonk's won over. "My country right or wrong," he murmurs. The balloons reflect in his eyes. "Oh dear God," say the Kents in unison. *Good grief!* I think, while far away, in a dark blazer, white shirt and red tie, face pale in the bright lights, arm waving, stands the American President, too far away for his features to be distinguishable.

Like everyone else, I know all the stories about Reagan, and about how he's a B-movie actor, and in a sense remains a B-movie actor throughout his presidency. And now, of course, we all know he eventually succumbs to Alzheimer's and ends his days—as a reviewer of *Dutch* puts it—"happily raking leaves off his swimming pool, unaware that they are replenished by his Secret Service guards." But as I stand there in 1984 he's nevertheless a historic—or at least a historical—figure: Reagan himself, a figurehead for an era, the black-haired, septuagenarian fortieth President of the United States, and I can hardly keep my binoculars still. I've had my little encounter with the Kennedys under the bush on the central reservation of an Oregon highway. But I'm edging toward *real* encounters. I've touched base in the Reagan-era. No less than that accommodating FBI agent, I'm an extra in the Presidential pageant. Like Woody Allen's human chameleon, Leonard Zelig, I'm in a crowd scene from history. The interest in American Presidents is that, at most, they define a decade. You're part of history precisely because *they* are so quickly part of history. And there he is, lighting up a drab November day with Presidential razzmatazz, "a picture of the future" so swiftly a picture of the past.

When he leaves, the crowds wave the little flags they've been given, and Reagan disappears to conduct our future. We bundle out of the stadium and line up to watch the motorcade zoom off. It's turned icy, and dim with a hint of snow. On Election Day, November 6, 1984, Reagan wins a landslide. People in upstate New York seem pretty happy. I'm happy too. I've seen a President, just as I dreamt of doing when I was eight years old and Nixon (of all people) came to power. I've seen a President and been moved by that fact if not by his words. I can admit that much to myself, and I've never been ashamed of it since, neither.

A few weeks later, Springsteen comes upstate and spends a good deal longer on stage than his number one fan did. There's a similar crowd, frantically waving Old Glory as he sings "Born in the USA." And such is Springsteen's popularity in his mid-eighties glory days that I'm just as far away as with Reagan. But they're both performers, both American figures, both with a hold on the public's imagination, both born in the USA, both made good in the USA from poor backgrounds. Even if there the similarities end. I'm talking about something much more personal than politics. Springsteen bares his soul, or at least draws on life's joy and pain. His music is a version of his personal history. Reagan's career, so extraordinary though it looks in outline, so cartoonishly successful, can be seen as a denial of personal history, a subsuming of the self into the country, into a picture of the future: a going for gold. Personally, I can identify with them both.

Part Two

Return

12

THE REAL ENID STEVICK

"Do you think that, as we get older, life becomes more real and less imagined, or less real and more imagined?"

"Knowledge increases unreality."

"Did you make that up, Enid?"

"No, but Yeats did."

It's late May and Enid Stevick and I are sitting on a wooden jetty by the Erie Canal in Brockport, New York, about to travel eight thousand miles. The notion of finding a definite purpose to traveling, and to my life, is the second part of my new aim. But I've still got the first in mind: to get real and not just live like a Walter Mitty of the road. Hence the companion. I'm hoping Enid might secure me to reality.

We've known each other much of the year and I've asked if she'd like to come with me. For her, the trip's a form of escape too. She started the year at Syracuse University on a Music scholarship. But due to some kind of "trouble" at Syracuse, she began taking classes at Brockport. She's quiet but very smart—much smarter than I am. She's thin with almost translucent skin and short black hair that would curl if she grew it. Her dark eyes stare at the world through pebble spectacles. I've never seen her blink. I've also never known her not to wear something turquoise.

She shares a flat with a mysterious ex-boxer, now

dope-dealer named Felix near the Strand Theater on Main Street. Our times together have always been rather secretive. Not that we're anything more than friends. She's firmly committed to this Felix fellow, but he's prone to jealous violence. Enid needs thick glass to help the sight in her left eye. I suspect Felix punched her, detached a retina or something. It's always seemed best not to take chances. In public we've mostly hung out at Casey's or Barber's with the McGuigans, a couple of hard-drinking Irish Republicans from Yorktown Heights, and an old hellraiser named Fiery O'Fuellan, who expounds sage advice while soldered to the bar. None of them likes Felix, and I think Enid sees their friendship as a form of protection.

A bird's whistling, "Skita, skita" in the branches of a maple. The green iron liftbridge that takes Main Street across the Erie Canal raises and a speedboat flashes through. The wave hits the dock and soaks the planks. We agreed to meet an hour ago but Enid's just arrived. It's okay because I anticipated this. I calculated what time we needed to catch the bus to Rochester, then took off an hour. When she arrives, wearing a turquoise cardigan, she's proceeding in a strangely staccato fashion across the lawn, swinging a green, cylindrical bag forward, dumping it, walking ahead, swinging it forward again. I go over and take it from her. It weighs a ton.

"Jesus, Enid!" I gasp, carrying it to the dock and slumping down. "What's in here?"

She sits down in her dainty way and curls her legs beneath her body the way women can and men—or at least I—can't. "I don't want to be in Nevada and wish I'd brought a different book."

"Or different clothes."

"I have five sets of clothing. They have laundrettes in Greyhound depots, don't they?"

"Are you crazy?"

"To want to be clean?"

"Even if they had, it wouldn't help. We're going Trailways."

"But I *love* Greyhounds! There's a very American sort of romance to those lumbering buses, especially at night."

"I thought you never traveled."

"Not widely. But back and forth between Buffalo, Lockport and Syracuse, oh my God! I've ridden Greyhounds for years and years."

"Trailways will make a change then, won't it?"

She pouts, but it's settled. Besides, I've bought the passes.

Enid's favorite author is Joyce Carol Oates. "She writes about where I'm from," Enid explains. "In fact she seems to write about *me*. She *literally* writes about this area, about the Erie Canal, and Lockport, where she's from, and Buffalo. She calls the area Eden County, her postage stamp of soil like Faulkner's Yoknapatawpha. She has a city named Port Oriskany which is sort of Buffalo and Lockport combined."

Neither of us know, of course, that within a couple of years Oates will publish a novel named *You Must Remember This* in which the main character is named Enid Stevick and shares certain traits and experiences with Enid. By the time this happens we've lost touch and I suppose I'll never know if somehow Oates got to meet her, or just tuned into her frequency in some mysterious way. Inevitably there are differences. Oates's heroine is young in the fifties, lives in Port Oriskany and never sets foot in Brockport. Also Oates—if she did draw on Enid's life—completely excised me from the narrative, thank goodness. But the fact is that Enid, *my* Enid, is the only whole-trip bus companion I'll ever have.

The trip is her suggestion. Our itinerary is loose, but the point is that I'll be completing something. Since my restless voyage in search of the unattainable place of inexpressible happiness has taken me to all the conterminous states except South Dakota, Nevada, Oklahoma, and Arkansas, she's suggested a trip where we take in these final four.

"Of course," she says, looking out over the green waters of the canal, "if you'd been a tad more careful on earlier trips, we'd not have to travel *eight thousand miles* just to finish it."

"Rarely have such distances been negotiated to so paltry an end."

"Maybe the journey *is* the end. Movement, motion, doing, becoming, has its own rewards. Arrive, and you have the question of where to go next."

"Still, it's a completion of a sort. Something against time's attrition."

"It's like the last payment on a mortgage."

"After this, you mean, America belongs to me?"

"Not quite." She slaps my wrist. "And you still won't have been to Hawaii or Alaska."

"It's been six years. I was nineteen when I started."

"Well, that's a great thing. To set foot in all the mainland states will be—"

"It's an accomplishment."

"That's right. You've got to have *something* to show for having lived."

"It's not much to show. I've dreamed my way through most of it. I want something concrete. Like this jetty we're sitting on."

"It's wooden."

"But someone made it."

"Come on, Biff. We'll be late. Let's head west."

I jump up and tug at her bag. "You really need all these books?"

"You *really* have to go to those four states?"

"You suggested it!"

"You didn't have to take me seriously. For all your talk of concrete accomplishment, you're going just for an idea. There's nothing real about it at all. Let's go to California."

"You think California's real?"

"It seems pretty real in *Do With Me What You Will*." That's another Oates novel. Enid's quite the *aficionado*.

"I don't mind going there again." I'm limping along hoping my shoulder won't pop out of its socket. "So long as we end up in Arkansas."

"What about Alaska or Hawaii?" needles Enid, almost skipping along beside me.

"I specialize in the bus, and it doesn't go that far."

She takes off her spectacles, cleans them and puts them back on, as if to see my insanity more clearly. She's got nice eyes, very big. "You're crazy."

"Thank you. You're wild."

"Thank you."

"You're welcome."

This is the way we get on. It can sound like bickering but it's not. She's arguing already but I like it. If you can have a perfect bus companion, it's Enid. Quiet but watchful, taking it all in with those dark eyes, wide as a watchful rabbit's, left eye bulging behind thick glass. She just likes to argue. That's all. I admire her. She's incredibly studious, works so hard, pushing and pushing herself. She wants to become a novelist or a musician or both. She's capable of achieving anything. She tells me she's mildly anorexic but it's under control. She still tends to survive on half a lettuce leaf some days, but she's intelligent about it. She knows the dangers. She's witty too, and usually too sharp for me. We're often impatient with each other. I don't like her tendency to be late. She doesn't like my lethargy. This is a contradiction, I know, but she's efficient and goal-orientated, while I'm inefficient and up to now in my life have had no goals. She's usually only late because she's been doing something more important than seeing me.

"You do realize, don't you," she says on the local bus to Rochester, "that even your aim to meet your heroes or even ordinary Americans, rather than just to fantasize, is itself a fantasy. Our real, true selves are interior. Meet people and you're meeting an image."

"Still," I suggest, "some solid flesh is better than pure imagination."

"Is it? We create others and we create ourselves. So who do you want to be? Don't you want to *become* someone?"

"I am someone. I will be remembered—or not remembered, as the case will probably be—for sitting on a bus for years. Maybe I can set an endurance record."

"Aren't you in pursuit of anything?"

"Happiness, like everyone. Our inalienable right."

"Don't quote my country back at me."

"Well, I'm also hoping to meet some of my heroes, successful people. Writers like William Styron and Arthur Miller. I'd also like to meet my favorite cowboy from childhood."

"John Wayne, you mean."

"Richard Widmark. Who knows, maybe one day I'll lunch with Joyce Carol Oates."

"You wish."

"I'd like to have met Marilyn Monroe—*really* met her, I mean: known her." I've mentioned our coffee shop encounter. "And Einstein, and Jefferson, and Thoreau. And I suppose Emily Dickinson, Neil Armstrong, Martin Luther King, Amelia Earhart, Babe Ruth, Custer, Crazy Horse, Chaplin—"

"Mickey Mouse?"

"Mickey I met at Disney World. Houdini, Superman, Faulkner, Laurel and Hardy, Pocahontas, Warhol, Billy the Kid, Debbie Reynolds and Minnesota Fats: the usual crew. Even Elvis, but then I'd liked to have known my parents, too: really *known* them. What are *you* in search of?"

"Me."

"Yes, you."

"No. I'm in search of *me*, of what I can be. The greatest mystery of an individual's life is who they will actually turn out to *be*. I want to feel I've become whoever it is that Enid Stevick is capable of becoming. That—and your relationship with others, in particular a few kindred souls—is life's great drama."

It's the longest speech I ever hear her make. What neither of us mention is that she has her "problem" and I have mine. But maybe everyone has something they don't talk about, and displacement activities to help avoid it. Some paint, some write, some work themselves to wealth or death or both as lawyers, doctors, teachers, circus performers, whatever gets them through the night. I ride the bus.

Waiting for the Trailways in Rochester, Enid's grumpy. "First we have to go to North Dakota, Nevada, Oklahoma and Arkansas, next I learn it's by Trailways."

"*South* Dakota."

"Same difference."

"No it's not."

"Whose country is this?"

There's blossom everywhere. Rochester is unrecognizable from that gray, barren November day I saw Reagan. We get off the local bus and Enid has to shop for something. I trail behind, switching her ten-ton canvas bag between shoulders while she carries my father's.

"Talk about Trailways," I mutter.

"Oh, hush."

We're going Trailways because Carlotta's father drove for them and said I should use them because— well, no reason, really, except there's a Bob Seger song called "Coming Home" with a line in it about a Trailways bus being on schedule. So it's part of Americana. Seger, however, clearly fictionalizes things as much as Oates will do in *You Must Remember This*. The Trailways bus is late. We wait maybe forty minutes at the depot before it pulls up and we settle down, disgruntled but excited, on the first leg of our month-long, anti-clockwise journey. First stop Chicago, via Buffalo, Erie, Cleveland, Toledo, South Bend and Gary.

"Wow," says Enid, "I've never been to Gary."

"Nice, is it?" I don't remember it as nice.

"It's probably awful," says Enid. "But Saul Bellow writes about it in *The Adventures of Augie March*."

The bus rumbles along the freeway. Bushes and trees whiz by close up but float in the distance. My arm vibrates on the cold metal sill above the "Smoking Prohibited" sign and the silver on black of the English and Spanish "Emergency Exit" plaque. Enid's never been west of Buffalo, but she's spent spring breaks in Palm Springs, Florida, where her grandparents have retired.

Twenty-seven miles distant, the Windy City is a haze of vertical gray brush strokes in the pale sky. I'm wondering if Pickawillany is around Chicago, or back for yet another summer at Pocono. I'm wondering what she'll think if I turn up with Enid. Enid won't mind. As I say, it's platonic. She's just a great companion, when she's on time and we're not squabbling.

A mud brown Chevrolet overtakes the bus across a concrete bridge. The green and white Illinois number plate flashes in the morning sun. The bus trammels over the ribs of the bridge, two beats a second like a magnified heartbeat. Even as we approach Chicago, I realize I'm growing out of youth. The trips are becoming more conscious. I'm beginning to see that the whole nature of my traveling has changed and I know this is the last trip of this kind I'll ever do. Where once I visited places I'd heard of and was seeing for the first time, now I mostly pass through remembered places. I'm not so much exploring as returning, and my motivation and feelings are more often about reminiscence than newness. This road into Chicago is the tail end of my very first bus trip, out of Michigan in 1979. And Chicago, for me, now means my six-year, sporadic friendship with Pickawillany. In total, we've known each other perhaps two months. The rest has been a correspondence. But such friendships—for me at any rate—have often had more impact than friendships with people I've seen day to day for years.

I tell Enid what I'm thinking.

"You think too much," she says. "Just live."

So I stop telling her what I'm thinking but go on thinking it, until eventually I say, "My early travels were about fulfilling dreams, going to places I had imagined, imagining my way into reality. Now it's about realities."

She doesn't reply. Chicago has changed for me even as we approach it. The *idea* of Chicago has changed. It's no longer the foreign city where I spent my first night in America, no longer a city of beginnings, but of memories, and mostly of Pickawillany. Still, as we reach Chicago on a beautiful spring morning in 1985, that's all past. Pickawillany's no more than a ghost in my crowded head. Enid and I walk down to Lake Michigan and sit by the trees. We're like two sides of the same person, she and I. her damaged left eye—I'm *assuming* from violence—mirrors my damaged right eye from that scuffle with my father. Neither of us is technically blind in our bad eye, but the stitches pretty much destroyed my detailed vision, so if we sit side by side the wrong way neither of us can really see the other. But, like a bird, we can look two ways at once.

"Funny," says Enid, taking off her spectacles and

looking out over the bottom lip of the lake with those enormous eyes, "It's like a sea but no smell."

"This lake brings back memories."

"Keep them to yourself."

That's the secret of our friendship: what we keep to ourselves. She knows there are things I don't tell her, and there are certainly things she doesn't tell me. We pass the spot where Pickawillany and I once sunbathed. I don't mention it. I think of Carlotta and the moon, but I don't mention that either. Enid is kicking sand.

"What are you thinking?"

"None of your business," she says.

"Suppose I do try to contact that Pickawillany girl I told you about. Would you mind?"

Enid shrugs. "Should I?"

"It's not like we're going anywhere," I say. "We're just going."

"I said okay, *okay?*" She punches my arm. She's always doing that. Sisterly. We find a phone booth and I call Pickawillany's home. Her folks remind me she's now at the Kansas City Art Institute. I call there and Pickawillany meets us in Kansas City where we stay with her and Splif, her brown-toothed, pig-tailed, post-punk, arty boyfriend in their furnitureless, carpetless garret full of Splif's very bad paintings that Enid and I praise. Splif barely speaks, but when he does Enid runs gagging from the room. "People with halitosis should be sectioned or summonsed or something," she says when we leave.

Pickawillany's hair, clipped short during my Chicagofest visit in 1983, is now long, tangled, matted, and dyed green. She looks like Medusa. We drink a few beers and discover that Kansas City is the home of Hallmark cards, and—one of Enid's whims—since we've on the Missouri side of the city, we find a bridge so that she can momentarily jump into Kansas. The last I see of Pickawillany for years is on our final morning. She calls a cheery goodbye while I'm still half asleep beneath a blanket on the bare floor. Such is the way with bus travel. Then we catch the bus for Omaha and stay with Carlotta. Enid doesn't mind this either.

"Girlfriend?" asks Carlotta when Enid's in the bathroom.

"No."

"No?"

"No."

"No?"

"*No!*"

Enid comes back and Carlotta says, "Did he mention the Waterloo Fair, Enid?"

"Oh yes," says Enid. "All about Dottie West."

Carlotta smiles. I wonder how things would be if I'd stuck around a long time ago. But I'm beginning to remember how I can't stand the Midwestern summer. It's only May and in the nineties. Blossom is out everywhere. The newspapers have a column or two about a catastrophic tsunami in Bangladesh, but mostly it's about the Midwestern crops and heat wave. I think of Roosevelt Franklin and wonder if he's still alive, wonder if he's changed his suit.

Three's a crowd and sooner than planned Enid and Carlotta are hugging each other goodbye—they've pretended to get on like old friends—and Enid and I are bussing west and north into South Dakota. From Sioux

Falls we head west to Rapid City, stopping on the way at the Wall Drugstore.

"This is a famous drugstore," Enid tells me.

"Why?"

"Because of all the signs to it, I guess. A man named Ted Hustead opened it in 1931. But things weren't going too well and he needed customers. In 1935 his wife suggested he advertize free iced water. Suddenly he got tons of customers."

"Ah, Ted *Hustead*," I say. "Born in Nebraska."

"How do you know?"

"An old man on a bus told me long ago."

It turns cold and rainy as we get there, and the ticket clerk casually points out that the only Trailways connection out of Rapid City is eastward—a four hundred mile journey back where we came.

"You'll see more of South Dakota," says Enid.

"I'll see the *same* South Dakota!"

"But from the other direction."

I ask the clerk the time of the next bus eastbound.

"Midnight," says the clerk, "or thereabouts." He looks apologetic but it's not his fault. "You might be able to get a ride out to Mount Rushmore," he suggests. "It's only a little ways south of here."

"I don't want to see Mount Rushmore," says Enid.

"I wouldn't mind."

"Why go look at four giant Presidential faces?" she says. It's an odd question and I don't have an answer. "Go if you must, but go alone. I'll wait here."

"I'm not leaving you alone." It's two in the afternoon. We have twelve hours in Rapid City. We leave our bags in a locker and step outside. Rapid City seems to be monochrome. I put my hand on Enid's skinny shoulder. "I'm afraid I've taken us on a four hundred mile wrong turn."

Enid shrugs. "Maybe something will happen." She's right. After half an hour, it starts to rain. "Don't mope," she says. "Rapid City is probably full of surprises." Rapid City might be, but we don't seem to be in the center of it. We don't really seem to be anywhere, except maybe on Main Street in a black and white movie. We wring away a few hours photographing each other before an eight-foot high cowboy boot. The two-foot spur spins. We spin it. The boot advertises the Stockman Boot Shop. There's a For Sale sign attached from Commercial Properties, with a phone number for Padgett and Mattson Realtors. "You reckon the boot's for sale?" says Enid.

"We couldn't get it on the bus."

"We could have it shipped."

"What, Enid, would we do with an eight-foot high cowboy boot?"

"It looks so lonely. You think it's one of a pair? Maybe a giant left it. Maybe it's got something to do with Mount Rushmore. Maybe some fifty-foot tall mechanical cowboy named Big John Gulliver is roaming the continent looking for his other boot."

"Then we'd better leave it for him."

I'm wondering if I've found my soulmate, or at least someone as odd as me. Or maybe twelve hours in Rapid City does this to anyone. The boot is incontestably the most interesting thing we find in Rapid City. Eventually we escape the monochrome by diving into a red-lit bar to hear a cowboy band. Buoyed by enough

Olympia beers to numb the journey back to Sioux Falls, I feel strangely warm toward my skinny companion, who doesn't touch alcohol at all.

Back in Sioux Falls the next morning, we take a local bus company. Rabbit Lines Bus 162 ("Make Tracks with the Rabbit," it says across the blacked-out back window and along the side) pulls us north toward Canada. Enid's reading *Lolita*.

"Is it good?"

"You want to read it? I've got two copies."

"No wonder your bag's so heavy. *Two* copies!"

"Only of light reading." She checks her page, chucks her copy over, and ruffles in her big green bag for the other. I can't help smiling. She's a strange, lovely girl, but that's the kind of thing we *don't* say to each other. I try reading but enter semi-conscious bus-mode. America passes by: Lake Vermillion—"Yield" signs—a place named Marsh—white cows—marshy landscape, rocks—Canistota—Alexandria. We stop at a rundown diesel station. We've slipped back to the forties. A man is filling a 1939 Chevrolet that looks new. In the depot a room-size glass cabinet creaks with stuffed elks, bears, deer, boars, mouths agape as if only the glass silences them. The display is advertising Frying Guest Ranch, Jackson Hole.

"Here," says Enid. "I've written a poem. Wanna see?"

"I didn't know you wrote poetry."

"Doesn't everyone? Don't you?"

"In adolescence maybe. It wasn't any good."

"It doesn't have to be good. It's just human expression, something we can do. It's fun. Here, take a look. I don't care what you think. It's called 'South Dakota Blue.'"

I read it aloud: "*Dim gray South Dakota Rabbit Buses / Rocking through the Badlands. / I rest my cracked feet / On the cracked plastic seat*—you haven't got cracked feet, have you?"

"Just *read*, will you?"

"*Smell gasoline, floor polish / See no Indians—no Sioux / Only tourist forts. / No roaming buffalo, / Just stuffed behind glass. / We travel fast, on, on, mad for pain / No Sioux, no living ornaments, / No You.*" I hand it back to her. "You want my honest opinion? It's better than I could do."

She beams.

"But it's not very good."

She's furious. "Your useless opinion doesn't harm my poem."

I'm feeling wicked. "Who is You?"

"Anyone," she replies. "Isn't there always a You?"

"Felix?"

"In fact, no."

"Well, anyway, it's just not very good."

"How do you know?" she says testily.

"Just live with the criticism, okay? Write another."

I don't know anything about poetry so shouldn't tease her, and resolve not to do so again. This is just as well because she turns to stone and doesn't say a word to me until Moose Jaw. We sit rumbling awhile. Through the dark glass a young girl sits on steps beside a Thunderbird convertible. A black puppy's asleep on the back seat. Blobs of rain splatter the gravel. The puppy twitches. The girl's T-shirt catches the light of a hotel neon sign. She pushes her hair into a bun, the nape of her neck open to the rain, soft curls blowing. Out comes a sunburnt man with tattooed forearms.

"There, see? She's someone's You."

But Enid is stone. She pretends to be engrossed in *Lolita*, her glasses off and her eyes practically smudging the print, and maybe she is. But she's also stone: a mini Mount Rushmore figure. The man strolls down the steps, the white, peeling door slamming behind him. He and the girl glance at each other. She tries to hold his gaze but he looks away. He drops into the Thunderbird, starts the engine, startling the black puppy awake, revs up, and jerks away in a puff of dust. The girl seems to look straight at me. But the bus windows are dark, so to all intents and purposes I'm in a movie theater. The film's real but I'm not connected.

"Don't you just hate some people?" I say as the bus moves off.

"Mm-huh," says Enid, peering in the book as if the page is a microscope lens.

"Good, is it?"

"Mm-huh."

"I've stolen all your money."

"Mm-huh."

We change to a Canadian Greyhound, and roll into Winnipeg, through Moose Jaw (where Enid says, "Are you sorry?" and I say, "Yes, it's really a very good poem") and Medicine Hat to Calgary. A Sioux Indian, wearing suit-trousers—Roosevelt Franklin's, I think—sneakers without socks, and a Montreal T-shirt, gets on at Calgary. He's carrying a yellow plastic bag with "Everyday Low Prices" printed in black.

"There's your Sioux," I nudge Enid, "if not your You." She's pretty stony even now, but I still enjoy being with her. In fact I'm totally happy, beginning to realize these travels are among the greatest times of my life, not because much happens or because the land and towns and cities are necessarily beautiful. There are real eyesores. But to sit on a bus can be bliss in itself. Nothing to do but watch the fields or rivers or mountains pass by, watch dramatic incidents in unknown people's lives, glimpsed for a minute before the bus rolls on.

And then, of course, the unexpected does happen. Onto the bus climbs Robert De Niro. Enid gives a start. It's De Niro as Rocky Marciano, and he's very convincing, a little punch-drunk, mean-looking, a wild scar on his face. Enid grabs my arm, either for protection or to stop me running, and says, "You're never Robert De Niro!" I put a hand over her mouth, but he's heard. He looks down with that lopsided grin and you can see the De Niro mole clear as day. He winks like De Niro, too.

"Na, honey," he says. "People always make that mistake. I'm Rocky. Rocky Marciano." And off he goes to smoke in the back of the bus.

From Calgary to Vancouver, the bus fills up with all kinds of people: parents and children, an old man with a beard and pigtails, a leather-jacketed, tousled-haired youth with a pencil behind his ear and a sleepy girl snuggled against his shoulder, two old ladies smoking cigarettes in holders in the "rear of the coach" and making eyes at either De Niro or Marciano, whichever he is. And our God-like driver, safely, reliably, courteously gunning us through day and night. The gray-jacketed drivers of the North, or blue-jacketed drivers of the South. Oh, the world of the bus! The people of the bus. The people of the road. I'm well on with *Lolita*, while Enid's finished it.

"Was it good?"

"Oh," she says, "I've read it before."

"Was it *good?*"

"Better every time."

"Did you see the Stanley Kubrick movie?"

"I don't watch movies." She fishes out of her library *Killer Angels*, a reconstruction of the battle of Gettysburg by Michael Shaara. We pass a lake in the midst of flat land, a clump of evergreens, a single-track railway like successful flypaper stuck across a pine table. The driver hisses open the door at the track to listen for trains. The clouds stir eerily through the green windows. Enid, quite apart from devouring books, is recording every place and name and the number of miles in the margins of the novels. "That way I remember the books better," she says. "Reading depends on place." I don't know what she means. That's often the case, and another basis for our friendship. It's no fun when you always know what a person means. A well-dressed young man hands me a note: Have you ever thought of becoming a Mormon? I haven't, but I do now. I'll consider anything.

From Calgary we head up to Edmonton—where to my chagrin there's a beer strike. "How Canadian," says Enid—then down through Kamloops to Vancouver via the snow-capped mountains of Banff National Park.

"Didn't you work in Vancouver once?" says Enid.

"Once." We glide past gurgling salmon streams, firs, snow-capped mountains. The time goes back another hour. (More regression, I'm thinking; I always seem to be turning back the clock these days.) My eyes are stinging from tiredness. "Enid, maybe I should go to Alaska."

"Maybe you should," she replies, not looking up from *Killer Angels*. "But what about Nevada, Oklahoma and Arkansas? You want to have your state and eat it."

"You think so?"

"Mm-huh."

On the bus there's another Englishman. He's just come *back* from Alaska. He took a ferry from Vancouver to Anchorage.

"You have to go," he says. "It's awesome."

"Na," I say. "We're going to Arkansas." He looks blank. Obviously he's never been to Arkansas. Or maybe he has.

We stay with an uncle and aunt of Enid's who live at Western Parkway, on the UBC campus. I go back to Duthie's but there's no sign of Lena. I phone her apartment. A man answers. He's never heard of her. Maybe she's in New Zealand. We head down the Pacific coast toward San Francisco. Enid shows me another poem.

"It's called Old Dog," she says. "Read it back to me and say honestly what you think."

"*Old Dog, run me through those names again—North Dakota, Oklahoma, Arkansas and Tennessee—Arizona, Carolina, children dream realities—every dog has its depot—and only alcoholics dream of drugs—America is wrapped and packed—so you and I are done—move on, old Dog, move on.*"

"What do you think?" she asks threateningly.

"Spooky," I reply. This seems to satisfy her.

Every day in San Francisco, we start with breakfast—usually scrambled eggs, smoked salmon and bagels—at a delicatessen called David's on Geary, then do whatever we want. One day we wander across Union Square down to Embarcadero Way and hire bicycles to the Golden Gate Bridge and over for lunch in Sausalito before catching the ferry back past Angel Island and Alcatraz. Another day we visit Alcatraz itself, trailing the path up to the prison, with the stink of guano dung in the air. Another day we take a streetcar advertizing Mug Rootbeer up to the Fairmount, and visit settings from *Vertigo*, including the Palace of the Legion of Honor where James Stewart spies on Grace Kelly looking at the painting of Carlotta. I tell Enid it's my favorite film.

"I told you," she says, "I don't watch films."

On our last afternoon we sit in the June heat and watch the San Francisco Giants routed 0-6 by the Montreal Expos in Candlestick Park. The half-empty stadium shimmers orange in the sharp sunlight. The Giants, bought from New York a few years ago, wear orange-trimmed white uniforms that dazzle in the sun, and black undershirts and black helmets. Montreal wear a cool, pale blue and steal the show. The crowd, munching on hot dogs and glugging cold beer in plastic cartons, seem none too bothered, and Enid and I, naturally, care not a damn, but enjoy the spinning baseball arc white against the gorgeous blue sky. We're soon back at the depot, a hole as deep and foul as The Golden Gate Bridge is wide and ethereal. Down one sleazy street a seven-foot transvestite is pinning a midget to a wall and slugging him. We can't wait to reach the safety and sanity of the bus, and soon we're heading for Reno. Nevada, I remind Enid, will be my forty-sixth state.

"Well, horty-torty."

Dawn in Reno, the light's bright even through the green tinted windows: white sand, white streets, white buildings, dark doorways. We arrive before six but a blotchy, evaporating old man in a crumpled suit is already—or still—pulling at a one-arm bandit. We weave across the red carpet, between empty tables and pulsing machines, up into the restaurant at the back with the promise of steak and eggs for $1.69. We've counted our money and are on a budget of five dollars a day.

The waitress smiles. "How's your steak?" The light's so dim you just see flashing mauve teeth.

Enid pushes it aside. "Sorry," she says, "but it tastes like a debt forfeiture."

Back in the brilliant sunshine, the air is already so dry and hot we're glad to retreat to the air-conditioned bus.

"Behold Nevada," says the driver over the intercom. "Between 1951 and 1963 the US Military detonated a hundred and twenty-six atomic bombs in the desert atmosphere."

"Well, that's a comfort," says Enid.

We head the five hundred miles south to Las Vegas in our dark shelter, past the treeless shores of Walker Lake, through the Excelsior Mountains and endless miles of white sand and barren, rock-strewn hills. Through Sarcobatus Flat and the Amargosa Desert, the sand curves like a naked body, but Nevada hardly seems a sustaining mother. The lakes, where they exist, are little more than dried milk streams, running from teat to navel across skin cracked and dry. The dunes resemble the body of the prostrate mother. The roads are dried mascara lines. Between these two mirage cities we stop near 20-Mule Team Canyon in Death Valley and escape the heat into a saloon. The paunchy proprietor tells us 20-Mule Team Canyon got its name from the mule teams that used to haul borax up a forty-two mile unpaved road in the 1880s. I drain my beer and Enid leaves half her coke and we're off again, through the rocks of Death Valley, past scrubland and gradually patches of green vegetation like water drops across the sand, and finally Vegas itself, shimmering on the horizon. The highway becomes a long, flat, venomous snake, the bus a tomb, a time-capsule, a swallowed mouse sucked like a bulge along the snake, as the road winds hissing into the belly of the city, the temperature now at 120 degrees just before five.

Enid's finished *Killer Angels* and is wiping her eyes with her turquoise sleeve. She puts her glasses back on and blinks at me. "Ask me if it was good," she says.

"Was it good?"

"Awful, as in sad. You'll love it."

The city itself is a sparkling oasis of hedonistic decadence; a mirage dedicated to illusion, a town begrimed with fake jewels, mechanized cowboys doffing giant Stetsons.

"Maybe we'll find Big John Gulliver with a boot missing," says Enid.

"Long limp to Rapid City."

"Can't you just picture this fifty-foot, mechanized, glittering cowboy with one bare foot, hobbling across America to Rapid City?"

"Remember John Wayne in *The Searchers*? No, of course not. *Why* don't you watch movies?"

"Too busy. I have too much imagination as it is. I might flood."

"You've never even seen Gary Cooper in *High Noon*? Or Humphrey Bogart and Ingrid Bergman in *Casablanca*?"

"*Casa-what?*"

"You're crazy. You have desert sickness. And bus-madness. You are sick and mad. I should never have brought you."

Enid reaches suddenly and pecks my cheek. "But I'm glad you did," she says. Excited as a schoolgirl, she's peering in casinos as if they're forbidden ideas. Green carpet lines the sidewalks to simulate grass. A dollar bill floats along the street like scrap. Enid snatches it. "This, she says, "is supper."

"It'll be filthy and tasteless. Let's get food."

"You're such a card. We put it in a machine."

We exchange it for quarters in a casino, away from the 100 degree heat even at midnight. Gambling machines stand in rows, like a phantom cohort, lined across the red carpets and along the red walls. The tinkling fanfares of one-armed bandits puncture the piped music ("The Green, Green Grass of Home"). It's a devil's gaudy graveyard. We feed in our four quarters. The last one brings three more. We feed them in, out come ten dollars.

"We've won in Vegas," says Enid. "Let's eat."

We celebrate with a three-dollar meal each and free champagne (for me) from an aluminum container in the middle of the room. It runs out after two glasses.

In Flagstaff a few days into June, we take the local Greyhound to the Grand Canyon, hike down a mile, clamber around the cliffs. The view from Lookout Studio over the Great Chasm reminds me of my first ever bus trip six years before, when leaving Muskegon seemed like launching into thin air, falling forever into the great chasm of the United States. By afternoon we're off again. Telegraph poles topped by upside-down triangles line a long, straight road somewhere between Albuquerque and Amarillo.

"Edwardian ladies walking to church in Sunday bonnets," says Enid, reading *Howard's End*. "Reading changes everything. In ways it's more real than life."

"Read too much and you'll *become* a book."

"I've had a difficult life."

"If you tell me yours, I'll tell you mine." But she shakes her head.

An old lady across the aisle asks if I've read Louis L'Amour. "He's the greatest writer ever lived," she says, peering at writing. "It's L'Amour, not Lamour," she points out, "and I'm *not* an 'old lady,' thank you very much. I'm Mrs Dorothy Wichita, an Ozarker, born and bred, though now I live in Oklahoma City." She crosses the aisle and sits close to me. I can smell a rather raunchy perfume for an old—let's say, aging—lady. Her fine bone-structure holds up her sagging, pale skin. Her eyes are liquidy and her teeth brittle and yellowish but perfectly aligned. "I'm from the Ozark Mountains, young man, the Missouri-Arkansas hills. You got that down? Just 'cos folks *look* old don't mean they *feel* old."

"Sorry," I say, scribbling down her name.

"You writing a book?"

"Recording a trip."

"To where?"

"Arkansas."

Mrs Dorothy Wichita claps her palsied hands in delight. "Oh my!"

Two hours from Amarillo, Mrs Dorothy Wichita is chatting away further up the bus and Enid is reading, so I get back to watching the passing world. By 7.30 p.m. we're in Oklahoma City. The red sun glows steadily on the red earth of Oklahoma all the way in. I've just finished *Killer Angels* and think maybe I'll visit the Civil War battlefields on the way home. Mrs Dorothy Wichita says goodbye and for us not to forget her, and I tell her I never forget *anyone*. Then I sleep and wake and it's two in the morning and we're entering Arkansas. I don't have the heart to wake Enid.

Reaching my forty-eighth state ought to be a momentous experience, but entering Arkansas by Greyhound in the middle of the night just isn't. Though I do feel something has ended. I've begun to see everything in terms of the future and past. I'm twenty-five with conflicting visions. How nice, I think, to have a wife and kids and a job and pets, but how wonderfully sad to be a lonesome traveler, trekking China, hiking Australia, living from coin to coin in a bitter world. I'm preoccupied with what I will or won't become. I'm no longer the adolescent who arrived in Michigan in 1979. But I've yet to become whoever I'm going to *be*. Will I ever meet the kind of American heroes who brought me here? Will I ever write a book? Will I ever reach Alaska? Will I sit on the bus forever?

Finally we stop and, gritty-eyed, I leave Enid on the bus and wander into the almost deserted depot at Fort Smith. It's 3.00 a.m. I buy a postcard with a red boar and "ARKANSAS" on it, and "Hoo-ey, hoo-ey! Go Big Red!" on the back, and inscribe it—

TUESDAY, JUNE 11, 1985
I've reached my final, conterminous United State

—realizing only as I do so that, by sheer coincidence, it is the same day and month, six years on, that I first flew out. I address it to "The Occupiers" of my old Chippenham address, since I can't think where else to send it, and in the box it goes. I'd like to wake Enid to share the moment, but she looks so peaceful, curled up by the window in her turquoise cardigan, still bespectacled.

"Enid?" I whisper half-heartedly. "*Enid!*" She's as stubborn a sleeper as she is a vulnerable, tough loner. Nobody at Brockport knows what to make of her, and I'm not sure I do. I kiss her forehead, a mere brush. Not a stir. "Enid, I did it," I whispers. But she's still asleep. I lie back as we speed northeast toward a St. Louis dawn.

When she does wake, she's furious. "Your big moment, and you didn't wake me? You didn't *share* it?"

"Believe me, it wasn't such a big moment. I sort of shared it. I didn't feel alone."

"It *was* a big moment, and I came on the trip to see it, you stupid schmuck. Big moments are all in the mind. It's not the thing itself, it's what it means to you."

"I don't know what it meant to me."

"But it did mean *something*."

In St. Louis we listen to jazz on a Mississippi riverboat in the shadow of the Arch, then visit its underground museum about the pioneering days, complete with a stuffed horse. I buy her a turquoise ring to remember the trip by and in no time we're Pittsburgh-bound. Our intention is to change for a bus to Gettysburg but the schedule scuppers us. Suddenly, we're in the Columbus depot, eating croissant sandwiches at the Burger King. The trip's all but done.

"It's been a good trip," says Enid. "I'll miss you."

"It's not over."

She touches my hand. "Yes it is."

She's beautiful in her own way. "In your own way," I say, "you're beautiful."

"And what way would that be?"

"I mean it."

"Maybe. But once we reach Rochester I'll go home to Lockport and you'll finish up and go to England, and that'll be that."

"How do you know?"

"In the same way as you."

"Perhaps I want to stay in upstate New York."

"You don't."

She's right, but I don't really want her to be. Our hands are on the table. Hers are delicate and skinny and make mine look oafish. She's put the ring on the middle finger of her left hand. It's a little loose. Three drunk men and a woman sit on a bench to our right. Pigeons flutter and perch around a fountain. By the time we reach Washington at seven on a sunny morning, we're so shattered that we fall asleep on the steps of the Lincoln Memorial to be woken an hour later by tourists clambering over us. We walk to the Washington Monument and slumber on the grass nearby. We do manage to stay awake at the Vietnam Memorial, seeing our own faces in the shiny stone amid the columns of names, but finally we fall deeply asleep for a couple of hours, back to back on a low stone bench near the Smithsonian.

In Brockport, Enid leaves for Lockport. I'd give her a hug, but I'm not the hugging sort and nor is she. She's barely a physical being at all. Felix notwithstanding, for all I know that peck on the cheek in Vegas and touching hands in the Columbus depot may be the most intimate she's ever been. I daren't tell her about my stolen, celebratory kiss in the middle of the Arkansas night. She doesn't tell me much and now she's leaving. She probably *will* become a novelist or musician or both. I hope so. I hope we all become what we want to be. All I need do is find out what that is.

"See you, then," I say. "Maybe I'll live in Lockport some day."

She smiles. "You won't."

"Will you go back to Felix?"

"Probably, if he's calmed down. Or else my mom's in Lockport." There's nothing else for us to say. She raises a skinny, be-ringed hand and touches my cheek with cool finger tips.

Enid Stevick remains a mystery to me to this day, not least because of our very last conversation.

"You should have woken me."

"When?"

"In Arkansas—your forty-eight state."

"You're a heavy sleeper."

She opens her dark eyes a little wider. "Am I?"

13

LILACS AND MAGNOLIAS

When lilacs last in the dooryard bloom, or when I last see them do so, I'm in Rock Hill, South Carolina, 6.30 a.m., April 8, 1986. The warm, sun-filled air is alive with a confetti of blossom and my life seems settled to experience an unending springtime. I'm here for a magnolian symposium on William Styron, whose *Sophie's Choice*, published the day I first saw America, so captivated me when I read my father's copy the following autumn. Since then, the 1981 film, starring Meryl Streep has secured it an even wider readership, and I've begun wondering if I might meet the man. For while there are better-known writers on the American map, I have a youthful conviction that the novel, for Sophie and for the way Styron so vividly dramatizes links between everyday behavior and our capacity to commit atrocities, will find a place among the American classics. On a personal level, Styron and I share a degree of survivor's guilt—he lost his mother to cancer when he'd just turned fourteen—and I have the idea that he's the kind of writer I can talk with. The symposium is my first stop on the quest.

I've arrived by Trailways. I say "arrived," though there's no place to arrive at as such, just a Trailways cabin. Assuming I'm heading somewhere else, I stay seated while the bus idles, and muse on the fact that South Carolina and *Sophie's Choice* share initials. A vicar is pacing the dusty gravel. Then the driver comes up and says the vicar is waiting for me. Wherever it is I'm supposed to be, it turns out I'm already here.

"A vicar? *That* vicar?"

"This is Rock Hill, and that there vicar says he's here to meet a passenger, and you're the only passenger for Rock Hill this morning, so it don't take much to couple you two up."

Gingerly, I disembark. But it's not Judgment Day, only another morning: excellent and fair, and full of the scent of lilacs and magnolias. The vicar is Reverend Art Stern, husband of Eve C. Stern, symposium coordinator. He drives us to their house, and says, "Call me Art."

Eve's prepared English muffins, "an English breakfast," she says. She's an Austrian Jew who came over with her parents in the 1930s, hence her interest in *Sophie's Choice*.

"So," says the affable Art over breakfast, "you like the bus?"

"It's taken me all over America."

"You ought to write about your travels," says Eve after we've talked awhile. "Have you ever read *The Road: In Search of America*? It's by Nathan Asch, a Hemingway-generation Jewish writer. He might have been a model for Robert Cohn in *The Sun Also Rises*."

"I think it was Harold Loeb, dear," says Art.

"Well, we have his papers here at the college. I went to see his widow in California. She gave them to us. We've a copy of *The Road* too. It's about bus travel in the thirties."

I'm in awe. "I've never met a writer," I tell them,

"or even a writer's spouse." I daren't tell them my ludicrous, ultimate aim.

"Here," says Eve, scrawling on a piece of paper. "This is William Styron's number. You should call him. He's ever so nice. I invited him to the symposium, but he said it would be a bit like coming to his own wake."

I fold Styron's number away in my wallet, already fantasizing our meeting. The personal interest aside, to understand American culture I have to take every opportunity that comes my way to witness all strata of society, and Styron—a Famous Author—would be quite a coup. Also, I realize that I *am* Stingo, to the extent that he's any young man, hungry for love and companionship when, that summer in Brooklyn in 1947, he meets Sophie trying to recover from her incarceration at Auschwitz and learns about a world beyond himself. I too seek the "fellowship, familiarity, sweet times among friends" that have always seemed so elusive or fleeting on my wanderings across America.

But much as I yearn to be a character in a novel, fated to be ensnared as "the hapless supernumerary in some tortured melodrama," I'm simply in Rock Hill, South Carolina. Art and Eve don't just *seem* welcoming and hospitable and uncomplicated, they *are*, in my experience, ordinary, pleasant, sane people. Art doesn't suddenly turn on me and say, "So, Brit, what about your Empire, what about the way Clive of India slaughtered Indians en masse? What about British anti-Semitism?" He simply says I'm most welcome in South Carolina and he hopes I enjoy the symposium. For perhaps the first time in my life, I understand "the gestalt" Stingo feels in the novel. The "blissful temper" of the sunny

April morning, the "ecstatic pomp" (for Eve knows *Sophie's Choice* well, of course) "of Mr Handel's riverborne jam session," and the Stern's festive breakfast room combine to "pierce me with a sense of ineffable promise and certitude."

After breakfast, Eve takes me to the Winthrop Library to see Nathan Asch's papers. As I browse, my bowels loosen: these are the first manuscripts I've ever touched. In between trips to the restroom, I devour letters from Malcolm Cowley, story manuscripts, rejection slips, all kinds of stuff the like of which I've never previously encountered. *Maybe this is it*, I write at a library desk while, outside, cherry blossom drifts down like pink snow on the lush green quad. *Maybe I've found my purpose at last, and my journey is my purpose. There's no island of happiness, there's only the journey toward it, and in the search for happiness lies the happiness itself. All my life's arrived.*

Excited about my idea to emulate Asch and write a book about bus travel, I spend most of my time before the conference making notes, reading *The Road*, and planning my own manuscript. At the college bookstore I imitate Styron, or Stingo, buying several yellow legal-size pads and a dozen 2B pencils, and begin to scratch away as the sun fires the pink blossom, startling the grass with notice that darkness is about to pass. *If I ever complete it*, I write, *it will be about my love affair with the bus, and out of the bus comes America, the country where I've been conducting my search for the unattainable place of inexpressible happiness.* But even as I sit scheming and dreaming, real happiness seems infinitely attainable, easily definable, and very much part of my present experience. *Happiness, I jot in my delirium, comes in meeting someone meaningful from your past you've not seen in a long time. It's when you get to see the manuscripts of a writer who seems to have felt some of the things you've felt. It's receiving an unexpected letter from someone you want to hear from. It's having no demands on you.* Suddenly I see it all. Everything seems to fit: South Carolina and *Sophie's Choice,* the publication date and my first flight. Life *does* have a pattern, if you help it happen. Leaving my notes and pens and library books on the table, I return, yet again, to the restroom.

Early that evening, back in my plush room looking out over the magnolia-bedecked, sun-drenched campus, weary from excitement, I catnap and dream I'm in Brooklyn in 1947. Sophie, Nathan and I are in Sophie's flower-bedecked room. Handel's Water Music crackles on the phonograph. I know nothing of the horrors to come, or of Sophie's loss of her children. Life is all promise.

"You do indeed look a great deal like Eve C. Stern did as a young woman," I'm telling Sophie, "but you, Nathan, look nothing like Reverend Art Stern."

"That," says Nathan, "is because I'm Jewish. Also, I'm really not Nathan at all but—surprise, ha *ha!— William Styron himself!*"

"I can't believe it," I stammer. Yet I feel so welcome in this world, that I'm willing to accept anything. Nathan barely drinks, of course, but lavishes Budweiser on me, "keeping my glass topped up with unceasing attention." For my part, I get a buzz fizzy enough to suggest my euphoria might overflow the measure. But even in ecstasy I quickly become aware that something is horribly wrong.

"He's lying," says Sophie suddenly, drawing me into their squabble. "Nathan's lying, I tell you. He's not William Styron at all. It is *I* who is Mr Styron, and I say *fuck him*, fuck my Creator. Fuck him and all his Hände Werk. He has made me in His image, and placed me forever in this hideous trap to endlessly—can you imagine, Stingo?—*endlessly* relive this Brooklyn summer, and my guilt over my dear children."

"But, Sophie," I say. "I want you to trust me. Nathan is death. Love *me*. Love *life!*"

"Oh, Stingo," says Sophie, "you are so sweet, but you do not belong here. You are not even Stingo. You must find your own book to be in. Stingo has gone out for groceries, and if he finds you here, there will be *four* of us!"

"But I *want* to be part of this world," I shriek. "Don't you see? I am solitary, nameless."

"You do not know what you are saying," Sophie responds softly, and begins to look, as is the way of dreams, like my own mother. "There are no insiders and outsiders. There is no center. There is only an unending prolif—how you say—*prolificacy?*"

"Proliferation?"

"Yes, of worlds, some real, some not. And this one you do not want to be part of."

At this point, Nathan, who has slipped out of the dream, or out of focus, perhaps at my elbow filling my glass with Budweiser, re-enters the fray. "I have an idea," he says. "We must phone this Styron schmuck. We must fucking phone our Creator, phone God Himself and get Him to sort out this mess, and tell us who we are!"

I spring up. "I have His number!" I shout. "I have His *number!*"

But even as the three of us dance with joy like a triumphant triumvirate trying out as models for the three graces in Botticelli's *La Primavera*, the door opens and my fabulous fizzy feeling evaporates like a billion beer bubbles. For there, in the doorway, holding two brown paper grocery bags, and wafting in with the smell of what can only be "a heroic squander of food" including bagels, lox, salami, pumpernickel, braunschweiger and bratwurst, stands the *real* Stingo, ready to prove once and for all that I am indeed an impostor and a liar, and not a fictional character at all. Except that Stingo, as he stands there challenging me—and it must be the shock of this, coinciding though it does with a flash of red sun through my window, that jerks me awake—is unquestionably *myself.*

The "sunset" turns out to be sunrise. I've not taken a catnap at all, but fallen fully clothed into a nightlong slumber. Faint with hunger, I jump into the shower then race down for egg, bacon and grits in a student building where Abraham Blue joins me. Abraham is a black scholar from Baltimore interested in *The Confessions of Nat Turner*.

"Styron's unwell," he tells me. "There are rumors of cirrhosis."

"He's a drinker, is he?"

"Was," says Abraham. "You can tell from the novels. But he's given it up, we hear."

"So he's stopped drinking?" I feel a little deflated. Still, I think, keep your goal in mind.

Soon I'm back on the bus, waving goodbye to Eve and Art and Abraham and assorted scholars, and heading North to Washington just to get some sleep before wheeling round to return south to Durham. The curator at Duke has invited me to view Styron's manuscripts, but I want to get back in touch with Busland first, since my quest for real Americans includes ordinary people as well as celebrities, and especially bus people.

Busland doesn't fail me. In the Columbia depot, a Chicano nurse is leading two men, one black one white, out into the sunshine. It's like a contemporary Norman Rockwell tableau: Picture of Brotherhood. The blind men turn their laughing faces upward so their heads are at odd angles. It's as if they're listening to the sun. By the depot doors as they pass, Margory Spindle (as I'm christening her) a sparrow woman in a safari suit, says to a freckled woman swishing a baby, "I meant for to get you a *large* coffee."

"That's okay," says the woman.

"Where are you traveling from?"

"Corpus Christi."

"South Texas? With a *baby?* You young people amaze me. It'd skin my hide, a trip like that." Margery is straight out of colonial Africa: safari hat, khaki jacket and shorts, khaki coat and handbag, khaki socks that rise like Plaster of Paris to her red knees. "Was the bus on time?"

"Sure it was," says the freckled mother. "Jes' a diff'n't time, is all."

That night, Haley's comet tracks our northbound bus and I feel back in my element amid the floor-polish smell of Busland. The People of the Bus form a separate community from the rest of America, a human river, souls floating like flotsam, invisible to carfolk or the mass of middle-class America who swarm the skies. Over the years, after all, I've become a bus person myself, when all the time I thought I was an outsider, an observer. In Washington, there's a black guy who calls himself Eddie Murphy. It turns out he's doing a panhandling routine but after all these years I still fall for it.

"Excuse me, sir," he says coming straight up to me in shades and carrying a white stick. He speaks a tiptoe English, part superior, part obsequious, entirely fake. "Excuse me but it happens that I have here a sequence of numbers to be used to reach someone by telephone. As you will no doubt note from my dark glasses, I am blind. Would you be so kind as to read them for me?" I do so, probably because of the two definitely blind men at the Columbia depot. After all, he *might* be blind. "Bless you, sir. I've been in such a panic remembering them I've now lost my quarter. Is it on the floor?"

There's no quarter in sight, so I fish one from my pocket and put it in his palm. He recites the number again, holding the paper in front of him. Because of the glasses, I can't see if he's reading or not. Then he turns and walks straight up to a booth and waits behind a majestic woman speaking on the phone. When she puts the phone down, Eddie Murphy says, "Excuse me, ma'am. I've got these here numbers but, as you will see from my dark glasses, I am blind and cannot read them. Would you—"

"Shame on you," says the woman.

"I beg pardon, ma'am. But as you can see—"

"What I see, you ridiculous man, is the same fella who last week told me he was deaf!"

Eddie Murphy shrugs. "Well I din' know it was *you!* I cain't *see!*" And off he goes up to an elderly white man, and says, "Excuse me, chile." He's learning fast.

Southbound again, night falls somewhere in Virginia. A pretty redhead across the aisle switches on her overhead light and begins conducting sheets of music to herself. Her right hand lifts and sways like a seagull, left hand in shadow, following and complementing, occasionally at odds, like the seagull's shadow on a stormy sea. When I turn away to sleep, the hands reflect in the window like ghosts lifting and falling over the black fields.

Then it's five in the morning in Raleigh and I'm eating grits and bacon and sourdough in a café. The light increases, revealing rain and greening trees, a Stars and Stripes flapping wet, and in the distance buildings gray and sombre in the drizzle, red lights twinkling on the highest like distant stars. Up close, red taillights speed by the window. My feet ache from too long in sneakers. The café starts to fill.

"You figurin' on eatin' inside?" someone says.

A black girl with a silver purse and beret sits at a table singing "Say You, Say Me." Ready Mix Concrete Company workers hunch over coffee. One taps another for a light. An old white couple huddle in a booth looking stunned, as if dropped from another Rockwell and unsure what to make of new surroundings.

By eight a.m. I'm in Durham and walking along a road between orange-sand verges for a day at Duke. All

I do is leaf through the eight hundred and ninety-five hand-written leaves of the *Sophie's Choice* manuscript. But it's enough to make me find a phone booth and call His number. No one answers. I wander in the rain around the flint-stoned campus. Books tight against their chests, beautiful girls cross the quads of another world I don't belong in. On the Trailways back to Atlanta I read a news report on a Florida execution. It says the man suffered from post-Vietnam stress when he stabbed his two victims. Soon, it says, more men will have died prematurely from having been in Vietnam than died out there. It's a sultry evening by the time I reach Atlanta, and I don't know what I'm doing in America. My aim has been to find a way of meeting Styron, but I also need a reason for doing so.

14

THE HOUSE OF INEXPRESSIBLE HAPPINESS

Through 1986 and into the autumn of 1987, I move to Nottingham and rent a stuffy ground floor room with windows sealed against the gritty fumes of Castle Boulevard. The house is in perpetual shadow beneath the cliff that holds Nottingham Castle. *The Trip to Jerusalem*, a pub a few yards away, is a façade for a cave used as a cellar since at least the twelfth century. It is here, with sandstone dusting my pints of ale, that I write William Styron a letter, requesting an interview, and explaining my quest for the unattainable place of inexpressible happiness.

The view of many a Professor of American Literature is that there are far more illustrious figures one should hope to meet. The British variety tends to ignore him altogether. To me, he is therefore as much a hero as he was to my father, and I've taken as an augury the fact that the day I first flew to America was Styron's birthday and the publication day of *Sophie's Choice*. So when a cream-colored envelope with his name printed on the back falls through my letterbox, I tear it open and read the following with not a little trepidation:

> *I would welcome the opportunity of meeting you when you come here next spring and I hope we could have a fruitful and enjoyable get-together. You must feel very odd being British yet writing about my work. I don't feel quite like Edmund Wil-*

son, who called your countrymen "the despicable English" and really had quite a vitriolic animus about Britain, but it is true that I've felt no warmth about your country over the years and plainly the feeling is mutual. Nothing at all personal, as we say, nor do I mean to be condescending when I say that not some, but many, of my good friends are British. But it is remarkable how some countries will take certain writers to their hearts and virtually ignore others. The best example, in my own case, can be seen in a list of books that was sent to me some time ago—a list I imagine you've heard about: the 20 "best novels" by living Americans, drawn up by some British book association or other. It contained novels by every U.S. writer I consider my peer (Roth, Updike, Bellow, Mailer, etc. etc) and quite a few novels by writers I would completely disdain—but not one of my works was on the list. Strangely, when I beheld this list I was not the slightest bit surprised. Totally aside from the absurdity of such lists (noblest dogs, best soaps, worst diseases) I had, through long experience with the British reaction to my work, always expected to be ignored and this list was a simple validation.

But I would certainly be happy to have you have a drink or two with me (I've gone off the hard stuff but still go for a little beer or wine) and also break bread and take walks in the woods with me and my dog, Tashmoo—although the glory of spring comes late to the Connecticut countryside— so plan to come ahead. I'm clueless as to how I *can help you in your search for what Thomas Mann (you say) calls "the unattainable place of inexpressible happiness" but certainly the pursuit of happiness is inscribed as one of our inalienable rights. So I'll be honest at least, and try to help you in your quest.*

That night, alone in my traffic-shuddered Castle Boulevard room, I consume a bottle of 1981 Bulgarian Cabernet Sauvignon in celebration of my potential savior. I feel as if I have just been given the most wonderful gift, as indeed I have. The next day I book a spring flight to New York.

I arrive in April and stay with Darius Desoutter at his apartment on West End Avenue. Darius has by now become a Manhattan attorney and almost entirely lost his southern drawl.

Many years have passed since that Bonanza bus drove me slowly out of a misty Manhattan and up through the Connecticut countryside to Danbury, but every moment of that day is etched in my memory like the most vivid and unforgettable dream.

I recall the bus trundling past Leonard Bernstein Place and the Alice Tully Hall, heading toward Central Park on 65th Street. I remember turning left on Madison and 74th Street and glimpsing the Dakota Building across the park, before passing over water on 124th and Madison and speeding north toward Yankee Stadium.

Across the aisle slept a girl. Her bleached hair rested on her leather jacket and caught the sunlight against the grubby black window frame. Her eyelids were so heavily made up—blue against the blue sky—it was if the weight of the mascara held them shut. Her red painted fingernails peeked out from beneath jean-clad thighs. She had one foot on the seat, one on the floor. Her delicate ear—the one I could see—shone translucent orange in the emerging sun. I imagined her dreaming of arriving, happy to be coming home, ensconced in a cotton-woolly semi-consciousness, floating in a cloud-strewn sea. But most of all I remember not who was in the bus but what was beyond it, and especially the Connecticut greenery.

Unlike Nathan Zuckerman in Philip Roth's *The Ghost Writer*, which, on Darius's advice, I've read in preparation for the visit, I'm not, when I arrive to meet the master, yet another "*Bildungsroman* hero" busy "contemplating my own massive *Bildungsroman*." I'm a rudderless vagabond and cultural tourist still, in my upper twenties, seeking a resort called Happiness. But just as Zuckerman arrives to meet Emanuel Isidore Lonoff in *The Ghost Writer* so I come to meet William Clark Styron Jr. Fearful of being late, I reach Danbury three hours early. I spend the morning on a bench outside the public library listening, on my walkman, to Mozart's Prague Symphony and the *Sinfonia Concertante* in E-Flat Major that so moves Sophie on pages 93 and 94 of the Random House edition of *Sophie's Choice*. My happiness is inexpressible. Vaguely conscious of distant traffic, I read Styron's novella, *Shadrach*, and, as the sunshine breaks into fullness, intermittently gaze at the billowing clouds that seem whiter than any clouds I've ever seen. In a dim liquor store, I buy Styron a bottle of Chianti (remembering that this is what Lonoff uncorks for his meal with Zuckerman. In the florist's next door, I buy his wife, Rose, an eight-dollar bouquet of flowers, then I sit with the wine and bouquet and wait.

When a pale green Mercedes slides up by the curb, it takes me something less than three seconds to open my mouth and say something stupid, which is, "Did you have a good trip?" Given that I've traveled three thousand miles and seven years, and in that sense maybe thirty-thousand miles of bus trips, to get to this morning meeting, while Styron has merely jumped in his Mercedes and rolled a few miles, this is stupidity in the extreme. I resolve to drop dead rather than say anything so idiotic again. But the great man takes the cigar from his mouth and, with what I look upon gratefully as extraordinary Southern restraint and hospitality, says that indeed he has.

His Mercedes weaves us almost silently through the green lanes to his yellow-painted clapboard farmhouse halfway up a gentle hill.

"Look at this crap," he says, pulling a wad from his mailbox. "Feel it. Junk. Ninety percent of my mail is junk. You have a mailbox and they stuff it with junk."

He leads me through to the kitchen, introduces me to Rose, and disappears upstairs. She smiles and welcomes me. She has a lovely smile, fine bone structure, and is altogether the most beautiful sixty-year-old I've ever encountered.

"I guess people come up here all the time."

Rose frowns. This is my second stupid comment and it's not yet mid-morning. "Oh no," she says. "This is real nice for Bill."

I try again. "I've read your poems."

Rose beams. I've made a friend. We get talking and she tells me about a disconcerting dinner they had with Ronald Reagan. "He's a nice man," she says, "he just doesn't know anything. We asked serious questions and he just laughed them off and went back to telling stories about Hollywood. It was the time of the Libyan crisis, and he tried to joke about it. He's a nice *man*."

Styron has come downstairs. "He's *not* a nice man. He's a complete jerk. An asshole."

"Well, I was just saying how we went to dinner and he was likeable enough."

"Mmph." He disappears again, this time down a narrow passage to some other part of the sprawling, L-shaped home.

"Maybe I'd better go in and talk with him."

"Maybe you had. I don't want to be found keeping you."

He's sitting reading the paper. A cigar smolders in an ashtray on a table beside him. I look around. The living room is as cozy, plain and neat as Lonoff's; a large, beamy room with beige carpeting, armchairs, two cream-colored sofas at right angles around a square rug before the hearth, long, crowded bookshelves either side of the fireplace, a grand piano in the corner, a staircase and balcony, a CD-player, a dining table and chairs, every surface, chairs included, piled with books, books, books. The walls are bare but for a large, sparse painting of a small building on a flat horizon and, above a bar lined with empty bottles, a snapshot taped haphazardly to a beam, and what looks like a death mask. To the right there's a stained-glass window, and to the left, beyond the dining table, a wall-length window with French doors and a view of dark limbed trees and a sloping lawn that stretches to fields and woodland. "Purity. Serenity. Simplicity. Seclusion. All one's concentration and flamboyance and originality reserved for the grueling, exalted, transcendent calling." I look around and mouth Zuckerman's words: "This is how I will live."

Only then do I notice Styron peering at me over his newspaper from the armchair that makes up the final section of the wagon-train around the hearth. He motions for me to take a seat, picks up his cigar and puffs. Blue smoke rises lazily to the beamed ceiling, and the pleasant aroma begins to fill the room. He seems content to let me start.

"Mr Styron—" I begin, before lapsing into an appalling silence.

"Friends and acquaintances call me 'Bill,'" he says eventually, "and you should do the same. This will make conversation easier."

I doubt this but, startled not least by the way he seems to be quoting almost verbatim from *The Ghost Writer*, I indicate my Zuckermanesque obedience with a smile. The great man then proceeds to dismantle my last, fragile struts of decorum by asking about my life so far. Needless to say, there's no more to report about my life than Zuckerman found to say about his—at least not, as I see it, "to someone so knowing and deep."

"I—I've spent a lot of time on buses," I say feebly.

"In America?"

"Yes."

"You've seen the South?"

"Yes."

And so, in a way, our conversation begins. I have with me my thirty or so three-by-five cards. Whenever I think I might dry up, I flip to the next question. I've set up a little tape recorder at his elbow. It's too weak to pick up my voice, but gets everything he says, and when, later, I come to turn the recording into writing, while everything he says is actual, my own voice is a kind of fiction.

And how the time flies. After a snack lunch of BLTs and Foster's lager, we continue for another hour, but all too soon I realize it's time to go.

"I'd better be off now."

"You're leaving? I thought you'd at least stay over, since you've come all the way from foggy Albion. Still, I'll drive you to the bus."

"Well, I—I'll stay then."

"Good."

I want to sink to my knees and bless him. From dull despair, I become the most elated young man who's ever lived. That evening, safely wrapped in the bosom of the Literary World, I imagine every moment as if it's as real as a written page. I stand around like Zuckerman as if I really am the "thoughtful man of letters" I've fooled the Styrons into thinking I am. We eat quail for dinner and drink a bottle of Chablis before Rose shows me to the bedroom off the balcony at the top of the stairs.

Unlike in Roth's novella, or in *Sophie's Choice*, nobody smashes a glass against a wall, or turns the light mood to darkness with a sudden rage or insult. Nothing seems inexplicably wrong. The farmhouse gives off no bad vibrations. I do have a sense "of a dwelling far removed from the city streets, of a place remote, isolated, almost bucolic." But beneath my royal mood I sense only that everything is inexplicably, and for the first time in my life, *right*. It's truly as if I've come, if not exactly home, then certainly halfway there. I don't completely, or perhaps even remotely, understand as yet, to further paraphrase *The Ghost Writer*, how desperate I am for Styron's recognition, or why. But I'm able to hold myself together and, like Zuckerman with Lonoff, avoid getting down on the floor to supplicate at his feet.

For I have, as surely as Roth's alter-ego with his Bernard Malamud-inspired literary hero, come "to submit myself for candidacy" as none other than William Styron's "spiritual son," in hope of "his moral sponsorship" and "the magical protection of his advocacy." No doubt this desire is in some way, and perhaps not obscurely, connected with my relationship with my own father. In one of our last meetings I suggested he and I go to the pub "to talk about life." This is something we'd never done, and he himself had never suggested.

"What do you want to talk about," he said, "my prospects?" Unfortunately the pub we found was dingy, and when I sat on a bench, he pulled up a chair that left him a foot lower than me. Every question I asked did indeed seem like an interview.

"What have been the highs of your life?" I began, knowing—or assuming—that my mother's death must have been the great low.

"I'm not sure," he replied. "My life has been sort of like this." He drew a horizontal line in the air, looking, for one of the few moments in our lives, directly at me. I think we were both glad to get down our pints and go our separate ways. But he may have been puzzled, even troubled, by my question, because as we were leaving, having awkwardly shaken hands, he said, "Easter Sunday, April 17, 1960."

At least, I thought, he recalls my birthday. "That was a high point?"

"No, no," he shook his head, pulling his collar up against the rain, his face in shadow, "the low point. It was the day Eddie Cochran died."

Maybe had we not been father and son we'd have got on fine, and maybe had I been Styron's actual son, Styron and I would have utterly failed to connect. But as it is, where my own father and I, try as we did, had almost nothing to say to each other, Styron and I—or this is my impression—rattle away like a couple of gatling guns. Gray-haired and jowly, Styron, when we're not talking, plods the same dogged, inward-looking way through the labyrinthine passageways of his house. When he focuses on me, he really does focus, but much of the rest of the time he just grunts in passing—and often we do pass unexpectedly at some intersection between rooms—or simply fails to notice I'm there. This is fine by me. I just sit around trying to look literary, leafing through some book or other from his ample shelves.

Even at the dinner table, as I "give my all to his cross-examination," I assume that it won't be long before he finds "a way of getting rid of me." Yet he's *invited* me, albeit vaguely, and I've no way of leaving until given a ride to catch the bus in Danbury. I make the occasional allusion to bus schedules, as if they're a hobby, just to give him a way out, but these go unacknowledged, and soon it's clear I *am* meant to stay. I go to bed that Friday night with no idea how I've got into this position and the strong sense lifted, like so many of my impressions of this visit, from Roth's novella, that I want to stay but feel I should go.

If I'm Ever Back This Way

I awake on Saturday April 23—a few days after turning twenty-eight—almost deranged by happiness. Sunshine streams across the bedspread. Dust motes float in front of the shadowed bookshelves. I jump out of bed, wander down the garden, and swim in the Styrons' steaming pool. On an old wooden desk in the pool hut, there are scrawled lines on a yellow legal pad in an unfamiliar hand—certainly not Styron's: *I did not mean / to fall in love with life / at least not twice.* Heart skipping at the sight of this original manuscript so carelessly cast down, I quell the urge to look around for more and instead return to the house.

Rose is making grits, eggs and bacon. The smell of coffee fills the kitchen, and "Bill," as I try hard to call him, reads aloud a letter he's received from a man in Nigeria. The man professes love and devotion and a wish to live with him and be a trainee writer. Again I think of Zuckerman sitting there while Lonoff complains about the various people who bother him and wonder what I've done to get so lucky.

And the days slide by. I almost forget the time. Over numerous meals and on walks along the Shepaug River at Judd's Bridge, "Bill" and Rose and I discuss Southern cooking, Herbert Aptheker, Eugene Genovese, Arthur M. Schlesinger (a friend!), Carly Simon (another friend!), Norman Mailer (they've made up), summer camps, young love, youth being wasted on youth, extra-marital sex, *Set This House on Fire*, Humphrey Bogart, literary thieves, quail, risotto, caffeine, Italians, Chianti, Chablis, insomnia, soft-shell crabs, Michelob, English women, a career as a writer—"I have no regrets, none whatever"—whiskey, abortion, President Bush, the Kennedys, Marilyn Monroe, Arthur Miller, Larry and Bertha (the Styrons' gardener and cleaner), the novel as a form of theater, the Styron's Irish au pair from the sixties, Mary Murphy, who worked for Pan Am and became chief stewardess and died in the Lockerbie disaster, Irish "Colleens" in Dublin, who put their hands over their chests when men look at them, dogs, music, Brahms's *Alto Rhapsody*, the slow movement of Beethoven's Fourth Symphony, and even as we speak I happen to glance at the fridge and see, pinned there, a note from a "Meryl" who can only be Meryl Streep.

When "Bill" disappears to write—to *write!*—Rose and I play tennis and talk.

"Three years ago," Rose tells me, "you'd never have gotten to see him. You have good timing."

"You mean since his breakdown," I ask nonchalantly, "he's looked up from his writing pad?"

"Exactly."

Styron has promised to read me from the opening to his new novel, so I'm constantly on alert. I daren't be absent when the great man decides on the moment. When it comes, it's only another of so many startling episodes during those marvelous days. It's near dusk a week after I arrive when I finally say, "Well, I'd better catch a bus."

"Aren't you staying the weekend?" he asks.

"I've been here a week already."

"Stay as long as you want."

"I fly home on Monday."

"Fine, you can stay until Monday morning and I'll drive you to the bus depot."

He's so accepting of me that I grow bolder. "What

have you been doing today?"

"I'm a writer," he replies, "so I've been writing. Would you like to hear some of it?"

Would I? "I'd love to, yes."

"Would you?" He looks concerned. "Just a few pages to see how it starts? It may be inflicting too much on you. I feel that since you're partially on a quest to see what I'm up to, this might be helpful. I haven't read a word of it to anyone. I'm trying to establish the voice, the tone, and it may be that I'll have to discard some of this." So as the evening draws in, he switches on a lamp and I sit opposite while he shuffles his yellow legal sheets, coughs, and begins. "In the year following the end of World War II, having returned from the Pacific to my home in Tidewater Virginia, I was in moral and physical disarray. My existence had become so aimless as to give new meaning to that gray old phrase 'at loose ends.' For the first time in my life I was faced with what appeared to be almost nothing to occupy my hours intelligently, or enliven my days. . . ."

"There," he says after reading for ten minutes or so. "Is it any good?"

"Oh, very good," I say, and offer rudimentary comments, such as, "Why not move this sentence to earlier," not a wee chuffed to hear myself telling William Styron how to write.

Then, on my last night, as the shadows of home and *la vie ordinaire* loom like my childhood hatred of Sunday evenings, I nearly collapse from shock.

"You should write something yourself," says Styron. "All that bus travel you've been telling me about. Maybe you have something to say about America. Why not write a book?"

Since I assume that, for a writer like Styron, I can only possibly be acceptable or worth his while if I'm a version of Stingo, I say, "Yes, well, I've started."

"Good," he says. "You can use my cottage."

"I beg your pardon." I nearly fall out of my chair.

"The cottage there," he continues, "it's where James Baldwin wrote parts of *Another Country* and started his seminal essay, *The Fire Next Time*. It's where I wrote much of *Nat Turner* and *Sophie's Choice*. Romain Gary stayed there, and Jean Seberg, and my good friend, Carlos Fuentes. You can have it for a summer, just pay the cost of the phone bill."

I look at Rose, who raises her eyebrows. *Please*, I pray. *I know I have to wake up soon, but please not yet, just a while longer.* But I don't wake up because I'm not dreaming. While for years I've imagined such situations, imagined meeting Marilyn Monroe in Michigan, and Ben Hecht in Pennsylvania, and the Kennedys under a bush in Oregon, here I am, sitting with a Pulitzer Prize winning novelist and his wonderful wife, being given the keys to the House of Inexpressible Happiness.

"I—I don't know what to say," I stammer.

"Thank you would suffice."

"Thank you."

"Just let me know when you want it."

The evening floats away. I remember at one point Styron calling me a "friend." "When one is sitting here, as now, with friends," he says. But I remember little else. When the Styrons go upstairs, I roam the house, and go out through the sliding French doors into the blossom-scented night and wander the lanes of Connecticut on a solitary, ecstatic walk to no purpose other than to rid myself of an excess of joy. I cannot possibly sleep, and don't hesitate, any more than Nathan Zuckerman, "to embrace trees" and kneel to kiss the dewy grass, so bursting am I "with a sense of gratitude and freedom and renewal." *I am a character in a fiction*, I say aloud. *At last, at last, I am in the Bright Book of Life.* Dawn comes, as always, and hour upon relentless hour passes with reckless speed. Utterly bowled over, infatuated with the man, with fame, with literature, with the gifts America is showering on me, I wave goodbye to Styron—"Keep writing," I say, or some such inanity—board the Bonanza bus to New York, and fly home with every intention of taking up Styron's offer.

15

A SPELL IN CONNECTICUT

"Are you going in there?" he asks, as I'm walking up the steps into the Museum of Natural History. "If you see old Phoebe, let me know, willya?"

"Phoebe?"

"My kid sister." He's sitting on the steps in a red baseball cap and heavy coat. "She's been ostracizing the hell out of me."

"What does she look like?"

"Somebody's given her a stupid haircut, and she's been taking belching lessons from a girl named Phyllis Margulies." I carry on up the steps. He gets up and climbs the steps beside me. "She's just a kid, and probably carrying some goddam heavy suitcase all around. She thinks she's coming west with me, but she can't do that. I've told her but she's just disappeared into the museum and I can't find her. You can't reason with her sometimes."

"She won't get far with a heavy suitcase."

"You don't know Phoebe."

"Well, we're agreed on something." Then, of course, I realize who he is, or thinks he is. "You're Holden, aren't you? Holden Caulfield?"

"I don't want to talk about it. I'm trying to get away from all that."

"You're one of the reasons I came to America as a teenager."

"Why come *here?* The country's full of phonies, for Chrissake!"

We enter the museum and stroll around the exhibits of stuffed animals set in half-real, half-painted woodland scenes.

"So what have you been doing all these years?" I ask as we gaze up at a giant brown Alaskan bear standing on its hind legs.

Holden sighs. "Chewing the rag with passers-by. I spend a lot of time in this museum looking for old Phoebe, and in winter I go sit by the lagoon in Central Park to see what happens to the ducks."

"What *does* happen to them?"

"Nothing. They slip and slide around on the ice until it thaws, then they go right back to what they always do: quack and paddle."

We pass a glass case of model Indians in a canoe.

"You don't look any older."

"I'm not."

"You feel trapped, being fictional and all?"

"I told you, I've escaped. I'm in the real world now, least I will be when I locate Phoebe and talk some sense into her. After Mark Chapman shot John Lennon and sat down and read my goddam book on the sidewalk I knew it was time to get the hell out."

In the end we find Phoebe looking at a Kaibab squirrel, which with her black beady eyes she rather resembles. She and Holden—or whoever they are—go off together and leave me in the gloom. Back in the sunlight I'm almost blinded. I stroll through Central Park and watch the turtles paddle in the lake. Then I meet Darius at a restaurant for a couple of Samuel Adams and a steak. The next morning I catch the Bonanza bus to Danbury and hitch a ride to Roxbury.

The bus trip is relatively short. The days of long-haul bus travel are all but behind me, and I wonder, reading the papers, if the buses themselves aren't near the end of their era. Violence has even invaded Busland. That March 12, according to *USA TODAY*, a Greyhound pulled into the depot in Hartford, Connecticut, with a suspected bullet hole in the driver's side window. The drivers began a strike on March 2, when nine thousand drivers walked out in a wages dispute. The situation worsened when a picket died on March 3 in Redding, California. The bullet hole was one of several incidents of snipers shooting at replacement drivers. Near another of my old haunts, Jacksonville, on March 11, snipers fired on a bus carrying thirty-nine passengers to Daytona Beach along US 1, about twelve miles south of Jacksonville. Seven were wounded by shotgun pellets and glass splinters and taken to St Luke's Hospital. Similar incidents occurred in Phoenix and Columbus. This was not exactly the kind of bus travel I knew, and light years from Clark Gable and Claudette Colbert's experiences in *It Happened One Night*. But all those safe, reliable, courteous drivers hardly seemed like troublemakers. "As far as I'm concerned it wasn't one of our strikers," said union official Bill Nicholson of Jacksonville, during Greyhound talks with the ACGLU, the Amalgamated Council of Greyhound Local Unions. "They've been like choir boys." Greyhound offered $25000 reward for information leading to the snipers.

So I head north for my month of what I expect to be almost uninterrupted Thoreauvian solitude with no great urge to move on. In some ways the contradictory desire remains both to stay put in a single room, at a desk, and to light out for the Territory. For Byron "there are wanderers o'er Eternity / Whose bark drives on and on, and anchored ne'er shall be," but I've grown to want a stable place so as to shape the past decades and give them meaning. This month in Connecticut is the compromise. I've traveled again to the States—my necessary Melvillian ocean—but not to roam restlessly from state to state. This time I want nothing more than to sit alone in a cottage deep in the countryside, and to summon up the ghosts of summers gone. In many ways my intention to stay put is the opposite of what I've usually done. Yet I've always tried, in Byron's words, to "become portion of that around me." To live, as Mr Thoreau advises, "one day as deliberately as nature."

The evening of my arrival is one of the pleasantest of my life. It's everything I want it to be: "sunny and mild, flower-fragrant." The days again seem "arrested in perpetual springtime." It's mid-May and I've at last reached a destination, which might just as well be the opening page of *Sophie's Choice*. By six that evening, I'm resting on soft moss beneath a tall pine tree in a wooded corner of the Styrons' sprawling garden. A cardinal flashes red against the sunlit green foliage. I lean back against the trunk, my feet held from slipping by some tangled roots around which a few large wood ants busy themselves for the coming night. Ahead of me the pre-Civil War house throws long shadows across the back lawn. To my left, the windows of my yellow cottage with its black shutters and white sills, sparkle in the last of the day's sunlight, with the glint of a blood-red side door puncturing the gloom beyond. The sun itself, warming my forearm and cheek, feels like the glow of companionship. Birds threek and whistle among the trees. Rose has settled me in and I've yet to see Styron. When he finally appears from his literary labors and ambles up the garden path to greet me I'm lounging in the lap of tranquillity with a cold glass of Michelob, at peace at last.

"Got a car?" he barks. I tell him sheepishly that I haven't. "You can't survive up here without a car. Got supplies? Come on. Let's get you some supplies."

So in Southbury that evening, Styron waits in his Mercedes while I purchase the kind of groceries I think Stingo and Sophie would buy, including bagels, bread, cheese, meat, beans, butter, fruit, vegetables and spam. The grocer's a strange fellow: an amiable, jaundiced-looking dolt with an alarming resemblance to Homer Simpson.

"Spam!" he says. "You picked the right product. Ask me anything about it!"

My arms are laden. Styron is waiting in the car. "I really don't have any questions," I tell him.

"Spam was first produced in June 1937 by G. Hormel and Company of Austin, Minnesota."

I put down the groceries and he starts bashing the keys of his cash register. "So just over a year before Eddie Cochran was born in the same state."

He looks up. "Doh, if you say so. You know why it's called Spam? Combination of spiced ham. I remember the first commercial, to the chorus of 'My Bonnie Lies Over the Ocean.' *Spam, Spam, Spam, Spam, Hormel's new miracle meat in the can . . . Tastes fine, saves time, if you want something grand ask for Spam.* That'll be forty dollars, twenty cents."

"And a bottle of Five Highs."

"Five Highs whiskey, that'll be $10.07 with tax."

"And three bottles of brandy."

"My, you're having a party." I pay and he opens the door for me, weighed down as I am with packages. "Know how many tins of Spam they reckon Americans eat a day? Thirteen thousand, six hundred and eighty."

"He's got no car," says Styron to Rose when we get back. "I took him for supplies."

"What about Al's jeep?" says Rose.

"We'll leave him one of the Mercedes."

Alexandra, the Styron's youngest daughter, is my equivalent to Nathan Zuckerman's encounters with Amy Bellette, the mysterious young woman in *The Ghost Writer*. As with the other three children, there are pictures of her all around the house, and Rose more than once mentions how attractive and gifted Al is, and how much we'd "enjoy one another." But, that summer at least, solitude suits me best. As the weeks pass and I write my bus book I find myself regressing to that teenage romantic I'm writing about, and dwelling deeper and deeper in the world of phantasms. My mind plays more tricks than ever. This is not helped by Rose's comments, nor Styron's as he bids me goodnight after our final dinner of veal before he and Rose leave for Martha's Vineyard in the morning.

"You afraid of ghosts?" he calls as I trudge up the path once used by James Baldwin.

"Ghosts?"

"There's a gang of ghosts up there. A lot of time

has passed."

I don't know the half of it, so for that first night sleep well. I awaken to dawn rain and walk outside where a warm mist gives the garden even more of the aura of a dream. I wander through the vegetation, past an abandoned swing, down toward the pool and jacuzzi steaming into the mist. There, in the pool, a naked woman, in maybe her early thirties and with close-cropped hair, is swimming lazily on her back. I dart behind the bushes, and pick my way through the damp grass up the slope to my cottage to make coffee. The rain becomes heavy again. I stand in the dark barn-like sitting room of the cottage and listen. It sounds like a kitten pawing its mother for milk, magnified a million times. I can't think who the woman can be. Rose has said that, apart from the retriever, Tashmoo, I'll be alone once she and Styron have left at six. It's gone seven.

Much of the day, I sit at the large oak desk and keep an eye out through the meshed window for the girl I saw in the pool. I've allowed Styron to think that I'm writing my bus book, but in fact, that day like many others, I just sit at the desk and watch the rain through the bug screen across the small window. I do get out my Venus Velvet 2B pencils, my yellow legal pads, and periodically write something about somewhere or someone in America. But I spend hours on the large bed once occupied by Baldwin, Romain Gary, Jean Seberg, Carlos Fuentes, and God knows who else, reading whatever I can find. This includes novels by Reynolds Price, Walker Percy, Maxine Hong Kingston and, to start with, since I feel like a fraud, Roth's *Deception*.

Around dusk I stand on my porch, Tashmoo at my

feet, and realize that for one month I'm master of all I survey. It's still raining so we go indoors. Tashmoo is fine company, but dozy and inclined to silence. For the sheer sound of other voices, I turn on the TV. Sammy Davis Jr., a newsreader announces, has died of throat cancer. Time weighs heavy upon me. I write a little essay on anxiety, and one on fraud. I cook myself a lousy supper of bacon and bread fried in its grease. What do I want? I ask myself. This is *it*, isn't it? This is happiness: to be given this famous writer's house and solitude for a month; to be befriended by a hero, and become the beneficiary of his extraordinary *largesse?* To be Stingo to their Nathan and Sophie? And yet something nags. Something is missing in the house of happiness.

Another day, having just read of Julien Sorel's demise in *The Red and the Black,* I turn on the news to hear of another death: Jim Henson, the creator of the Muppets, a young, unexpected death. What is my life? What do I want? What is Meaning? ("Where is Truth?" asks Stendhal's hero.) The rainy days and nights wear on. The beams creak. I take to drinking Five Highs, then the brandy, trying to figure out where to go next. Much of the time I think I can hear voices, but I can never be sure. Old barns creak so much it's like chatter. I've seen no further sign of the mysterious woman in the pool, though when I swim the water sounds like gentle laughter. Only when I find a visitors' book with the scrawls of all the people who've stayed in the cottage do I decide maybe I'll spend a while in the main house. I've been reading about each person. Romain Gary, I learn, shot himself in 1980. Jean Seberg, I've known for years, committed suicide after being hounded by the FBI for her links with the Black Panthers. James Baldwin has died of cancer in France the previous July.

Finally spooked out of the cottage by a second sighting of the woman—this time sitting on the steps, staring at me, again with short hair, blue eyes—I grab a glass and the brandy and go down to the main house. It's never locked, Styron has told me. The place is yours. I walk through the empty kitchen and into the large sitting room where I interviewed Styron two years before. I sit at the bar. Tashmoo sprawls on the carpet. To my right the garden falls away.

"What falls away is always and is near," I whisper. Theodor Roethke's larynx guffaws across the years.

On the terrace, against a backdrop of misty green trees, droplets of water plop onto abandoned chairs. I leaf through the books on the bar: George E. Vaillant's *The Natural History of Alcoholism* and Camus's *The Fall*. Ahead of me empty decanters line the wall where, two years ago, Styron's "death mask" hung, made, said Rose, while "he was real sick." In its place now hangs what looks to me like the death mask of James Baldwin. Around it is slung Styron's Legion of Honor medal. Another new addition is the presence of full spirit bottles on a lower shelf of the bar. To my left, innumerable books lie piled on the piano stool. I pad across the carpet and look at some of the books on Styron's shelves: Langer's *The Holocaust and the Literary Imagination*, *Malcolm X Speaks*, Aptheker's *American Negro Slave Revolts*, the complete works of Montaigne, Fuentes' *The Air is Clean*, Chaim Potok's *The Chosen*, Buchwald's *The Buck Stops Here*, Malraux's *The Twilight of the Absolutes*, Kemble's *Journal of a Residence on a Georgia*

Plantation, Lester's *Look Out Whitey, Black Power's Gonna Get Your Mama*, Plato's dialogues, Steiner's *Language and Silence*, the letters of Faulkner, the letters of Mencken. . . .

I drink a goblet of brandy to Tashmoo, then one to the Styrons, and one to Baldwin, and several to myself. Time collapses in on itself and eventually whatever book I'm reading begins to swim before my eyes. Whether something even stranger than the ghost woman really *does* happen around midnight, or whether I dream it, I don't know. But it certainly seems real. I've had too many goblets of brandy to count, and am too afraid now to venture out into the rain to take the slippery path back to the cold, dark cottage where the ghost woman awaits. I had no intention of staying in the main house so long, but it has a warm feeling the cottage lacks, and I've become utterly absorbed in Styron's library. I have my notebook with me, and have jotted a few lines about James Baldwin, the thought of whom has increasingly haunted me as the days pass. I know he—a *real* writer—has occupied that cottage a quarter of a century before. If the Living could be hoodwinked by a traveling fantasist, the Dead might see all. The narrator's comment in *Sophie's Choice* that he's "a person who is too often weakly misguided by the external masquerade" and "quick to trust," may have encouraged me in what I am fast coming to fear is my dissemblance. But Baldwin's writings, in contrast, shows that he knew all too well how people, and not just black Americans, playact. "The Negro," he writes in *Notes of a Native Son*, "learns how to gauge precisely what reaction the alien person facing him desires, and he produces it with disarming artlessness." If I am indeed a literary fraud, Baldwin, I begin to think, will know it, and might seek to avenge Styron.

I forget momentarily about Baldwin as I lie on the carpet behind the grand piano and read a poem by Rose in a book called *Thieves' Afternoon*.

Romancer, I write letters / that I never send, / to gambler and tree-surgeon, / cardinal and prophet, / a lover I still covet / as a friend. / You who married me / when the urns of child-scarred / stone were tall / ivy fountains, and patience / bloomed in the irongate garden, / and image was all, / could scarcely guess / how faithful, full of faith / for you I'd be. / Nor would I want you to. / Image is all. Just then, I hear something, but continue to skim read: . . . *your arm around her / (You, stronger than you'd been, / she, as I was then, / graceful and seventeen) / your world, / I wonder for a moment: / where is mine? Your bare fine arm, / your eyes and wit like hers / were mine in Rome*

This is the point in the poem, mid-sentence, that I feel a breath—a presence perhaps, but breath seems closer to what I actually feel—on my neck. Rain gusts against the large windows. Night has turned the window into a mirror reflecting back the whole room, as if, like the displays in the Museum of Natural History, Tashmoo and I are in a glass case. I turn and see her sprawled on the carpet snoring. But though I glimpse no one behind me, I do catch the reflection of the room in the window. I see immediately, and of this I'm certain, sitting facing one another on a chair and sofa respectively before a blazing fire, a tall, thin, white man—a darkhaired, young William Styron, I would say—and a small, delicate-looking black man who can only be

James Baldwin.

I look back at the cold, dry hearth. Then back at the window, and there, in reflection, beside that *blazing* hearth, sit Styron and Baldwin, snowbound on some cold night in the winter of 1960 to 1961 during the first year of my life. I get up from the floor and walk across the room. Tashmoo is nowhere to be seen and there indeed now the hearth is alight, and Styron and Baldwin sit talking in its glow. They don't seem to notice me, but they too cradle brandies, sloshing as they gesticulate, cigarettes in hand, catching the light of the fire with a glint of glass. I sit on the sofa and listen, but though they seem to talk so animatedly, I hear only snatches. A snowdrift lies piled against the foot of the French doors. Just above the crackling fire, I hear Styron explaining how his grandmother, Marianna, "had two little slave girls, Drusilla and Lucinda." "My own father was a victim of slavery," Baldwin's saying. "He was never a slave himself but his father was, and in Virginia where you're from. Both their lives were poisoned by the bitterness they felt. A deep, corrosive bitterness, the kind that breaks people who won't bend."

But it's as if there's an invisible force in the room, some kind of wind that blows away their voices and their words are lost to me again. The room's becoming cloudy with cigarette smoke. I can no longer see myself in the window's reflection. The smoke thickens the harder I listen, until eventually the whole room clouds over and I fall into a coughing fit and pass out, only to awaken hungover, beneath the piano, the sun already high. Tashmoo's nuzzling my face and I sit up with a start and bang my head on the bottom of the piano.

From here on the days pass almost benignly to their end. I sit in the cottage writing by day, and each evening sit on the deck at a white table in dappled sunlight. Maybe, over by the old swing, a Red Admiral butterfly or a cardinal amid the greenery catches my attention and I toast the wildlife with a Keystone beer and get back to *The Heart is a Lonely Hunter,* or *Crime and Punishment,* or Peirce and Hagstrom's *The Book of America,* or Zinn's *A People's History of the United States*, listening to, say, Chopin's sonatas. I'm content enough, none too bothered by anything, and slowly the beers overtake me and drown out my concentration. I wake on my penultimate morning realizing I've not written to anyone all summer. In the past I've come to the States and searched out people. But now, finally, the restless movement has gone out of me. I desperately *haven't* wanted to move anywhere. Some aspect of my emotional journey is nearing completion. The solitude is the same solitude, the same privacy I attained on the bus. But I can't seem to care enough about the outside world to even let people know I'm here. This spell alone in a cottage far from home has brought back all my melancholy from earlier days and I want to try to capture the ephemeral past that constitutes my sense of self. So, as I try to write, I pin words from Shelley's "To a Skylark" to the wire netting of my window: *Our sweetest songs are those that tell of saddest thoughts.* The fact that I no longer seek out friends from past years means that something has ended.

For one final time, I return to the main house and sit beneath the awning on the veranda to continue with my bus book to the sound of the first movement of Mozart's Flute and Harp Concerto. I'm describing how I went through Billings, Montana. To my left, by the French doors, Tashmoo lies flaked out, perhaps dreamily listening to Mozart. To my right, on the low wooden wall around the terrace, a gray cat whom I treat with only the occasional stroke has decided to be near Tashmoo and I, and is asleep on its stomach, chin thrust forward on the warm stone, no doubt purring in appreciation of Wolfgang Amadeus. The guttering creaks above me, the wind rises and drops like music, and in my mind there's a mixture of Billings, Chippenham, Nottingham, *Walden*, and memories of my parents. I'm altogether serene, contemplative, and untroubled by the agitation that has beset me for so much of the past ten years. My ghosts and I have come to an accommodation. I'm getting ready for home, or perhaps someday to make one.

During my final night I'm beset by dreams of the oddest kind. I tour battlefields with Hitler in the back of a minicab, interviewing him about his part in it all, ride a bicycle that's towing a yellow van driven by Sean Connery, and have tea with the Brontës. (They've moved to Sauk Center, Minnesota and have a mother but no father, only a step-father who shares the slightly weird physiognomy of a particular c1930 photo of Sinclair Lewis. Charlotte's talkative and pours the tea, but Emily's like one of those distant stars that you can't see if you look at it directly). Finally I have the dream to end all summer dreams. I'm at a dinner party with Bob Hope one side of me and Pope John Paul II the other.

"I know you're a Polish Catholic," I say, "but do you *really* believe in God?"

John Paul's very nice about it, but he's wincing.

Bob Hope's embarrassed, and keeps trying to distract me with jokes about World War II and Bing Crosby. It is then, at about three in the morning, that something jolts me awake. Through the dim light I see what at first I think is the word "Sophie" across the door. As my eyes adjust I see it says, "Seberg," and at that same moment I become aware of the crop-haired woman in the chair across from the bed.

"What do you want?" I ask.

"If we spirits have offended—"

"Not at all, but—you're Jean Seberg, right?"

She shrugs. "I'm told I was born in Marshalltown, Iowa. But names are just names, whether of places or people, nothing more."

"Why are you here?"

"This place is a sanctuary for spirits, haven't you noticed? We like to be in places we can be accepted."

"If you're who you look like, you died the year I came to America."

"Did I?"

"Do you wish you'd never left Iowa?"

"Maybe I haven't."

"Why do we reject where we're from?"

"You tell me."

"What do you do?"

"Nothing. I just am. Or am not. It's hard to say. But I'm in good company. I like to offer advice."

"Okay. Let's hear it."

"Be careful what you set your heart on," she says softly, "for it will surely be yours."

Only on my Bonanza bus for New York do I read a paper again. Busland, I discover, has continued its turmoil during my stay. The *New York Post* reports some repercussions of the strike, now in its fourth month. The bus authorities are using reserve drivers. One of these hapless fellows, it turned out partway through a trip from Norfolk, Virginia to New York, was having a little trouble. After jumping the bus around the place, and nearly crashing, he finally admitted that he didn't know how to drive stick-shift. A woman passenger, Diane Monteiro, took over and drove the bus herself the hundred and twenty miles from Delaware to New York. "He should not have left the terminal," said an official at Dallas headquarters, "if he was not familiar with the stick shift." The bus had left Norfolk on the Thursday at 11.10 p.m., and there was a change of drivers around 4.00 a.m. at Clement Travel Center. For a few minutes everyone was silent, mostly sleeping, but one great lurch after another bundled people awake and they began screaming at him to turn the bus around. At this point Diane Monteiro took over and, through darkness and heavy rain, drove the three or so hours up to New York to arrive, finally, at 8.00 a.m. In the words of another passenger, Rosa White of Crown Heights, Brooklyn, "It was like a ride through eternity." Such is Busland at this time. But without my further realizing it, Busland has become almost exclusively a part of my past. I no longer feel the need to travel but just the time to *be*, or more particularly to record.

"I'm beginning a new chapter in my life," I tell Darius in McSorely's in Greenwich Village, with all those ancient photos cramming the walls. "The eighties are over, and my youth with it."

"You're barely thirty," he replies.

"But thirty I am. How are you enjoying the beaten track of the professions?"

"I love it." he sips his McSorely's Dark. "I love New York, but I'm lonely. Not like you, who always seem to have another place to go."

"Whatever happened to Daniella?"

"We saw each other, and then we didn't. What happened to Mary-Ann Steiner?"

"You told me her teeth were held in by her wealth."

"I didn't say that."

"Anyway, she went off and became a doctor in Harrisburg or married Barry Buck, or both. I've no idea. *Gather ye rosebuds while ye may*, I told her."

"What did she say?"

"So that's what I am—a goddam rosebud."

Darius laughs. "Still, that's all behind you now."

"Yes. Onward to the future."

"Where else? Another beer?"

We talk on through the summer afternoon. I feel this is the start of a new kind of life. I'm no longer the youth who began these travels. It's time to realize that the life I've been looking for is the life I'm living.

The larger History that has shadowed my little voyage now reaches its own changes right on cue. On November 22, Margaret Thatcher resigns after eleven years, five months and eighteen days. It's the end of an era. I feel gleeful at first, then sad. When she came to power I was nineteen and about to see America. Her leadership has exactly coincided with what may one day seem like the most exciting years of my life, and her end finds me trying to refuel for another decade.

"I think I was in love throughout my summer in Connecticut," I tell Darius, "and sometimes I think I've been in love all my life."

"That's not the real world up there," he replies. "It's where the Styrons, Roths, Hoffmans and Millers of this world live. It's not where you or I belong."

"A lot more people live up there than you think, and it was real while I was there."

He gives me a knowing look, and says, "Was it?"

And I really can't say that it was.

16

PISTACHIOS WITH ARTHUR MILLER

During that summer I do have one verifiable encounter, or rather a double encounter, that breaks my solitude. While much of the time I'm alone, I'm aware that all kinds of famous people are hidden away among the trees and up private lanes. The signs are everywhere. Two years before, Rose drove me around, casually pointing out Arthur Miller's house, Walter Matthau's summer home ("Where Jack Lemmon's daughter, Courtney, sometimes stays. You should call her"), Richard Widmark's Connecticut retreat. "That's Dick's house," she said. "What a shame they're not back from California yet." On this current visit I even play tennis with "Dick's racket," wholly conscious that I'm gripping the same handle as the man who played Jim Bowie in *The Alamo*. I've felt closer than ever to fulfilling my father's notion of a glamorous life. After all, the man who gives me a lift to the court claims to be Dustin Hoffman's gardener. But signs—including tennis rackets, adjuncts and brandy-induced ghosts—are almost all I see, and it seems time to engineer an encounter with the real thing.

All summer I know that Arthur Miller's house is only four miles up the road, and I spend much of my less productive time in the cottage thinking of excuses to meet him. It's not exactly a yearning, but I feel I should at least try to meet one of America's most famous post-

If I'm Ever Back This Way

war playwrights, not to mention the one-time husband of my old friend hiding out in Michigan, Marilyn Monroe. In fact, how could I *not* seek out such a "real" celebrity? Several Americans I spoke to in the years after that summer believed Miller had died long before he actually did, in 2005, and his stock seems fairly low in his own country, whereas in Britain he was, and is, a kind of literary god. "Arthur and I joke about it," says Styron. "He has Britain and I have France." Certainly he's a writer the British have adopted with an interest they've never shown in Styron. The University of East Anglia has an "Arthur Miller Centre."

In Roxbury, that summer, I discover that Miller's reputation precedes him not just as a playwright and one-time Monroe husband, but as a friend and neighbor.

"Arthur!" is the kind of comment I hear. "He's the biggest cheapskate in literary history. I mean I *love* Arthur, but—"

"Arthur! We used to play tennis with him. He never provided balls himself, and then one day when he did he wouldn't let us hear the end of it."

"Arthur! He wouldn't build Marilyn Monroe a swimming pool!"

So of course I'm curious to make my own assessment. I also want to see what he can tell me about America, and the pursuit of happiness. Part of my procrastination involves reading Miller's autobiography, *Timebends*, so I know, both from there and from people's comments, something of his wife, the photographer Inge Morath, and their daughter, Rebecca. Rebecca is reputedly both beautiful and talented. Already a successful artist and actress, she's just been in *The Cherry Orchard*

If I'm Ever Back This Way

in New York. Needless to say, I see Rebecca—in my dreams—as just the girl for me.

So, duty-bound to try to meet Miller, and perhaps his daughter, I take my copy of *Timebends* and drive up to his house to ask him to sign it. Miller's white house is set just back from the road. I pull into the driveway and walk through an archway to a large porch facing a sloping lawn down to a small lake. There's an old lady sitting just inside the French doors.

I poke my head in. "Hello," I say. "I'm after Mr Miller."

She narrows her eyes. "You're not one of them McCarthyites, are you?"

"No, they died out years ago. I'm using the Styrons' cottage for the summer."

"Oh, the Styrons," she says. "Well, come in. Arthur's somewhere in the house. He'll be here in a minute. Make yourself at home, Mr Styron."

Where Styron's house is bourgeois, Miller's is bohemian. There are no carpets, just the odd rug. All around the living room hang paintings by—I imagine—Rebecca, and photographs by Inge, and everywhere, of course, books. I peek into Miller's paper-strewn study. Styron is a neat, orderly man. He clears his desk at the end of each working day, piles his manuscript neatly to one side, his Venus Velvet 2B pencils all in a bunch with a notebook to one side. With his habitual writing schedule and habitual walks, he's a man who enjoys, and probably needs, routine. Miller's study, in contrast—when I see it—is a tip, the desk awash with papers, the bin overflowing. His typewriter has a single sheet of notepaper with "Arthur Miller" printed at the top. Beside his chair stuffed files hang from a cube shaped file holder.

Just then I turn to see a beautiful, dark-haired girl with large blue eyes. She bounds in and greets me with the kind of enthusiasm reserved for, at the very least, someone who has some sort of business here. She shakes my hand, and I recognize her as Rebecca. Not far behind strolls a tall, well-built, balding man in spectacles. It's Miller himself. He's casually dressed in jeans and an un-tucked shirt. I think he's going to bellow, *What the fuck do you think you're doing sticking your nose into my study?* But he's as casual as he looks.

"Hi," he says.

"Hi," I respond automatically. "I'm just a—well, I happened to be passing, and I happened to have a copy of *Timebends*, and I wondered if you'd sign it. I'm a friend of the Styrons."

"Oh, the English fellow staying there. Well, sure."

"And I wondered if we could have a photo."

"Sure," he says again, "let's go outside."

What I mean by this is a photo of us shaking hands or chatting affably as if at a drinks party or something. But once outside, Miller immediately backs up against the wall in the sunshine and poses smiling for me to take a picture of him, so I do, and thank him.

"Sure." He pauses. Rebecca's with him, smiling at me. He looks at her. "I fancy a walk," he says. There's another pause, then he looks at me. "You want to walk with us?"

"No, thanks all the same, that's okay. *No.*"

No.

The word is out before I can stop myself. Miller

seems surprised and Rebecca, I like to think, mildly disappointed. I feel sick.

No.

"I've got things to do," I say. *Things to do!* I'm thinking. *I've got nothing to do all summer except write my bus book, and I get a chance to walk with Arthur Miller and the beautiful Rebecca and I say, No!*

"Suit yourself," shrugs the counterpart of Tennessee Williams and Eugene O'Neill, author of *Death of a Salesman*, *The Crucible*, and *After the Fall*, former husband of Marilyn Monroe, friend, contemporary, or acquaintance of Clark Gable, Elia Kazan, Lee J. Cobb, Laurence Olivier, John Huston, Montgomery Clift, Dustin Hoffman, Saul Bellow, John Steinbeck, Paul Newman, and whoever else. "Suit yourself." He even sounds mildly offended.

We look at each other. He's quite a bit taller than I am, remarkably straight-backed for seventy-four. He's smiling. He's welcoming. Rebecca's beside him, watching me with those stunning blue eyes.

"So," I say hoarsely, "I'll be going. You must be busy."

"Not really," he says. "I'm off to England tomorrow for a few weeks." The full horror of what I've done won't register for another hour or so, but I'm beginning to realize the extent of my decision. By the time he's back, I'll be gone. "Will you still be here?" he asks.

"Home in England, I'm afraid."

"That's too bad. So long, then." He shakes my hand. Rebecca smiles at me. I nod at her feeling, absurdly, like Darcy in *Pride and Prejudice*.

"See you," I say, very un-Darcylike. *See you!*

With total dismay at my own mouth's betrayal of me, I walk numbly to the car, and drive slowly back down the country lanes toward Rucum Road. In a daze, I wander into the cottage, climb the stairs, sit at my desk, and begin my self-immolation. What I had to get back for I have no idea. Why I've said No, I've even less idea. Maybe he was just being polite, I reason. *That's* why I refused. Maybe he just wanted to be with Rebecca. *That's* it. But all the time I'm groaning as I slice open my guts, and pull them from my belly to place them on the desk and study them.

"You idiot," they bubble and spit at me, "you complete imbecile. You've spent all these years traveling and imagining—living your pathetic fantasies—and you get this kind of opportunity and what do you do, turtle brain? You fuck up. You say, *No*."

"Arthur Miller is just a man like other men."

But my guts have had enough of me. They twist and pull, and finally sever from my belly. I'm almost entirely hollow, and nauseous from the stink.

"America's greatest twentieth-century playwright asks if you want to go for a walk and you say, No. You asshole!"

"Yes, but it's done."

"Done! You complete and utter prick. Try again!"

So I gather my guts together in a hot, slippery armful, stuff them back in my belly, do up my shirt tightly in the hope they won't fall out and cause further embarrassment, run out of the cottage and drive back to Miller's house. I'm like a man in love. I've no idea what I'll actually do, other than go up to him and Rebecca and say, puffing and panting, "Sorry, I made a mistake. Actually, yes, I would like to go for a walk with you." But it hardly matters. When I open the French doors only his old mother is there, looking more bemused than ever.

"Hello Mr Styron," she says. "Arthur's gone for a walk."

I've missed them. I drive home.

And continue, for days, to torture myself. What would we have talked about? Who knows now. It's history. I realize, given the way the bus book's shaping up, that I can always exaggerate, invent, even lie. But my goal has been to move from the imaginary to the real, and rejecting such a prolonged encounter has screwed up the whole plan.

That night I have appalling dreams that are virtually exact replicas of those dreamt by Stingo at the end of *Sophie's Choice*, "a compendium of all the tales of Edgar Allan Poe: myself being split in twain by monstrous mechanisms, drowned in a whirling vortex of mud, being immured in stone and, most fearsomely, buried alive." Half the night I'm smitten by "the sensation of helplessness, speechlessness, an inability to move or cry out against the inexorable weight of earth" as it's "flung in *thud-thud-thud*ing rhythm against my rigidly paralyzed, supine body, a living cadaver being prepared for burial in the sands of Egypt." The rest of the night, I'm walking dumbly with one playwright after another through a maze. First I'm with Chekhov, then Chekhov disappears and Strindberg takes his place, succeeded in turn by Beckett, Ibsen, Aeschylus, Aristophanes, Marlowe, Webster, Tourner, Sheridan, O'Neill, Tennessee Williams, even David Mamet takes a hedge-turn with me. I'm reaching the center of the maze. "You really ought to start talking," says Wycherley, as we pass a statue of Arthur Miller with *Arthur Miller Centre* written on the plinth, "because unlike Arthur there, we're not statues, we're not representations, we're the real thing, and we're ready to chat." We turn a corner and there, on a white bench in a large, central garden, sits Shakespeare, an Olivetti on his tighted knee.

"Won't keep you a moment," he says, "I'm just completing *The Dream*."

"Oh shit," I say before I can stop myself. "You mean it's a *dream?*"

And of course I wake up.

And lie there in the dark, and think. I *could* invent. I could turn the Miller episode into a shaggy dog story, or a tall tale. After all, isn't half my life—and half these travels—fantasy anyway? Isn't America a trip of the imagination? And would I really have much to ask him? And what did I expect to happen? Would he have left Rebecca and I alone to wander through his thousand acres, suddenly realizing that we were made for each other, and. *And nothing.* I'm thirty years old, not twenty-two like Stingo, or nineteen as I was when I first came out. It's time (I scold myself) to realize I should be *living* my life, not dreaming of another one. It's time to accept who and what I am, and to understand that I'll never be the husband of Rebecca Miller, any more than I'll marry Marilyn Monroe.

But why limit yourself? says the snide little voice of self-torture, or else my personal motivator. *Are you going to give up? Suppose Miller's flight's delayed?*

So I do phone again, two or so weeks later. Not out of unfounded optimism, but because I hear through the grapevine that Miller's back from England earlier than expected. It's Tuesday, June 12, 1990. I take three deep breaths, one for luck, one for courage, and one for the hell of it, and phone.

"Hi," says a voice on the line.

"Hello?" I say. *Courage, courage!* "Arthur!"

"Who's this?" he says.

"You remember the Englishman who called to have you sign *Timebends*?"

"The guy who didn't want to go for a walk with me?"

"Yes."

"I never could figure that out."

"Well, anyway, I have more books. Could I come up and get you to sign them?"

"If you think you've got the time. Drive on up."

By now the Styrons have the Mercedes on the Cape, but I don't want to tell Miller I have no car. "I'm going to jog," I tell him. "Daily exercise." I haven't jogged in years.

"Jeeps. It's quite a ways. It's maybe four miles."

"No sweat."

In fact, when I finally turn up at Miller's handsome, hilltop home in running shorts and a Nebraska T-shirt, after jogging the hilly, dappled roads with a *New York Times* plastic bag holding three plays, another copy of his memoirs, and a tape-recorder, I'm sweating like Walter Matthau in *The Odd Couple*. It's 4.30, but still hot and sunny. Miller seems as bemused as his mother did when I came back looking for him The Day I Said No To A Walk.

I can barely speak. "Drink?" I gasp. "Please?"

"Sure," he says. "Come on in." His kitchen is fairly small with a central table, and crowds of pans and utensils around the walls. He runs the kitchen tap and hands me a glass of water. "Help yourself," he says. "Plenty more where that came from. Let's go on the deck."

We sit down and talk for an hour. Really, I want to talk about meeting Marilyn Monroe in Michigan seventeen years after her supposed death, but I have to work up to it.

"So," I stall, "tell me about writing plays. Do you say the words aloud when writing?"

"I used to," says Miller. "I don't now, but it's a good idea."

"Have you any thoughts about the phenomenon of time, and memory?"

"Theatre time is different to novel time," he replies. "It's more condensed."

"But *Death of a Salesman* has a kind of novelistic time," I suggest. "Willy lives half in his memory, which is also a fictional re-imagining."

"Even so," says Miller, narrowing his eyes as if he suspects I'm getting at something, "it's finally caught in theatre-time. Theatre dialogue, too, is different to novel dialogue."

"Could you have written your plays as novels?"

"You can turn a play into a novel," he says sententiously, "but not a novel into a play. *Sophie's Choice* is an example of how film is a bastardized cross between a play and a novel."

"You think film are a bastardized genre?"

"Well, it's much newer, of course. It's evolving."

"And novels and plays are not?"

"I don't believe in the Death of the Novel. But maybe it doesn't have quite the impact it once had. It's no longer a primary source of important information, not the way it used to be."

We sit quietly for a moment, gazing out over the woodland Miller himself planted. I think of the walk we never had and how maybe it would have led to more, or maybe I'd have been left with no excuse to call again. My current addiction to encountering famous, successful people, I realize, is akin to the intoxication of love, or at least infatuation, which explains my interest in Rebecca, whom I've met for just under two minutes, and never expect to meet again.

"Rebecca not here?" I say without much hope.

"She's in New York."

Then through the archway comes a short-haired woman. I stand to greet her.

"This is some English guy who's jogged to see me," says Miller from his chair.

"Hi," she says, "I'm Inge. Do sit down." I sit and she looks at us facing each other across a low table, then says, "Arthur!"

"What, dear?"

"Arthur! Really! Have you got the poor boy a drink?"

Miller's beady eyes plead with me through his spectacles. "I got you a drink, didn't I?"

"Sure."

Inge looks at me aslant. "What did he get you?"

"Water," I explain. "It's very good."

"Arthur!" she turns back to her husband. "*Water?*"

She tuts and turns to me. "I'll get you some cider."

She brings out two glasses of non-alcoholic cider, and a large bowl of pistachio nuts and goes back indoors. Miller looks at me, then at the pistachios, then back at me, and pushes the pistachios toward me. I take three before he pulls them back to himself.

"I've read *Death of a Salesman* and *The Crucible*," I tell him. "*Death of a Salesman* had quite an impact on me, and it's sort of stayed because I'm getting nearer and nearer to the ages of Biff and Happy."

Miller laughs. "And I'm way past Willy, and heading for Uncle Ben territory."

"He's in Willy's imagination, of course. Do you think we fictionalize the past?"

"Sure."

"But is *Salesman* in any sense autobiographical?"

"No," he says, finishing the pistachios with some voracity. "But it's personal."

"Linda tells Biff he's such a child because he doesn't realize that he can't keep going away and coming back to expect his parents to be there. One day he'll knock and there'll be strangers at the door."

"That's very true. You can't go home again, or anyway not forever. *I years have been from home / And now before the door / I dared not open, lest a face / I never saw before.*"

I suddenly feel lightheaded. Am I *really* sitting here while Arthur Miller quotes Emily Dickinson at me? An image flashes before me of sitting with Dickinson quoting from *Death of a Salesman. Steady*, I tell myself, *steady*. "Did you know the play would touch a vein?"

. "You can't predict things like that."

Miller's a little distracted. He's looking round peevishly, as if he must have missed a pistachio somewhere. He's even peering into the empty shells.

"You talk about it in the autobiography. Why did you write *Timebends*?" He's not listening. "There's one on the floor, just there."

"I see it." He bends down and reaches under the table and holds up one final pistachio, hidden away in a half-shell. He's beaming like an eight-year-old. "Why did I write *Timebends*? So many people have come to me asking if they can do a biography that I thought, Jesus, I'd better—"

"Tell the facts?"

"Well, tell my version." He gets interested again. "I got a letter the other day about Native American mythology. It was about ghosts, and time as continuous. Fascinating stuff."

"Does it make any sense?"

"I think so. We can't quite believe the past isn't out there somewhere. We know it's in us, but you tell someone the past doesn't exist beyond us and if they agree it will probably only be in an intellectual sense. Emotionally, we believe the past's still out there."

"There's no such thing as *was*, said William Faulkner. You could take that either way. Everything's in the present, meaning there *is* no past, or the past is still somehow here."

"Exactly. Time is continuous, say ancient myths. Time is continuous, says Faulkner."

"Is it painful to talk about Marilyn Monroe?"

"It depends what you ask."

"I wish I'd met her. But the past *has* passed, hasn't

it? There's no going back. Time *can't*—when we get down to specifics—be continuous. Yet images remain."

"Hell, what do *I* know? But there's a tremendous psychological hunger in people, and in our culture generally, and in an age of mass media, we attach that hunger to the stars." He smiles. "By which I don't mean some cluster in the Tarantula Nebula."

Inge returns with more cider. "You two seem to have a lot to talk about."

"Any more pistachios?" says Miller.

"All gone," says Inge, disappearing again.

Miller sips his cider. "I got another letter that was from New York school kids about *The Crucible*. They were complaining about the ending. There's a great demand for justice. You should have let her die, they said, not Proctor."

"What do you think of contemporary American writing?"

"Maybe I'm just getting old," he sighs, "but what seems to be missing in a lot of contemporary fiction is a sense of history. Faulkner, Dreiser, they all had a sense of carving out an expression of their own time as part of a continuum. I don't see that today, except in writers like Styron or Doctorow. My problem with contemporary American fiction—and I don't read a lot of it—is that it lacks history. In other times, writers, whether you go back to Faulkner, or Dreiser or to Cooper or Hawthorne or Melville or Twain, tried to distill their times in history. You don't have that anymore. And if you do, it's only in a writer like Styron. I don't understand why he's ignored in Britain. He writes more in an English tradition of eloquence. Maybe I'm getting old, but with a handful of exceptions, the novel no longer conveys important information."

"Do you watch much television?"

He laughs. "Y'ever watch our newsreaders? I know what they're thinking. I see it through their glazed eyes. They're thinking, I'm talking to Oregon, New Mexico, Canada—I'm talking to hundreds of millions of people. In England it's cosier. As for the entertainment side, the only reason they do it is to make money. By the way." He leans forward. "They're showing my adaptation of Ibsen's *Enemy of the People* tonight at nine."

"What do you think of academia?"

He laughs again. "It's about making a career out of jealousy. I remember an English academic friend lecturing an audience on the history of American Literature. He was eloquence itself but it made no sense to me whatsoever. To understand it, you had to be hip to that jive. But what do *I* know. Maybe I'm just getting old. You think I'm getting old?" I mean it when I say no; Miller hardly seems old. But time—continuous or otherwise—has passed swiftly. The sun's begun to set and I begin to make a move. We've been talking a couple of hours or more. "I'll drive you home," says Miller. We start down the road. "Where are you going after Roxbury?"

"I once thought I'd head for Alaska like Uncle Ben. But it's New York and home."

"You like New York?"

"I've yet to be mugged."

"New York's always been a hard, violent place. I remember people stepping over bums fifty years ago. I was walking down Broadway the other day, and there was this black guy and a big white guy and a large white girl, and the black guy was smacking the white guy in the face, and the white guy was ignoring it, and the girl, who looked moronic, was watching it too. The guy kept punching him, the girl kept watching, and no one else took any notice. That, for me, was typical New York."

As we near Styron's house, I remember the tape-recorder. During the conversation on the porch I didn't want to spoil the casual conversation, but while we're talking of the scene in *Salesman* where Willy's conversation with his boss is interrupted by the boss's new recorder, I can't resist clicking the On button inside the plastic bag that carries the books. Miller drops me at the gate and I race up to my study and scribble down everything I can remember. Even as I do so, I realize I'm on the right track. It's time to get a grip, and to write, seriously now, a book myself, a *proper* book; a book about life. I begin to honestly believe I can do it, must do it, will do it. The whole logic of my travels, I see, has pushed me to this.

Postscript: some years after this I learned that Rebecca had married Daniel Day-Lewis in Vermont. I didn't get an invitation. I cannot help but not bother to wonder what might have happened had I agreed to the walk. It's after I tell him this story, and about Rebecca, that Darius rightly says, "That's not the real world up there. It's where the Styrons and Roths and Hoffmans and Millers of this world live."

Not the real world: no, of course not. But it felt real enough. I've lived vicariously with the stars, and perhaps I'm the lucky one. "As an artist I began by admiring others," wrote Albert Camus, "which in a way is Heaven on Earth." Which is real happiness: to be an old man sitting there impressing a starry-eyed younger man, or a younger man, sitting with a hero, and a whole life ahead of him? The one who's got there, and seen and been all that he wants to be, and lost a great deal on the way, or the one who's still early in his journey?

"You taped it?" asks Darius, a long-time admirer of Miller.

"Yes and no. I taped maybe thirty seconds at the end, through a plastic bag. I'm now the proud possessor of a muffled conversation on the last half-mile recorded for posterity."

"How much of it is intelligible?"

"Not one word."

17

DOUGLAS AND DONEHOGAWA

When I finally get back on a Greyhound, it's the 2121 Cleveland-bound bus from Columbus, Ohio, five years later, in 1995. Where once to fly was a luxury, now a bus ride is a luxury because I've much less time. I've flown in from Baltimore and am taking the bus to Brockport to visit friends and maybe to get in touch with Enid Stevick. The real point, however, is to return to Busland and see how it's changed. It's mid-March but there's a cold snap. I'm spending a day at Ohio State University. The part of campus I'm on is like a chemical plant. Snowflakes fall through the bitter air beyond Professor Kelvin Kestler's office window, and settle on the bleak, gray buildings. Professor Kestler is droopy-eyed, maybe forty, and resembles Kevin Costner, in features, voice and name. He's sipping hazelnut coffee from a BUCKEYE mug.

"How can I help you?"
"I'm doing a little research."
"What's your subject?"
"America."
"Big subject."
"Can you tell me anything about the Greyhound?"
"You're thinking of taking a *bus?* You don't know what you're doing."
"I just thought I'd try it. Cultural experience."

"Cultural experience, my ass!" He sips his coffee. "To tell you the truth, I've never given it a thought since I was a student. You ride the dog because you're dirt poor, haven't got a car, can't fly, whatever. You don't take the bus because you *want* to. It's a doggone easy way to get you down."

"Bus travel's for the poor?"

"Well—," he swings back on his leather chair and looks through the window. Snow blankets the campus below and the room itself is snow-bright. "Far be it for me to sound politically incorrect, but you've got to understand that in America nobody who is anybody—whose got *any* decent income—takes the bus."

"Not even students?"

"They might, but since the strike even that's less likely. It was okay maybe ten, twenty years ago and I'm no expert. But from what I hear it's not even what it used to be. It's all collapsed. Services cut all over. You've never taken one before?"

"Maybe a couple of times."

"When was the last?"

"Seven years ago."

"You'll see a difference."

I get up and thank him for his time.

"That's all you need to know? You don't want to talk about Toni Morrison, our famous daughter from Lorain, or James Thurber? He lived right here in Columbus. We have bits of his wall in our special collection."

"His wall?"

"He drew cartoons all over it. The people who moved in were going to paint over them, so we took the plaster. It's in the library."

"Anything else I should see in Columbus?"

"Downtown there's a scale replica of the *Santa Maria*."

"Maybe I'll catch it from the bus. Thanks for your views, anyway."

"No problem." He stands and we shake hands. "Come visit us again." As I walk out he calls in that voice he shares with Costner. "Those bus terminals are full of desperate people! You *really* don't want to take the bus." But the die is cast. I'm going back to Busland. I'll dance with the wolves.

Six a.m. the next day, I'm at the Columbus depot thinking maybe Professor Kestler is right. An icy gale howls through the doorway as passengers shuffle forward to board a bus for St. Louis. The signs have letters missing. The floor is stained and strewn with receipts. Trash spatters the tables of the Burger King. People stand around like Segal sculptures, string-tied bags for baggage. They're mostly black though, beneath a radiator crowded with empty beer and whisky bottles, three white drunks slump like executed bodies. In fact the depot's sheltered them from a night cold enough to kill. I climb aboard Bus 2121 and we explode into life.

"Come on, driver," shouts someone from the rear seats. "Where's your heat?"

We roll out past the streetlamps and over the Ohio River. I put on my personal CD. Joan Armatrading's singing "All the Way from America." The sky's lightening to reveal rolling, yellow-brown hills and leafless trees. Soon I feel happy as a baby in a womb. The driver's a short, silver haired lady. It's the first time I've seen a female driver.

"Let's roll this dog," she says as we hit the freeway.

Next to me a bespectacled black girl reads a leather-bound Bible. I read with her out of the corner of my eyes. We're on I Chronicles 16-17. She's underlined 16:10, 16:20, 16:22. It's all about David and Nathan the prophet. David's reciting the first psalm over the Ark of the Covenant, citing the promises of God to Abraham, Isaac and Jacob. *Glory ye in his holy name*, she's underlined, *let the heart of them rejoice that seek the LORD*, as well as *when they went from nation to nation, and from one kingdom to another people.* She turns the page and I read another underlined section, 17:9-10, beginning *Also I will ordain a place for my people Israel, and will plant them, and they shall dwell in their place, and shall be moved no more.*

She props her coat on the window ledge, closes her Bible and her eyes. Armatrading fades out and on comes Chris Rea, singing of the dubious skill of "hiding" rather than "confiding" what one feels. US 71 unravels northward and I, too, close my eyes. This girl doesn't seem desperate at all. She's got her Lord the living God to comfort her. She's got her warm coat and her ticket to ride. I remember a driver saying once that bus people were running to or from somewhere. I'm not running anywhere any more. In spiritual terms I remain a vagrant, but once on the bus I've felt my soul spread out again after five years cooped up in England. You can go all dreamy on a bus but somehow you're more able to watch and listen than in day-to-day life. The wide highway from Columbus to Cleveland curves through farmland. Winter's brown grass is turning green between the patches of snow. Billboards intersperse red clapboard barns, farmhouses, silos gleaming silver. Meanwhile Chris Rea's singing "Gone Fishin'" about spending a life doing what you think you ought to and never being free. I think of a note found on the underside of Melville's desk after he died: "Stay true to the dreams of your youth." The girl has her Bible. I have music: whatever gets you through the ride. May as well sit on a bus, free from the frenzy to make something of the day. Hemingway wrote of the depression he felt at the end of each day wasted. But even that can be a trap. You define your sense of waste. I'm reading Joyce Carol Oates's *What I Lived For* because I've decided to write about her novels.

What I lived for. What indeed.

The gray freeway threads either side of a shallow dike. We cross numerous rivers. Cars and trucks flash by. The white license plates have pale blue writing and "the heart of it all" scrawled in red beneath Ohio. Rea sings of turning wheels and dusty tracks and the joy of driving to a place that's still far off. Or is it? I suspect I won't need the bus much longer. The trips are already few and far between. In Brockport, I'll hire a car, then fly to New York.

The girl sleeps. Her Bible slides off her lap. I prop it next to her. Her open hand reveals a cream palm with brown creases. Bus windows used to be green, now they're just tinted. Sometimes they started dark green at the top, and paled to the bottom. Once there was an upside down window. It started pale and became dark by the bottom. I sat by it: my kind of window. On sings Rea of living for the present, between the signs and bridges on our way to a still far-off destination.

A loud voice rouses me. The black girl sits up. Her Bible falls to the floor. I take off my headphones and pick it up for her. She thanks me, but doesn't smile.

"Ah, my two baby boys," a black lady across the aisle's saying, "one is a construction worker, the other works for the FBI, so we pretty proud right now."

"You has a *right* to be proud," says the old, black man in the window seat.

"My daughter, I don't want to snatch her from school. But we gonna haul out and move to Charlotte. I don't want her getting into trouble." We pass signs for Lodi and Chippewa Lake. "My father," she says, "he came to me at school but *one* time. That was enough. I got the message. Those kids really think they hurt somebody, but they ain't hurting no one but theyselves. My mother, she been dead thirty years. My father's mother, she raised me and my sister. I just has to take this trip up here to see my daughter face to face. She wanna join the Marines. I told her the fifteenth but I'm here *today*."

They chuckle at her cunning. "Oh man," he says, "you gonna really catch her."

"She phoned home last night and said, What y'all doin'? I said, Nothin', but I was *packin'*, ready to come." We pass a Big Western, a Suburbanite Motel, a Sunoco gas station. The white guy in front has a green jacket with MSU in white. He has swept back hair and a thick moustache. The lady starts up again. "I worked ten year in the operating room of the City Hospital but my sister got cancer and I never went back, jis went from job to job. I shoulda gone back. But they layin' off real bad now, and hirin' people back at a lower rate."

"Now *me*," says her companion. "I am what I am and what I am is what I is. But it's not what I was." He chuckles, a syrupy, deep-down, not-very-desperate-sounding chuckle. "I got laid off in eighty-one." He's pulling at each finger in turn. "Laid off in eighty-three, laid off in eighty-six *twice*. Every time you go to a new plant, you go as a new person. Experience don't get you more pay. 1988 I don't think I worked at *all*."

Disciple of Studs Terkel that I am, I'm scrawling all this down. The black girl's looking at it. I doubt it's readable. All that time I rode the bus in the eighties, this old guy was doggedly trudging from dead-end job to dead-end job, a cog in a wheel of a bigger wheel that was part of a vast production machine that didn't really need him.

"I'm tired of ridin' the Dog," laughs the lady. "It stops in every turn."

"Every little place."

"Every little *hole*, man. I'm tellin' you." They both laugh, the man with his deep, rich, guttural cackle, the lady rocking, wiping tears from her cheeks. I want to join in, tell them who I am and where I'm from. But I'm invisible, outside their lives and have that familiar feeling that all this is no more than a film, and I'm just here to record the script they improvise.

"And as soon as you git to sleep," she says, "he pops them lights on and says, Hello! Last night was a *trip*, man." We pass the Ford factory on the outskirts of Cleveland. She points out of the window. "There's the Metro. The hospital. It's beautiful. I worked there ten years, through to eighty-nine. Got my lungs too busted up with those helicopter fumes. I worked in the trauma unit. It's a nice hospital."

We come to Jacob's Field, the Cleveland Indians' new stadium, except there's a strike.

"Sure is a nice stadium," says the old guy.

"Too bad ain't nobody to *play* in it!"

People all over the bus chuckle. Maybe everyone's been listening to this dialogue. The guy in the green jacket leans over. "They played one or *two* games, at the end of last season."

"At the start," says the black guy. "There *ain't* no *end!*" They all laugh. "Hard to tell which is end and which is beginning nowadays, since they lops bits off!"

The whole bus seems to be joining in, making jokes about the baseball strike. All except me, since I know little about it, and the girl next to me. She's opened her Bible again. Maybe she's naturally shy, or doesn't care about baseball.

Even the lady driver throws in a line. "To your left going back behind us now is the famous Jacob's Field baseball stadium," she says over the PA. "Word is they gonna take it down and rebuild it in Japan or Cuba or some place they play baseball."

The bus judders over a bridge as if rocking to the laughter. At last, I think, I'm out of the sterile world of airports and campuses. And I see more than ever that the bus *is* the journey. No bus, no America. Sever it and you sever vital arteries because you don't see America when you fly. You don't hear it. Not the stuff on the ground, the roads between depots, the people of the bus, and therefore of the ghettos and tenements, and the open road, thrown together on their journeys somewhere, to visit, help, rescue, reprimand, or just to get away. I'm back in love with America, and life.

Sunshine floods through the glass-roofed Cleveland terminal, sparkling on the chrome of a counter where I'm eating breakfast. I buy a toy Greyhound Bus in the gift shop for some child I may one day have, then switch to bus 1964 for Rochester, and pile up my bags so I can lean in comfort and watch the view. I'm ready for the final leg, tracking Lake Erie up US 90 through Erie to Buffalo and across to Rochester for a local bus back to Brockport.

Ahead this time is a youth stroking the long mane of his Mohican haircut. He's wearing a bead necklace, shades and a PROUD TO BE AN IROQUOIS T-shirt. He's as young as I was last time I came to upstate New York. *The Iroquois Struggle For Survival* nestles on his forearms, and he has a bag of other books including one on American Indian Lacrosse. Over the aisle a Hispanic couple cuddle. The girl has a violin case on her lap. The guy has a munched left ear with great lumps above and below it, gruesome scars where it's been torn during football or boxing. Ahead of the Iroquois an older black man in a straw hat taps a silver cane and looks out of the window through shades like a bluebottle's eyes. His thin shoulders convulse as he quells his frequent cough. Each time he coughs, the Iroquois looks up from his book.

It's been sunny the whole trip, but two hundred miles north of Columbus the patches of snow are larger, joining up the landscape between icy fields and rivers. Our "operator" hasn't put up his name. For years I've sat in this mobile environment and hardly glanced at the signs. Now, sensing I'm nearer the end of my bus days than their beginning, I record them, including the change to a No Smoking policy. They resemble a poem.

> For passenger safety,
> Federal law prohibits
> operation of this bus
> while anyone is standing
> forward of the white line.
>
> This coach is
> restroom equipped
> for your convenience
>
> NO SMOKING By order of the ICC.
>
> Drinking intoxicants
> on the coach prohibited

I feel my old exhilaration. Dion's "The Wanderer" comes on my personal CD, and then Johnny Tillotson's "Poetry in Motion." We pass Lake Erie white with ice.

"You should get something for that cough," I hear the Iroquois saying above my headphones. He's talking to the old bluebottle fellow but still reading his book. "I said you've got quite a cough there."

The bluebottle's staring back at the Iroquois as if he's a festering slab of meat. "Number one, you're born," he barks. "Number two you go to school. Number three you go to college. Number four you go to jail. Number five you retire. Number six you die." The Iroquois looks up from his book. "Yes, Injun Joe. I'm talkin' to you."

"My name's Donehogawa."

"Douglas," nods Douglas. "So what do you do, Doneho*gawa?*"

"Go to college," says Donehogawa languidly.

"When you gonna work?"

"I got a job pays tuition."

"You ain't *never* gonna work."

"I will."

"I thought that too. How much they pay you?"

"Twenty-five an hour."

"Twenty-five an *hour?* What you learnin'?"

"American Native languages. I speak Iroquoian and I'm learning Chippewe in Minnesota. We don't want it to die out."

"I seen *Dances with Wolves.*"

"That's Lakota. It's died out. There's no native speakers."

"*All* Indian language is dead."

"There are two hundred living Native languages."

"It's *dead.*"

"No it's not. I'm Native American. I speak it."

"*I'm* Native American," says Douglas, pushing up the brim of his straw hat. With the light on his bluebottle shades, I can see Donehogawa in them. "I's *born* here!" They both look out of the window. A funnel of white smoke plumes on the horizon. "Your language is gibberish," presses Douglas. "*You're* speaking gibberish."

Donehogawa speaks calmly and quietly. "I don't want my culture to die out."

"*Every*thin' dies, man. People, trees, languages. Everything. You know what you should do? Speak *English*, the King's English."

"When a language dies out it's genocide."

"No it ain't."

"I don't want to see anything of my people die out."

"Well, you *gonna* see it."

"My parents are assimilating."

"Assimilate and you annihilate."

"I feel sorry for you."

"Don't feel sorry for me."

"I hope you see the light. You should have gone to college."

"College?" snorts Douglas, sweeping off his bluebottle shades to reveal yellowed eyes. "I bin to college. I bin to NYU. I bin to Columbia, to Brown, to Stanford. I bin to most all of 'em one time or another. I studied *five* places. More'n you'll ever see in your life."

"I hope you see the light."

"I see it."

"No. You just see the one thing." Like a flash storm, the argument abates as fast as it started. Donehogawa himself puts on shades and headphones. Douglas returns his bluebottle shades to the bridge of his nose, turns round in his seat, pulls the brim of his straw hat down, and starts fussing with his bag on the seat next to him. "You want a book to read?" says Donehogawa.

"I read every book ever existed," states Douglas without looking round. And there they sit, a young Native American and an old black guy, both in shades, the one with his headphones, the other with his straw hat, nothing more to say. Only Douglas's quelled coughs break the silence. We're passing Brockport and, though I'll have to double back westward from Rochester, I'm almost there. I follow Douglas off the bus, gather my baggage from the hold and enter the depot to see I've an hour or more to wait for the Brockport bus.

Douglas, slumps down into one of those black plastic seats with a TV attached, and peers at me over his shades. "Where're you heading?"

"I'm trying to get home."

He humphs. "We's all doin' *that!*"

And this, I want to tell Professor Kestler, or maybe myself, is why I've been riding the Dog for so many years. Like Burt Lancaster in *The Swimmer*, based on a John Cheever story about a man who decides to swim home by way of different friends' pools, I'm trying to get back somewhere. Never getting "there," perhaps, but getting *somewhere*, or somewhere else.

18

JOYCE CAROL GHOST

Eddie Cochran and Joyce Carol Oates were both born in America in 1938, and there the similarities would seem to end: a man and a woman, one brought up in Lockport, New York, the other in Los Angeles. One died in 1960, the other took after Sylvia Plath, in 1959, by winning the *Mademoiselle* college fiction award. But unlike Cochran or Plath, Oates has survived. The year after Cochran's death, she found one of her stories cited in the Honor Roll of Martha Foley's annual *Best American Short Stories* and decided to become a writer. The year of Plath's death, 1963, Oates published her first book, *By the North Gate*. By the time she accepts my invitation to lunch, in July 1998, she's a professor at Princeton and the author of twenty-seven novels under her own name, six under a pseudonym, twenty-two collections of short stories, four novellas, eight collections of poetry, eight collections of essays, and dozens of plays. She suffers from tachycardia and, unlike Mary-Ann Steiner outside the infamous Stroudsburg Laundromat so many years ago now, she's always taken seriously Robert Herrick's advice to gather ye rosebuds while ye may.

    Why she should bother to have lunch with me I've no idea, but my reasons are clear. As a chronicler of post-war American culture, she seems to play some small part in the American pantomime, and I think she must know a thing or two about the pursuit of happiness. It's nearly the third millennium and I'm close to the end of my thirties. Eddie Cochran, that twenty-one-year-old whose death ushered in my birth, would have been, like Oates, all but sixty. I've decided this visit to the States will mark the symbolic end of anything I can remotely imagine as my "younger days." Moreover, I'm aware that Oates is currently writing a novel about Marilyn Monroe, so hope to find out whether or not she's had an encounter with Monroe similar to mine in Michigan at the start of my travels.

"Rhapsody in Blue" is on my personal CD for the bus ride from JFK into Manhattan. We crash over metal sheets on the road like the clash of cymbals and trumpet our way past signs for Junk Cars Wanted, Tire Shop, Flat Fix. No Shoulder, says a brilliant red diamond sign before the Triboro Bridge. Harry Van Arsdale Jr. Avenue runs off to the right, and now Gershwin's trumpets blare like traffic horns, and his drums rumble like the clatter of vehicles over the bridge. In Queens, there's sudden greenery, water and yachts through willows. Planes take off into the sunshine from La Guardia. Soon we're past Flushing Meadows and the bright blue of Shea Stadium. The music slows as we turn down a side street, bounce past an Amoco filling station, and signs for Jamaica and Hillside Avenues, with still no sight of the glorious chords of Manhattan. When we slow up behind a dusty Dodge Ram van, the cabbie wipes his face and neck with a grimy handkerchief. Then we're off and Gershwin's jaunty again with the promise of Manhattan ahead until, after some piano-tickling, bam! Manhattan's a thunder chord. We flash through the great canyons to

West End Avenue. Suddenly I'm in a playground with Darius and his wife, Juliet, whom he married two years ago, and their little boy, Daniel. The Desoutters live in that same, spacious three-bedroom Upper West Side apartment Darius bought a while ago, but he's high up the lawyer's ladder so they can also afford a colonial reproduction getaway home in the Hudson River Valley. No one's called him "Redeye" in years.

The day of the lunch is a Friday so Darius is dressed casually. I, on the other hand, put on a blazer and tie like every other man in my imaginary Princeton.

"You *definitely* don't want a tie," he says, "you don't even want a blazer." He's right. I get off the subway at Seventh and Broadway dripping. "Got your wallet safe?" he says. "This is a notorious pickpocket area."

But turn-of-the-millennium New York is not the New York of 1979 when you hardly dared set foot in Central Park and where Port Authority was a cesspool. It's all cleaned up. The once rotten core of the Big Apple has been genetically modified back to freshness. Times Square boasts not just Darius's firm but a Disney Store, Good Morning America and MTV studios.

We take the elevator away from the shirt-prickling, sweaty-neck streets and shoot upward to the icy brightness of Darius's air-conditioned attorney's office. The thick, tinted windows look out one way on the Coca-Cola neon sign and the other way on the back of a billboard. Dozens of yellow cabs funnel silently down Broadway and Seventh like toys between books on a playroom floor. New York this July is a city of two temperatures, the cool of the enclosed and the heat of the streets.

If I'm Ever Back This Way

Soon I'm at Penn Station drinking almond coffee on the 9.32 New Jersey Transit to Princeton Junction. The train pulls out and we move through darkness into light. I'm nervous but ready. I've got my Gant shirt on with its little USA logo and my blue blazer and cream slacks. My shoulder bag is crammed with hardback Oates novels. Dictaphone jammed in my top pocket, I'm smart, clean, organized, and heading for the supposed paradise of Princeton, one-time hangout of F. Scott Fitzgerald and Albert Einstein.

We pass truck-sites for K-Mart and Consolidated Freightways. Half the trucks of America seem to be parked along this stretch of track. A bridge disappears in the haze over a swampy river and uninhabitable scrubland. *I once dreamed I went to Princeton for lunch with Joyce Carol Oates. But that was long ago.* As it will be! As it is! But how happy you can feel on the way to a special rendezvous. A routine day for Joyce Carol Oates will be a special day for the not-so-young man meeting her. Twelve years have passed since my, for me, momentous first meeting with William Styron. Over twenty years have passed since Dimmerstamm met me off the plane in Muskegon and asked how I liked America, and Carlotta Domarski asked about my experience of American girls. Nineteen years ago this summer I smoked cigars with Pickawillany. I still write letters to Carlotta, but they might as well be blasted into outer space with the remains of Timothy Leary.

"There's nothing out there," Styron told me once, "Some people are appalled that we're a little freak of a planet, marooned in the middle of nowhere. But it appeals to my sense of life. Unless our intuitions are totally haywire, we know that the Earth is going to be turned into a cinder. We're on our own, and since we're alive we have to do what we can."

Meanwhile, scientists keep probing both inner and outer space. It's only fairly recently that researchers at San Francisco State found clear evidence of another solar system when they detected three huge planets spinning round *Upsilon Andromedae*, forty-four light years from Earth among the two hundred billion stars of our Milky Way. Since then they've found dozens more around different stars. But no one knows if there's life out there, and astrobiologists like Peter Ward and Donald Brownlee in *Rare Earth* claim to confirm our lonely plight. As for all my teenage love-angst, neuroscientists now say love or its antidote could soon be bottled. It was all just chemical overload after all, for me as for everyone else. So much for romance: Ben Hecht was right after all. Only love can believe in love. Presumably only life can believe in life. "Everyone feels they're above New York," said Darius this morning, "but we're all part of it." I assume that includes me, though I've never felt a part of anything much. So much for Whitman's notion of "the floodtide below me." We *are* the floodtide.

The man next to me has brown hair graying on short sideburns, heavy spectacles, hair flopping across his furrowed brow. He says he's Lewis Thomas, a biologist. "It's an illusion to think that there is anything fragile about the life of the Earth," he tells me. "Surely this is the toughest membrane imaginable in the universe, opaque to probability, impermeable to death. We are the delicate part, transient and vulnerable as cilia."

"What is one person among so many people?" I

ask him, adapting some lines from Wallace Stevens. "What are so many people in such a world? Can one person think one thing and think it long? Can one person be one thing and be it long?"

He narrows his eyes behind those heavy spectacles and says, "What are you going to Princeton for, smart ass?"

"To have lunch with Joyce Carol Oates." He raises an eyebrow. "Surely, from a biologist's point of view, this is no big deal."

"Quite," he agrees. "We're a bunch of ants, really. In fact ants are so much like human beings as to be an embarrassment. Like bees, termites and wasps, they seem to live two kinds of lives. They are individuals going about the day's business without much evidence of thought for tomorrow, and they are at the same time component parts, cellular elements, in the huge, writhing, ruminating organism of the hill, the nest, the hive."

"The city."

"Exactly."

"So my having lunch with Joyce Carol Oates probably has some purpose beyond my own thrill in doing so, and whatever curiosity or kindness made her agree?"

"This is what a biologist would suppose."

We pass a wrecked factory, piles of old tires, a warehouse for Admiral Steel Equipment Company, the gray hell of Newark Station. After Europa Motors we speed up past once red-painted buildings, a smashed half-missing billboard of a Buckingham Palace guard in a bearskin hat, Faitoute Steel, a Budweiser factory. *Budweiser!* How much that name once meant to me! Symbol of my youth and freedom! Neat suburbs come into view, and a ballpark, a softball diamond, an open-air pool. This is suburban New Jersey, a little shabby but still the New World. By Rahway, it's all rather bucolic. I glimpse a park through trees, people jogging, rows of smart clapboard houses: suburbia. *Don't just sit there*, reads a billboard at Metropark. *Okay, just sit there.* Next to it are posters for *Home News Tribune* (Your local news first) and for various films including *Gladiator*, *Road Trip* and, in Metuchan, for *Mission Impossible 2*, and several for BMW with the phrase, *Ultimately, you'll come to Princeton.* We speed through Edison, New Brunswick, Jersey Avenue. Lewis Thomas is asleep, his spectacles tilting on the tip of his nose. We cross a river into the maroon-stanchioned platform of New Brunswick and ads for *Big Momma's House* and more for BMW.

By the time we reach leafy little Princeton Junction, the day's overcast. I cross to the shuttle train. As the shuttle crawls toward the university I feel like all these trips have been leading to this meeting with a person who may end up considered one more, hard-working ant, or come to be seen as one of the great American commentators. *Ultimately, you'll come to Princeton* keeps appearing like an augury. Lewis Thomas has changed to the shuttle with me and I tell him this.

"That's not an omen," he says, "that's an advertisement."

The shuttle hoots, shuffles through a tunnel of trees. Only three of us on it: Lewis and I, and a female student in sandals, jeans, T-shirt. She smiles at me and I smile back. Princeton is overcast, sultry. I'm awkward in my redundant blazer when everyone else is in shirt-sleeves and knows how to dress for the weather. I walk up to Nassau Street and find the Alchemist and Barrister at 28 Witherspoon an hour before we're due to meet, then hide out in a coffee shop to avoid bumping into Oates before our arranged time. I order a *Mocha Frappé* and sit down at the next table from an elderly man with white hair like cream on top of a peach-colored face. He's taking notes while reading Maupassant's *Bel-Ami*. There's still over an hour to go but I don't want to venture outside again and get sweaty, so I scan my questions and check my Dictaphone for the hundredth time.

Then I see her across the room: a frail young girl in a plain green dress. She has tied-back black hair and big dark eyes. Round her neck she's wearing a mandala. Sitting in a corner talking to a friend (who in fact *also* has dark hair, only a bit frizzier, and a similar build, but has her turquoise-cardiganed back to me) is the *young* Joyce Carol Oates. Or at least she looks like her. I'm not sure she sounds like her.

"You know, Enid," she says, "I'm so sick of people staring at me thinking I'm you." They seem very involved in their conversation but when Enid ups to leave I'm stunned. It's *my* Enid. I haven't seen her in fifteen years but she looks just the same. I jump up to catch her. Momentarily a short, puffy-faced businessman blocks my way. He pushes past me and sits down with Oates who, barely missing a beat, says, "Hi, Jerome."

"Call me, Corky," says Jerome.

I run to the door and look up and down the street, then laugh at myself. As if Enid could be here, and still young! Of *course* I was mistaken! I return to my table.

Jerome, who exactly fits my image of Corky Corcoran in *What I Lived For*, has been replaced by a drunken woman with a bad cough and mussed up hair. It's a No Smoking coffee shop but she lights up. "Come on, Persia," says Oates. "What would Iris think?" She's just as involved in talking to Persia as to the other two friends of hers, and no more concerned when this woman lurches suddenly away from the table to the restroom. When Persia staggers out again, yellow bile dribbling from her mouth, she walks past Oates's table without acknowledgment. Oates in any case is now talking to a blonde with heavy lipstick and the even heavier aroma of Chanel No. 5.

She seems to be conducting coffee shop tutorials with her own characters, and were it not for the fact that I know this cannot be *the* Joyce Carol Oates, because the person I'm due to meet was born in 1938, and this dark-eyed waif cannot be more than twenty-five, I'd be mighty spooked. But whoever the young girl is, it's an extraordinary performance. The sheer involvement she registers with each passing individual, the immediate, empathic concentration, is as wonderful as the sudden switch-off is alarming.

Monroe, or whoever she is, leaves, as does the professorial peach-and-cream man. Suddenly the shop is all but empty. The young Oates stares at me with those big dark eyes. But even as I assume it's finally my turn and gulp my *Mocha Frappé*, I put down the cup to find she's gone. I look at my watch. It's one minute to one. I race down Nassau Street, turn left up a shady alley to the Alchemist and Barrister, and there, scribbling in a notepad, sits the *real* Joyce Carol Oates. She's in jogging gear, her frizzy black hair half hidden beneath a purple baseball cap.

I introduce myself and she takes off her cap, looks through me from behind her pebble glasses, and says, "Take a seat, I'm so pleased to meet you." At which point, true to form, I am struck dumb. It's worse than first meeting William Styron. Total silence except for my heavy breathing. "How are you?" she says. I wipe my brow, look into her dark brown eyes. I'm the only person in New Jersey wearing a blazer on the muggiest day of the year, and I begin to sweat again. It drips down my temples, down my neck, down from my armpits and along my sleeves. "I said, How are you?"

Finally, on the second prompt, I manage to speak. "Sweaty."

"Why don't you take off your blazer?"

"Thank you."

"Have you been here long?"

"I just sat down."

"I mean in Princeton?" Miserable, wordless, I can do no more than shrug. "I've got something for you," she says, breaking another looming silence. "You won't want to carry much when you're traveling." It's an edition of *Billy Budd and Other Tales* with Oates's introduction. "Let's order," she says, probably wondering why this blazer-wearing Englishman has come all the way to Princeton to talk but has nothing to say.

I know I must summon forth some vestige of a personality if I'm to stop her gulping her food and escaping back into the literary world from which she comes, so I say, "Have you ever read a biologist named Lewis Thomas?"

"Oh, yes," she replied. "I reviewed *The Lives of a Cell* for The *New York Times* but a long time ago. I don't know how to praise him most accurately. For a research pathologist, if one can say such things, his prose is extraordinarily effortless, beautifully-toned. Many of the chapters, I think I said, are masterpieces of the art of the essay. The underlying thesis of the book is that divisions are really illusory. It insists on the interrelatedness of all life, and it's very persuasive without being dogmatic."

I remember the review. It's quoted on the back of an edition of Thomas's book, and she's essentially repeated her words. "Have you a photographic memory?"

"Hasn't everyone?"

"Did Thomas's ideas influence your writing?"

"I'm influenced by almost everyone I read and I've read almost everyone."

I don't tell her about my encounter in the train because I've no idea if I *really* met Lewis Thomas or just someone with the same name who was paraphrasing him. I don't even know if he's dead or alive. But it hardly matters. Our voices so easily become the voices of others and others' voices so easily become our own, and the world of the imagination, I've long known, cannot be satisfactorily or permanently separated from the world of fact. I try putting some of this to her but I'm merely echoing what she's already said. We start talking about delusions and psychopaths and the conversation gets so interesting—at least to me—that I ask if I can turn on my Dictaphone.

"By all means." She looks concerned. "Are you sure it will work?"

If I'm Ever Back This Way

"Oh yes. It's new."

"Are you sure it will pick up my voice? They so often fail." But I'm certain, so between mouthfuls of sandwich she answers my questions leaning toward the Dictaphone. Since, in mimicry or out of some misplaced politeness, I do the same, we soon look like conspirators and I become barely conscious of a world beyond us.

I ask her, of course, about Enid Stevick. "I knew her in Brockport," I tell her. "She had a boyfriend called Felix, just like in your novel. I took a trip with her. . . ."

"There's a real Enid Stevick?"

"You never met her?"

Oates looks at me as if contemplating connections between my neurons. "I made her up," she says eventually. "Enid Stevick is a fiction."

I shake my head. "We traveled ten thousand miles together. I'd have noticed."

"People see what they're looking for."

My heart thumps. "I heard that a long time ago."

"From?"

"It's something Marilyn Monroe said."

So we discuss her current book about Monroe and finally I ask what brought it about. "After all, she *was* real."

"Well, that was her screen name, her persona."

"You didn't—meet her, did you? You didn't have some kind of encounter that made you want to write about her?"

Oates's penetrating gaze stings my eyes. "It's just a novel," she replies. "I identify with her."

"So you haven't met her?"

"Have *you?*"

"I got that impression."

"Where?"

"In a Grand Rapids café some twenty years ago."

"She died August 4, 1962, so how come?"

"Perhaps she was an Oates—I mean, a ghost."

Oates just looks at me. My eyes sting worse than ever. I'm saved only when a pretty young waitress comes to the table.

"Excuse me," she says in a breathless rush, "I hate to interrupt but I just wanted to say, Miss Oates, that I'm a grade-school teacher and one of my pupils *loves* your work and wants to be a writer and he'll be *so* jealous that I've met you and served you and, oh, I'm sorry, I shouldn't interrupt."

In other circumstances, or in previous years, there'd have been no contest for my attention between this older woman and this pretty waitress-teacher. But Oates mesmerizes me, and the whole two-hour lunch goes by in a flash until the appalling nadir. When she excuses herself to go to the restroom, I check the Dictaphone. Nothing. For two hours, even switching sides, we've sat there with only the "play" button pressed. The tape is blank.

Oates returns, ready to get back to the real world of her writing.

I look at her sheepishly. "I forgot to press record." I feel like a little boy telling teacher he's wet himself.

"These things are always happening," says Oates without a blink. "I'm resigned to it. People are always setting things up—tapes, videos, cameras—then admitting their equipment didn't work, or didn't have any film, or finished too soon. It's quite humorous." I keep a manly face and we stand up. She's surprisingly tall. "You know," she says, "men are so different from women. They have this male thing, this persona. Hemingway had it. Corky Corcoran in *What I Lived For* has it: a mask they put up as a front to the world." Obviously "it" includes my stiff-upper-lip acceptance of the disastrous mishap with the Dictaphone, but I retain my brave face.

"It's nothing," I tell her. "Like Julien Sorel, I have a pitiless memory."

"Like Julien?" she says. "Well do be careful how you use it. I must be going."

"Will you run?"

"I run everywhere."

"Before you go, tell me: did you see that joke press release from Bangor, Maine, about Stephen King announcing that he had acquired Joyce Carol Oates in a 'win-win' deal allowing him to boost his output to a novel a month under the name 'Stephen, Joyce, King, Carol, and Oates' and at the same time become one of the most violent and critically acclaimed of contemporary writers, and make inroads into new markets like college literature classes?"

"Yes, I saw that."

"Did you find it funny or did it irritate you?"

"I thought it was funny," she replies, but changes the subject. "Do you run?" she asks. I tell her I play tennis. "I don't like to play tennis," she muses. "I don't want an opponent. I just run. There's no end, no goal. Just running. It's a little like dreaming. Dreams in succession."

"Like meeting people, or traveling. The going not

the getting there?"

"Maybe." She dons her purple baseball cap, clasps my hot palm with cool fingers, and jogs off into literary history. I shrug on my blazer, double and treble-check the Dictaphone to see if I've captured *anything* of the conversation, and discover despairingly that I haven't. I wonder if, after all, I've met another ghost. I stride manfully back down Witherspoon, cut across Nassau, quelling my desire to head butt a wall, and try to re-enact our conversation into the Dictaphone. But most of what I remember is my own chatter. On the train back to New York I conduct a frantic monologue into the Dictaphone, recalling every snippet I can, and drifting into a commentary on how, just as you can imagine meetings, so you can actually meet people but feel as if you've only met yourself. That evening, partly to reassure myself that we really *did* have lunch, I phone her to thank.

"Not at all," she says. "You're a charming man. I felt so sorry for you in that blazer. And to be honest, while I personally never met Monroe, I haven't the slightest doubt that your meeting all those years ago was just as real as your meeting with me today. As I said about your poor little Dictaphone, these things are always happening."

19

REDSHIFT

After my real—I think—lunch with Joyce Carol Oates, I get back on *terra firma* by visiting Brockport one last time to see a former professor of mine, the poet William Heyen, and visit the Styrons on Martha's Vineyard. Heyen, a friend of Oates, has invited me to meet her parents, because he and his wife, Hanne, have promised to watch out for them.

I pick up my Alamo white Mazda 626 near Newark Airport and drive to Brockport along a highway edged with purple flowers. It's a long, carefree journey and I spend it dreaming back over a West Coast visit last spring to see Pickawillany Dinwiddie. She found my hotmail address through the Internet and e-mailed to say she was living in Carmel. I flew out. This was thirteen or fourteen years after Enid Stevick and I left her in Kansas City. Despite being in her thirties, she could still pass for seventeen. She'd cropped her hair and remained small, slim, tanned. Her gray-blue eyes still had enlarged pupils (not, it turned out, because they enlarged whenever she saw me, but from amphetamine abuse in her youth). Only the raised veins on the backs of her hands betrayed the years.

We spent time in San Francisco and drank at *Vesuvio's* on North Beach, where the Beats used to hang out.

"That's what I remember about being with you,"

she said as I fetched more beer. "I never drank so much in my life." I asked if that was all she remembered. She didn't answer until we'd climbed California Avenue and taken the elevator up the outside of the Fairmont to watch the mist engulf everything lower than the stars. Then she told me about how, when she was little, her father explained that the universe was expanding. "He said the galaxies are all getting further away from each other, and that scientists know this because of something called 'redshift.' The light from distant galaxies appears slightly redder than it would if they were stationary. You know what I did?" she laughed. "I burst into tears. Sometimes I still feel that way. I don't like to think about the past, and distance."

"So you don't remember much?"

"Not if I can help it." She seemed part friend, part stranger. Her laughs were sudden, false coughs. The past few years she'd spent no more time in America than I had. For two years she'd taught English in Taiwan, and was off next to teach in China. "It was always my father's dream to live in the Bay Area," she told me, "but I've done that now. What was *your* father's dream?"

"America."

People call Carmel a paradise, but Pickawillany's tiny lodging saddened me. It amounted to no more than a large closet with outfits evidently chosen to suit her different hairstyles. I fixed the broken shower handle in her cell-like bathroom and realigned her cabinet. It contained a dozen kinds of vapor rub and rheumatic ointment. She'd suffered for years from curvature of the spine and a disc she'd dislodged doing "Active Sculpture" at the Kansas City Art Institute. There was almost no food in the house, little of anything, really, except a shelf of books about the Orient: Robbins Burling's *Hill Farms and Padi Fields: Life in Mainland Southeast Asia*, Marguerite Yourcenar's *Oriental Tales*, Mulk Raj Anand's *Coolie*, Frank Chin's *Ancestors*. She was living in her father's fantasy world, but dreaming of somewhere else. Before leaving, I wrote a brief note and left it under a book on the coffee table. It was to wish her luck. That same day she was due to take an HIV test.

"You'll come to Europe?" I asked as we walked one last time down the sloping street, past shops with her colorful paintings on display, through the wild cypresses to the white beach and fierce blue sea.

"I doubt it," she said. "I've had a bad time. I lost three friends to AIDS, including an old boyfriend. Two more friends died on the TWA 800 crash out of New York."

"And your sister? Still a despicable yuppie?"

"Chrissie has one child, a second husband, and virulent skin cancer. Her body's a mass of scars. Pregnancy fucked up her hormones. Plus she's getting another divorce."

"What time does to us!"

She smiled. "You're just the same as you ever were."

I let it go.

Not that she was wholly wrong. That same trip I had my usual encounters with American ghosts, notably James Dean, Otis Redding, and John Steinbeck. Oh, and Melville turned up again. James Dean—or at any rate a tousle-haired youth driving an open-top, silver Porsche 550 Spyder with 130 on the side and front—gave me a

If I'm Ever Back This Way

ride to Monterey where I caught the Greyhound back to San Francisco. He had a slight squint and kept his head down, peering through the windshield with upward-looking eyes.

"Say," he said, "you heard of James Dean?"

"You're a fan?"

"Kind of!" he cackled. "Me and the others meet up every anniversary at the Crossroads of Death. We congregate at dusk at the intersection of 466 and 41 north of Bakersfield where there's like this huge great James Dean statue. This year I hooked up again with Marilyn Monroe, Ritchie Valens, the Big Bopper, Buddy of course—"

"Eddie Cochran?"

"Eddie's always there. Otis Redding, Patsy Cline, Harry Chapin, Jim Croce, Jim Morrison, Jimi Hendrix, John Lennon, Montgomery Clift, William Holden, and new guys like River Phoenix and Kurt Cobain. Just about anyone who died young and famous."

"Wasn't William Holden in his sixties?"

"He may be old but he's cool. He died alone and maybe drunk. Hit his head and died from blood loss. A sad death, if not a young one."

"Macabre Americana."

The youth cackled and clapped his hands. "Yeah, real macabre Americana."

"What do you think of Elvis?"

"You know, I don't get it. Elvis is always the no-show."

"And Jesus?"

He frowns at my dense interjection. "He didn't sing or act or nothing. Plus he's not American." He wrenches the silver Spyder round a bend, squinting against the rush of wind. "It's real disappointing about Elvis. He worshipped Jimmy like Jimmy worshipped Brando. Elvis learned the script of *Rebel Without a Cause* by heart."

I started thinking about how I, too, once imagined being James Dean, until Jeremiah ate my red jacket. "So where are you from?"

"Fairmont, Indiana. You should see me fly the open road. I'm a pistol, man, a *pistol*."

"Don't you worry about dying?"

"Death is mind over matter. Not that I tear around. I intelligently motivate myself through the entanglement of the streets. That's what Jimmy would say."

"Were he alive."

"Mind over matter."

"What's your real name?" I asked when he dropped me.

"Jimmy. Jimmy Dean." He winked and cackled, "Mind over matter. Real macabre Americana. I *like* that. So long, Buddy-o."

Just another fifteen-minute celebrity, I thought, climbing aboard the Greyhound. America is full of these kind of people. I'd met James Dean. Mind over matter. I promptly fell asleep and dreamt Steinbeck was driving me in a black jalopy. We were sharing a bottle of Jack Daniel's and as he handed it to me he wiped his chin like they do in old cowboy movies and splashed bourbon on the dusty dashboard. One day, he said, all this will be called Steinbeck Country, and it will be yours. I shook my head and said, But I'm not your son. Hell, he replied, it's not about *material* ownership. It's dreams and memories. It's a country of the mind. You've got it in your *head*, see? I passed him the bottle and he showed me the places he loved. We drove through a green valley into Salinas, and turned onto Central Avenue where he stopped the jalopy in front of a Victorian house with big trees and a well-kept lawn, pointed to a window on the first floor and said, That's the room I was born in. Then he pointed to the window above and said, That's the room I wrote in. I asked him when he began to write. He said, almost in wonder, I don't remember a time I didn't write. I wanted to ask him more, but, as sometimes happens with dreams, he'd turned into Melville.

Ah, Herman! I said. You know what they think nowadays? Time is not linear: time *bends*. It looks linear when you're young so you think you're going somewhere. Melville looked at me wearily, as if a sophomore had just told a professor that *Moby-Dick* should be cut by half. There is no steady, unretracing progress in this life, he told me. We do not advance through fixed gradations. (He paused here, fingering his beard.) But once gone through, we trace the round again. I told him time makes less sense to me now I'm older. *Older?* he replied. You don't know the meaning of the word.

Finally, Otis Redding actually did turn up—not in a dream, I mean. I was sitting on a grass bank by the Bay, gazing at the Golden Gate fading toward Sausalito, when this voice said, "Hang out, brother! Don't you dig the sunshine?" I looked up and this big black guy with a guitar held out his hand. "Otis," he said, "how's the world hangin'? Everything still remainin' the same?"

"Oh, we're plugging along, you know," I told him with nonchalance learned from years of spooky encounters. I didn't really think this *was* Otis Redding—I'm old enough to know better—but I didn't want to chance it and leave him feeling he'd missed out since dying in 1967. "AIDS is killing millions," I said. "It's out of control in Africa. The environment's the biggest problem. Global Warming could end humanity. But we have computers and videos and Virtual Reality so think we're okay. You can write on a computer, click your mouse and someone the other side of the world can read it."

"Click your mouse?" he laughed. "Dig it!" I asked him to sing "Dock of the Bay." Otis laughed again. He laughed a lot. "You think I'm *the* Otis, brother?"

"I don't know what to think."

He put his hand on my shoulder. "I'm just kidding you. You want 'Dock of the Bay'? I'll play you 'Dock of the Bay.' I don't get much call for it nowadays."

So I got a one-on-one concert including "Dock of the Bay," cover versions of "If You're Going to San Francisco" and "Do You Know the Way to San José?" and even a Sheryl Crow song, "If It Makes You Happy," that he must have plucked from the ether.

"Well," said Otis, whistling and stroking a perfect C. "I gotta go rest my bones."

"I thought the dock was your home?"

"Got no home, brother. Gotta roam forever, and this loneliness won't let me be. I'm just a posthumous song groovin' in the same old groove." He shook my hand, said, "Click your mouse, brother," picked up his weary bones and wandered back to the Summer of Love.

And suddenly, as if time has jumped, here I am, a year on, back east in Upstate New York, reaching

Brockport on a sunny, July day. Brockport looks much the same. Ghosts of old friends call out to me from the shadows of sundecks and porches. Faces from the past watch me through screen doors. I rest my weary bones outside a canal-side bar named Jimmy Mac's, and watch the young people, the students, no longer one of them. You're young: you feel like an outsider. You get older: you *are* an outsider.

"Hey," calls some dude student, baseball cap on backward, shorts to his knees, cigarette drooping from his downy lip, "where yo' guys goin'?"

Where indeed?

It's much later than I've let myself realize. *Redshift*, I think, *a melancholy thought*. I down a weisse beer, return to the car and turn on the radio. Someone's talking about the dangers of impotence from cycling. I've had seventeen tries at sex, says some young man, aged twenty-seven, and only two were successful and neither of them satisfying. I start the car and take it over the bridge and across to Frazier Street. I'm happy enough, I tell myself, but America is not my home and never will be and never was. It's not even my home-from-home. I've still got the radio on. There's a call-in competition, but both the host and caller are shaky on their facts.

"Can you name any novel turned into a movie?"

"*Schindler's Choice.*"

"*Schindler's List*, I think you mean, but it was never a book."

"I thought it was a novel by William Styron."

"No," says the host. "It was an original screenplay."

"How about *The Magus*?"

"Yeah, a 1972 Stanley Kubrik flick—a Brik-Flick, ha, ha—of Anthony Burgess's famous novel."

Musing on why Spielberg changed the title of Keneally's novel, *Schindler's Ark,* to *Schindler's List* (because of *Raiders of the Lost Ark*?) I pull into the Heyens' driveway. Their house is utterly tranquil. I've got my own space down in Bill's study in the basement. There are hip-high windows out to sun-flecked greenery. A pine desk looks out on pine bookcases stretching round the room. Bill's own books are all in one case. He's recently sold his huge collection of signed books of contemporary American poetry to the University of Rochester. "I've gotten slowly rich from collecting inscribed copies," he tells me in his soft Long Island drawl. He's six foot five maybe, taller than I remember. He wears a short-sleeved, checked shirt, white T-shirt, black jeans with a belt, like the fifties of his youth. He and Hanne are so calm, so relaxed. We eat steak at the Brockport Diner, newly rebuilt after it burned down, though you wouldn't know it. They want to keep historic downtown Brockport historic. It's like Main Street out of the fifties, like *Back to the Future*, and Bill is right out of that past. His one novel, *Vic Holyfield and the Class of '57* is about a guy who gets rich and buys his old high school and invites all his old high school buddies for a reunion. He wrote it listening to Elvis. He's always liked my father's story of knowing Elvis, though he assures me I bear no resemblance. "If anything," he says, "you look like Russell Crowe."

"Have you seen much of Fiery O'Fuellan?"

"I thought I wrote you. Fiery died a year ago."

Bill drives Hanne and I out to the cemetery off Route 19 just outside Brockport. "This is where old Fiery lies now," he says. "It's where we'll all be buried. Except this Englishman, who'll be cremated in Blighty, where there's less space. You know, half my colleagues who were around in your day, they've retired, or gone, or had strokes, or heart attacks, or cancer, and died. Several of them lie here."

"But some things stay the same, don't they?" I try, "like Main Street, Brockport."

"The old part of town, maybe," says Bill. "But, boy, we're growing. All this out of town stuff. It's a tide of modernization that's going to surround this cemetery one day. Modern America is upon us. Even Brockport's getting violent. A guy disappeared from Wegman's. Turns out his wife paid someone to abduct and murder him. They found his body dumped near Niagara Falls. Not long ago a man out hunting in the fields near Spencerport was shot and his gun taken. Shot for his gun!"

"Don't you want a gun to protect yourself, every American's right to bear arms?"

"There's a guy over the road, *he* has guns. He's a regular Capone."

But that night I lie in bed and feel calmer than ever on the trip. All that Brockport has meant to me comes back. This is what we live for, I think, this peace. The Heyens seem to have found happiness, even if in truth they've just come to a plateau that they want to stay on as long as they can.

When Hanne wakes me early with extraordinary news, I know my travels are coming full circle. General George Armstrong Custer's coming to town.

"*Custer?*" I'm incredulous. "Cochran aside, he was the first American I ever heard of!"

I can identify with the poor fellow. He's confused by time. Advance leaflets suggest he thinks it's 1864 and he's a Civil war hero. In fact, when we reach the town hall of nearby Clarkson at the busy intersection of Routes 19 and 104, where Custer's due, the crowd amounts to a dozen people and a band playing "Gary Owen" just below the noise-level of the traffic. Morning, says a short, muscled fellow with a white beard, cigarette pack rolled in one sleeve of his T-shirt. I ask him if he's waiting for Custer.

"Always like to greet a relative."

"You're a Custer?"

"Sure," he says. "Alvin Custer. My grandpappy's grandpappy, I believe, was his cousin, though he didn't take after him much. This here's my brother, Jim."

Jim's hair is gray, shoulder-length. He shakes my hand. "Jim Armstrong Yellow Hair Custer," he says. "Our sister's over there. She's married, so she's a Poulin now, not a Custer. But she changed her Christian name to Custa with an a, so she's Custa Poulin."

Then up comes the head of the clan, George Armstrong himself, dressed in black with gold trimmings and a crimson scarf, in a horse-drawn carriage with his wife, Lavinia. He helps her out of the carriage, is introduced to the small gathering of maybe forty people now, and above the traffic noise, makes a little speech then poses for photos beside a regimental flag.

I go up to him. "May I call you George?"

"My friends call me Autie," says Custer.

Used to interviewing by now, I launch in. "Are

you sympathetic to the Indians you're policing?"

"Very much so," says Custer more politely than I deserve, "and 'policing' is exactly the word. You see I'm caught in a double bind. On the one hand the farmers and travelers want the Indians kept in check, on the other hand we've got to do the right thing by them since it's their land. The settlers get us on one side, the liberals on the other. We're caught between."

"Surrounded, you might say. Well thanks," I tell him. "I've hoped for years to meet you. Good luck with future police actions. Look after the Seventh Cavalry."

Custer smiles wryly. His expression suggests he's seen the future. Meanwhile Bill's taking it all in. He's written a book of poems about Custer called *Crazy Horse in Stillness*. Custer's going to be given it this evening at some reception. I think it'll unnerve him. Take this, for instance. It's called "The Tooth."

> After the beheading, they found
> the one gold tooth in Custer's mouth.
> They propped open his jaws,
>
> cut away his upper lip,
> & looked into the tooth in firelight.
> It was like a small television
>
> tuned to the news, & a white man
> in a white suit was already
> stepping down onto the moon.

Custer's very concerned to be sure I know everything I want to know. He gives me his card. Genl. G. A.

Custer, it says on the front, and on the back, his name and title—Foremost Custer Living Historian—with an e-mail and street address in Monroe, Michigan. (*Ah!* I think, Michigan: *Monroe*, Michigan!)

Down in the study that evening, Bill shows me some of the things he's collected besides poetry. They include a ton of Beanie Babies, a Peace Pipe wrapped in a red cloth, three Civil War bullets, and an SS Death's Head ring.

"It's a ring of *der Totenkopfring der SS*, instituted by Himmler in April 1934, recognizing the wearer's personal achievement, devotion to duty, and loyalty to the Führer and his ideals. I showed Joyce," he says. "She put it right on her finger." I hesitate, then try it on. It's too big for any of my fingers. "They were supposed to be returned to the *SS Personalhaupt* in Himmler's castle in Wewelsburg."

Half the rest of the night I'm awake and reading books from Bill's library about Nazi rings, and Peace Pipes. By around one a.m I'm reading Ian Frazier's *Great Plains* and Francis Harries' *The Buffalo*, getting dizzy just looking at all the other books I want to read and wondering what I've been *doing* for so many years, when you have to find your focus pretty fast. By three, I'm reading Mailer's *Of A Fire on the Moon*, about the Apollo missions, then Al Gore's *Earth in the Balance* and a book of Hubble photographs of distant nebulae, then fall asleep with both books open on my lap.

The next day we drive just beyond Lockport to Millersport to visit Oates's parents. Frederic and Carolina live in a tiny bungalow set back fifty yards from the six-lane highway. They're both over eighty. Fred helped build the bungalow himself, in 1962. The old house would now be right by the highway, a single road when Oates grew up. There's no more to the bungalow than a tiny kitchen and living room, a bathroom, and two bedrooms, one of which is Fred's study. It's maybe eight foot square with a small bookcase on which he has copies of novels he studied at the University of Buffalo where he enrolled in his seventies. They discussed one of his daughter's novels in class without knowing who he was. On his small desk there's a large magnifying glass attached, maybe a foot in diameter.

"I've got bad eyesight," he explains, "bad heart, bad everything. I'm falling to pieces. I can't hardly see to read her books any more."

"But you still do?"

"Oh sure, every word, even when I don't understand them." The wall in front holds a series of photos in a line of his younger daughter, Lynn. On the wall to the right there's a large framed picture of Joyce graduating, or with an honorary doctorate, and a kind of collage from the portrait on the back of *Foxfire* and the cover of *Conversations with Joyce Carol Oates*. "Don't you want to ask more questions?" says Fred. I'm learning more from seeing Fred's study than from any questions I could ask. But back in the lounge I do ask Fred about his flying. *Man Crazy* opens with a flying sequence in a light aircraft. "It was kind of expensive," he says. "I had to give it up."

"Did Joyce fly with you?"

"Sure, when she was little."

"You took her to boxing. Did she want to go?"

"Not much," says Fred. "But she's worked a lot of

that stuff up into her novels. I see myself all over the place. She makes me out to be all kinds of people."

On the wall there's a painting of a sunset, and a detailed drawing of Wuthering Heights, a small, sombre house amid the heaths. It's signed, JCO.

"Oh, she did that in high school," says Carolina. "She was always doing something. We just let her be. She wasn't much use around the house."

"You gave her time and space."

"We sure did. She was always reading and drawing and writing. You want to see the creek she sometimes writes about?"

We all walk out through a lean-to porch to a garden buzzed by relentless traffic.

"It never stops," says Fred. "Never." To see the creek we have to negotiate the edge of the six-lane highway. "Used to be nothing but fields and a track here," says Fred. "We used to be country people but now we're urban, yet we haven't *moved*." Look one way and all you see is a stream and a boulder in the middle. But the cars are like gusts of wind at your back. "We're worried," Fred confides in Bill. "We've been swimming in the same public pool every day for twenty-one years and they're closing it down. I don't know where I'll get exercise, how I'll keep my strength up." He's a strong man, or was, with big hands, muscular, brawny. But he's got a burn or abrasion on his arm, as if seared from a passing vehicle while protecting Carolina as they age together beside the six-lane highway.

"Couldn't you join Joyce at Princeton?" says Hanne.

"This is where our friends are," says Fred. "This is

our life."

We walk back along the hard shoulder with Applebee's and Arby's and gas stations, and Pizza Huts in the distance. The three of us shield Fred and Carolina from the gusts of traffic and we walk, a strange little group, back over the bridge to their garden. I look back at the river. There's not enough even to see your reflection. No one pays it too much attention any more, or pays them too much attention either, in their little bungalow off Route 1, just past the Denny's and McDonald's and just before the Exxon sign.

Dawn the next day I bid farewell to the Heyens, and gun my Mazda down 19, then east all the way to Cape Cod, blasting Elvis and a fifties and sixties CD. Basically, I'm playing all the songs my parents used to have when I was a child. The music that made them dream of America, and the music that first brought me here. I sing them all out loud so the sky pops and the car rocks and I'm in love with life again.

20

STAR SPANGLED MAN

The Cape bursts before me over the breathtaking sweep of the Bourne Bridge. I catch the Wood's Hole ferry to Martha's Vineyard and at Vineyard Haven am welcomed by Rose as if I've never been away. Styron walks out haltingly, not from decrepitude but an eye complaint which means he's seeing double and will do so until he can get the operation he's scheduled for. Left to my own devices late in the afternoon, I stroll across the lawn with its view of the sailboats dotting the harbor and sit on the jetty. The wind's blowing everything out of my mind in one huge spillage. I'm contemplating a midlife clean-out. It's a belated end to youth, but why not? I won't get it *back*. I plunge into the sea in T-shirt and shorts and bob with the yachts in the wild fresh weather of the Atlantic coast after the warm glow of small town America. The Styrons are well into grandparenthood now. There are grandchildren running everywhere. I think of the children I will one day have, and see how the Styrons, among others, have been surrogate parents for me, just as America has been a surrogate country and given me a role and a sense of myself.

At five a.m. I'm awake in an enormous, white-sheeted, white-painted bed in a white and sky-blue room with white furniture and white net curtains billowing inward in the dawn light. The Atlantic gusts suck in the cries of seagulls. There are photos on the wall of sand dunes, and a montage by Sylvia Cooper. On a white table stands a stack of books about Martha's Vineyard including one called *Vineyard Summer* inscribed to the Styrons—with a wink at history, their full names written in it—from Bill and Hillary Clinton. The signs of fame are everywhere. Styron's turned down a dinner invitation with Margaret and Denis Thatcher and Nancy Reagan. I ask him why.

He raises his eyebrows. "Do you *blame* me?"

Around six I'm out of bed and heading across the damp grass to the jetty to swim. When I get back Daphne, the Styrons' Jamaican housekeeper who works as a nurse in Toronto all winter, gets me scrambled eggs, bacon and coffee. We talk about my bus travels.

"I take the bus, too," says Daphne.

"So we're both bus people."

"Perhaps," says Daphne.

"Come on," says Rose a little later. "We're going to a farewell lunch for Dick Widmark and his new wife, Susan Blanchard. She's lovely, and as deaf as he is. She used to be married to Henry Fonda."

I'm about to tell her I had a ride with Henry Fonda in Michigan years ago, but then I realize I didn't. I started my American travels imagining meeting such people, and here they are. Fantasy becomes reality.

Off we go to lunch in West Tisbury at the house of the painter, Kib Bramhall. The house is up a winding track and looks out over woodland to the sparkling Atlantic. Inside, the spacious, airy feeling is reinforced by the numerous paintings of Cape Cod landscapes with billowing clouds, yawning beaches and dazzling color.

Richard Widmark—or Jim Bowie, as I remember him from childhood—comes out to greet us. He's in his eighties, but slim and tanned, wearing large spectacles: altogether remarkably fit and well so long after what happened to him at the Alamo. A circle of six people sip iced tea in a rectangle of sunlight from the window facing seaward. Widmark's daughter, Annie, is there, an attractive, warm, blue-eyed, gray-haired woman of maybe fifty. She was once married to baseball legend, Sandy Koufax, Styron has told me. Widmark himself is unpretentious, deaf, but very funny. He looks much the same as in his movies except the spectacles enlarge his eyes. He's modest and self-deprecating, and seems to find most of his career hilarious. There are lots of laughs about *The Long Ships*, a film he did with Sidney Poitier.

"Sid was a brave Moor with a great, curving scimitar to slice me up," says Widmark, "but I was an even braver Norseman." He's laughing as he says this, clapping his hands, tears in his eyes. "And there was a golden bell," he booms, "made of plastic, so when it fell off the cart, which it kept doing—" he bellows now, this rich, sonorous laugh, "—it *bounced!*"

Lunch is lobster salad. The talk ranges from Hollywood to bus travel—a hazy memory for everyone but me—but keeps coming back to arthritis. "*Everyone* has arthritis," says Bramhall. Everyone at the table, evidently, except me. Yet. I talk with Annie about England and Los Angeles and why she's coming to live on Cape Cod and what a wrench it is, and how she wants to travel cross-country. ("I'll go with you," says Rose. "What a trip that would be!") Styron talks of getting drunk with Jackson Pollock and watching him paint.

There's a joke that maybe Styron did one of the paintings and it's hanging somewhere with Pollock's name on it. Annie talks about her time at Sarah Lawrence where she studied under Joseph Campbell.

"I didn't enjoy it much," she says. "He was complicated, like most brilliant men."

I tell her of how I once heard Campbell's advice to the young. Follow your bliss, he said. If you do that, you'll enjoy yourself and you're more likely to succeed. If you don't it doesn't matter because you've been doing what you want to do.

"Follow your *bliss!*" mocks Styron. "When I was in hospital recovering from my depression they said, Let it wash over you, Mr Styron. *Woosh!* I don't like that stuff."

"You know what I don't like?" says Widmark. "Texas. I don't like Texas or Texans and they don't like me. I'm walking down the street in Austin or somewhere, minding my own business, when along comes this woman and, thwack! She whops me one. I don't like you, she says. Another time I'm in a bar in Lubbock, talking with some friends, and this guy comes up and gives me the eye, and thud! *He* whops me one. You miserable, dirty coward, he says."

"After all you tried to do for Texas at the Alamo." I shake my head. "Incidentally, did you like John Wayne?"

"John Wayne!" says Widmark. "America's greatest cowboy. He was a pretty brave man, ha ha—for a, shall we say, non-combatant!" He and Styron laugh. "He's a bigger myth than the Wild West. He's the greatest myth in our culture. No I did not like John Wayne."

My final evening, Styron and I sit out watching the yachts in the harbor across from his green expanse of lawn. I tell him about my travels, and how I'm going home to finish my book about America, and that I think I've found what I was seeking. "How about you?" I ask him. "You're a grand old man of American literature."

"Ha-ha!" he says flatly.

"Well, you've got health, grandchildren, houses in Connecticut and Cape Cod, the respect of your peers. Aren't you satisfied?"

"It's okay."

"It's happiness, isn't it? Total satisfaction?"

"I'm bifurcated," he replies. "I'm both more dissatisfied than I thought I would be at this stage in my life, and more satisfied. It's hard to describe."

"Why are you dissatisfied?"

"Oh, I'm dissatisfied that I didn't turn out something else, you know, but even as I say that I realize that you cannot look at your career as what you failed to do but what you *did* do. I've done far better than I thought I would ever be capable of doing. I also feel my work has at least acquired a kind of permanence. But, well, the world slips away from us all."

"Ah yes," I say, "Redshift. The past looks a little pink as it recedes." Styron just sits there, looking out over the bay, so I ramble on. "I'm not sure that I've ever met anyone who has been at all successful who hasn't said, when you ask them, that they're dissatisfied. It's the nature of the beast that if you're ambitious to reach your potential you're going to be dissatisfied because that's what drove you in the first place."

"Precisely," says Styron, "and I *am* dissatisfied.

If I'm Ever Back This Way

I'm *profoundly* dissatisfied. But it's dissatisfaction that's combined with satisfied acceptance. It's a kind of schizoid feeling. Sometimes I feel a miserable insufficiency about myself, and other times I say, man, I've done this. Who else has done that? You see what I'm saying?"

This largely confirms what I've come to realize. There is no place of total happiness. There are just moods, a range of feeling you get whoever you are and wherever. There are happy people and unhappy people, but most of us are middling, and circumstances have something to do with where we fit on the scale, but not everything. We *pursue* happiness, and some of us are happy in the pursuit.

When I last see him on the Cape, Styron's lying in his dressing gown reading on his bed, as he seems to do between about nine and eleven most days. "Finish your book," he says and raises a fist. Rose drives me to the ferry. I kiss her cheek. "Hurry back!" she says. I sit on the ferry and wonder how easy it would be—or so it feels as I watch their shoreline house recede—to stay forever in this fantasy land of beautiful, successful, wealthy, talented, generous people. But this is the world of the Styrons, the Kennedys, Widmarks, Clintons. Of *course* it's intoxicating. This is a place full of powerful or highly successful people. This is where the Thatchers and Reagans dine—if anyone will dine with them—but it's a world I only visit. I'm an outsider, but no less happy for that. On the ferry I chat with a Polish girl. She says she's studying here. She has beautiful eyes and sounds like Meryl Streep as Sophie. I ask if she likes America.

"I don't like how people say, Have a nice day

when they don't care if I do or not."

"You miss Poland?"

"I'm fed up with these Americans. They're spoiled. They complain about any little thing. And all that stuff about Lewinsky and the President. This kind of thing doesn't happen in Poland. Americans have got too much money. You've either got everything in this society or you've got nothing. And they don't care about those people. I can't wait to go home."

There are people who have to leave home and people who have to get home. But I don't know how much difference there is between them. Off the ferry, we say goodbye and I drive back over the Bourne Bridge to the mainland, away from paradise.

I stop at a tollbooth on I95. The operator who takes my money gives the impression he's worked there all the time I've been traveling America, and he's *not* happy. He's shouting at the operator of the next booth, who must stand opposite him day after day. "You could just try to be a little bit nice to me, you know? A *little* bit nice!" I can't hear what the man in the next booth says but it's not nice. They've maybe both worked the same adjacent booths for a decade and are as heartily sick of each other as of the fumes. Two American worlds, I think—Vineyard Haven and the tollbooth on I95. I pay my seventy-five cents, and shoot away from the tollbooth to Connecticut.

In Hartford, presumably only blocks from Wallace Stevens's old office, I stay at the Hyatt. It's a long way from Hotel Busland. There's an enormous double bed with soft sheets, power shower, a black desk and elegant lamp and leather desk chair. I don't feel either old or young. To be forty is better than being fifty or sixty, but not like being twenty-something. That evening I stick in the Elvis CD, put on my shades and roll downtown listening to "Heartbreak Hotel." There's an open-air music festival. Two women named Laverne and Shirley sit next to me on the low wall, watching the band. They work at a Budweiser factory. They're holding cups of beer and have blue stamps on the back of their right hands to show they've bought them. Laverne's muscular with thick eyebrows. She's a supervisor. Shirley's red-haired and slim with a nice green dress on and a down-curved nose. She's smoking a cigarette and narrows her eyes at me, head raised to blow a stream of smoke.

"Wanna beer, nature boy?"

"No, thanks."

"You're not from round here, are you?" She's rather nice, but she's wearing a wedding ring. I'm happy but sad, too, and not sure why. *Don't you realize how old you are?*

Willy Loman sits on the wall next to me. He looks like Dustin Hoffman. "To be forty and still looking for the unattainable place of inexpressible happiness," he tells me, "is a *disgrace.*"

"It's all right for you," I tell him. "You're just words on a page."

"Maybe that's all you are, too," he says, turning into Hoffman playing the dying Rizzo in *Midnight Cowboy*. He gets up and hobbles off muttering, "Gotta catch a Greyhound to Florida."

Down sits Susan Sarandon, who seems to think she's playing Helen Prejean attending Death Row inmates in *Dead Man Walking*. "What were you looking for?" she says. "What do you think happiness is?"

"An unalienable right," I suggest.

"Ah, yes," she says. "But there are so many of us! And even when you think you've found it, there's still something missing, isn't there? Don't spend your life looking and find, as Joni Mitchell once put it, that you didn't know what you had until it's gone." She gets up, and looks back with those kind eyes. "At least you haven't killed anyone," she says cheerfully.

Just then someone nudges me. "Hey, Buddy, wanna buy a toothbrush?" He's a scrawny black guy with no teeth and twenty toothbrushes. "They givin' them as a promotion," he says. "I got no use for them, but I took what's free."

"If they're giving them away free, why would I want to buy one?"

"The Land of the Free Toothbrushes don't gonna help me get *dentures*."

I give him a dollar, throw the brush away and drive back to the hotel. My restaurant seat is beneath a tree filled with white lights that spangle the table.

"*Carciofi Ripieni al Granchio*, please," I tell the waitress.

"Artichokes stuffed with crabmeat? Yes, sir."

So long, Busland and Burger King. I follow it with pasta and spicy Italian sausage, washed down with Molson and a glass of Louis Jadot. The piano man plays "The Way We Were," then Don Williams's "Good Ole Boys Like Me." The artichokes and crabmeat are excellent. The bread's soft and fluffy as a cloud. After the pasta, I order cognac and decide maybe in another life I'd fall for the waitress who first served me, but she's gone home, and besides, I'm older now. The waiter who brings the cognac turns out to be Bob Dylan. "The times they are a changin'," he whispers.

"You're not kidding."

"Don't talk to me," he says, "I'm not really here. The guys on the next table will think you're nuts." I glance at a young Japanese couple eating pasta. "They'll think you're Willy Loman, mad from too long on the road. *Death of a Salesman*'s big in Japan."

"I met the man who wrote it," I tell Dylan. "I met Arthur Miller."

"Sure you did, Willy," says Dylan, "and I met the Jack of Hearts."

Like a lot of people, I've always wanted to talk with Dylan. "Congratulations on not becoming a casualty like Janis Joplin or John Lennon or Elvis or Eddie Cochran," I tell him. I'd mention the circumstances of my birth, but I'm just about growing out of that feeble need. So I tell him my father knew Elvis. He looks at me as if I've said I wrote "Blowin' in the Wind."

"Sure you did, Willy. Sure you did."

"Hey, you," says the Japanese youth at the next table. Dylan looks at him. "The pasta's no good."

"It's the best we have, sir," says Dylan.

"Well, go tell the chef the pasta is way over soft."

Dylan acts obsequious. "Shall I change it, sir?"

"It's soft, too soft. You've overdone it."

"Would you like me to fetch the cook, sir?"

"Do what you want."

Out comes the cook. It's Frank Sinatra.

"Oh, my God," I exclaim, even as I realize "Imagination" is being played as background music in

If I'm Ever Back This Way

the restaurant. "I can't believe it!" But no one's listening to me, which is probably a good thing. I drain my cognac, and nudge Dylan for another. "When you're ready." He nods as if I'm requesting an autograph.

Ole Blue Eyes bends to the youth. "Is it good?"

"The pasta's soft. You did it the wrong way. You boiled it up with the water. You should've boiled the water *then* put the pasta in."

"I did it my way, sir."

"Well it's too soft. Go away." Away go Sinatra and Dylan, and he starts in on the girl, who's muttered something. "If you're going to be a bitch about it, I don't want to know," he says. "You're too ugly."

"Don't say that."

"You can't help it, but you're too ugly for me."

She sits on her hands and puckers her lips. "I can't believe you."

"Believe me. The pasta's soft and you're ugly. If you fitted my ideal, you'd be a West Coast, blue-eyed blonde."

"And how would you be?"

"What I am. The fact is, the pasta's soft, and you're ugly." Just then, Wallace Stevens enters in a post-war corporate suit, and recites the first opening lines of a short poem, "Gubbinal." *That strange flower, the sun, is just what you say. Have it your way. The world is ugly, and the people are sad.* "Oh, go away," says the youth.

On my last day before my flight home I go, from curiosity, to the Strand Bookstore to find out about Richard Widmark's relationship with John Wayne. There are no Widmark biographies there, but several on

Wayne, with titles like *John Wayne: American*, on the back cover of which are "What famous Americans have said about John Wayne."

John Wayne was bigger than life, Jimmy Carter tells me. *In an age of few heroes he was the genuine article. But he was more than a hero; he was a symbol of many of the qualities that made America great—the ruggedness, the tough independence, the sense of personal conviction and courage—on and off the screen—that reflected the best of our national character.*

Next up is Ronald Reagan. *There is no one who more exemplifies the devotion to our country, to its goodness, its industry and its strengths,* says Reagan.

Frank Sinatra joins in. *No man's lifetime of work has better expressed the land of the free and the home of the brave*, says Sinatra. *No man's life time or work has given more proof to the world that our flag is still there. John Wayne is in truth a star spangled man whom so proudly we hail. To the people of the world, John Wayne is not just an actor and a very fine actor. John Wayne is the United States of America. He is what they believe it to be. He is what they hope it to be. And he is what they hope it will always be.*

John Wayne: America. Certainly that's the kind of image I first had of the country. America as an idea: Westerns, Elvis and Eddie, Marilyn Monroe and James Dean. But Wayne died the day I first flew out, of course, and quickly waned as one of my images of America too. The headline-grabbers of history and culture are a small part of the panorama. The Richard Widmarks of popular culture are another thing again: known without being icons. In his own way, Widmark's the quintessential cowboy. He just never (like say Gene Autry) made a song and dance about it. I look up Widmark, Richard, in the index of the Wayne biographies.

"Duke had heard rumors that Richard Widmark was difficult to work with," says one book, "and the rumors proved understatements." Filming *The Alamo*, Wayne placed an ad in the *Hollywood Reporter*: "Welcome aboard, Dick. Duke." But Widmark was nobody's Dick. He felt miscast. There was also an argument over contracts. Widmark relented but was, say the books, difficult on set, criticizing Wayne in front of the cast. I look up the film in *Time Out*'s Film Guide. It's described as "an elephantine, historically inaccurate, stridently patriotic tribute to the handful of Texans who faced assault by 7000 Mexican baddies."

My final afternoon I picnic in Strawberry Fields, dedicated with money from Yoko Ono, and lurk the dappled lanes, taking monochrome photos. Bodies sprawl in the sun. A paraplegic man sits in his wheelchair in the shade and I'm reminded of Drum Desoutter's one-time fiancé up in Oregon, Christine Svenson. I buy a Miller draft at Summer Stage. Machel Montano and Xtatic, a Carribean band, fill the air with the beat of summer in the city. New Yorkers dance round in all shades and shapes of humanity. Manhattan is a country, the world, or any kind of world you want it to be this July Sunday so near the new century. Rollerbladers swing past a Hare Krishna gathering on a patch of grass between lanes. A plane writes LOVE in red smoke above the trees. The word disperses into the pale blue sky.

In the late afternoon, I take a bus downtown and go up one of the towers of the World Trade Center. I forget which. It's one of those things I've always meant to do, but thought of as something for another day. It's not, I've been thinking, as if they'll disappear.

21

IN THE TWINKLING OF AN EYE

And the years pass, ever faster now, just like we were told they would: "acceleration toward the point of impact," as Joyce Carol Oates would say. We hurtle forward at 500 miles an hour, but seen through the cabin window, the future seems an endless blue sky and the plane merely to float and tilt. Only when you compare it to a still object, getting closer, do you see the truth.

    By now marriage, parenthood, and a generally settled life have irrevocably shifted my perspective. Transatlantic trips are no longer about Novembers of the soul, or the equivalent of Cato's sword or Ishmael taking ship. But to recall that note of Melville's, they still feel like opportunities to stay true to the dreams of my youth. So in October 2001, less than a month after Nine Eleven, I fly out to Omaha via Chicago on United Airlines. Oates is reading at the Cornhusker Hotel in Lincoln and I can combine this with a reunion, out of curiosity, with Carlotta Domarski, long since married, with a teenage son and daughter, to a grain exporter named Orlin Sundberg. But even as the plane arches over Michigan I ponder one last Greyhound journey for the following spring. On the TV screen a cartoon plane edges across a green cartoon Michigan and directly over Muskegon, Star Lake, and Camp Jakalak. In the end, I know, my Odyssey must return me to that starting point of so many years ago.

Carlotta and her parents still don't reach my elbows. Sherwin Domarski has long since retired from Trailways and mostly naps in an armchair. Irma Domarski, far from having spent the intervening decades sharpening her pincer eyes to ever-finer precision, now seems like a kindly old lady with no strong views on America or me. Meanwhile Orlin Sundberg overflows with a quiet largesse that matches a physique as high and wide as a Nebraskan barn. Brought up on a farm outside Kearney, west of Omaha, his prairie-born enormity seems eminently suited to the driver's seat of the giant green combine harvester he demonstrates on our visit to the family farm.

"Orlin," I tell him, "you grew up with the life I dreamed of, a prairie farm boy. I bet you even had dungarees and a checked shirt, and a dog and stick."

"Guess I did," drawls Orlin, crunching the combine's gears.

"Just like Ricky in *Champion, the Wonderhorse*." Orlin scratches his fair hair. "You know, that old black and white TV program?"

"Never heard of it."

Omaha is crisp, sunny, mellow and magical, and—with Carlotta working at UNO—I spend a couple of days downtown or just wandering the bending avenues that connect with their house on Shirley Street, past pole after pole of sun-lucent Stars and Stripes, garages with basketball hoops, driveways strewn with crisp red and yellow maple leaves. On the trees, the leaves burn against the rich blue sky while single leaves twist down as if an orchestrated part of the autumn.

The modest houses stretch across generous allotments. Carlotta's, like the one her parents still inhabit, is a split-level bungalow. Enter the hallway and you have steps down to the basement or up to the living room. Along one otherwise bare wall in the living room, a single light draws your attention to a sideboard display of small American flags and a flag-cushion. Aside from two armchairs, a couch beneath the net-curtained window and a piano, the only other large object in the room is a giant TV spewing CNN's 'Breaking News' of the latest threats. US air strikes continue against Afghanistan. Osama Bin Laden says America will reap God's revenge. The Taliban are ready for the Jihad. Richard Gephart, the House Minority Leader, talks about international teamwork.

"We need to do it," he tells me, "we have to do it, we will do it."

Carlotta drops me at the depot to catch the Greyhound for Lincoln. "I *never* come here," she says. "I haven't since I was a student. Orlin has never set foot in a bus depot, and nor will my children. I could drive you to Lincoln."

"No, I need to remind myself of such places," I tell her. "It does look different."

"It is. They closed down the old Greyhound depot when the lines merged. This used to be Trailways, where Pa drove from for years and years. You know, Orlin can't understand why you want to take the bus."

"And you?"

We're standing outside the glass doors, which look smeared with dried blood. Momentarily her Slavic eyes hint at the girl who took me to the Waterloo Fair.

"I'm glad you kept in touch for twenty years, or

whatever," she says. "It certainly wasn't *me*. But now I've seen pictures of you and your wife and little girls and home and everything I'm grateful to you for persevering. Who knows where we'll be in another twenty years."

"Life is full of circles."

"Well, here I am. I told you this acorn would never fall far. At least you haven't brought up the Waterloo Fair episode."

"I've left that for you."

Carlotta drives off in her eight-seater People Transporter to fetch her daughter, Dorothy, from the same jungle restaurant she herself once worked at, while I push open the blood-smeared door of my latest Greyhound depot. It's nothing like the spacious building I spent several early mornings in as a youth. In fact, it's about the seediest hell-hole in Nebraska. You wouldn't want to spend an hour in there, let alone dusk to dawn. The dinginess matches the smell of fried food and greasy atmosphere. Shadows cough at corner tables. A silhouette passes the glass door, sharp against sunlight.

To the bemusement of the Asian girl behind the counter, I buy a Greyhound baseball cap that lies beneath the glass amid other murky novelties like a wreck on an ocean floor. Even behind glass it has absorbed grease, and retains the smell of frying to this day. For all I know it was first on sale at the old depot when I was last there so many years ago.

In Lincoln the next morning I wake in the Cornhusker to Al-Qaeda warning that hijackings will not stop. Thousands of Islamic fundamentalists stand waiting to carry out such actions. The anthrax investigations continue. Tornadoes tear through Oklahoma. The western world is envisioning its own demise. In my hotel room I hear my old bus-loving friend, Jim Lehrer, announce on Channel 12 News that the FBI are warning of new attacks. To cover all eventualities, I write letters to the family to be opened in the event of my death etc.

Down in the bar-restaurant a pale girl sits down on the stool next to me and orders red wine. Her name is Maya. She's a twenty-two year old biochemistry major from Tulsa. We talk about our different countries, and this brings us to populations.

"What's the population of Britain?" she asks.

"What do you think?"

During the pause I notice, in a corner booth, a well-fed, ruddy-faced priest. He resembles George W. Bush as he might have been had he not become teetotal at forty.

"A million?"

"What's the population of America then?"

The priest raises his hand but only, it turns out, to scratch his head.

"A billion?"

I ponder whether it's a good or bad thing she'll be a biochemist. As our conversation stumbles on, I contemplate the restaurant's eccentric murals. Highly colored and full of bizarre detail, they are interspersed by fake columns, some in relief, some painted, in a half-hearted *trompe l'oeil*. One depicts gondolas, another peacocks, another a Grecian urn on flower-strewn steps, another a windmill and tulips. The various inscriptions include Wordsworth on daffodils: *Along the margin of a bay: / Ten thousand saw I at a glance, / Tossing their heads in spritely dance.* Pictures of a ram, a bull, fish and stars decorate the ceiling.

"Was the muralist mad?" I ask Maya.

But we've run out of conversation. It's after midnight, so morning UK time. I phone and talk to my wife and daughters in turn then sleep well before breakfasting on pecan French toast with bananas and bacon. When, after a day roaming Lincoln, I take the elevator down to hear Oates talk, the door opens on a huge man in a black suit and trilby. He might almost be Orson Welles.

"Are you going up or down?" I ask him.

"Descending," he replies, "gracefully."

Oates reads to a huge, yellow-lit hall of perhaps two hundred people. "No blazer, this time?" she says when we meet afterwards.

"Did you get the bus book?" I've sent her a draft.

"Oh yes," she replies, opening her large, dark, all seeing eyes. "I know all about you and Enid. What a bold, original, undefinable book!"

Before I can request clarification, a brutally mascara-ed, forty-ish woman strides up. Oates plucks at her cardigan and gazes around like a shy rabbit.

"Young man," she says, "are you married? So am I. My husband is a surgeon and the father of my children. I hate him."

"Excuse me?"

"I've come to ask advice of Joyce Carol Oates and you are in the way."

I happily stand aside. Oates is now the proverbial rabbit in the headlights.

"Ms Oates," says the woman. "My name is Mrs Mildred Schiller and I've written a novel about a man I knew in college. I've e-mailed to ask him to read it and get together with me. He has said no. Well, I won't allow him to be boring and just live out the rest of his life, so I'm going to insist. What do you think? The alternative is I kill myself."

"How interesting," says Oates. "But maybe he has a life of his own. I must go."

She turns from Mrs Mildred Schiller, smiles at me, waving her fingers in a strangely girlish farewell, and disappears. I extricate myself from Mrs Mildred Schiller but later see her haranguing the desk clerk.

"I've written a novel about a man I knew in college," she's saying. "I've e-mailed to ask him to get together with me. He has said no. Well, I won't allow him to be boring and just live out the rest of his life, so I'm going to insist. What do you think?"

Flying back east, Chicago is like a dream city on the lip of a pink lake that recedes upward to where Camp Jakalak must be. It seems no time at all before I'm flying back out from Britain and landing at JFK to attend a Steinbeck conference at Hofstra University as an excuse both to spend the weekend with the Styrons and to embark on that final Greyhound trip. New York is blustery and bitter. I take the free bus to Holbeach and Far Rockaway and the subway across Queens and Brooklyn to Manhattan. We pass Ground Zero and sweep up the West Side. I catch a local at 59th Street for 86th and wheel my suitcase along Amsterdam and Broadway to West End Avenue for a shower, pizza, bottles of Negra Modelo, and a reunion with Darius, Juliet and their now-three young children.

If I'm Ever Back This Way

The next morning I'm on the Long Island Railroad, listening to Springsteen's *Born in the USA*, for nostalgic reasons, I suppose, and watching the colorful, clapboard houses pass to the melancholy strains of "Downbound Train" and "Dancing in the Dark." The latter song stays in my head throughout the conference and provides a strangely comforting soundtrack against the icy winds of that bright but bleak March week at the about-to-be-demolished Quality Hotel, Hampstead.

Serendipity strikes once more, though, with the appearance of long-time Long Island resident, Budd Schulberg, as a Guest of Honor.

Budd Schulberg! Budd Schulberg, who wrote *The Disenchanted*, a book resulting from his acquaintance with F. Scott Fitzgerald in Hollywood in the 1940s. Budd Schulberg, who wrote *On the Waterfront* and put the words, "I could have been a contender" into Marlon Brando's mouth in a film directed by Elia Kazan, the first director of *Death of a Salesman*. Life is indeed full of circles, I'm thinking, as I watch the old man sitting in the midst of the gathering, waiting to give his talk.

"So may I present to you . . . Long Island's very own *Budd Schulberg!*"

The old man struggles, ever so slowly, to rise, and edges toward the microphone. "Talk among yourselves," he says. "I won't be long."

He turns out to be the nicest of men. I buy a copy of the *On the Waterfront* screenplay and get him to sign it. I ask him what F. Scott Fitzgerald was like.

"Disenchanted," he says.

He and his wife seem to know the Styrons.

"How is he?" says Mrs Schulberg. "I keep phoning but never get an answer."

"I don't know yet," I tell her.

"Well here," she says, pulling out pen and paper. "I'm going to write a letter for you to take to him." She scribbles a note and seals the envelope. "It's asking how he is."

First thing next morning, collar upturned against the icy air, I catch the 7.20 Long Island railroad back into Manhattan. Who should be sitting opposite but Van Morrison.

"'Brown-Eyed Girl' is perhaps the song of yours that means most to me," I tell him. "But there's lots I like. 'Wonderful Remark,' for instance. That line about sighing sighs and telling lies."

He nods. "To myself."

"I also like 'Bright Side of the Road.' Time passing and all that."

"In the twinkling of an eye."

And indeed, the Long Island Railroad carries me fast toward Manhattan's diminished skyline. When Morrison's not warning to seize the moment, my companion is Springsteen again, but now *The Rising*, and as we re-enter Manhattan the whole vista seems to rise up with Springsteen's nation-carrying voice. I wheel my suitcase to Port Authority just in time to snatch my ticket, take the elevator down to the waiting bays, and catch the Bonanza bus.

Beyond my window bright sunshine floods the highway but there's ice on the rocks, frozen water caught in the act of flowing. By 9.45 we're at Westchester, near enough to Yorktown Heights and the McGuigan brothers I knew from Brockport, now lost in the wreckage of time. We hit Interstate 684, and I ponder what I will find when I reach Southbury and meet Styron, now that he's seventy-seven.

I arrive at Southbury just before noon and wait for him over corn cake and vanilla coffee. I'm a little early but want to savor the joy of being back in a place that has helped to shape my life. A half hour later a dark blue Mercedes rolls up and out steps Bill. "Bill" "Styron." I've always had a little trouble with the power of names, not having one myself. I call him "Bill" to his face, and I might call him "Bill" to people who know him. But in my head there are two men, "Bill" and "Styron." Perhaps I should grow up.

Styron's gait shows the early signs of Parkinson's, a hint of a shuffle, right leg always a little ahead of his left, right arm less than mobile. But he's the same old cheerfully glum Bill, brain as sharp as ever, and that same old occasional, guttural cough, hacking at the icy Connecticut air. Back in the old, yellow-painted Roxbury farmhouse that was once a form of Heaven for me, we sit in the lounge and talk over a couple of Pale Ales. I tell him I met Budd Schulberg.

"How is the old goat?"

His wife gave me a letter to hand you."

"Ah," he says.

Late in the afternoon I drive Styron to one of his favorite walking spots. I recall it from my summer in the haunted cottage. In place of warm sunshine, greenery, long grass, and Tashmoo chasing butterflies, a grim wind flaps our coats and the trees are skeletal against a salmon sky. The track, streaked with ice, has rutted solid. In the ditches, clumps of snow slump purple in the twilight.

Our walk is slow but dogged. While Styron's left arm swings normally, his right is close to his ribs and the hand that wrote the novels is clenched, raw red against the cold. As we turn back the sun blobs beneath the stubble. We have no dog with us now. Both Tashmoo and a black labrador, Dinah, died two years ago, precipitating Styron's most recent depression.

"Not that the death of a dog leads to clinical depression," he says, "but these things lurk, and get triggered. You know I had shock treatment, don't you? Well, it was my decision, and it worked. But it's left me feeling spacey much of the time. It's hard to describe." He holds both hands up, either side of his jowls, as if to represent a helmet around his head. "Oh, by the way, we've got dinner guests. I hope that's okay. You've met Arthur, haven't you? Arthur Miller? And Becky?"

"Becky?"

"His daughter, Rebecca. She's staying with her father because Inge—did you meet Inge? Well sadly, she died. It happened only last month. She came back from a photography trip in Europe complaining of a pain in her back that everyone assumed was the result of lugging cameras around. But then she felt unwell, unable to get out of bed, and then she died, suddenly, and for Arthur and Becky, shockingly. Lymphatic cancer."

We are now entirely in shadow. A pink line streaks the horizon, but otherwise it's that time of evening when your skin glows against the dying light. It's as if not just the darkening sky but the dismal news itself makes the trees more skeletal, the wind harsher, the road icier.

"They were together so long," Styron is saying, "about forty years. His beloved Inge with whom, one would guess, he found real happiness."

By the time we're back to the car in all but darkness, we've talked more about Miller, about Rebecca, about her husband, Daniel Day-Lewis, about what a fine cook he is, a motorcycle daredevil who—one time—drove up from New York in an hour, not much more than half the usual time.

"Oh, one thing," says Bill as we get in the car, "I know you wouldn't do this, but do please remember. I've been with Arthur on numerous occasions, public and private, all over the country and in Europe. I can't think of a single time when someone hasn't brought up the subject of Marilyn Monroe. It *never* fails. You just wait for it to happen and someone says something like, 'Er, Mr Miller?' and your heart sinks."

"I wouldn't dream of raising her. I probably did when I met him years ago."

"Well, it honestly never fails but this time—especially at this sensitive time—let's hope it does. Also, don't expect anything of Arthur." The car headlights seem to draw the bone-white trees toward us as we sweep down the tunnel-like road. "We've had him eat with us once a week or so since it happened. Up to now he's hardly spoken."

"Do you know him well?"

"We've been neighbors for years. But even when we came up here in the fifties Arthur was already a legend, even to himself." Styron chuckles. "He was married to Monroe then, and I drove by hoping to get a glimpse, same as everyone else."

"Did you ever meet her?"

"We invited them to a party, as you'd expect. They were supposed to be coming, but it got later and later and eventually Arthur turned up alone. He made his apologies for her. Apparently this happened a lot. She'd be getting ready but never be so. I guess she didn't want to go out and be Marilyn Monroe. She didn't want to perform. As for Arthur, I know him, and I don't know him. Arthur is Mr Enigma."

"He's very talkative, or was the day I met him."

"Oh sure, Arthur'll talk all day. But what was it Nietzsche said? To talk a great deal about oneself can be a way of hiding oneself? I've always found Arthur hard to fathom. There are areas you don't go into. Anyway, just don't mention *Marilyn Monroe!*"

Back at the farmhouse, I take a bath and go down to the lounge with a beer. Upstairs I fancy I can hear Bill reading drafts of my bus travels, laughing perhaps. Or is that a cough?

Arthur and Rebecca appear. Rebecca is seven months pregnant and, of course, she's lost her mother. With those blue eyes, she remains exceptionally beautiful. But this is the most terrible of times. She looks as drained, emotionally and physically, as would any pregnant, grief-stricken woman, and those blue eyes often fill with tears. Arthur, whom I remember as tall, striding, powerful, walks carefully and has a bent-over back. His beady eyes crinkle more than ever now, as he edges through his eighties, sometimes reflective, sometimes scrutinizing, sometimes twinkling: *he* knows all about *tempus fugit*. But they both say they remember me. I doubt it, but it's possible.

"I remember your face," says Rebecca, "if not your name. Who does he remind you of?" she says to her father.

"All Englishmen look alike to me," Miller replies, "now my eyesight's failing."

We chat over cheese and Chablis. Well, in truth we don't really. Styron and Miller talk, Rose and I listen, and Rebecca holds herself together on the sofa, eyes frequently welling up. Miller has two plays on in New York, one being *The Crucible*, which has played, he tells us, to packed audiences since Nine Eleven.

As we settle in the candle glow at the Styron's kitchen table, Miller to my left, at the head of the table, Rebecca to my right, Styron and Rose across the table, and an empty chair the other end, I ask him what he made of all this, and the War on Terror.

"We live," he says, as if allowing me time to write it down, "in Rome."

The food is fabulous: cod roe, veal in bacon, asparagus, and a Meursault, the quality of which (a 1998 Charmes premier cru) Styron alerts me to, before ceaselessly topping up my glass. No one else, I imagine, feels like drinking much.

"What's the name of the other play you have on?" I ask Miller.

Eyes twinkling, he replies at dictation speed. "The Man Who Had All the Luck."

"Can one man be one thing and be it long?"

"I have no illusions left," he tells me. "None at all. I've seen so many people come and go, so many slide in and out of fortune, so many famous writers slip into oblivion, so many good people never achieve recognition, so many charlatans lauded."

"By other charlatans?"

"Not always. Well-meaning people do it to, and sincerely. But what of it? We're all insignificant in the long run. You know, the first discovery of a planet orbiting a star beyond our own was less than twenty years ago. But since they found what they unromantically called 51 Pegasi B they can't *stop* finding new extrasolar planets. I reckon soon enough they'll have found hundreds. It's already clear that many stars have planetary systems, so it's likely some must be suitable for life. They'll find an Earth-like planet in a year or two."

"Does time really bend, do you think?"

The deep ridges around his twinkling eyes call to mind the cracked, icy crust of Europa, or perhaps I'm just thinking of March in Connecticut. "They reckon that within a few years we could have proof," he touches my arm, "*proof*, demonstrated in laboratories, that all human experience has been confined to a four-dimensional sheet floating in an unimaginably larger, higher-dimensional universe. Every educated person ought to know such things."

"Does it help?"

"To know the subjectivity of time is to accept that we really are a long time young and a short time old. Sure it helps."

"Joyce Carol Oates once wrote that time devours us in the name of wisdom."

"She's not kidding."

"So what matters is to live by heartthrobs, not by hours?"

"Did she say that?"

"Emily Dickinson."

"Ah yes! *Opinion is a flitting thing but truth outlasts the sun. If we cannot own them both, possess the oldest one.*"

"More wine?" Styron looks me in the eye and fills my glass with Meursault

Everything goes swimmingly, until Rose leans across the table and says, "Did you say, 'Joyce Carol Oates'? He met her parents, Arthur. That must have been *fascinating!* What's that big, recent novel of hers?"

Before I can hold my tongue I've said "*Blonde.*"

"*Blonde*? Isn't that the one about—"

To my left sits a grief-stricken octogenarian coming to terms with the loss of his wife of forty years. To my right sits their pregnant, grief-stricken daughter. Across sits William Styron, known to me as an esteemed novelist, but more particularly at this moment as The Long-Term-Friend-And-Neighbor-of-Arthur-Miller-Who-Has-Reminded-Me-Scant-Hours-Earlier-Not-Under-Any-Circumstances-But-Especially-At-This-Sensitive-Time-To-Mention-*Marilyn-Monroe.*

There at the table with us, in the empty chair at the far end between Rose and Rebecca, where perhaps Inge Morath has sat for the first half of the meal, unbeknown to us, sits the ghost of Norma Jean Baker, aka Mrs Miller, aka Marilyn Monroe. She looks at each of us in turn. We who notice her lower our gaze.

"Oh my goodness," laughs Rose, who hasn't, of course, been privy to Styron's warning. "I was in Ireland with Joyce. She gave readings from *Blonde*. It was amazing! She looked down, brushed up her hair, gazed out at the audience and began to read. She had the voice, the mannerisms, everything! I've never seen such a performance! She simply *was* Marilyn Monroe."

I search for something to say. Miller's eyes crinkle, reflecting the candle light that casts dancing shadows across the table to the empty chair. Rebecca gazes at her half-finished food. Styron looks at me. Rose grows thoughtful.

I turn to Miller. Good as I am at saying the wrong thing at the wrong time, I now surpass myself. "Erm, have you read *Blonde*, Arthur?"

Idiot. Fool. Behead yourself instantly! Cut a hole through the floorboards! Throw yourself through the kitchen window!

Miller crinkles his eyes at me. "No," he says.

"Joyce approaches many subjects," winces Styron, "and sometimes bites off more than she can chew."

Well, we survive the moment. I don't defenestrate myself. Rebecca brightens as she tells me of her book of stories, *Personal Velocity*. Doubleday has just published it in Britain and she's directed a film of the same title to be released this year by United Artists. I assure her I'll see it, and do so, though I have the cinema to myself. She also talks of her mostly female crew, and how little money there is to work with. Miller talks animatedly about, of all things, Medicare, and how cheap it is for pensioners. I'm struck by such concern for money in presumably wealthy people. But Miller's reputation, among peers, as the biggest cheapskate in literary history is matched by affection, surely, for his utter lack of pretension. He is the most boyish octogenarian I'm ever likely to meet. Perhaps—who knows?—the child and the cheapskate are psychologically linked.

So the supper in the Styron kitchen is surreal in its normality. How is it, I ponder in bed that night, that I could be accepted there? I, who amount to so little, sitting there with a poet, a Pulitzer Prize winning novelist, a film director married to a film star, and America's most famous playwright who, if the award really meant anything in terms of merit, would long ago have won the Nobel Prize? I am, I conclude, accepted there because these people do not think of themselves in these terms, but are simply seen so by others. They are not Ben Hecht's "mindless, moodless hunters of success," as he put it to me in that dusty library in the Poconos so long ago, but have found their path from within. Like Hecht, to such radiance I will always bow.

Mercifully, that night, in the midst of my ponderings, I fall into what for me is the unusual experience of a dreamless sleep.

All the time on the bus down into Manhattan the next day I have things on my mind. Partly it's Miller and Inge Morath and Rebecca, and birth and death at the same table. Partly it's the Twin Towers, another form of bereavement, two ghosts against the blue sky. It's a feeling that someone or something somewhere has gone. I find myself looking for what isn't there. New York is, and isn't, what it was. On my walkman, Sinatra is singing "What now, my love?" As so often with songs, the words seem spookily appropriate, especially when I scrawl them with a few revisions. *What now, New York, now that it's over. . . ? Nothing but sky, where those towers should be . . . .*

We pass the Guggenheim on 88th and 5th Avenue,

a building that always lifts my spirits, and now New York is thundering above me, as if arising, as Springsteen urges, from the ashes. On cue Sinatra launches into "New York, New York" as I've never heard it before, with a full panoramic backdrop, and I'm swallowed up anew into what Baudrillard called the city's "baroque verticality." I leave the bus and go for a New Amsterdam at a little place called French Roast, where a young waiter with a long chain attached to the keys in his pocket, a goatie beard and tattoos all over his arms, is kissing each waitress in turn before leaving the bar.

Outside a yellow cab pulls onto Broadway. I leave the café and walk down to the intersection with 51st to buy a *Post* at a green sidewalk booth. Inside it, surrounded by a cut-price cornucopia of candy, magazines, postcards flapping in the breeze, today's papers, cold drinks, a Pakistani man looks out at me, at us, at New York, as we pass across his box of vision in the twinkling of an eye.

But there's another thing on my mind besides New York and bereavement. Just before I left for Manhattan, Styron and I spoke again of *Sophie's Choice*.

"I reread it not long ago." I said. "All that emotional chiaroscuro, don't you think, is quite operatic."

"I hate to tell you," said Styron. "But they're making an opera of it to be performed at the Royal Opera in Covent Garden this December. Want to come?"

22

THE FINAL ACT

And so distorting, proving what he proves
Is nothing, what can all this matter since
The relation comes, benignly, to its end?

Wallace Stevens

The December 2002 premiere of *Sophie's Choice* at Covent Garden mingles with memories of my final Greyhound trip in 2004, along with Styron's Memorial Service at St. Bartholomew's Church in Manhattan on February 2, 2007. All were, for me, endings. All seem to set an appropriate seal on this narrative. To sit in the darkness of an auditorium watching an opera unfold is perhaps not so very different from sitting in the darkness of a bus, watching the bright world pass by, or amid a thousand-strong congregation watching the story of one man's life unspool before us ("with negligent haste" as Styron might say) in a succession of testaments from family and friends and photographs from childhood to old age.

Off I go, in 2004, from the Port Authority, on an absurd journey of closure, down into Texas to roam the real Alamo in the heart of San Antonio, and then up through Arkansas, the edge of Tennessee, Missouri, and Illinois into Michigan, to my *Paha-Sapa*. The Alamo visit is in homage to my cowboy-enthralled childhood, with a nod to my brief encounter with Richard Widmark. That such a trip makes sense is reinforced by a comment Larry McMurtry makes to me, while I'm reading his essays on Texas, *In a Narrow Grave*, on the southwest-bound bus.

"It only remains for you to perform some *acte symbolistique*," he says, "to give the journey coherence, the present to the past."

It's early April and the weather dodges back and forth over the many hours of travel. One moment the sun shines, the next hailstones the size of softballs clatter the windows. McMurtry, whom I've flattered by talking admiringly of *The Last Picture Show*, tells me of a trip he made to San Antonio, which he considers to be "the one truly lovely city" in Texas.

"Already the doors of the many small bars were propped open to the soft air," he says. "I walked by the San Antonio River awhile and had breakfast at a café by the waterside only a few blocks from the Alamo. The green water flowed quietly past. . . ."

"Yes, Larry," I say, "but you're just quoting verbatim from your 1968 book. San Antonio may have changed by now."

"San Antonio," he says, "will always transcend Texas, as San Francisco transcends California, as New Orleans transcends Louisiana. Not a little of its charm, like that of El Paso, is attributable to the presence of Latins, who almost always improve an Anglo-Saxon town."

If I'm Ever Back This Way

Encouraged by McMurtry's pronouncements, the bus and I trundle west round Houston on the Sam Houston Bellway and filter right, up over a massive overpass. "The Rising," Mozart's Horn Concertos, the Everly Brothers, and the Beach Boys, sustain me on my iPod toward San Antonio—especially "When I Become a Man," with its haunting refrain of ages, fading out, alarmingly, at thirty-one. The verges are a mass of wild flowers. Every time we skim a bridge, house martins swoop from their nests beneath the arches, dark against the blue sky. Buzzards circle, an orange butterfly meanders by. Trucks with silver chimneys tootle past.

San Antonio is a surprisingly small city, and not how I remember it from 1981. The Marriott on Commerce Street dominates the skyline. Night falls soon after six. Urged on by McMurtry, I settle in at the Marriott bar and consume a Chicken Fried Steak Sandwich in a cheese sauce. The stools are lined with latter-day Lomans who seem much the same as those I've seen in hotels across the country and the decades. Back in my room on the nineteenth floor, I turn the armchair to the plate-glass window, pop a Lone Star beer and contemplate the sparkling city. The curtain to the left suggests a stage show and straight ahead—so fittingly you'd imagine it couldn't be true—above the Bank One sign and the hotel pool, shines Venus, lone star in the Lone Star state, watched by a man with a Lone Star beer.

After a first, generic American breakfast in the Marriott, I resolve to eat only Mexican during my stay, so each mealtime after that I dine at the Villa San Antonio in Alamo Plaza. I've bought my wife and daughters bracelets, and the girl who sold them to me tells me this,

If I'm Ever Back This Way

rather than the cafés on the Riverwalk, is the place with the most authentic Mexican food. The plastic tablecloths are orange and yellow. A gigantic plastic Shiner Light bottle stands on the counter. Cactii line the shelves. I work my way through the menu, breakfast one morning on *chorizo de heuvos*—spicey pork and peppers, mixed into the obligatory refried beans—another morning on *chilaquiles plate*—eggs with onions, peppers, refried beans, then *migas plate*, then *huevos a la Mexicana*, then *huevos rancheros*. I take light lunches and gorge myself in the evenings, along with side dishes of cheese *enchillados*, and a merry accompaniment of mango marguerites, Dos Equis beers—oh those Oregon nights of twenty years ago!—and my favorite beer there, Tecate, *Lo auténtico se reconoce* (my beer mat whispers to me). Villa San Antonio brings me great happiness, and I vow to eat there again if I'm ever back that way.

Across Alamo Plaza, glimpsed between the trams, the police cycling by in shorts, and the trees in the raised central square that holds the monument, stands the familiar outline of the Alamo's eighteenth-century church. The first time I go there, after a downpour, it emerges through steaming streets and a yellow mist of sunshine. Entry is free, so I wander through the site most days and listen to the guides in red waistcoats, white shirts and black trousers recite the official Texan version of the Alamo, merging it with movie trivia, such as the fact that Wayne filmed his epic at a reconstruction two miles west, in Bracketsville, and that a new version will reach multiplexes later in the year. Away from the guides and their stream of listeners, the place is fairly empty and much of the time I have it to myself. I peer through the glass case at the artefacts—a knife, a gun, a ring, a lock of hair—run my fingers over the walls from bullet hole to bullet hole, and stand listening alone in the room where twenty women and children survived while their husbands and fathers died outside.

After a few days, San Antonio feels like a cruise ship stranded in the desert. Besides the Alamo, there's really only the Riverwalk to see, and the sunken square of the Riverwalk Center, where the tourist boats turn beneath the looming glass of the mall that merges into the Marriott. Alamo-ed out, and numbed by the endless, piped rendition of "A Fistful of Dollars" in the Riverwalk Center, I'm stir crazy enough to sample the outlying districts by bus. It might as well be Baghdad. I've been reading Cormac McCarthy's Border Trilogy and *Blood Meridian* and am ready for the road again.

On my last night, accompanied by Zora, a pretty black woman with a blueberry-sized mole on her chin, I take the elevator up the Tower of the Americas and drink marguerites as the revolving restaurant spreads the little city and the Texan plains at my feet. Zora is a committed Christian and an Assistant Professor. Naturally I'm impressed. We talk about Styron, Baldwin, Nat Turner, Sandra Cisnero's Chicana stories in *The House on Mango Street*, Gloria Anzaldhua's *Borderlands / La Frontera*—a book written partly in Spanish, partly in English—racism, Texas, and Zora's burgeoning career.

"Best of luck," I tell her.

"And you," she says. "Where next?"

"Michigan." She gives me a quizzical look. I tell her there's a sandy draw there that leads to Lake Michigan. "It's my *Paha-Sapa*—my spiritual home."

"And what'll you do there?"
"Remember."
"How lovely to *remember!*"
"Most of the time."

The Michigan trip probably makes no sense but it makes me happy. From Muskegon I hitch a ride out to Star Lake. The softball diamond is still there, but the picnic tables have gone, along with the shack Dimmestamm called a "supermarket," and there's no more trace of Camp Jakalak than I'd probably have found of Marilyn Monroe's non-existent café had I stopped in Grand Rapids.

I climb over a KEEP OUT sign and walk into the overgrown woods. The cabins have gone, but I reach a clearing and the remains of the Council Circle, and find my way to the sand dune called Shifting Mountain. I stumble down through Shifting Mountain Draw to the tufted grass and dunes overlooking Lake Michigan. *Twenty years!* I think. *I've been a waif for twenty years!* But it's more than that even. Soon enough it's a quarter of a century and more since Carlotta and I watched an orange moon loom to a hard bright disc doubled in the lake, and complete a circle with its watery reflection. The stretch of beach feels like the loneliest place on the planet. There are no voices. No one says, *Have you got the spirit?* No one calls out, *damned dogfuckin' worms!* No voice whispers, *We're like painted spheres in the Universe.* Even the Paschenslaag Memorial Chapel, fallen to ruin, is being reclaimed by the woods. There's nothing but the sound of the wind in the sound of the grass tufts across the dunes, and it's the sound of the

If I'm Ever Back This Way

lake full of the same wind blowing across the Wisconsin or down to Illinois. Like Stevens' snowman, nothing myself, I feel "nothing not there and the nothing that is." If the Native Americans were right that their ancestors' spirits haunt the land, then maybe, beyond my sight or hearing, the ghosts of that first summer are all around me, just as my travels and meetings are still happening somewhere in the incomprehensible continuity of time. But, whatever else, the Indian past, the American past, and my past, are all on a level now. What I did experience, what I only imagine I experienced, and what I've consciously distorted, are bound together as an emotional truth. So I turn away from Lake Michigan, clamber back over Shifting Mountain Draw, down through the woods, back over the KEEP OUT sign, and hitch back to Muskegon, and, from the very place I started out, board my final Greyhound.

Yet here I am, as well, back in 2002, high up in the darkness of the Royal Opera House, Covent Garden, wearing a hired Moss Bros dinner jacket, my skin sore and sweating, my neck chafed, as if I were somehow in school uniform once again. Only this time it's my choice. I'm wearing it out of respect, and not even thinking about it much, because I'm only half in this cavernous darkness and half on stage, at least during the Brooklyn scenes. After the thunderous applause I'll leave the auditorium and wander the empty stairwells for too long trying to find the backstage party. But when I do so there, across the room will be, not Styron, but a face I recognize.

As she walks past I'll say, "Excuse me, you're not

Chelsea Clinton are you?" and Chelsea Clinton—for it really *is* Chelsea Clinton—will turn and say, "Yes?"

"I—I just wanted a word."

"Yes?"

She'll turn and look at me as she might if an Oxford professor called to her in a cloister about an essay.

"I just wanted to say," I'll improvise, "that I think your father was one of the best Presidents."

But Chelsea will prove, to me at least, to have something of what I take to be her parents' charisma. Instead of snorting with derision, she'll break into a delightful smile.

"Oh, thank you so much," she'll say.

Left to fill the gap, I'll talk books, for some reason *Anna Karenina*.

"Oh, that's like my most *favorite* book!" she'll exclaim.

No doubt our exchange, which will seem to me to be a fifty-minute seminar on Tolstoy, will last no more than a minute, before she's off to greet other well-wishers, and I'm left to reflect, not for the first time, on the oddities of our celebrity age.

The babbling crowd are like a mass gathering of characters from some idiosyncratic book—some famous, some talented, others just happy to be included. Over there is the director, Trevor Nunn, and beyond him the conductor, Sir Simon Rattle, talking with Styron's biographer, James L. W. West III, and look: over there Nathan, played by Rodney Gilfry! And over there, yet another Stingo imposter, Canadian Gordon Gietz (Stingo Canadian? Whatever next?) And there! Sophie herself, the stunningly beautiful, wonderfully named mezzo-soprano Angelika Kirschlager is talking with the operatic narrator, Dale Duesing.

I barely talk to Styron on this last occasion I'll see him. Shamelessly, and without regret because I know that this, like all moments, will vanish even as it appears, I tout my program sheet for signatures. It hangs, framed now, on my study wall even as I write this years later.

"I've got those opening night blues, Bill," wrote Styron, in a shaky yet still elegant hand. But that nervous comment came subsequently to be surrounded by the almost uniformly triumphant, exhilarated signatures of the composer, Nicholas Maw, of Stingo, Sophie and Nathan, or rather their operatic counterparts, of Trevor Nunn, and, most triumphantly of all, by the curling, flourishing composer's hand across the centre of the sheet, as if Sir Simon Rattle were still composing, even now, as I look up at it in the early morning shadows.

"I've got those opening night blues," Styron repeats in the top left corner.

Sir Simon wraps his conductor's arms around the author's shoulders, and scrawls across the page: "What's wrong with the blues? Love Simon."

It's a fitting finale, framed on a wall, sealed in a book.

Later, as cast and audience separate across the London night, I'll see Rattle again, easily recognizable from his shock of white hair, in an overcoat, hailing a taxi at the roadside. Even the Chief Conductor of the Berlin Philharmonic Orchestra has to leave the stage and party for the humdrum, rain-speckled pavements of everyday life. As for Styron, the last I see of him is in the bar, surrounded by family and friends, and fêted by a jostling, exhilarated crowd. Something is complete when the crowd opens up a little and, arms outstretched, Styron shuffles forward to embrace Angelika and I think of Stingo finally, in old age, being able to embrace Sophie and let her know that he has come to understand her, and come to understand his own, dead mother perhaps, as the young man never could have. At this point, I am happy to slip away.

But, in my memory of the opera, all that is ahead. I'm still sweating in my dinner jacket in the darkness, watching the drama unfold across the stage. When Stingo, Sophie and Nathan are in New York, I, too, am there. It's 1947, and 1979 and 2002, or 2004, or 2007, or any other year I've a mind to recall. In particular the events on stage and the operatic voices, merge with my last ever bus trip, down into Manhattan in 2004. At the end of my last Greyhound journey, as I recall, I hire a car to drive up to Maine and swirl down through New England, then drop the car in Newark in the compound off Route 1 & 9, and catch my last bus home: an Olympia Trails to the Port Authority.

My final driver's a black guy who looks like he was once an athlete. His vest's outlined through his pale blue shirt with its Olympia Trails patch on the arm. Jinx, I call him, after an Oates character. I see him in his domestic environment. He has a wife and two kids. He's got a carefully trimmed beard. He has dignity. He's got a chunky ring on his right hand. I decide his father gave him that when he was eighteen, and said, "You do good, son. Make your dad proud. If you're a star you're a star, but if you drive a bus, you be as good a driver as possi-

If I'm Ever Back This Way

ble." I'm no judge of bus drivers, but we have a rollicking ride into Manhattan.

I'm thinking, as the bus rolls in, about how to put across my version of America. I remember a conversation with Bill Heyen about a squirrel. "See that squirrel darting from tree to tree," he said. "Sometimes you see it, sometimes you don't, but you always assume it's there. Imagine living in a world before we had rational explanation. Things are there. Then they're gone. The Indians assumed that what was gone could still be there, of course. What a magic place the world must once have seemed deep in the woods or in the mountains of this continent before it became America." My America is as much to do with what you don't see as what you see.

The bus heads for the Lincoln Tunnel. I'm looking out for my last Greyhound. Bam! There's Manhattan across the water. Bam! There it is again. Thunderous chords. Through the tunnel there's a rushing sound. Rain sparkles on the bus windows like the sweat of an athlete. It's a wild ride. Jinx nearly crashes. He takes wrong turns. He blunders into Manhattan, and as I get off at the Port Authority, I hear someone behind me say, "That's it. That's the last time I'm taking a bus. I'm never riding the bus again!"

Me neither.

Back in the city, I sit at a bar on Broadway called The Republic. I could be anyone, everyone. After a beer, I *am* everyone. After another three beers I'm Walt Whitman himself. I know I'm in Dreamland but I know you have to have Dreamland somewhere. I'm still invisible after all these years. New York's not what I thought it was. It's everything and I'm a speck of it.

If I'm Ever Back This Way

Everyone thinks they're above the city, as Darius said. *But we're all part of it.*

The rich and the poor, all the people I've met, they're all part of the tapestry. The people I've met, the people I've dreamt of, the people I've known and the people I've only heard of. Carlotta Domarski, Dirk, Drum and Darius Desoutter, Pickawillany Dinwiddie, William Styron, Joyce Carol Oates, Richard Widmark, the Clintons, Marilyn Monroe, Ronald Reagan, Bruce Springsteen, the Heyens, Reverends Fish and Fina Flesch, Jeremiah the Jacket-Eater, James Baldwin, Ántonia agreeing to marry me *maybe*, Rabbi Bruce, Custer, Arthur Miller. They've all been part of my America, and part of America as one century has metamorphosed into another. And not only are they part of America but now, in finishing this narrative, I too am part of America, and my journey, I realize as I sit there at The Republic, has been the most American of journeys. Out of my solitude, I've found myself to be, *not* above anything, nor below it, nor apart from it, but *it*. I am part of the pulse of the city, part of the interconnectedness of all life, part, at least for this while, of America. Dazed by the sun streaming into my face up Broadway, dazzled by beautiful passers-by, I feel like old Walt, feel I've recorded something meaningful at last about the land that has given me so much. After all these years, the great happiness of America is to sit at a table on Broadway and watch America pass by. On I sit as the sun lowers, in love with the pulse of the city, the pulse of America. Finally, I rise, a little woozy, and stagger up Broadway. Outside a cyber café called DotCom a woman watches her boyfriend talk to his cell phone. I catch her eyes and she rolls them at me as I pass by in my essential solitude. Groggily, I walk down West 84th Street, also known as Edgar Allan Poe Street, and Poe's there beside me and says much the same as Oates quotes him in the epigraph to her 1998 novel, *My Heart Laid Bare*.

"The road to immortal renown lies straight, open, unencumbered before you," he tells me. "All you have to do is write what you experienced. But remember: the book must be true to the *spirit* of your travels. You can lie about facts, but never about the *emotional* truth."

I say goodbye to Darius and Juliet. "You've finally finished traveling," nods Darius. "Phone or e-mail once in a while."

I catch a limousine to the airport, and the trip ends, as all trips end, all dreams. There's the usual, primal, visceral fear of crashing. But I'm a changed man.

"I can't get *all* of America in," I told Bill Heyen a few years ago in Brockport.

"Yeah, well," he said. "Write your book like you're watching that squirrel before we invented rational thought. You know, America is a place of the mind."

Like the supposedly unattainable place of inexpressible happiness, it turns out not in fact to be unattainable but ungraspable, and only inexpressible beyond approximation.

So it is as if, now, I sit in three places at once: the auditorium, watching the *Sophie's Choice* opera in December 2002, the New York café after my last bus trip in April 2004, and amid the congregation at St. Bartholomew's in February 2007. Reminiscences dangle before me: images of the states of my youth, the states of my mind, intermingled with the opera and with the

If I'm Ever Back This Way

Memorial Service. The latter proves to be the epitome of all I could have imagined when I set out on my American odyssey. Among the succession of friends and family members—most notably Al, who spoke of her father's "epic, wretched descent"—up to the pulpit to talk or read, came celebrity after celebrity. Peter Matthiessen talked of their first meeting in Paris, and how, after too much plonk, Styron fell face first, "lachrymose among the oysters." Bill Clinton spoke of how "the Human Genome Project has shown us that 99.9% of our genetic make-up is identical to every other human being on Earth," and that "all that we have that's different is mind and heart and what matters most is what we decide to do with these."

"We become what we care about," he said. "William Styron was a great man."

Mia Farrow read from the ending of "A Tidewater Morning." Ted Kennedy told some anecdotes and quoted JFK on art and literature. Carlos Fuentes told a Magical Realist anecdote about Styron signing a book for a girl in Paris just as a sudden downpour washed the autograph away.

"But I knew," said Fuentes, "that the next morning, for that young Parisienne, when the page had dried out, Styron's signature had returned."

Finally, Meryl Streep read from the ending of *Sophie's Choice*, and as she finished I glanced across the aisle, looked idly at a tall, dark haired man in a long, gray coat, and caught the steely eyes of Philip Roth.

Were I still young, I'd have accosted him after the service, pummelled him into discussing *The Ghost Writer*, or *Operation Shylock* or *The Plot Against Amer-*

ica. But even as we exchanged glances—with me knowing him instantly, and he seeing just another face in the crowd—I was under no illusion. Those days are gone.

Bus riding has been like being a swinger of birches, in Frost's phrase, and one can do worse. To leave and return has been my life's pattern. That little capsule, that inch of history through which I lived it, recedes like a blue sphere into the expanding universe, drifting, like Voyager, ever outward, far away into space even as the Solar System will eventually incinerate, until one day, perhaps Voyager will view the universe from a world near the Siamese Squid Nebula, or the yellow star, Alpha Centauri. Yes, Voyager is a redshift candidate for sure, and I'm glad to have been even a small-time voyager on my own tiny journey, following Arlo Guthrie's call to sail into the void, swept along the open road without end. And who knows, maybe I'll be back again.

But I'm thinking too, not just of America, but of the home life that I rejected while I found myself, but that I could never get back, as well as the one I've found and intend to keep as long as I'm wanted. I think of my parents, long gone, and their largely unknown youth; of my grandfathers in *their* youths; of an uncle who died in the First World War, aged twenty-one like Cochran, saying, "For God's sake, *live it!*" Each photo is fainter and smaller, the further back I look. If you blew them up the grains would widen and disperse and, really, there would be nothing there but illusion. The past is theory. But in my study I see the present and future too. My computer wallpaper is a Viking photograph of the rust-red rocks of the surface of Mars. I'm not only married and a father but aware of all the children on the horizon—not mine, but others'—unborn, unknown, or just unseen, perhaps the way the sun must once have seemed not to exist between dusk and dawn. But if you *are* there, you have your own youth before you, and your own bus ride. And don't let anybody tell you it's not yours to have.

So when—back at the opera—Sophie screams as her daughter is wrenched away, I suddenly realize that I am no longer even remotely Stingo. I am Sophie: the parent, not the youth. The lump in my throat throughout the four-hour show swells as Sophie's fate unfolds, and bursts amid the standing ovation as the show fades to silence. All through the opera I've pictured Bill Styron sitting with his family somewhere in the midst of the crowd. What must it feel like to sit in old age while a novel you've written unfolds as opera? Or is the lump in my throat also for my own, now vanished youth?

Well, the opera has ended—along with the Memorial Service and the bus ride—the curtain has closed and the audience has risen and I, too, have finished my story, and if I'd known what trouble it would be, I'd still have done it. The years have passed and I sit now, in my study, my fading map of America on the wall before me, with its inked-in routes crisscrossing a country I've edged with passport-sized photos of Styron, and Heyen, and Fiery O'Fuellen, of my young self beside a bus, of Eddie Cochran, Joyce Carol Oates, Marilyn Monroe and others, and of my parents.

We're well into the new century. There have been bomb attacks in London and flooding in New Orleans. The Arctic is melting and the very fate of the Earth is uncertain, even as Earth-like planets have been discovered. Arthur Miller died in 2005, three years before mathematicians Irina Aref'eva and Igor Volovich first suggested that the atom-smasher at CERN, the European laboratory for particle physics, might just create suitable conditions for time travel. William Styron, at least, got to read all but this final chapter of the book, but time currently outdoes us all. I've reached the top of my personal climb. Now comes the plateau, where I'll watch younger people scramble up, and shed and don identities along the way. I'll help if I can, as I've been helped, and perhaps do so through this book, mostly written for imagined beings who no doubt are or will be real: a flawed but honest book, because why would I lie to them?

Like the music that accompanies me, I veer between reflection and vitality. Springsteen now jostles for my ear with his energetic admirers, The Hold Steady, a Minnesotan band whose songs from *Separation Sunday* and *Girls and Boys in America*, performed at Asbury Park's Stone Pony during the Memorial Service trip, reinvigorate me toward the future. But just as often I listen to Mozart or Miles Davis and am more likely at such times to reflect, with Wallace Stevens, on the notion that death is the mother of beauty. It's in the going not the getting there that we live, of course, and, even as I approach the thirtieth anniversary of my first trip, that too becomes history. Yet journeys do end, and we do arrive. Every dog has its depot, and the depot's in sight for this old hound. I gather my bags, shake my pages into one neat pile. The bus brakes. The driver mumbles, "Thank you for traveling Greyhound," and I prepare to meet a new world. Were this a film, we'd fade out with

If I'm Ever Back This Way

the bus pulling away from the terminal and heading into the distance on one last ride into the past. I'm on it, thinking of all that I've seen and whatever it is I am or am not. It occurs to me, as Allen Ginsberg put it, that I am America. I know that what I now know is as much as I'll ever know, at least of certain things, so to that extent I'm satisfied that my search is over.